The Petitpaon Era

Henri Austruy

The Petitpaon Era
and Other stories

translated, annotated and introduced by
Brian Stableford

A Black Coat Press Book

ISBN 978-1-61227-294-8. First Printing. June 2014. Published by Black Coat Press, an imprint of Hollywood Comics.com, LLC, P.O. Box 17270, Encino, CA 91416. All rights reserved. Except for review purposes, no part of this book may be reproduced or transmitted in any form or by any means, electronic or mechanical, including photocopying, recording, or by any information storage and retrieval system, without permission in writing from the publisher. The stories and characters depicted in this novel are entirely fictional. Printed in the United States of America.

TABLE OF CONTENTS

Introduction

This is the second of three volumes of translations of the fantastic fiction of Henri Austruy; the first is *The Eupantophone and Other Stories*, which contains, in addition to the title story, "The Tavern," "The Statue" and "The Castle," and the third is *The Olotelepan and Other Stories*, which contains, in addition to the title story, "A Samsara" and "Master Flaver's Revelation." The introduction to the first volume contains a full account of Austruy's literary career, and the few details of his biography that are presently accessible.

L'Ère "Petitpaon" ou La Paix universelle, here translated as "The Petitpaon Era; or, World Peace," was originally published by Louis Michaud in an undated edition released in 1906. (The Bibliothèque Nationale catalogue mistakenly gives the date as 1908, but it was reviewed in the *Mercure de France* in 1906 and the advertisements at the back of the book are all for 1906 titles.) It was Austruy's second novel, following *L'Eupantophone* (tr. in *L'Eupantophone and Other Stories*), which Ernest Flammarion had published a year earlier, following its serialization in 1904 in the *Nouvelle Revue*. "Le Pays d'Humanie," here translated as "The Land of Humania" was published in three parts in the *Nouvelle Revue* in September-October 1902. "Miellune" was published in three parts in the same publication in August-September 1908. "La Jungle républicaine," here translated as "The Republican Jungle," appeared there in three parts in November-December 1919, under the pseudonym "Diogene Anonymus."

"Le Pays d'Humanie" is the neatest and most effective of Austruy's Symbolist allegories, and brought that earnest phase of his career to an end; all of his subsequent works were satirical comedies, albeit of a rather black hue. *L'Ère "Petitpaon"* is perhaps the blackest of them all in its concluding section, reflecting an anger in its fierce sarcasm that faded away there-

7

after, perhaps expended and perhaps suppressed for reasons of diplomacy. The novel evidently set out to be controversial, and to give offense in certain quarters, and might have succeeded rather too well for the author's career prospects.

The preliminary material in the Michaud volume lists another book as "*en préparation*," entitled *Les Joies de la Vie et de la Mort*, but it never appeared, and Austruy never published anything else thereafter outside the pages of the *Nouvelle Revue*, He was the editorial secretary of that publication from 1901 to 1913, when he took over as editor-in-chief—and presumably its owner—for the remainder of the periodical's life, and, it appears, his own. Both disappeared within weeks of the German occupation of Paris in August 1940. Given that Austruy's regular articles on foreign affairs in its pages had been uncompromisingly harsh in their treatment of Adolf Hitler ever since the Nazis took control of the German government, Austruy's name must have been close to the top of the Gestapo's hit list of potential targets for suppression and reprisal.

From the viewpoint of the twenty-first century, *L'Ère "Petitpaon"* seems harmless enough in its assault on the supposedly-evil triple alliance of Capital, Catholicism and the military establishment, especially in view of the fact that its treatment of the far left tendency in the French parliament is also rather scathing. It undoubtedly ruffled feathers at the time of its publication, however, although not in the productive fashion of generating loud publicity and increased sales. The book appears to have been largely ignored, in fact; the only review preserved on *gallica* is a very brief notice in the *Mercure de France*, once the chief organ of the Symbolist Movement, which carefully refrains from stressing its satirical aspects. By virtue of its pacifism as well as its humor, the novel invites comparison with the fantasies of Albert Robida, but its illustrations—by Lobel Riche—are considerably more mundane than Robida's, who would certainly have made a great deal more of the two perverse battles fought in the course of the plot, the second replaying Waterloo on a much grander and ultimately more tragic scale. Its prose, however, it can easily stand comparison with Robida, and so can its wit; although the greater savagery of its sarcasm would not have been to everyone's taste at the time, that aspect of the work has worn well.

The satire in *L'Ère "Petitpaon"* has some striking touches of grotesquerie, but that was an aspect of Austruy's work that was still in development at the time, and it comes out much more forcefully in "Miellune," which moves from a relatively staid commencement to extremes of surreal bizarrerie that are quite remarkable. Austruy must have been well aware of the directions in which some his contemporary ex-Symbolists were moving, and presumably observed the proto-surrealist elements in the work of Alfred Jarry and Guillaume Apollinaire with some interest. He does not appear to have had much sympathy as an editor for that kind of work, and was far less hospitable to the work of Symbolists and ex-Symbolists than his predecessors as editor-in-chief of the *Nouvelle Revue* had been—perhaps ungratefully, given that it was presumably his Symbolist credentials that first attracted the attention of P.-B. Gheusi, who bought "La Statue" and "Le Château" before hiring him as editorial secretary—but as an author he retained a strong attachment to the grotesque, and "Miellune" is one of the two works, the other being "La Révélation de Maître Flaver," in which he gave it fullest rein.

"La Jungle républicaine" is also an exercise in the theater of the absurd, but the fact that it is brought back from an imaginary location to the world of Parisian politics forbids it to go to the extreme of "Miellune"—and, indeed, even to go to the political extreme achieved by the futuristic *L'Ère "Petitpaon,"* the whole point of the story being to poke fun at the apparent inability of the contemporary system of government to contrive any significant change at all. The theme of the story, involving anxiety in the face of possible ecocatastrophe caused by soil erosion, has helped it retain a certain relevance into the twenty-first century, although its anticipatory acumen is not tested by any attempt to map social change in response to the challenge.

In between the publication of "Miellune" and "La Jungle républicaine" the Great War was fought; Austruy, born in 1871, was too old to be mobilized, and he spent the war at the helm of *La Nouvelle Revue*, helping as best he could to maintain morale with his regular editorial feature on "Paris during the War."

The actual war must have made the black comedy of "Petitpaon warfare" described in *L'Ère "Petitpaon"* seem far milder than it had in 1906, and perhaps considerably less amusing, but no less pertinent. It is entirely possible that Austruy had decided to give up writing fiction in the years before the war, perhaps wounded by the fate of his second novel and his inability to follow it up, and it might well have required a new beginning for French society to prompt him to make a new beginning himself.

Austruy never became prolific as a fiction writer, his non-fiction and his editorial work evidently taking up almost the whole of his time and energy, but his subsequent endeavors, although limited in their circulation, nevertheless justified his efforts abundantly, all of his post-war work being quietly remarkable.

It is arguable that he never did anything else quite as remarkable in its bizarrerie as "Miellune," but the imaginative work he put into that exceedingly strange story certainly did not go to waste. He was never as cruel again in his treatment of Churchmen as he was in "Le Pays d'Humanie" and *L'Ère "Petitpaon,"* but that was probably because he saw no need to repeat himself, and felt that there was no point in flogging a horse that was dying anyway. Indeed, insofar as the allegorical component of his work is concerned, the works contained in this volume do provide, between them, a summation of sorts, while laying the foundations for subsequent endeavors of a different but no less interesting kind.

The translation of *L'Ère "Petitpaon"* included herein was made from a copy of the Louis Michaud edition. The translations of the three shorter stories were made from the relevant volumes of the *Nouvelle Revue* reproduced on the Bibliothèque Nationale's *gallica* website.

Brian Stableford

THE LAND OF HUMANIA

In a time not marked by any event worthy of the attention of chroniclers, a young man and a young woman left Panbiole, the capital of the celebrated land of Humania, now vanished from the map of the world.

In the bosom of the spring night the breeze, precursor of the dawn, became excited, and the two travelers, passing the scattered houses of the extreme outskirts, went on to the road that climbed a steep slope toward the east, all the way to the distant horizon where then sun quit the earth in order to scale the high vault of the blue sky.

At the hasty pace of pursued runaways, the young man and the young woman were marching side by side, and yet it seemed as if the woman was pulling along her companion, whom she held by the hand.

The crowns of the trees were agitated by long frissons and the belated shadows, still prisoners of the dense foliage, escaped one by one into the light, which now poured down the slope like a torrent.

Doubtless inconvenienced by the dazzle of the fluid avalanche, the young man bowed his head, which he sometimes tried to turn away, while his companion, her eyes intoxicated by the unfurled waves, marched with her head high, drawing to her lips the hand tenderly squeezed in her own.

Under the caress, the man straightened his drooping shoulders, and his stride became bolder. Soon, however, as if vanquished by fatigue, he made a gesture of irremediable distress to his guide, whose high-heeled boots were sounding resolutely on the roadway.

Then the woman, slowing her pace slightly, darted a backward glance over the man's shoulder toward the city asleep at the foot of the steep hill, and, in a hesitant voice trembling with the fear of a response that might not be the desired response, said: "My Aiglor are you leaving some regret down there?"

The man shivered; he seized the hand that the woman extended toward the city still buried in darkness as if it were an unexpected aid; his breast heaved violently and, lowering his eyelids, which crushed large tears beneath their lashes, he said in a faint voice: "Féliah, omnipotent queen of my heart, you know that marching in your footsteps is my sole hope, but forgive me…while bathing in the tenderness of your gaze, my eyes have lost all strength, and the cruel sun is wounding them terribly!"

"Oh, don't blaspheme the triumphal sun, whose noble light has passed through my eyes…my eyes, which were your joy, are frightening you now…"

"My dear…dear…to flee Humania…to quit Panbiole… to die…but to follow you always, my eyes sunk in the radiance of your tender, infinite pupils!"

"My lover, don't veil with mourning the memories of the bright morning of our love. Oh, if you could know all my jealousy of that horrible city, which retains something of you in its shadow!"

"Féliah! I swear to you upon our love that only the most indifferent of my thoughts remain down there! Féliah, my soul is entirely yours, I swear to you on my adoration of your beauty!"

"Thank you, my Aiglor. Oh, thank you for our love…forgive me for the funereal idea that causes me anguish. I have in a horror in my heart at thought of abandoning a little of you, of you who belong to me…"

"Yes, Féliah, all my soul is exhaled into your soul, and my entire body has fainted in the delirium of your body; the victorious sensations of your caresses have abolished my being in your being. I am no longer anything but a shadow attached forever to the splendor of your desires…but suffer, oh, suffer that my gaze should look down on Panbiole one more time, in order to carry away from that city you hate all our joy of being loved there! It's a caprice Féliah…"

"Aiglor, your caprice is dearer to me than my will; let us both look back at the dense darkness that our dawn will dazzle with its fires in a few minutes. On those friendly rays, let us flee the supreme reflections that the shadow of life has left in our eyes…our eyes, in which the light ought to give rise henceforth only to the eternal image of our love!"

The young woman sits down on a large bank of grass; she draws the young man to her, who sets himself at her knees; their lips meet in a long kiss; the woman's bosom rises and fall in a violent rhythmic movement that animates the fabric of her silver mesh corsage. The man seems paralyzed in the grip of the arms cast around his neck. Slowly, their lips separate; Feliah's fingers are now caressing her lover's head, which rests on her knees, and both of them gaze silently before them at the city, one of whose steeples progressively raises its rosy silhouette against the gray wall of the sky.

"Look at the steeple of our church," murmurs Féliah.

"Yes…the steeple," Aiglor repeats, mechanically.

Suddenly, he removes the two hands placed on his temples and, getting up with a violent effort, asks in a contracted voice: "My house—where's my house?"

"Your house, Aiglor. Oh, for a long time yet it will be plunged in darkness; the towers and steeples of all the churches will emerge before that, and the high roofs of princely dwellings; the white mosaic terrace of my palace will appear before that, and only when the entire city is bathed in light will the humble thatch of your house form a bump in the ground, like a wreck blackening the clear mirror of the sea!"

Motionless, Aiglor makes no reply. He turns to Féliah, but an invincible force draws his eyes in the direction of Panbiole again. The pink shadow of the steeple whitens gradually, while the confused forms around become gradually more distinct.

As if to himself, having forgotten his companion, Aiglor says: "Poor house! You were very dear to me, though; your thatch sheltered people who loved me…my mother…my father…my brothers and sisters…oh, all the good things that I have left behind…!"

Féliah has risen to her feet; she goes to her lover, whose words she has overheard, and in a tender voice, scarcely marked with indulgent reproach, she interrupts him.

"Why are you talking about your mother, your father, your brothers and your sisters? Am I not your entire universe? Have I too not left, for you, a father of whom I was proud, a mother whose only joy I was? For you, have I not left a palace, a palace that the greatest people in Panbiole envied me? Is not the abandonment of my wealth worth as much as that of your poverty?"

Aiglor extends supplicant hands toward the young woman and, as his thoughts stray, words emerge from his mouth at hazard. "Why leave Panbiole, Féliah? Why flee that life, rich in all good things of which one dreams?"

Féliah takes her lover's hands in hers; with a kiss she stops on his lips the regrets that are ready to expand, and while dragging him to the grassy bank she speaks to him softly.

"Perfidious good things, Aiglor! Good things that would be the certain murderers of our love! Oh, my lover, do you believe, then, that in that city down there it's permissible for a woman who lives in a palace to love a man whose head reposes beneath a modest roof?"

Hands enlaced, the two lovers, huddled together, are sitting on the grassy bank; Aiglor listens in profound delight to the harmonious voice that is whispering the infinity of their tenderness in his ear.

"We are in love, my Aiglor; is that not the only concern of our two beings? Are our hearts bound by other bonds than our love? Are our eyes made of another light than the sunshine of our joy? Aiglor, hatred is always on the lookout for love, as shadow is always on the lookout for light. Look at the sun chasing the last of the darkness away; its victorious rays will soar, for a few hours, from the height of the glorious sky; but this evening, darkness will resume the battle, and, vanquished in its turn, the resplendent star, having bloodied its agony, will fall asleep in the impenetrable shroud of night. Aiglor, I'm shivering...I'm trembling...I can see, hidden in the folds of shadow, men who are lying in ambush for our love, like snakes lurking in the dry grass.

Aiglor stands up abruptly; his wide open eyes are lost in the vertigo of the sunlight and his voice rings like that of a herald of victory: "Féliah, love is a holy thing and all powers break against it. Féliah, we will crush the venomous snakes under our heels!"

For a few moments, he remains in that heroic pose, in which he seems to be defying the world. Féliah contemplates him at length, in a sort of tender admiration. Then, in her turn, she gets up and, coming to lean on her lover's bosom, murmurs words in a voice so low that Aiglor is obliged to tilt his head in order to hear them: "Aiglor, has the thought never occurred to you that other lips than yours might press my lips? Have you ever thought that other arms might embrace me?"

Brutally, as if to drive away a pressing danger, Aiglor seizes the young woman—but she, suspended from her lover's neck, soothes his sudden anxiety seductively: "Let your heart be reassured, my Aiglor...of all my person, men have only brushed my fingertips, abandoned as if to domestic animals that it is necessary to retain in one's power."

Slowly, Aiglor kisses his mistress' eyes; gently, he lets her slide to the ground, and she smiles at him while he turns his gaze, full of haughty indifference, in the direction of Panbiole, which is brightening rapidly. Suddenly, his eye pauses, and fixes attentively on a white patch that grows amid the tangle of steeples and towers; his right hand points it out to his companion, whose waist he sustains with his left arm.

"There's your palace, on the threshold of which I saw you for the first time. It was one morning when, as usual, your blessed hands were doling out charity to the poor of Panbiole; all of them knew the generosity of your soul and all of them came in search of a little relief of their misery; dawn had scarcely broken than they lined up at the foot of the terrace, mute and silent for fear of troubling your repose; but your pity was anxious to abridge their waiting. Almost immediately, the door of the palace opened; as soon as you appeared, the unfortunates prostrated themselves as if before a divinity.

"Oh, you were so beautiful, my Féliah, that my knees, too, buckled at the sight of you. You advanced between the ranks of the poor to whom your white hand gave a silver coin, and all of them blessed you with tears in their eyes. You passed before me, and you deposited a silver coin in the palm of my hand. Oh, that silver coin! My lips wore it away so much with my kisses that it undulated before my breath like the leaf of a tree in the breeze.

"Every morning, for many a day, I came, dressed as a beggar and lost in their crowd, to receive your daily alms. Often, on contact with your hand, my hand became so tremulous that the silver coin escaped from my fingers. When you had passed by, the poor, mocking my clumsiness, helped me to find the coin, which I placed with the others over my heart, in a narrow bag.

"One day—do you remember?—you passed before me without your hand putting the customary alms in mine. Oh, I thought that my heart would break...my knees remained nailed to the ground...I saw you draw away...you climbed the white steps and my eyes closed in order not to see the large door separate you from me forever. My head was filled with strange noises, like those of a storm thundering in the distance, and the sudden hope awoke in my heart that a lightning-bolt might annihilate me in that square brushed by your feet.

"Then, my burning forehead felt lightened by a cool caress calming the furious beating of my arteries, and my eyes, incredulous at first, saw you before me. All the poor people had gone. We were alone, Féliah! I dared to raise your charitable hand to my lips. Oh, Féliah, your heart had understood that the silver coins were not the alms that were necessary to my life.

"You took me into your palace; your hands, with tenderness, decked me with festival garments, and the following morning, holding hands, we appeared on top of the terrace.

The poor saw in me your fiancé. They addressed a fervent prayer to Heaven for the eternal happiness of our union. You gave them gold coins, and forced me to distribute the silver coins that you had found piously preserved in my bosom. 'Souvenirs,' you told me, 'are the guardians of dead things, and our love alone has given birth to eternal life.'

"Every morning, the unfortunate received their alms from our hands, until the day when, in tears you told me that henceforth, you would go to the poor alone. You told me that danger was lying in wait for me outside and begged me not to cross the threshold of the palace again. What did you fear for me? Then, you no longer left me. One of your servants fulfilled your charitable duty and the poor, who thought that you were ill, sent us flowers. Do you remember the sadness with which those flowers filled you? Féliah, why was the sight of the poor, who loved you, forbidden to you? Why, Féliah, did your eyes weep over the flowers?"

At the last words pronounced by her lover, the young woman has become very pale, and, making a sudden effort, she holds herself tightly against him.

"Aiglor, my love, I don't know...perhaps I was afraid that contact with those poor people might tarnish our joy...and then, I was jealous of eyes that saw you. Forgive me, Aiglor for my jealousy of the poor. Let's go...oh, let's go, quickly!"

Suddenly, she extends her arms. She has just perceived human forms climbing the slope.

"Men! Look! Oh, let's flee!"

"They're unfortunates, Féliah. Once, your charitable soul didn't want to make the poor wait at the threshold of your palace; now, let your generosity cede to those desperate individuals the first place on the road of hope. Come, let them pass by; we'll leave afterwards."

As if fearful that the human beings who are advancing rapidly might recognize them, Féliah seizes Aiglor by the hand and draws him behind a thick clump of giant rose-bushes that rises up by the roadside near the grassy bank. Both of them are completely hidden by the roses of all colors expanding in an immense perfumed spray, from which a few petals have fallen to strew the edge of the road and the grass of the bank.

Half way up the hill a man and a woman appear, they are walking separately on the two sides of the road; they are talking, but only the voice of the man is distinctly audible at first from the place where Féliah has drawn her companion.

"Oh, how long it is since the day when we loved one another for the first time! Since then, many joys have blossomed, expanding our hearts for the desolation of immense sadnesses, and yet, forgetfulness cannot come of the summer evening when, treading the green path, my feet walked in the odorous intoxication expired by the breeze. It was like a perfume of flesh that fled before me. For fear of dissipating the floating caress with which my blood was inflamed, I dared not run, and my desire rose in bounding waves to my maddened temples! Finally, at a bend in the path I perceived a woman who was slowly drawing away, turning her head from time to time, from which loose blonde hair hung down all the way to the ground. As I approached, she smiled..."

The man and the woman have quit the two sides of the road; gradually, they have moved closer to one another; now, they have arrived beside the grassy bank. They stop, and the woman completes the suspended sentence.

"And that woman was me. Oh yes, I remember. The muffled sound of your footsteps on the moss filled me with an immense joy, the proud and sovereign joy of sensing that I was desired. Oh, your desire! I wanted it burning like the mid-day sun, thirsty from its journey toward refreshing night! Your desire! I wanted it exasperated by mystery and by delay, and I fled, leaving behind me the penetrating scents escaped from my hair and my shaken veils!"

Those two beings resemble one another strangely; their faces are covered with an unhealthy pallor and their entire individualities reveal cruel dolors recently suffered; their eyes, profoundly sunken, shine with a sharp gleam in the blue circles that surround them; they are staring, and shudder as if at the memory of something terrible whose return they dread. At the same time, with identical gestures, they place their hands on one another's mouths to impede the words giving new life to the haunting of the frightful past—but almost immediately, they take their hands away, in which teeth have left imprints; with despairing expressions, they follow the slow effacement of the violet-tinted marks.

Their eyes meet again; their nostrils flare, and, matching breath to breath, in voices as hoarse as those of rutting beasts, they say what their oppressed breasts are impotent to hold back.

"Oh, your kiss, which crushed me in your arms!"

"Oh, your arms, which bound me to the hectic caress of your body!"

They are both speaking at the same time, and the shrill tone of woman's voice dominates the deeper voice of the man.

"Oh, our hearts transported by the same emotion!"

"Our bodies reddened by our kisses!"

"Our flesh united, exhausted!"

Then their voices lower, and become more bitter.

"Our bodies writhed like green branches thrown on to a fire!"

"Our backs creaked like trunks broken by the tempest!"

"Our flesh quivered under the bites of our kisses, determined to make a single being out of our two beings…one blood out of our blood!"

They shove one another violently in order to escape, it seems, the carnal folly ready to reconquer them, and the man groans, dully: "Oh, how many times I fled into the paths to rediscover the sweet intoxication once inhaled! The hard stones lacerated my feet. Until I was out of breath, I pursued, as before, the white mysterious phantom!"

The woman continues in the same moaning voice: "And always, that white phantom…was me! Oh, I tried to run, but the sound of your footfalls put a leaden weight on my shoulders!"

And both of them, in common lamentation: "And always, we found one another, thirsty for one another, searching, in the fury of our embraces, forgetfulness of vain treasons. The languid bites became scarlet again. Our flesh howled at the crushing of old bruises!"

Their quivering lips can no longer articulate any sound; haggard, the man advances toward the woman, who throws her arms around his neck; they totter, as if gripped by vertigo; the woman, dragging her companion, whom she holds narrowly enlaced against her bosom, falls backwards on to the broad grassy bank.

They embrace with a long cry of dolorous rage, which is prolonged in a gasp in which their lives seem to be hiccupping their last strength...

Now they are lying side by side, on their backs, the woman with her breasts erect and her mouth open, the man with his arms in the form of a cross, his teeth clenched; multi-colored petals, dropping from the tops of the rose-bushes, fall one by one, covering their bodies and their faces, and they seem to be two cadavers over which pious hands have scattered a dusting of rose-petals...

Convulsive tremors run along their bodies; gradually, they are reanimated; like people awakening from a profound sleep, in which all their consciousness has been obscured, they rub their eyes, mechanically casting aside the flowers, which slide down the grass of the bank; then they raise themselves up on their elbows and dart anxious glances around them. They recognize one another, and lower their heads silently.

Suddenly, at a sound of footsteps coming up from the direction of Panbiole, they stand up, and, perceiving two men clad in long white robes followed by an entire procession of human beings, they utter the same cry of terror: "The priests! The priests!" And they flee along the road that disappears eastwards, while the two men clad in white make bizarre signs toward them with their right hands.

Aiglor and Féliah, clinging tightly together in the cradle of verdure, have followed the scene that has just unfolded before them without saying a word; at the sudden flight of the two strange individuals, they both open their mouths, but the questions pressing upon their lips are arrested once again by the sight of the cortege that is advancing along the road, broadening opposite the grassy bank into a kind of ledge where the slope seems to rest momentarily before commencing its paid ascent immediately thereafter.

It is a very disparate troop; behind the two priests clad in long white robes with floating sleeves, following in the greatest disorder, come a band of young women and young men; there are also children, and, to distract themselves from the length of the journey, they are jostling one another. Whenever one of them bumps into one of the priests marching ahead of them, laughter bursts forth, quickly suppressed by the severe glance of the man in white.

Then, in a compact group, come mature men and women; the latter are enveloped by long black veils that cover their faces and hand down all the way to the ground; the men, bareheaded, are walking with their eyes fixed on the ground. These people, by their costume and their entire external appearance, seems to belong to all ranks of society; the majority are carrying precious caskets in their hands; some of those caskets, as if they have been carried away in haste, are poorly closed, letting out the ends of golden chains, which swing back and forth heavily.

Then, some distance away, but stimulated by the priest who closes the procession, trail several old men, leaning on their staffs, with whose length they try in vain to straighten their curbed backs.

The two priests, occupied in maintaining order in the ranks of the children, have just gone past the grassy bank; they stop, facing the puerile swarm, which their gaze suddenly reduced to silence and immobility.

The old men have caught up with the group that had a slight advance on them; now the whole troop is mingled. The priest marching at the rear comes to stand beside the first two, and all three of them, with their arms extended, address a prayer to the heavens, which is repeated, with the same gesture, by the entire audience.

Fixed on the breast of each priests, cutting through the whiteness of the robes, is a large square of red fabric embroidered with a silver disk radiant with gold; it is the symbol of the new religion, but only the priests and privileged adepts have the right to wear it.

From a black velvet pouch suspended from his belt, the oldest of the priests takes a square of red cloth similar to the one he bears on his breast; he holds it in his right hand and, showing it to the faithful, who immediately bow their heads devotedly, he begins to speak in a solemn voice.

"My brothers and sisters in the Unique and Almighty God, our feet are finally treading solid ground. We are like shipwreck victims lost in the torment on the angry sea; in our flesh, the hours of suffering and anguish have counted, one by one, their lancing pulsations. The frightful tempest has been unleashed, hollowing out the waves with unfathomable gulfs, animating them with gigantic waterspouts enlarged by inevitable tentacles. The lacerating summits of innumerable reefs have reared up against the whitening foam. But the terror of gulfs is vain! The enlacement of waterspouts is impotent! The spurs of rock are blunted! We have escaped all the traps, resisted all the assaults, and the frail raft of our hope has finally reached the shore!

"There, on the unshakable rock, indifferent to the waves that break at its feet with a great din, the castaways, still trembling at the dangers confronted, throw themselves to their knees to thank heaven for their salvation; above the abyss, eager to reconquer them, they beg God to deign to accept the humble offering of their riches, miraculously saved from the tempest! On the lost ship, at the first blasts of the storm, men and women have charged themselves with their most cherished possessions, and now, from fingers soiled by the foam, slide jeweled rings obscured by mud…the ears of women are stripped of long precious pendants stained green by viscous algae…innumerable jewels tarnished by the sea emerge from hiding places..."

The three priests examine, with anxious eyes, the men and women kneeling in front of them; the voice of the one who is speaking rises with increasing violence.

"Ah! Your fingers too are charged with rings! From your ears, I see heavy pendants hanging! Metal chains run over your shoulders! Yes, you have followed the order given in the name of the God of light whose glorious message I bring! Yes, you have adorned yourselves with that which life in Humania has devolved upon you in the puerile name of wealth! Ah, sad wealth, soiled with all kinds of mire, veiled with all manner of shadows!"

After having exchanged a furtive glance with his two fellows, his right arm raised, he launches a furious interrogation.

"And there, in those caskets, what else have you brought? Oh, doubtless obscure things prestigiously qualified as treasures!" And, his voice resonant with scorn: "Ah! Treasures, those vile metals? Treasures, those poor stones that the Almighty Sun, our sovereign God, deigns to dress with the bright adornment of his radiation? Go, quickly! Humiliate before the glare of the divine flamboyance that miserable wreckage of earthly pride!"

The caskets open, awakening the triumph of their riches; there are supple chains of gold, like sparkling snakes that flee between the fingers; large medallions quivering in blinding disks; diamonds that the sun traverses with fulgurant darts; rubies bleeding their redness over the azure of sapphires and the milkiness of opals...

The three priests follow the hands occupied in stirring the rippling stones within the caskets attentively; their irises, invaded by too much light, contract in order to see more distinctly, and as the inestimable treasures are revealed their visages gradually lose their troubled expression; the voice of the priest, gradually becoming less aggressive, ends up relaxing into words that are almost soft.

"In the infinity of his mercy, we have the temerity to hope, God will bestow upon you forgiveness for your attachment to these despicable possessions, as he will suffer your audacity in making the offering to him..."

The faithful remain motionless while the three priests confer in low voices, The latter make a sign of acquiescence and the youngest among them, taking a few steps forward, leans over to rummage in the casket open before a man dressed in black, whose long white hair is silvering, on his nape, the golden links of a necklace, from which is suspended a diamond crescent that brushes, as it sways, the jewels heaped in the casket.

The priest's fingers, plunged into the gems, cause flashes of light to spring forth. The hands finally take hold of a gold star with six points forged in a dark shiny metal reminiscent of jet. The priest holds it in his left hand while his right hand is placed on his breast, upon the little square of red cloth. He straightens up and, at the sight of the star with the black points, the other two priests also piously cover the silver disks radiant with gold, embroidered on the squares of red fabric that clash with the whiteness of their robes.

All the men and women have bowed their heads before the mysterious object that the priest is considering, while his disdainful words spill forth.

"Ah! Here it is, then—the criminal image of the error that so long enveloped Humania in the unfathomable depth of its obscurity! Here it is, then, the frightful symbol of the ancient belief, denying immortality! Oh, accursed star, your golden center irradiates black rays! Yes, it means that life is the prisoner of the darkness that surrounds it, does it not? It means that only the realities enslaved by the earth are alive, outside of which you proclaim the unique existence of nothingness? Ah, here it is, the deadly face that you employed, puerile old man, to inform your fellows of your unique love for the life that, down here, is annihilated in a few ephemeral years! What am I saying? A few years...but no...rather, a few minutes, a few seconds, miserable intervals of time so fleeting that in eternity, the most sensitive sand-glass would be unable to count them!"

The old man whose casket contained the star with the black points, without daring to raise his head, holds out his imploring hands toward the white-clad priest, who continues to rail at him, shrugging his shoulders.

"Oh, now your hands reach out for the forgiveness of your crimes?"

A dull and tremulous voice emerges from the man's breast; several times it repeats the same words of pitiful appeal: "Forgive me, Master! Master, forgive me!"

"Forgive you? For sure, you were one of the faithful servants of that execrable cult of life! Human spectacles prostituted your eyes, which God had given you to contemplate his glory! From your mouth, which should have opened solely to praise the Master, emerged coarse songs celebrating the deceptive splendor of terrestrial joys! You hands, made to remain joined in holy prayer, you dishonored by accomplishing mortal toil! Oh, wretched madman! Poor stray on the frightful road to damnation! Finally, faith has conquered you! The blindfold that hid the truth from you has finally fallen from your eyes; from the accursed starless night you have come to us, charge with repentance!

"This offering, sinner, the glorious Master will receive; like the wind that purifies the azure of the clouds that burden it, his hand will efface your sins and your crimes! Let your forehead, washed clean of its soiling, look up toward the heaven that divine grace will permit you to enter."

The old man abruptly raised his head; in that movement, the chain supporting the diamond crescent caught on one of the corners of the casket; a link broke, and the golden thread, sliding under the gray curls spreading over the shoulders, fell to the ground.

At that sight the priest stopped, as if nonplussed; the star with the black points escaped from his fingers and went to join the golden necklace on the ground. His lips murmured rapid words, a prayer—doubtless immediately granted, for, extending his arm toward his two companions, who interrupted the conversation in which they were completely absorbed, he cried, in a prophetic one: "A benediction upon up, my brothers! The ardor of your faith has touched the Lord Almighty! He has condescended to signal his august presence in our midst by the most striking of miracles; his hand, invisible to the weak eyes of mortals, has extended through the clouds to one of our brothers, whose soul, once the most obscure, has illuminated today with the radiant clarity of faith!

"Rejoice, old man! In accordance with the spirit of humility and on a laudable thought of contrition, you have come to God, your shoulders charged with the shameful sign marking the criminal sacerdocy once filled by you with such a frightful zeal that your eternity would be accomplished in the most frightful tortures if God, whom you once had the madness to hold in contempt, had not wanted to give you a living proof of the infinity of his clemency!

"Rejoice, old man! God has touched your body, vowed to eternal flames! His hand, the creator of worlds, has made the abominable chain that sealed your soul to the rack of eternal expiation fall from your shoulders!

"Rejoice, brother! Now your person is sacred, for God has approached it! Now, your mouth is florid with innocence, like that of all small children. Now, your hands are pure, equal to those of the servants of God!

"Rejoice, brother! In my ear, just now, his ineffable voice made itself heard, ordering me to place on your heart the sacred symbol whose intimate essence you have penetrated. Is that not so? You know that that silver disk is nothing other than life, sad and temporary life, the dolorous career in which the creature whom the weight of sin has precipitated into the darkness crawls inexorably.

"In the first hours of the fall, night weighed over the universe unremittingly, and cries of distress rose from the depths of the black gulf toward the Almighty, whose pity open to the wretches justly struck by his wrath; he leaned over them, and suddenly, the damned saw their prison illuminated by an immense light; some recognized in those floods of light the very person of the God they had betrayed, and, repentance entering into their souls, they begged the Master to let them approach the hearth once again where the original flame burned whose reflections had come to animate them; and gently, along luminous rays, one by one, they rose into the ether, sustained by invisible wings.

"The celestial apparition did not strike the multitude, however, and the majority of the reproved, attributing to their own strength the advent of that beneficent light, hurled further imprecations toward the one who had expelled them. In vain, the Being of supreme bounty, tearing himself away from the adoration of his faithful, came every day to show his dear rebels the road to grace—who, still convinced that they had half-vanquished the darkness, struggled, with the hope of conquering total light!

"Oh, miserable mortals, the centuries have passed, filled with your sufferings, also consecrated, alas, to the exaltation of your pride, and when, despairing of ever seeing your eyes reopen to celestial light, God assumed lamentable human form in order to enable your ears to hear the eternal word, your sacrilegious hands were raised against him!"

His eyes lost, the old man seemed to be listening to a distant song; the priest's last words snatched him abruptly from his bliss, and as before, his throat sobbed the same supplication: "Forgive me, Master! Master, forgive me!"

From the black velvet pouch suspended from his belt the priest had taken a square of red cloth similar to the one that marked his own breast. He put it to his lips, and then, holding it in his right hand, he approached it to the old man's face.

"Look, Brother, at the sovereign sign whose virtue effaces the memory of even the most frightful crimes. Your crime was the crime of all other men, and your fate is linked to the culpable fate of your forefathers. Your eyes, too laden with shadow, would have refused to recognize God in the simple living man who once appeared in Humania clad in a white linen robe; he preached the principle of all things, and the sun itself is merely one of his attributes; he came to return mortals to the road of light, which their footsteps had fled, and in Panbiole, laughter and gibes welcome the divine messenger who, in order to compel the faith of the most incredulous, consented to give a striking proof of his supernatural power.

"One day when the people were gathered in the main square, to listen to him in the manner of a spectacle, he raised his right hand above his head, and immediately, in spite of the ardent sun, a bright star appeared in the depths of the sky, attentive to follow his movements. At the sight of the prodigy, the laughter suddenly stopped, and after a brief moment of stupor, a slow growl of anger rose up from the crowd, followed by ferocious howls clamoring for the death of the impostor; the most intrepid ran upon him, and, because he only opposed calm words to the furious, showing them the star scintillating above his head, he was thrown amid cries and threats into a the depths of a dark dungeon.

"The judges of Panbiole brought him out of it and, recognizing him as a magician dangerous for the security of Humania, condemned him to suffer the execution reserved for the worst criminals. Since the remotest times there had existed in Panbiole a well dug by unknown hands, so deep that the fall of stones dropped into it was not followed by any echo. Into that abyss, where malefactors whose crimes demanded the most ignominious of punishments were precipitated, the divine Master was to perish. As his death was a sacrifice made to the light of day, the oldest of the judges of Panbiole, clad in the functions of executor, waited to shove the chained body into the gulf until the precise moment when the sun, marked at its center by the star born of a reproved power, reached the highest point of the shy, directly above the infernal void.

"The executioner's action was carried out amid the unleashing of a vengeful joy, but the frightful moment, when the victim tottered on the edge of the gaping precipice, was extinguished in the darkness that suddenly surged forth; mouths paralyzed by horror, could no longer articulate any sound, and eyes widened by fright were obstinately fixed upon the pale golden star that remained in the depths of the sky from which the sun had vanished.

"Oh, if only remorse had entered your hearts! If only faith had brushed your souls! But no! It was by the impotence of your rage that your features were contracted! It was the infinity of your hatred that blemished your faces, and when, tremulously, the voice of the sovereign judge rose up to accuse the man who was about to be executed for a further crime of disrespect for Humania, an immense call for terrible vengeance, triumphing over anguish, escaped from all throats.

"In a supreme effort of his horrible power, the execrated magician had just dragged after him the day star, the glorious witness of the victory snatched from the darkness, half of which had given way to light.

"The Council of Panbiole met before the gulf into which the rays of the motionless star plunged, shimmering, and in spite of a minority opinion estimating any such attempt futile, it was decided that someone would descend into the well in order to take possession of the talisman creative of such extraordinary prodigies.

"The heralds, raising torches arranged in a circle around the Council of Panbiole, proclaimed the decree and ordered the man to come forward who would offer himself for the accomplishment of the gigantic task.

"Everyone recoiled, and it was necessary to go into the prison in search of a condemned man who was awaiting the expiation of the murder of his own father. The wretch, who howled that darkness was an inviolable safeguard for him and that they did not have the right to execute him at night, was brought forth with his wrists bound. With great difficulty, the judges finally made him understand that he could save his life by rendering Humania a service so great that not only would his crime be effaced but that he would also become the master of all the gold to be found in the richest quarter of Panbiole.

"The unexpected salvation and the fabulous offer did not calm the terror of the wretch, whose haggard eyes stared fearfully into the gaping mouth of the somber precipice, and when the judge had explained to him what Panbiole expected of him, his head fell inertly on to his breast. Without making a movement, as if death, for him almost immediate, had stiffened his body, he learned that soon, sustained by ropes, he would be allowed to slide down to the bottom of the well. There he would find the cadaver, still warm, of a man who had just been thrown into it; he was to attach it to the end of the cable, which would bring both of them back up to the surface, where the promised reward would be ready.

"The judge asked the man whether he had understood; he raised his head imperceptibly and let it fall again in a sign of assent.

"Then the judge, taking off his cape, wound it around beneath the man's armpits, in order that his flesh would not be too badly bruised by the rope, and instructed him to tug the rope three times when his feet touched the ground; he was to give three similar tugs as a signal for the ascent. After having touched his trembling lips to the golden star with the dark rays, the symbol of existence in Panbiole, the judge handed him over to the servants of the Council, who carefully looped beneath his arms a chain chosen from the heap of cables of every sort that had been brought out.

"That chain, made of a light metal whose resistance was proof against any strain, was the sacred witness of the grandeur of Panbiole; every year, on the same day, it was deployed in great pomp around the city, of which it had to surround all the houses, and when the construction were extended into neighboring terrains, links prepared in advance permitted the chain to be lengthened to embrace the city's new domain. For fear of not finding a number great enough to express it, no one had ever dared to calculate the length of that chain; they limited themselves to saying, in low voices, how many more rings would suffice to surround the entirety of Humania.

"The frightful descent began; for hours the shining cable sank into the hole; the men moistened their fuming hands, armed by the rapid slide. Several times, consumed torches fell from the hands of the herald. Suddenly, the inexhaustible chain ran out, and the astonishment was such that the judge, with great difficulty, only just had time to seize the last link as it was about to disappear into the gulf. The rigging of ships, the bronze chains of war machines and those that served to keep ferocious beasts prisoner were connected end to end, and nothing remained but an enormous package of slender cord fabricated for the daughter of the king, who amused herself by having herself raised up into the clouds by huge captive sea-birds.

"They hesitated, because they feared that the frail cord might break under the excessively heavy weight, but one of the judges observed that it was ridiculous to entertain so many reservations, since it was merely a matter of the life of a criminal condemned to death. It was knotted to the last link of an enormous chain maintained by three men on the edge of the well, a hawser that tended to vibrate with shrill sounds like the highest notes of a harp. In incalculable length was then unrolled, and the packet was almost exhausted when the servants of the Council finally perceived the agreed three tugs.

"An indescribable emotion took hold of the audience at the thought that, for the first time since the birth of Humania, one of their fellows had reached the bottom of the mysterious well, and that his hands were about to touch the blooded remains of the magician whose horrible crime had been so justly punished. Minutes as heavy as centuries went by before, once again, the cord was agitated by the signal awaited by the haulers before commencing their task.

As the different fragments of ropes and chains reappeared, the judges calculated what the abyss still retained. The brilliant girdle of Panbiole finally emerged from the darkness and the judges, in the light of inclined torches, leaned over in order to attempt to be the first to penetrate the mystery. Slowly rotating at the end of the chain, which thinned out in the opaque atmosphere, something inert rose up, covered in the black cassock of parricides. The sovereign judge, stiffening his muscles, by means of a violent effort exerted on the chain, brought the lamentable human form level with the mouth of the well, and, seizing it with both arms, laid it on the black marble rim. The man did not move and the judge, in order to interrogate his heartbeat, applied his right hand to the left side of the chest.

"Suddenly, an oblique ray of sunlight lit up on the edge of the horizon, and came to brush the fingers of the judge, who nervously took off the garment of infamy in order to lay bare the breast in which life was perhaps not entirely extinct. The sun, rapidly rising several degrees into the vault of the heavens, inundated the man's breast, discovering a small red patch marked at its center with a silver disk radiating slender golden darts.

"A slight frisson passed through the inanimate body; the eyes opened very wide to the light, and the hands agitated, seeming to want to approach the breast. Then the judge, taking possession of the square of cloth, raised it up before the eyes of the man, who put his hands together while his lips were animated by an imperceptible tremor. The judge leaned over to hear the words that were scarcely proffered, and were an account of the terrible adventure revealed by the man lying on the black marble rim of the well: 'A dazzling light, like that of the sun, reigned in those depths, striped by a floor whiter than the paving stones of a church...'

"The sovereign judge listened breathlessly to that whisper, which, vacillating on the pale lips, gradually died away, to be reborn after a long moment, for the evocation of the infernal secret. 'No bones lay at the bottom of the well, and on the white flagstones, illuminated by a blinding glare, not the slightest trace of blood...'

"And slowly, slowly, without effort, as if his body had become imponderable, the man raised himself up on his elbow. His lips, approaching the judge's hands, kissed the mysterious square of red cloth, and at the same moment, the creature sitting on the black marble rim vanished in the sunlight suspended from the summit of the vault of the heavens, and some people saw a human form glide and disappear into the bewildering blindness of space...

"The redemptive sign of the sin whose atrocity weighed upon Humania, God left in the ignorant dazzle of the well of shame, from which hands red with the most culpable blood extracted, it in order to render it to your adoration, criminal old man, who has become my brother.

"Look at it, my brother: the certain symbol of your salvation. The sparkling golden darts departing from the pale silver circle proclaim the praiseworthy desire to go beyond the life enclosed in that red square, reddened, it seems, by the floods of human blood shed for the conservation of an accursed existence!

"There, formal and vivid, is the promise of grace descending from divine pity for repentant hearts. So long as the sun is radiant over the world, the radiant ladder whose summit attains paradise will be raised toward the sky; but so narrow are its rungs that there is only room for one body at a time, and one soul at a time. Solitary, in expiation of a common crime, creatures must march, along the road that leads to eternal happiness!

"Old man, on your breast, wherein divine love beats, I will place this sign, thanks to which you will be able, when our steps have followed the entire route, to climb the vertiginous summit of the temple, where the hand of God will take you, to sit you down at his side on his glorious throne of infinite splendor...as the first, you will climb toward the light from where, down below, you will see your brother kneeling, waiting for the road to bliss to open for them too!"

Quiet tears surged from the old man's eyes. They ran slowly down his transfigured face. He seized the hands of the priest who had just attached the mark of forgiveness to his breast; he covered them with kissed while a murmur of prayer rose from the ranks of the faithful, still immobile, heads bowed.

The other two priests have followed with approving eyes what their fellow has done. The latter frees his hands from the effusions of the old man to go past the men and women whose hands were entirely empty, rapidly and without stopping. Hav-

35

ing arrived beside an adolescent who is silently weeping large tears, which are trickling into a little filigree basket, he perceives feminine adornments heaped up: rings, ear-rings, necklaces and belts set with large precious stones.

"What is your despair, child? Why darken with your tears the gleam of the jewels of which your basket is full?"

"My fiancée loved them, Master."

"Ah! Your fiancée loved them, as you loved your fiancée. The straying of the eyes! The straying of the senses! In the reflections of those topazes, sapphires and rubies, the features of that woman still reside. Those necklaces seem to you to be still warm from the perfumed contact of her throat, breathless with the promise of kisses. Those belts she had to undo, did she not, for the work of the flesh that caused your being to leap? Ah, damnation! Where is your fiancée?"

"In heaven, Master; she is dead."

"She is dead! And the debris of your soul that she has left on earth, you are going to offer to the Lord? You are going to ask the Lord to take your body, bruised by the horrible bonds of the flesh?"

"Oh yes, Master, let God take my body—I'm suffering so much!"

"What? You speak of suffering, child? What is your grief, then, if not the deliverance of your flesh, escaped from the flesh that would have tortured it, after having put it to sleep with the mirage of deceptive caresses? Oh, you have been robbed of your stupor? God, with the seal of eternity, has closed the lips that poured into your heart the devouring poison of love—and you call that suffering, child? The glory of Heaven is already shining for your young eyes. Of that which you call your suffering, child, Heaven will cure you."

"My fiancée, Master, shall I find her there?"

"You will find the perfection of all things there. If your love truly merited quitting the earth to live in Heaven, if the beauty of your fiancée was worthy of ethereal dwellings, you will be united on high for eternity with the one who aspired your desires in this world."

"Thank you, Master, thank you!"

While speaking, the priest has examined the jewels thrown pell-mell into the filigree basket; his fingers have palpated the precious stones amorously, one by one, and their contact seems to have cast a disturbance into his mind that he is having difficulty overcoming. From time to time he wipes a diamond tarnished by the young man's tears on his robe, looks again at the translucent stone, and contemplates its dazzling facets lovingly. After a final glance full of tenderness, as if regretfully, he places the little filigree basket on the ground and stands up, after having attached the symbol of redemption to the adolescent's breast.

He continues to file before the ranks of the prostrated faithful, sometimes pausing, retained by some casket more sumptuous than its neighbors. At each of these brief stops, he distributes emblems that he takes from his black velvet pouch. He finally arrives before a woman enveloped in the veils of mourning; she is holding to her lips, outside layers of black muslin, a large gold crown with silver leaves. The priest tears it away violently, and the woman follows the brutal hand that might break the frail golden circle with a dolorous gaze.

"Ah! Your nuptial crown, woman?"

"No, Master."

The priest considers the precious object and, prey to a violent indignation, says: "What is this crown, woman?"

The woman utters a cry, and in a scarcely intelligible voice, sobbing, babbles: "My daughter...my daughter..."

The priest examines the creature kneeling before him for a long time, and suddenly remembers.

"Oh yes! Féliah the sinner! Where is she, then? Still down there, enmired in her stupor, is she not? Ah, when she swore the oath to follow us, I saw the mortal flame that devoured her glinting in her eye; I sensed that it was impossible for her to abandon her jewels and riches! Let her wallow, then, in the warm mire of sensual pleasures, in which her body softens to become easier prey to the dolors that await her! Let her go to sleep, then, in her abhorrent luxury before the avenging hour of the awakening sounds! And you, woman, to obtain pardon for the heavy sin of your maternity, is this all that you have brought: your daughter's festival crown? The ornament with which she embellished herself to fortify the attractions of her execrable beauty?

"Listen to me: you will retake the road to Panbiole. It is your duty as a mother, you understand, to return to your daughter. It's necessary that she marches on the road to salvation, thus adorned—and remember, if the sun discovers the narrowest part of her body unprotected by a shield of gems and gold, your daughter, woman, will be on the field devoted, for eternal time, to the most frightful tortures! So, you will dress her in her jewels, you will charge her..."

The woman has tried to speak several times, but only a dry croak has emerged from her taut throat. With an almost inhuman cry, she interrupts the priest. "She has gone, Master!"

And, in jerky phrases, she says that her servants saw her leave at nightfall, after remaining for several days hidden in the depths of her palace, dressed in white, on the arm of a man.

The priest has listened with an almost indifferent expression, but when he learns that Féliah has distributed to the poor of Panbiole the totality of her wealth, he throws the crown down on to the ground. It breaks, and in a voice trembling with wrath, he says: "She's gone? With her lover? Dressed in white?" And he repeats, furiously: "With her lover... with her lover...dressed in white!"

His eyes come to rest on the grassy bank, which is still compressed by the imprint of two bodies.

"Ah! It was them who fled as we approached! There, they have embraced before the face of Heaven, hollowing out their indecent abyss even further. We'll find their bloody bodies lying at the bottom of a ditch, where the road has opened up beneath their feet to annihilate them!"

The woman utters groans while the priest, who has been rejoined by his two companions, continues howling until one of them stops him by tugging on the large sleeves of his robe.

All three begin a very animated discussion, in the course of which one of them points a finger at the grassy bank, making energetic signs of negation, which seemingly end up winning the approval of them all.

They count the squares of red cloth remaining in their pouches, thus finding the number they have distributed; they converse together for a little while longer, then they embrace one another three times, and the oldest of the priests, moving a few paces away, orders the faithful who have received the sign of forgiveness to gather around him.

"Follow me, you who have merited salvation! As for you, children of golden bubbles for whom, one day, grace will shine with all the brilliance of holy faith...old men, whose stride no longer triumphs over the fatigue of the route and whom, down here, if you are worthy of it, God will come himself to seek you out, go back to Panbiole with the two sacred servants that I leave you...listen, repeat their words, which are those of the God of light and joy!"

Slowly, the faithful who bear the silver circle radiant with gold on their breasts separate themselves from those who are to return; the two groups are now standing some distance apart. The old priest has already given the signal to depart when Féliah's mother, until then prostrate in her grief, races to join the cortege that has already taken a few strides along the ascendant route. One of the priests grabs her, and, in spite of her cries, he drags her back by force in the direction of Panbiole, followed by the crowd of children and old men that the other priest is driving ahead of him.

The cries of Féliah's mother are still audible when Aiglor, in spite of all the efforts made by his companion to hold him back, emerges from his hiding place. He seems utterly distraught at what he has just seen and heard. He covers his face with his hands and stands immobile until Féliah, approaching softly, takes his hands, which she passes around her neck, and their breasts come together, her eyes interrogating her lover's eyes.

Under that gaze, Aiglor, shivering, murmurs in a very low whisper, as if afraid of hearing the sound of his own voice: "Your mother, Féliah! Your mother, whom you're abandoning…your despairing mother…"

Féliah has thrown her arms recklessly around her lover's neck and, lip to lip, her head slightly tilted back to render the contact of their bodies more complete, she says: Leave, my love…leave…you alone, my Aiglor, you alone occupy my thoughts…"

"Your hear, Féliah…your heart…"

"My heart is full of you, Aiglor. Only that which concerns you causes it disquiet…"

A shadow passes over Aiglor's eyes, and after a long silence, he goes on: "Think, Féliah: our hands are empty; no adornment brightens us…and did not the priest say, a little while ago, that gold and gems…?"

"Shut up, my friend! Am I not rich in affection? Are we not dazzling in our common happiness? Does our love not shine as brightly as gold and gems? Is not our love, my Aiglor, as radiant as the sun?"

Aiglor is weeping softly and his tears dampen their two faces. Finally, he attempts a supreme argument.

"Did you not hear, Féliah? In the stairway to the temple, there is only room for one body and one soul at a time! It will be necessary for us to separate, Féliah…to separate…do you understand?"

Violently, the woman has thrown her head back; she launches a long glance at the flamboyant sun, full of hatred and defiance, and, with her fingers interlaced around the nape of the man's neck, she says: "Separate, us? One by one, you say, one climbs to the summit of the temple? Well, are we not one being? Is my body not your body? Is your soul not my soul? My Aiglor, we shall be so narrowly bound together that a single ray of sunlight will fuse us together in the same ascent!"

Aiglor and Féliah are no longer speaking; they look around. At the same time their eyes pause on the grassy bank where the blades of grass are straightening one by one, gradually erasing the trace of the two bodies that lay down there. Standing on tiptoe, Féliah crushes her lips upon those of her lover; enlaced, they are gradually drawing nearer to the bank, which seems to be calling them with an invincible attraction, when the sound of breaking branches suddenly becomes audible. A man, who had hidden in order to allow the troop going back down to Panbiole to pass by, emerges from the trees bordering the road, and Féliah only just has time to drag Aiglor behind the clump of rose-bushes.

The man advances slowly; a black cloak envelops him from head to toe, and his face is entirely hidden beneath a large hat the same color as the cloak. He is walking with his shoulders drooping and his head bowed; unintelligible sounds emerge from his mouth.

Féliah presses herself against her lover's bosom, as if gripped by a sudden terror at the sight of the strange individual, who, having arrived on the level ground, stops and darts an empty, indifferent glance around him. His cloak opens, and with his right hand he removes his hat, uncovering long blond hair, which hangs down to his shoulders in thick curls brightened by the sun. He has turned toward Panbiole and his lips are incessantly repeating the same syllables, mechanically, with indifferent inflections, sometimes murmuring them like a prayer and sometimes roaring them like an anathema.

Without worrying about the man—who is, in any case, too absorbed to pay attention to what is happening around him—Aiglor has straightened up suddenly. Trembling, he stammers: "Féliah, it's your name that he's pronouncing!"

But the woman, smiling in spite of the increasing pallor of her face, forces the man to sit down again beside her, and, in a voice only marked by a slight emotion, says: "Of my name, my lover, your lips alone can pronounce the syllables. It is your love that makes them audible in all the noises arriving at your ear…about what is your heart anxious? One day, do you remember, did you not tell me in the garden of my palace that you recognized the name that is dear you in the songs of

41

birds and the quivering flight of butterflies? It's your tenderness, my Aiglor, that is sighing your lover's name in your heart...thank you, my Aiglor!"

And while Féliah, by means of her caresses, tries to deflect her lover's attention, Aiglor listens breathlessly to the pilgrim, who is exhaling the plaint of his betrayed love in a lamentable fashion.

"Oh, your beauty blossomed in my heart as the breeze, floating over the sea, swells bosoms avoid for its odorous breath. But alas, the breeze rose into a murderous tempest, unchaining icy gusts and bruising hailstones in my heart. Oh, the infernal power that has poured the devouring poison into the tenderness of our love! Alas, I was still very young when a seeress discovered over my heart a tiger-claw ready to rip it...that claw, Féliah, was your white hand with pink fingernails...the seeress told me that a day would come when the tiger would vanquish the lion.

"A sinister prediction! Yes, the lion has fallen, his heart ripped by the cruel claw! Yes, Féliah, you have vanquished me—me, Prince Lowenol! My heart, broken by its torture, is no more than a palpitating rag in my dolorous breast...and yet, the blood of the masters of Panbiole ran in my veins. I was born to rule over all Humania, but alas, if I had been king, would I have been able to become your slave? So I quit that court, fearful of the divine clarity of your eyes, and my father, refusing to believe that someone of his race could be foolish enough prefer the beauty of a woman to the glory of sitting on a throne, and no longer recognizing his own blood within me, disowned me.

"My mother died of shame and chagrin, and on her deathbed, while swearing to her fidelity, she covered me with her malediction. Oh, poor mother! Is it your anathema that has made a sinister, moaning ruin of the life of your child? My life, Féliah, was breathing the air that you breathed. My life was seeing your eyes smile. Oh, Féliah! I had made you the queen of a palace of light in which you gave me the eldest of our loving kisses. The hectic hymn of our tenderness rose in the splendor of our joy; but into the bright palace, the treacherous shadow slid, veiling my gaze even to your dear presence. In the thickness of that darkness, I pursued in vain your fleeing phantom. My hands, open before me, have wandered, groping, along lugubrious walls into which my head bumped..."

In a voice as heavy as a groan, Aiglor exhaled: "Oh, Féliah! Your name! Your palace! It's you..."

Still smiling, Féliah interrupts him softly.

"Let it go, my love. That poor fellow isn't talking about me. In Panbiole, there are other palaces than mine, and am I the only woman in the world named Féliah?"

Aiglor remains nonplussed for a moment, his eyes looking into his the eyes of his mistress; then he exclaims, in a tone of dolorous adoration: "There is but one Féliah on earth, as there is but one God in Heaven! Oh, our love, Féliah…!"

Féliah, putting her hand over his mouth, stops him speaking, because Lowenol has been staring at the rose-bush for a few moments. Again, however, he turns toward Panbiole; his stooped body gradually straightens and his pale face brightens with a sudden radiance.

"Ah, your palace! That is what is as resplendent down there as a sacred altar to which the absent priestess will bring back life, Féliah! Would the darkened palace shine if your beauty had not rendered it brilliant? Is it not the sun that comes to illuminate the black tomb of the sky? Féliah, impotent death has fled without touching our love! My pious breath will reanimated the momentarily wearied flame. Lightened, it will launch our ecstatic hearts into the sublimities of harmonious joy!"

Suddenly, his arm, extended forwards, fall back alongside his body. A cloud extinguishes the radiance of his face.

"And if the shadow returns to menace your palace, I shall pursue it with a burning torch! Your palace will catch fire one last time and our united beings with soar in the ardor of a similar death!"

43

He stops, frightened; his knees buckle and his voice, now beseeching, seems to want to cover his last words with forgetfulness.

"No, Féliah...life watches jealously over our love. Féliah, the night, in brushing with its wing my excessively suspicious heart, has broken it forever!"

He places both hands on the left side of his breast, as if to appease a stabbing pain; then, with infinite precaution, he takes from his bosom a withered rose, whose thorns, remaining on the long stem, tear his flesh and catch on his garments. He looks at the faded flower for a long time, plunged in his sadness.

"This flower I took one morning from those scattered in your room, from which you had fled...since then, its frightful bite has remained upon my heart...but it is dead now, the flower of treason, leaving in its place the rose of hope!"

He stands up abruptly, and, swinging the withered flower by the extremity of its stem, he hurls it far away from him with a great gesture of deliverance.

"Go to oblivion, infamous souvenir!"

And, approaching the clump of rose-bushes, he climbs on to the grassy bank. From the summit of the flowery massif, he picks a barely-open rose, whose petals, timidly tinted with red, are sheathed by four mossy points of green velvet. He lifts it to his lips and magnified, it seems, by his passion, he utters a long cry of triumph.

"Love, down there is resplendent! Down there our love is summoning me!"

At a hectic run he launches himself down the steep slope that goes down to rejoin the houses of Panbiole, and his cloak, only fastened at the neck, floats behind him.

The flower thrown by Lowenol has flown over the clump of bushes to fall at Féliah's feet, after having brushed Aiglor's head. The latter, his features contracted, has seized Féliah's arm, which he is shaking violently.

"You have betrayed me! You have betrayed me!"

Insensible to the brutal grip, the woman seems to be searching for the words that will calm her lover's anger.

"Betray you, my Aiglor? Oh, death would be the thousand times preferable to the perjury of our love!"

As Féliah speaks, the man's grip relaxes, and ends up opening completely. The woman picks up the rose fallen at her feet, and mechanically plucks away the stiffened petals, one by one.

She has fallen silent, but Aiglor, on his knees, begs: "Speak, Féliah...speak..."

Suddenly, the woman, joyful at having finally found the explanation from which absolute confidence will be born, exclaims: "Oh, how foolish I am! Do you not remember that man who has stirred up your jealousy?"

As Aiglor remains motionless, without replying, she continues: "Remember, Aiglor...do you not recall having seen, at the theater, an individual who said the same words, in the same voice? It was one of the best-loved actors in Panbiole. Frenetic acclamations greeted his appearance, and before his harmonious voice had concluded the final words of the play, an avalanche of bouquets, falling from all the galleries, thanked the actor for the emotion that his genius had caused to pass through the souls of the spectators..."

Aiglor is still listening, but his eyes, charged with a mute interrogation, say clearly enough that he does not understand what his mistress means. Féliah continues in a voice that is almost cheerful, in spite of the sadness of her story.

"That is what he has become, the sublime actor! By dint of playing the role of duped lovers, he has ended up believing himself to be an unhappy lover...his reason has capsized in the fictions that he makes so much effort to live in order to render them truer and more poignant...and you know very well, my Aiglor, that in the theater, the amorous are always the elder sons of great individuals, and the objects of their amour beauties like none that exist on earth. So, the poor madman has come to believe that he really is the son of a king...that his name is Prince Lowenol, and that he is madly infatuated with an infidel baptized with the name of Féliah, which caused you to believe momentarily..."

Aiglor contemplates Féliah tenderly; he takes her hands, which he is kissing gently when a slow melody becomes faintly audible. They both listen, in a profound delight, to the nebulous song that is gradually detached from the silence that envelops them.

It is a plaintive voice, droning indefinable words, which are, in any case, soon completely drowned by a great tumult, and a band composed of about ten individuals advances in the wake of a man with graying hair on a head that seems almost juvenile; under his left arm he carries a small lyre made of dark wood veined with red. In order to make himself more clearly audible to his companions he turns toward them, while walking with an uneven and unsteady tread.

"Thus destiny is accomplished! We are going toward this goal, which is not the one of which we have dreamed. Here we all are, docile pilgrims of eternal rest, we whose hands have molded wings of clay in order to attempt gigantic flights into these heights, where no azure has ever seemed to us serene enough! Alas, we have all fallen, one by one, through the blue spaces that we hate, on to the implacable ground! Our bodies are bruised! Our blood has been drunk by the soil and that reddened earth, warm with our blood, our hands have taken up endlessly, to knead it again into new wings—but always, we have fallen back from the full height of our broken dreams! Now, it is finished. Our veins have dried up, the vanity of our efforts has appeared in bright sunlight! Oh, the sunlight!"

To ward off the imprecation, the plaintive voice rises again, and, with two hands extended, a man clad in a dark doublet decorated with bright embroideries detaches himself from the approaching group.

"No, no, I beg you! He is good, the God who will forgive us. Our temerity has gone as far as the absurd folly of wanting to be creators too. The just God has removed the scales from our eyes, and at this moment, his clemency deigns to welcome us, to pour over us a healing balm for our disappointed dreams..."

Another tearful voice emerges from the mouth of an old man with an ecstatic gaze: "Our dreams! Our poor dreams remain down there, in the mansards of Panbiole! Our etheric dreams are lying in the gutters, in the depths of narrow streets, like punctured balloons! Our lamentable dreams, broken by the jolts of life like uncertain flames extinguished by the wind...!"

He represses a sob, and the young man with the gray hair, brandishing his lyre of dark wood veined with red, interrupts him.

"Come on, pious singers of defeat, enough humility! What? Has the struggle not cost us enough? We have made the complete sacrifice of all joys and all pleasures; we have accepted the formal menace, long since realized, of all anguish and the worst suffering! We have locked up our pride in the deepest recesses of our hearts, and there, like a captive driven mad by the chains with which he is laden, without respite or release, it has rent the walls of its prison! Our convulsed flesh, ever ready to weaken, has howled to infinity its distress and its dolor, sprung from our souls toward the Beauty with which we were infatuated!

"Oh, poor Humanians! You have all passed by, indifferent, curbed by the somber weight of salvation, like mules laden with leather bottles swollen with precious wines, who go over the burning sand, their desiccated tongues hanging out; if one of those goatskins opens, letting out the ambrosia, the mules pass by disdainfully, their tongues still grazing the ground, in which the liquid that would slake their thirst drains away...

"Ah, but if you had wanted it, Beauty would have become the glorious mistress of Humania; her august harmony would have delivered matter, captive of time and space, and the liberated earth would finally have attained its destiny, the freedom of eternity! But it is in vain that we have struggled, in vain that we have suffered! The fearful slaves have fled the ardent breath of our hearts, which blazed to reignite the extinct torch! Eyes have not wanted to see, or ears to hear, because God came to affirm that Beauty had once been sent to earth by him, as a punishment for distant crimes, to torture men with inextinguishable love, and that he promised to deliver the world from her if the world would lay down at his feet. Then, the Humanians had faith in your word, deceptive God, perfidious God!"

A cry of horror emerges simultaneously from all the mouths, breathless with fear, but the blasphemer, raising his lyre toward the sky, continues furiously: "God the thief! Under the weight of years you have crushed our youth. You have extinguished our pride while cradling our dolors with mitigating hopes, and our own essence, the Beauty that we love, the Beauty that makes us greater than you, slyly, by night, like the most infamous of sneak-thieves, you have taken her from us!"

Grabbing hold of the old man with the ecstatic gaze, who tries to stop him, he continues: "He has taken her"! He has stolen her! Listen to me, you: do you remember the festival of Beauty in which you rode in glorious triumph? Alas, it was the last of all. We were ranged around the statue raised by you for the magnification of the ideal feminine form. The people of Panbiole, piously, came to contemplate your work, and the women, grateful to the artistic celebrator of their beauty, spread before you the flowers from their baskets; the ground disappeared completely under the litter, which, in large patches of different colors, in accordance with the flowers offered, in a carpet that feet did not dare to trample, extended from the statue into the distance..."

All the watchers are listening silently, and each new detail seems to remove a little of the ecstasy from the old man's eyes.

"At the edge of the iridescent field, naked, amid the flight of amethyst waves scattered around her, in the splendor of her flesh, a woman appeared; like the marble statue, she stood motionless, her hands, clasped behind the nape of her neck, arrested the black undulations of her hair; her solemn gaze was fixed upon you, and, responding to the mute interrogation of her eyes, you bent down to pick up a rose with red petals from the ground, which you held out to the living image of beauty..."

"How beautiful she was! How beautiful she was!" murmurs the old man, whose features are rejuvenated by the evocation of the glorious day.

"Slowly, in order not to injure the harmony of her stride, the woman advanced; the veils of amethyst squashed beneath her feet, whose whiteness was bloodied by the red of roses, to be washed subsequently in the milk of jasmines and lilies, and, pausing at all the spots on the ground, like the fur of some fantastic animal, she did not seem to be the same creature from one moment to the next; on the changing colors of the spread flowers, she gave birth to an infinite succession of new forms, all alive with ideal beauty, and when, in order to take the rose with the red petals from your hand, her fingers came apart, allowing the black tresses to obscure the ivory of her shoulders, the woman appeared to be the twin sister of the one hatched from your soul in its marble dream..."

"How beautiful she was! How beautiful she was!" the old man repeats, incessantly, in an increasingly forceful voice.

"Yes, she was beautiful! And also beautiful were the eurhythmic creatures who, one by one, undressed themselves; first the courtesans, sure of their power, proudly displayed their victorious charms; then, like impatient flowers, ready to open at the brush of the first caress, blushing virgins, frightened of an ardently sighing unknown...and brunettes with heavy flesh impregnated with heavy perfumes, like fruits gown in the depths of valleys, and blondes with the slender contours of plants stretched by the sunlight on the hillsides, all bearing within them a fraction of the absolute beauty..."

"They awoke the holy joy of eyes and came to pluck the roses of our adoration from our hands," the man in the somber doublet puts in.

"And, judging themselves unworthy of that honor, they offered them to the one among them who was the most beautiful, the woman who, emerged from veils of amethyst, now stood immobile, lost in the odorous dream exhaled by her rose with the bloody petals. The queen of beauty held the sovereign flowers to her bosom for a few moments; then her knees bent before the marble statue and, abdicating her royalty, she deposited the bouquet of triumph at the feet of her rival..."

"Yes, Beauty was victorious!" roars the old man, his fists raised against the sky.

"Beauty, you reigned over Humania, when..."

"When," resumes the brazen voice, "the God came, the annunciator of a new faith! In vain was he annihilated in the well of infamy! Alas like the poison that runs through all the veins in the vertigo of an instant, his lying words had already corrupted all souls, and behind the veils of illusory promises, he had already hidden Beauty! Oh Beauty, created of the purest of ourselves, finally to open the era of eternal happiness, the perfidious God learned to hate you as the most terrible of scourges! Into the hearts of women he put horrible jealousy, and their hands broke your image one night..."

"The night! The night!" moans the dolorous chorus of artists.

"And now, all is finished...God has stolen Beauty from the earth...my lyre is dead!" sobs the poet. Mechanically, he sets it against his shoulder; his fingers, clenched upon the strings at first, gradually recover their suppleness, and harmonious chords make themselves heard. The poet, dreading that he might be the victim of a hallucination, interrogates his companions with his eyes—who, full of surprise, also listen religiously to the melody with which an improvised song soon mingles.

> *Pure and radiant child of men,*
> *O Beauty!*
> *the master of the azure envies your sovereign light,*
> *and comes among us to take possession of you!*
> *Humanians, credulous in your fallacious word,*
> *deny the white daughter of their dream!*

O perfidious God, she becomes your prey,
and into your heaven you bear her away
our Beauty,
pure and radiant child of men!

By force you sit her down at your side
on your throne of deceit,
the white daughter of our dreams!
but your caresses cannot dry up her tears,
which the meadow grass drinks in the morning.
Without cease, her sobs make the seas quiver;
her heart-rending plaint whistles in the tempest;
and from the one who laments on your throne of deceit,
the hectic dolor has cried out to us!
Your dolor is our dolor,
pure and radiant child of men,
Beauty,
whose light was the envy of the master of the azure!
O perfidious God, between her and us,
in vain you put insurmountable space,
sown with moving reefs of cloud and lightning!

Yes, we shall go to rediscover her,
the white daughter of our dreams
who calls to us for help!
We shall deliver her, our exiled saint,
your saddened captive who weeps by your side!
Her collected tears will shine in our hearts
like bright diamonds mounted by our love!
Her eyes will open again to the sovereign clarities
momentarily obscured by your hateful power.
We shall bring her back to Humania,
the white daughter of our dreams,
our Beauty,
stolen by trickery from our adoration.
The earth, beneath her footsteps,
will be clad with flowers,

and eternal happiness will be born of her kiss!

Pure and radiant child of men,
O Beauty!
to take you back from the perfidious God,
toward you we shall climb,
to cross the insurmountable space,
sown with moving reefs of cloud and lightning!
Among us your sovereign light will revive,
O Beauty!
mother of eternal happiness!

Suddenly, the song that the poet is accompanying, on his lyre, with long chords, is intoned by all the artists, impotent to contain their emotion, and all the voices repeat, in an enthusiastic chorus:

Pure and radiant child of men,
O Beauty!
to take you back from the perfidious God,
toward you we shall climb,
to cross the insurmountable space,
sown with moving reefs of cloud and lightning!
Among us your sovereign light will revive,
O Beauty!
mother of eternal happiness!

The artists become increasingly excited by the sound of their own voices. A kind of frenzy takes possession of them; some shout insults, raising their closed fists at the sky—and all of them, behind the poet, hurl themselves on to the road along which the religious cortege of the faithful promised to the kingdom of heaven has preceded them.

The last echoes of the song of revolt fade away into the distance, and, after a long time, seemingly fearful of troubling the silence, Féliah whispers supplicant words into Aiglor's ear, to which he makes no reply.

Finally, they both emerge from the clump of rose-bushes, Féliah dragging Aiglor after her. Féliah extends her arm toward the road that rises upwards into the powdering of the sunlight, while Aiglor turns his head back toward the city. Then they look at one another for a long time, without speaking. In their eyes a supplication is legible of similar intensity, that of the woman wanting to vanquish her lover's last resistance, that of the man hoping that the weight of the past will be sufficiently powerful to make his mistress resume the road to Panbiole.

Aiglor, however, has lowered his gaze before that of Féliah; he confesses his definitive resignation with a gesture in which the complete abandonment of his will is expressed.

The woman takes hold of both the man's hands; she covers them with kisses—and, retaining one of them in her own, Féliah, followed by Aiglor, begins to climb the steep slope that rises up toward the east, all the way to heaven.

THE PETITPAON ERA
or
WORLD PEACE

I

In the indecisive pallor of dawn, formidable detonations burst forth at multiple points in Paris.

"It's cannon-fire!" shouted multiple cries from hastily-opened windows, in tones of anguish or joy, in accordance with whether those proffering them were enthusiastic about war or horrified by it.

However, the prospect that some of them were hoping for, and which frightened others, vanished instantaneously; the windows closed again, violently slammed by the bellicose, disappointed by the false alarm, and carefully replaced by the placid, secretly grateful for the brutality of the awakening, which brought a more intense sensation to their quietude.

The artillery salvos, perfectly innocent, simply announced the anniversary of a great event.

A year ago, to the day, the Earth had followed France in the path laboriously prepared by several phases of the Republican government.

The giant charm of the three words *Liberty, Equality, Fraternity*, once inscribed, in hours of provocative delirium on the front of monuments, had transformed human nature in its intimate essence; it was a veritable new era that had risen over the world.

International treaties, solemnly agreed, had assured, without it costing the parties present the slightest drop of blood, the solution of differences emerging between nations.

A few emperors or kings, by divine right or brute force, still seated on the worm-eaten thrones of their fathers, had not renounced military ostentation, however, and even France, the glorious heroine of the sublime action universally revered under the name of the Great Revolution, had accepted as peremptory the reason of a moral and economic order invoked in favor of the maintenance of permanent armies.

In every country, in fact, the prestige of the uniform was still so powerful over great ladies and pert young women that the sudden suppression of generals, officers, sergeants, corporals and soldiers would have caused excessively profound perturbations in social mechanics.

An ecumenical congress, in which every temporal power capable of establishing regular jurisdiction over a minimum of a hundred and fifty subjects was represented, had been held in Paris, and, as much out of gratitude for a hostess overflowing with charms as deference to the country that had taken the initiative of the assembly, the members of the congress had unanimously placed exclusively in French hands the care of finding the means to abolish war, while conserving for warriors the integrality of their natural attributions.

The problem was arduous; after the accumulation by the hundreds of unrealizable projects in which the most various cerebral originalities had been given free rein, the President of the Republic had put forward an idea whose simplicity was pure genius.

Before having climbed, one by one, the steps leading to the supreme magistracy, Bernard Petitpaon had been in the theater.[1] The "Or de Perpignan" had generously employed the

---

[1] The literal meaning of *petitpaon* is "little peacock," and that might be the author's intended implication in attributing it to his dubious hero; it is, however, worth noting that the term is most familiar in French with reference to the "*petit paon de nuit*": the heathland moth *Saturnia pavonia*, known in England as the Emperor Moth, or sometimes as the Small Emperor.

son of the people to form its larynx.[2] Previously equipped with all the laurels of which the Conservatoire de Musique et de Déclamation can provide for the glory of its most illustrious pupils, Bernard Petitpaon, favored by a renewal of Antique form, had triumphantly baritoned on the greatest stages in the two hemispheres. Then, yielding to the pleas of a southern Minister glad to mark his succession to the Ministry of Fine Arts by a nomination satisfying both his compatriotic duties and the esthetic interests of France, he had descended from his singer's pedestal to preside over the artistic and commercial destiny of the Lyrique Grand-Mondial.

Bernard Petitpaon knew that the functions of director of the Lyrique Grand-Mondial did not consist solely of mounting, in the best possible frame, lyric productions of more or less appreciated vintage. He was aware of the tradition that made ballet the soul of the House, and he dreamed of fusing the soul in question with the soul of France.

With that aim, while conserving for the subscribers a legitimate respect for their fortunes and titles, he opened wide the Eden of the wings to everyone connected with the public powers: ministers, senators, députés, functionaries and influential journalists, stars of all shades and all shapes, invited by him, came into conjunction with the variously colored stars of song and dance.

With a satisfied Olympian eye, Petitpaon attentively followed the variations of curves of tenderness established between the members of his troupe and those of the governmental troupe. An ostentatious handshake, given at the right moment to a cavalier disdained by his lady, immediately reheightened the fellow's prestige, and Petitpaon, like a cockerel

---

[2] The phrase "*Or de Perpignan*" [Perpignan gold] is nowadays used more generally in a metaphorical sense, but its original use seems to have been closely connected with the famous Masonic lodge once possessed by the town, which was reputed to be a significant hotbed of Enlightenment thought in the twilight years of the *ancien régime*.

voluntarily descending from the breach, watched the joys of false marriages of which he was the parent blossoming gratefully around him.

One evening, a young député from the Midi to whose heart he had rendered many services, confided in him, in a fit of sincere admiration: "What damage a man like you could do in politics!"

"Yes, that's true!" Petitpaon cried, without making any attempt to put the slightest hint of modest into his brazen voice. "The fact is that my thoughts have never settled upon a personal political view—but it's an idea, my boy. Thank you! We'll talk about it again."

Bernard Petitpaon did talk about it again, and waited impatiently for the general elections to take, from the young député who had shown him the road to Damascus, his own seat.

Petitpaon entered parliament, the aureole with which the profane are pleased to ornament actors worn with swagger but without any arrogance, and the former director of the Lyrique Grand-Mondial was seen in the corridors of the Chambre, untiringly shaking the hands extended to him; his lowered voice, still thunderous, posed a question that always made the other blush slightly: "Still obliging, the girl?"

The time that public affairs left him, he loved to consecrate to irregular hearths for which he had provided the first spark, and whose flickering flames he reanimated with a tutelary breath, like a vestal.

The amicable frankness of his relations was soon translated, during a Cabinet reshuffle, into the portfolio of Agriculture, which a delegation of different groups in the two Assemblies begged him to accept.

"Agriculture lacks arms? I shall put mine at its service! It's quite natural," Petitpaon had replied, without the slightest hesitation, adding: "Besides which, I once guided a plow! It was in *Cincinnatus*, the opera by Pistonnet."[3]

Never had France possessed a minister endowed with a similar vocal power. In the four corners of the land, great cities and small towns inconvenienced by inaugurations, agricultural shows and scholarly or patriotic fêtes competed for the sonorous Excellency.

Bernard Petitpaon never declined an invitation; he spent his life under triumphal arches of cardboard and verdure, on stages embellished with tricolor flags and notable indigenes, in decorative corteges of gendarmes, soldiers and foremen; he presided over countless banquets, celebrating with ardor and conviction the benefits of peace, the grandeur of war, the pleasure of being young, the glory of being old and the joy of being French for everyone who is not a foreigner.

Unfailingly, he declared the absolute superiority of the people, livestock and products of the region where he happened to be, and among the citizens there were surges of enthusiasm; as for the women, those of the people, who left to bluestockinged ladies the literature and perverse idea of Pasiphaean love, they compared his male organ to that of a bull.

In the same way that he had resisted the intoxication of his artistic success, Bernard Petitpaon did not allow himself to get drunk on an enormous popularity of excellent quality.

One day, in Perpignan, his cradle, between two members of the Académie des Beaux-Arts, his compatriots and friends, he was occupying the place of honor at a banquet organized to celebrate the twentieth anniversary of the foundation of the Syndicate of Turnip Farmers when a coded telegram brought

---

[3] Cincinnatus was a Roman military leader and statesman who was recalled in a time of crisis to serve as dictator after retiring to work on his farm, having fallen from favor. He created a startling precedent by resigning his dictatorship once the crisis was over, and thus became an emblem of civic virtue. The opera and its supposed composer are fictitious.

him the news that a coronary embolism had just abruptly robbed the Republic of its President.

An instinctive sign of the cross escaped the right hand of the Minister of Agriculture, who rose to his feet in order to ask the official representatives of the cruciferous vegetable for permission to retire, as a sign of mourning. Forced to give further explanations, an immense clamor responded to him:

"The President is dead! Long live the President!"

Slightly pale for the first time in his life, Petitpaon was not sure that he understood. The chorus of turnip-merchants made it more precise with loud cries of: "Long live Petitpaon! Petitpaon for the Élysée."

The Grandmaster of Agriculture caused a few tears of emotion to roll down his cheeks, took out his watch and ran to leap on to a train departing for Paris.

Mitrouffe, the President of the Council, who thought himself the natural designate of a vote of the National Assembly, summoned his colleagues in order to render his candidature official. Favored with a mediocre exterior and excellent health; full of illusions regarding his physique, he began by declaring that, in his opinion, France needed a decorative man.

By means of a rapid glance in a mirror, Bernard Petitpaon assured himself that he was, in every respect, the man of that dream.

Mitrouffe continued to enumerate the qualities indispensable to a good President of the Republic, and, throwing into the balance the renown of his invincible health, he desired above all that the man chosen to receive the grandees of this world should be endowed with a good constitution.

"Like that of 1875!"[4] approved the Minister of Agriculture, toward whom the Cabinet's ten pairs of eyes turned.

---

[4] The three fundamental acts establishing the Third Republic in France, which became known as the Constitutional Laws, although they did not constitute a formal Constitution, were passed by the National Assembly in 1875. They were eventually replaced by the Constitution of 1946.

A few seconds of solemn silence went by—a silence that it was Bernard Petitpaon's prerogative to break with the simple words: "I am the man that France needs."

Forty-eight hours later, Bernard Petitpaon returned from Versailles in the traditional landau hitched to four horses, two of them mounted by postillions, escorted by artillerymen.

After having accompanied to the Panthéon the mortal remains of his predecessor, the President of the Republic devoted himself body and soul to his duties. He doubled his domestic staff, had the ceremonial carriages repainted, ordered the purchase of horses so large that it was necessary to raise the stable doors in order to let them through, recommended the Service du Protocole to mount guard with jealous care, and demanded that the courtyard of the Élysée be swept every day and washed in the summer.

With a sumptuous ease, Bernard Petitpaon received kings, emperors, a shah, Indian princes and potentates of various colors and extractions, sometimes of vigorous strength, from distant islands and mysterious continents.

However, a man of Petitpaon's scope could not restrict his functions as the first magistrate of the Republic to foreign affairs alone. He had adopted as his motto: "I think, therefore I act!" and often, in the company of his intimates, he slapped his forehead, saying: "I feel that there's something there!"

The question of world peace came up, bristling with reefs, complicated by difficulties of every sort; diplomats and thinkers of all countries had lost therein the strength of the sturdiest legs, or what remained of their gray matter, when, a new Minerva of whom Petitpaon would have been the Jupiter, peace emerged fully formed from the presidential brain.

Every profession exercised for some time leaves its indelible mark on the body and the mind; in the great circumstances of life, men often seek points of reference and analogical relations in their métier to judge all things. Bernard Petitpaon instinctively thought of what had come of peace and war in the theater. He remembered the evenings when, sword in hand, he had engaged in frantic battles; he recalled the boards of the stage strewn with the dead and wounded; he added up the total of the Philistines that he had slain with the homicidal jawbone of an ass, at the rate of a thousand a time for more than three hundred performances.

However, those horrible carnages had never shed veritable blood. The curtain had scarcely fallen than the dead rose up again, the best places in the distribution of roles responding with bows to the applause, the simple spear-carriers returning to their dressing-rooms to take off their costumes, ready to be killed again tomorrow of the script demanded it.

The President asked himself why it was not the same in what is conventionally called "real life." The response came so rapidly that he only just had time to convene the government.

The Cabinet then had at its head General Croppeton, senator and Minister of War. He it was, therefore, in his double capacity as President of the Council and head of the department most directly interested in the question, that Petitpaon addressed.

"My dear Croppeton, could you give us an exact definition of war?"

Before replying, the general introduced into his mouth almost the entirety of his moustache and beard. A few minutes later, the attributes of his virility reemerged, mingled with fragments of phrases: "War is…is… War is a…a…a necessity. War is..."

"The shame of humanity!" put in the curt and passionate voice of the Minister of Commerce, Pierre Phosphène, who represented the color red in the spectrum of the Council.

"It seems to me that that affirmation, although it does you great honor to proclaim it, might perhaps be qualified as exaggerated," conciliated Arthème Flopinte, the Garde des Sceaux and tutor of Themis.

"It's certainly exaggerated!" agreed Henri Verbuis, Minister of Foreign Affairs.

"It is, however, sustainable," hazarded Charles Mirandet, Minister of the Interior.

"What do you think, Admiral Théhyx?" asked Bernard Petitpaon

"Oh, me, I only think about water. I like that more than anything else, except above my head. I fight when I have to, but I don't insist on doing any more than that."

"Of course—me neither!" added General Croppeton. "Do you think it's agreeable to get yourself killed or crippled for reasons that, three-quarters of the time, no one knows? In spite of everything, though, soldiers ought to love war as children love their mother!"

"She's a fine one, your mother!" howled Pierre Phosphène.

"In any case, I'll ask you not to insult her, Monsieur Mercury![5] Do I call you a thief under the pretext, however plausible it might be, that you're the Grandmaster of Commerce? It seems to me, however, that the difference between theft and commerce is merely one of terms!"

"Messieurs, please!" Bernard intervened. "Neither wolves not ministers should devour one another!"

"That's fair," opined the holder of the national scales.

"So, it's a matter of establishing a plan that permits, as the general so aptly puts it, soldiers to continue to love their mother, and which, at the same time, safeguards the most elementary rights of humanity, to borrow from our colleague Phosphène the key term from his own phrase."

"Choose between barbarity and civilization," snapped the aggressive henchman of Mercury.

"That intransigence is entirely to your glory," said Petitpaon, soothingly, "but my dear minister, it's necessary not to get hung up on words. What are barbarity and civilization if not two sisters—I don't say twins, since their respective births were separated by an abysm of time, but two sisters—of whom, the elder, is brunette, tragic and strong, while the

---

[5] The Roman god Mercury was, among other ministerial functions, the god of the marketplace.

younger is blonde, delicate and frail. Let's make a bouquet of them!"

"A bouquet of women!" giggled Abbé Mortol, responsible for agricultural, postal, telegraphic and religious manifestation, hysterically.

"And let's present the world with a favor in the colors of France!" concluded President Petitpaon.

"It would be a nice gesture!" the four individuals holding the portfolios of Education, Public Works, Finance and the Colonies sighed, admiringly.

"Well, let's make it! It's as easy as convincing a egg to stand on end—which contributed as much to the glory of Christopher Columbus as the discovery of America. I declare first of all, that my plan will not involve the slightest prejudice to the soldiers of the armies of land and sea."

"On their behalf, we thank you," said General Croppeton and Admiral Théhyx, in unison.

"As for economic interests, collective and individual, they too will be scrupulously safeguarded."

"That's admirable!" baaed the eleven voices of the ministerial chapter, simultaneously.

"You've said it!" agreed Bernard Petitpaon. "Now listen."

And in his voice, marvelously adapted to all the degrees of the sonic scale, he read the revelatory monument, inscribed on the back of a visiting card with which he as playing negligently.

"Article One. War is and will remain the argument that nations can and ought to invoke with respect to one another.

"Article Two. Each of them will retain sovereign rule, in number and in specialties, of its manpower as well as the nature and quality of its armaments.

"Article Three. The laws and regulations relative to the exercise of war, whether continental or maritime, will remain in force.

"Article Four. With respect to everything concerning the persons of the belligerents, war will consist purely and simply of theoretical effects."

The Excellencies applauded, while darting anxious glances at Bernard Petitpaon, who concluded his reading with an "And that's it!" proclaiming the great simplicity of the resolutions that he had just proposed.

"You must be content, Monsieur Phosphène," General Croppeton said, going on the attack.

"I don't know!" confessed the Minister of Commerce, scratching his head in order to launch his riposte. "And you?"

"Me, I find the ideas ripened in the wise and profound brain of our dear and esteemed President are a trifle green for us."

"Who are blues!" concluded the black-clad man of Agriculture, Posts, Telegraphs and Religion.[6]

"The first three articles are very clear, but the fourth seems to me to be a trifle obscure," General Croppeton added.

"It is, however, light itself!" said Petitpaon, with a smile.

"I confess that I don't understand."

"The most elementary politeness would force me to say I'm astonished by that, if I were convinced that there really were grounds for astonishment. It's my duty to give you a few clarifications. Thus, as all of you have so admirably understood, I am changing absolutely nothing in what is the very essence of war. As in the heroic centuries, the most glorious epics will unroll their sublime pages; the fields of battle will still..."

"Be fields of carnage—abattoirs!" interjected the brilliant Phosphène

---

[6] I have translated "vertes" and "bleues" literally to conserve the wordplay although both are intended metaphorically and both meanings would be gathered under the metaphorical means of "green" in English—the General means it in the sense of unripe or sour, the Abbé in the distinctively French sense of a new or raw recruit.

Bernard Petitpaon winked maliciously. "That's where my article four comes in. I have said that was will be restricted to theoretical effects. Thus, not a drop of blood should redden the international arenas. Let's take an example. Two very extensive enemy armies confront one another, animated by the most ardent patriotic zeal, amply provided with the most improved accessories of combat. Men and horses are ready to rush upon one another at a signal from their leaders, the cannon to roar, scattering amid the crackle of rifle fire and the clash of steel flesh torn from human bodies..."

"I've seen that," General Croppeton testified, courageously.

"The soldiers deploy their standards, utter their rallying cries, and would fight like lions if their officers were not there to demand respect for a discipline that is strictly necessary to arrive at the result that I hope to attain, of supposed steel."

"You talk like a soldier!" sanctioned the Ministers of War and Marine, in chorus.

"I hope so!" Petitpaon granted. "However, I intend to remain a civilian, just as I emerged from my mother's womb. But I shall close this parenthesis..."

"We'll open our ears!" affirmed the scene-setter of Justice.

"Thank you. So, on either side, the belligerents maneuver in accordance with the norms of the strategy most appropriate to the circumstances; all ruses are permissible; brilliant actions retain their place; the field of honor is open!"

"Glory to those who, falling as heroes, die for their fatherland!" cried General Croppeton.

"Exactly!" approved Petitpaon. "But henceforth, the heroes will be content to fall; they will no longer die."

"That won't change them!" Pierre Phosphène groaned.

"Possibly! But at any rate, they'll no longer die," the Head of State went on. "Steel is free to clash, throwing off sparks, but as soon as it encounters a breast it must stop its homicidal momentum dead; the human target will merely be brushed by the tip of the bayonet or the cutting edge of the blade. The dead will be conserved alive, thanks to my system, and the wounded perfectly intact.

"And what of the rifles? And the cannon?" Phosphène shot, aggressively.

"They will fulfill their function!" Petitpaon declared.

"But then…?" said Croppeton and Théhyx, anxiously.

"Then?" the Head of State continued. "Listen: I've told you that it's necessary for my war to conform rigorously to ordinary warfare. Thus, it will have the virtue of international conventions; the engines will be carefully cataloged according to their exact power of destruction. The munitions of all sorts that accompany them will be submitted to very rigorous expertise, as well as a severe accountancy immediately after each war. You understand that it's necessary to render to Caesar what is Caesar's, and to conserve for the soldiers of all nations their true value."

"They'll fire in the air?" suggested Phosphène.

"So that the shells, bullets and machine-gun fire fall back on your heads?" mocked Bernard Petitpaon. "You can't think so, my dear Minister."

"Every instrument of ballistics, like its steel sisters, will only make a mark on its victims?" asked Admiral Théhyx.

"That would evidently be one means," Petitpaon granted, "but its realization seems to me to be very complicated. My presidential sagacity has found something else: cartridges and shells will be absolutely identical to those in use today, and the cost will be the same; it will merely be necessary to enjoin pyrotechnical artificers to place the projectiles behinds the explosive material instead of in front of it. Thus, one will continue to enjoy the odor of powder and the noise of the detonations will remain essentially similar."

"Artillerymen can continue to go deaf?" asked Charles Miraudel.

"If they so please!" concluded the wily Petitpaon, with a smile. "It's now a matter of passing on to the military personnel. It's essential that the most senior general and he humblest private soldier are absolutely equal before the rifles, as they are before death. After each engagement, on the sight of the expenditure on either side of men and munitions, arbiters will establish the outcome of the day and will calculate, in accordance with ready-reckoners approved by all the countries in the world, the number of dead and wounded."

"So there will still be some?" queried Pierre Phosphène.

"More than ever," Petitpaon replied. "But the physicians will have no need to finish off the wounded, and the dead will continue to live in perfect tranquility."

"I no longer understand," confessed General Croppeton and Admiral Théhyx, simultaneously.

"It doesn't matter—you'll surely understand soon. A capital problem arises here; it's a matter, in fact, of knowing to whom we should address ourselves in order to individualize the dead and the wounded with all the guarantees of impartiality that such a delicate operation requires."

"One could appoint a committee," ventured Charles Miraudel.

"I thought of that," Petitpaon went on, "but all men have their weaknesses, and it would be highly probable that bias, deriving from political issues or personal ones, would intervene in the question of life or death with regard to a greater or lesser number of citizens enjoying the same rights and subject to similar duties. I deem that it is necessary, above all, to avoid having the lists of dead and wounded drawn up by human hands."

"If, in his infinite bounty, God would..." Abbé Mortol put in.

"Oh, you can rest easy—he wouldn't!" Pierre Phosphène interjected, brutally.

"What do you know about it?" replied the man of God.

"Now, now! Don't start arguing about God in a debate that doesn't concern him, and in which I, Bernard Petitpaon, have anticipated everything. Is it not to chance, that motor as powerful as it is marvelous, that we ought to address ourselves? Lots will be drawn. Slips will be put into a secret urn bearing the serial numbers of all the officers, superior or subaltern, as well as all the sergeants, corporals and private soldiers of the armies at odds; after the battle, and the verdict of the arbiters, the urn will be brought to the front of the troops; the youngest canteen-waitress in the service of either camp will plunge her innocent hand into the urn..."

"It's desirable that the waitress should be a virgin," observed Abbé Mortol, prudishly.

"If you wish!" Petitpaon granted. "So, a virgin waitress plunges her hand into the urn; the emerging numbers first designate the dead, then the wounded!"

"It's absolutely the same as ancient warfare!" the General and the Admiral proclaimed, in unison.

"The bullets and cannonballs won't choose," Croppeton continued.

"It's a matter of chance!" Théhyx concluded. "Once, a shell carried away my helmet and a lock of hair, and without the luck of...a hanged man, I'd have been killed!"

That indirect allusion to the compensation that fortune had reserved for the Admiral—whose conjugal misfortunes were notorious—made the assembled legislators smile.

"What will become of the dead and wounded?" asked the steward of the Treasury, Thunasol.

"For the dead, it's quite simple," Petitpaon explained. "They're erased from the registers of civil status. They'll no longer exist, and if people talk about them, it will only be in the past tense. For the wounded, it's more complicated, for they'll continue to have the right to take part in the social body to a greater or lesser degree, according to the seriousness of their supposed wounds. Thus, a one-armed man..."

"Will no longer be able to make use of the arm he lacks. That's obvious!" put in Croppeton.

"And quite natural," added Admiral Théhyx.

"Will prisoners be taken?" asked General Croppeton.

"Why? There's absolutely no need. As ardent pioneers of progress, everything that has no intrinsic purpose ought to receive no mercy from us!" said Petitpaon. "But I can't emphasize too strongly that our new *modus belli* should be considered purely from a public and official angle. The private lives of the dead and wounded, like those of the living, should not be afflicted in any way by the slightest inquisitorial or vexatious imposition.

"Long live liberty!" proclaimed Pierre Phosphène.

"You said it!" sanctioned the President. "We cannot repeat that phrase too frequently, synthetic as it is of all the individual aspirations summoned to melt, for the good of all, into the bosom of common constraint."

Unanimous applause saluted that brief and significant proclamation. Bernard Petitpaon returned the salute by applauding himself with the ardor of a Roman of the great epoch.

"My dear Verbuis, in your capacity as Minister of Foreign Affairs, it will be up to you to open fire for the realization of this project by skillfully explaining the fundamental points—on which we're all agreed—to the representatives of the Powers..."

"I request the floor!" interjected Abbé Mortol, lowering his eyes.

"You have it! You have it, my dear Abbé," granted Petitpaon, promptly.

"The reason with which the Lord had deigned to endow his humble creature causes me to feel the immense weight of the change that will be produced in bodies and souls by the application of purely figurative war. It is for me an unavoidable case of conscience to consult, before forming an opinion on the subject, His Eminence Cardinal Pecari, of whom I am temporarily, as Minister of Religion, the temporal superior, but who nevertheless remains, in his capacity as Archbishop of Paris, my spiritual superior..."

"Act to the advantage of the salvation of your soul!" approved President Petitpaon, rising from his armchair to signify the end of the session.

II

Three months after that memorable discussion, the negotiations undertaken by the Minister of Foreign Affairs were completely concluded.

Throughout the world, not one nation had been found to reject Bernard Petitpaon's plan. The most warlike countries were those that exhibited the greatest enthusiasm, and the only people to put up opposition were a few celebrated and powerful representatives of religions, who all protested that war, such as it had been practiced since the earliest ages of humanity, was divine in essence and that it would be sacrilegious to make any significant modification to it.

All peoples were called upon to subscribe to the contract that bound them in honor to one another. The signature of autocrats was sufficient to engage peoples curbed under their yoke, while a vote of their respective Chambers was necessary for Republics and empires or monarchies provided with constitutions.

In France, President Petitpaon's idea had been acclaimed by an enormous majority, but it would have been an insult to parliament not to open the question to passionate debate. In the bosom of the Chambre des Députés, among the adversaries of the plan, some were easy to win over; a manufacturer of surgical instruments declared himself satisfied by the addition of lancets, scalpels, saws, forceps and other operative adjuncts to the nomenclature of accessories of war of variable but assured consumption; an intractable merchant of mourning dress was returned to the finer sentiments on a formal promise of a sumptuary regulation obliging the relatives of the pseudo-defunct to dress in black for a lapse of time at least equal to that presently customary.

The question of inheritance raised innumerable difficulties, as can be imagined. On behalf of the Government, Minister of Finance Thunasol made a promise to the families of the victims of "Petitpaon warfare," as the *modus vivendi* to be adopted was already being called, to triple their income, not in the ordinary form of cash but the much more democratic and no less sure form of public employment, tobacconist's shops or collecting agencies, according to the sex and aptitudes of the interested parties. The dead and the wounded, of course, remained the responsibility of the families that the State was deeming it a duty and a glory to indemnify.

Jurisconsultants presented a few observations on possible filiations. Many children, in fact, would be born of fathers figuring in the registers of civil status in the columns of the deceased. A feminist député argued the blatant injustice there would be in dishonoring widows under the fallacious pretext that they had become mothers of children of husbands presumed dead by the law, but who nevertheless remained capable of successfully delivering themselves to reproduction.

The Minister of the Interior, Charles Miraudel, explained that a well-organized society, having the family for a substratum, had to do everything possible to ensure the legitimacy of the descendancy of citizens, without class distinction. In the midst of applause he declared that birth certificates would bear, along with the names of the child and the mother, that of the father, followed by the note: "Presently dead for the fatherland."

Several other specific and particular points were elucidated to the full satisfaction of those raising them. It was only with Abbé Mortol and Louis Méripal that the debate rose to the level of general considerations and the examination of principles qualified as eternal by the orators, doubtless because of their role in nourishing interminable discussions.

Abbé Mortol, ceding to the pious injunctions of Cardinal Pecari, had resigned in order to avoid associating himself with the act of relative pacification, estimated as extremely injurious to the interests of the whole of Christendom. His conscience as a Catholic satisfied, but his ambitious heart profoundly ulcerated, Abbé Mortol had resumed his place on the benches as a mere député. All of his hatred was turned against General Croppeton and Bernard Petitpaon, holding them both

71

solidly responsible for the sacrifice that he had been forced to make to his religion.

With a violence and a shamelessness only excusable by their attachment to a fervently exalted faith, Abbé Mortol launched an attack against the President of the Council of Ministers, of which he suffered so painfully from not being a part, which resounded under the vaults of the Palais Bourbon like a heroic and unusual appeal to some modern crusade. With tears in his voice, he deplored the abandonment of integral war.

"War is the admirable school, eternal and synthetic, of all the Christian virtues, the inexhaustible source of the dolor and suffering that God, in all his bounty, permits his creatures in order to liberate them from the illusion of this miserable life and give them the hope and the thirst for a future existence made of intrinsic happiness and unalloyed joys."

He spoke about the "imprescriptible rights of God" over the blood flowing, thanks to him, in the veins of men, and which it was absolutely necessary to shed, following the example of the savior, the voluntary hero of the crucifixion, less glorious, without any doubt, than the joyful passing on a field of battle transformed into an essential cataclysm by the rain of iron, the lightning-flashes of blades and breastplates, the sometimes-continuous and sometimes-stuttering fire of fusillades, as well as the grave speeches delivered by the cannons "spitting out the thunder of their rifled souls."

He threatened General Croppeton—who had taken the responsibility of excluding humanity from violent death, henceforth only assured, as a rare and precious thing, by a few isolated and unforeseen accidents—with the thunderbolts of Heaven.

"You have betrayed the Épée... and the Épée is merely a servile instrument in the candid hand of Faith! Épée is synonymous with saber, and the Cross, in Heaven, in what the saber is on Earth! The Cross we conserve with the fervor of the azure and the whiteness of souls, and you are refusing the Épée its natural nourishment: human blood! Do you believe that you can deceive God and cause him to bless a saber that, in your perjured and renegade hands, is a wooden sword at best?"

General Croppeton received the anathema head on, without blinking, like a soldier accustomed to looking worse things than death in the face.

The orator continued in the midst of a frightful tumult: "Debase war, then, to the point of officially proclaiming it a caricature! Make that tragic shadow of the flag, which has seen the proudest courage falls to its knees before God puerile and derisory! Woe to you who dream of stealing from people the almost celestial joy of the renovative exterminations of the Faith! To expel death from the battlefields is to expel religion from the hearts of men!

"We have, with the aid of God, tamed the human beast! Our hands have gripped the steel rein flecked with bloody foam! And today, you are liberating from that rein impatient mouths that will howl with hunger, thirst and dolor! Oh, madmen that you are!

"Promises made in God's name ordinarily suffice to soothe dolor, receive thirst, appease hunger. And when wretches bare teeth that are to sharp, when their excessively dry throats make disquieting growls heard, we throw them to feed on one another, and they devour one another in epic feasts, in torrents of blood, all of them, as many victors as vanquished, intoxicated to the point of the drunkenness that engenders slumber. That slumber is peace! Oh, beware Monsieur Coffre...!"

That name, howled at the top of the voice had the effect of a torpedo operating simultaneously on all the benches of the Chambre. Honorable gentlemen young and old stood up in a sudden tumult, launching coarse insults and hyperbolic acclamations toward the first floor gallery. A man was standing there, his arms folded on the red velvet arm-rest, his eyes bleak in a frame of white side-whiskers fusing at the ears with discolored hair emerging capriciously from the bumps of a shiny polished cranium. That cranium belonged to Hermann

Coffre,[7] the great banker, who, with his long and emaciated hands, the fingers of which only took on the aspect of claws during socialist speeches and writings, played like a cat with a rat with the economic life of the entire world.

Next to him, the legitimate Madame Coffre, née Pulcelette, assured with her opulent person the stability of a chair in the back of which she was leaning, either because she was trying to hide from the manifestations or because she wanted to approach the nape of her neck to the blond moustache installed behind her under the straight and slender nose of Alexandre Sylphe, a captain corseted in the black tunic with white decorations of the cuirassiers, who was reputed to be her lover.

As motionless as a statue, Monsieur Coffre did not seem to hear or see anything. The President of the Chambre, Perruquet, clutched his hand-bell in his right hand, which he agitated frenetically, brandishing in his left hand a paper-knife full of menaces for Abbé Mortol, who, in spite of the prohibition on launching an attack on someone unable to respond, continued nevertheless to vociferate against Monsieur Coffre.

Finally, breathless and exhausted, with white foam in the corners of his lips, his feature contracted with impotent rage, the not-very-ecclestiastical abbé quit the podium, to which another député, hastening from the heights of the Extreme Left immediately climbed, making grand gestures to attract the attention of his colleagues. It was Louis Méripal, whose thirty years represented the revolutionary spirit of a Parisian arrondissement.

Never had a collectivity been synthesized in a more complete and more exact fashion than the electoral body that had elected Louis Méripal. As nervous and impressionable as a crowd, as passionate as one, to the point of injustice, following his slightest reflexes of sympathy and antipathy with re-

---

[7] Coffre's forename is given here as Anacharsis in the original, but is given as Hermann everywhere else, so I have altered it is the interests of consistency.

gard to people and things, without even trying to make his reason intervene, he did not belong to any group, and every one of his votes was a white or black counter with which he marked a fleeting sensation that he made no attempt to analyze.

Essentially impulsive and spontaneous by nature, Lois Méripal was ignorant of what the accountants of human conscience termed "rights" and "duties." Free of all prejudice, liberated from any social bond, perhaps hiding, beneath a total absence of self-regard and vanity, an absolute pride in himself, he allowed all his actions to display themselves on the same plane, as items equal in their intrinsic value. Incapable of a calculation or a dissimulation, he professed the paradoxes that skill is the ultimate clumsiness and that instinct, for humanity and for the human individual, is an infallible guide so long as intelligence and reasoning do not disturb it.

Louis Méripal was, in fact, the least political of the six hundred-and-some legislators of fur and feather habitually combined to form a majority apt to bring to the functioning of the social estate changes qualified as inestimable benefits by some and atrocious calamities by others. He opened his mouth and his thought poured out without reticence, in its entirety, such as he conceived it.

Méripal's colleagues experienced in his regard a kind of fear, struck as they all were by a man whose mind had never been crossed by concern for the electors, and who marched through life without a gesture of ostentation or hypocrisy. Sometimes, they listened to him with curiosity, as one listens to a child uninstructed in good and evil, without irritation and without anger. From his lips, conservers of the most distant past and socialist prophets of the most nebulous futures collected the flower of truth—a poor flower, dead as soon as it blossomed, stifled in the feverish hands of base ambition and vile interest. But sometimes, too, that pitiless speech and absolute frankness, unsparingly enouncing the calculations and secret motives that made others act, unleashed furious tem-

75

pests in the bosom of the Assembly, by which the modern Chrysostom had the naivety to be astonished.

Partisans and adversaries of Abbé Mortol cut short the customary manifestations and various cries in order to hear Louis Méripal speak.

He began by calling "Petitpaon warfare" a poor joke.

With the utmost gravity, President Perruquet forbade the orator to pronounce the name of the first magistrate of the Republic, evidently more at home in a lewd song or the couple of an end-of-year revue than a parliamentary debate.

To General Croppeton, who claimed the responsible paternity of the project, Méripal riposted: "So be it! You, Courage, are the father, but where is the mother, Fear?"

"I have never known her!" Croppeton declared.

"She has, however, given you a child—this project that you are presenting to us, ridiculously smeared."

"You're insulting world peace!" President Perruquet intervened.

"You call this world peace—this lamentable pantomime that you're organizing to safeguard the privileges of soldiers who no longer want to play their roles to the end?"

"We are not actors!" protested General Croppeton, with dignity.

"You're the posturing hams of Death!" Méripal continued. "Go, then, and put on your most flamboyant uniforms; take up your rifles, sabers, revolvers, bayonets; to the sound of brilliant fanfares, make the emblems of murder flutter in the wind, drag cannons and machine-guns to some corner of the world where, for years on end, you will render illusory any hope of a crop, and perform the spectacular play of which Monsieur Coffre and his like will collect the authors' royalties in the form of equipment and munitions! And it's that frantic wastage, that cleverly organized destruction of human effort, which you're baptizing with the name of peace?

"Confess, then, that you're afraid of peace—of veritable peace! Oh, because that's the day when human labor will only serve to assure the well-being of life, which will appear to

76

everyone sufficiently worthy of being lived for no gaze to be tempted any longer by the afterlife, and every priest will be charged with imposture!"

A frightful racket drowned out Méripal's voice, who threw his speech to the stenographers: "Peace will come in spite of you, Monsieur l'Abbé Mortol, zealot of the eternal Moloch, in spite of you, Messieurs the warriors, and in spite of you, Monsieur Coffre, all united like fairground thieves around the Mère Gigogne of Faith, to bring about the earthly reign of the tyranny of iron and gold!"

Beneath the boos and ironic applause, Louis Méripal calmly went to the bar, and did not even deign to go back into the Chambre to vote against the plan, which was passed with an enormous majority.

In the Senate, the discussion was brief; only Monsieur Jadis raised his voice, alleging that it was his duty to declare that times had changed a great deal, and that when he was twenty years old, he would never have suspected that he would one day see such things as living dead men.

In his capacity as the Executive, Bernard Petitpaon promulgated by decree, countersigned by all the ministers, the idea that he had had, and which was to become, under the name of the "Petitpaon law," not only a French law but a law inscribed in all languages on the pages of the codes of all the peoples, to enjoy full international effect from noon on the first of September of the present year of the Gregorian calendar, as measured at the Paris Observatory.

III

The first of September thus became a universal feast day, as if the most highly-reputed saints of the various sects and religions presently in use had been given the word to accomplish on that precise date a miraculous gesture worthy of simultaneously attracting the attention of all their faiths.

The French Republic was obliged, in its own eyes and those of the world, to celebrate with royal sumptuousness the first evolution accomplished around the sun by our planet under a regime that would, in the opinion of historians—the more-or-less clear-sighted and faithful concierges of the past—throw the doors wide open to an era that it was legitimate, although infinitely flattering for France, to call "the Petitpaon Era."

Paris had made grandiose preparations for that solemnity, which was not merely the anniversary of a notable event but also the commemoration of a victory that the valiant French tricolor had won over a negro people.

Almost the day after the international convention, to which he had subscribed by having his ambassador hand over an ivory tablet engraved with solemn engagements, a potentate reigning in the heart of Africa over half a million pairs of anthropophagous jaws had indulged in gastronomic deviations with regard to the persons of two Marseillais travelers, whom he had accommodated in a bouillabaisse of which he was fond. No country worthy of the name could permit an African king to treat its nationals as mere comestibles, and it was the most elementary duty on the part of France to trouble the digestion of that lover of white meat. She took care not to fail in it; the Chambres voted unanimously, save for the votes of Louis Méripal and Abbé Mortol, for the immediate mobilization of a small army of forty thousand men, of which a renowned tactician very much in fashion, General Marquis de Foiraubilles, took command.

The newspapers published the portrait of that anticipated victor over one of the corners of the map approximately depicting the hereditary domains of King Haricot VII, which explorers, save for the two unfortunate Marseillais, had only visited in their boldest dreams.

The coefficient of destructive power accorded by the treaty to French arms was ten for the dead and ten for the wounded. In other words, every French infantryman, cavalier or artilleryman, operating globally and in the proportions prescribed by the general staff regulations and sensibly equal conditions of combat, would kill or wound a number of enemies equal to ten times the proportion established by the coefficient appropriate to the antagonistic nation.

In the cafés and the brasseries, the regulars, young and old, abandoned their favorite games in order to occupy themselves exclusively with the expedition. Mathematicians, blackening marble tables with giant rules of three victoriously penciled, demonstrated with a very natural patriotic emotion that in the first total engagement bringing the French army into conflict with that of Haricot VII, the latter would, *ipso facto*, be annihilated.

The eloquence of figures is justly reputed to be unequaled. It was, in fact, indisputable that, one Frenchman being able to kill ten enemies and wound as many, forty thousand Frenchmen could therefore kill or wound four hundred thousand negroes. The result of that arithmetical operation, every time it was proclaimed, was welcomed with delirious acclamations, and everyone drank, to the point of the most complete drunkenness, to the health of the triumphant Republic.

In an estaminet near the École Militaire, a former accountant in a bank was manhandled for having claimed that, from that number of four hundred thousand dead it was necessary immediately to subtract the number of wounded, which would similarly be four hundred thousand. Savage cries of "Death to all the Haricots!" responded to him. In vain the poor man tried to demonstrate that on a battlefield, wounds always precede death, even in the cast of apparent instantaneity.

In the Rue du Croissant, a gang of students attacked and sacked the offices of a newspaper that had published the losses that the French army would suffer. In vain the editor tried to discuss the matter with the demonstrators, to prove to them that his figures were the rigorously exact result of the international tables that attributed to the soldiers of King Haricot VII a coefficient of one nine-hundredth for the dead and one two-hundredth for the wounded. In other terms, their individual value produced a ninth of one percent and five wounded per thousand among the enemies they encountered. The chauvinistic scholars did not want to hear it; they hit the unfortunate journalist so hard and often that the police—who arrived, in conformity with the customs of their organization, once their presence had become an unnecessary luxury—only found a cadaver, which they transported to the Morgue.

He was the first victim of the war.

The concentration of the army took place in Marseilles. The embarkation presented serious difficulties because of the population, which could not resolve to be separated from the soldiers to whom France had confided the care of avenging the two sons of the Cannebière.

For General Marquis de Foiraubilles, the hour of the departure naturally sounded last.

Bernard Petitpaon accompanied the supreme leader of the expedition to the Gare de Lyon personally.

All along the special train, decked in tricolor flags, the classic scene of adieux unfolded. The officers of the General's staff boarded the saloon-carriages first, immediately putting their variously-plumed heads out of the windows.

Captain Sylphe was the last of them; he kissed the cheeks of Mademoiselle Hermine de Foiraubilles, to whom he was engaged. His future mother-in-law hugged him in her arms, catching her horn-rimmed binocle in his regulation feathers. As he pulled away, the captain broke the cord passed around the neck of the general's wife, and the frail optical instrument fell to the ground. Gallantly, Bernard Petitpaon bent down to pick it up; he observed that one of the lenses was broken and, as he was superstitious, he had a moment of dizziness that obliged him to lean on General Croppeton's arm.

After handshakes and countless accolades, General Marquis de Foiraubilles, his bicorn hat in battle order, his right hand over his heart and his left on the hilt of his sword, climbed into his carriage, of which Admiral Théhyx closed the door.

The Messidor decree reserved to the representative of the ecclesiastical authority the honor of giving the train, with his supreme blessing, the signal to depart.[8] Cardinal Pecari having forbidden the most modest aspergillum to put in an appearance, however, the director of protocol had been obliged to laicize the ceremony. A silver whistle had been specially constructed for the august lips of the President of the Republic, operating in the stead of the sulking God.

Bernard Petitpaon made the gesture of raising to his lips the whistle that had been presented to him by a gold-braided individual, but his arm fell back and, in response to a few briefly-articulated words, the obedient servant disappeared, as if by enchantment, to return a minute later brandishing a bugle.

Bernard Petitpaon wiped the mouthpiece of the instrument with his dogskin-clad palm, and, with his singer's lungs largely dilated, he drew a formidable blast from the bras instrument.

The locomotive-driver leaned on the lever that set the engine in motion with all his strength; the train drew away so brutally that heads collided with one another at all the open windows, without any respect for the hierarchy of plumes and pinions.

For several weeks, there was no news of the army, the probable situation of which was calculated day by day and hour by hour. Finally, a telegram from General Foiraubilles announced that a first engagement had just taken place in the northern section of the Niger bend. Details were lacking, but it was evidently a victory.

Events followed one another with an extraordinary rapidity and in the early days of March, Haricot VII, surrounded in his capital, Cirajoum with all his warriors, accepted the deci-

---

[8] The decree in question is that of 24 Messidor, an XII (13 July 1804), instituted by Napoléon I, which defined the roles of civil, military and ecclesiastic authorities is state ceremonies. This passage was written before the modification of the relevant decree in 1907 by Georges Clemenceau.

sion of the arbiters who declared his army completely destroyed.

The French, therefore, entered Cirajoum; they found the
shoulder-blades of the two Marseillais suspended in Haricot
VII's dining room. The officer charged with unhooking the
funereal remains, with great ceremony, discovered an inscription on each of them in Negro verse, which an interpreter
translated as:

> *These bones were covered with the delectable meat*
> *Which the great Haricot VII was pleased to eat.*

All the cannibals filed before the remains of the feast so
flatteringly commemorated, and nothing further remained than
to regulate officially the consequences of the war and the losses on either side.

On the black side, there were vastly more than the complete annihilation, since Haricot VII had only been able to
raise two thousand warriors and the French could have killed
four hundred thousand.

In conformity with the treaties, the dead had to be dis-
armed and dressed in long white robes, but as His Majesty
Haricot VII's subject were completely ignorant of the use of
garments, it was agreed that the negroes would limit themselves to painting themselves from head to toe with ceruse, of
which French commerce would have the sole right of supply.[9]

---

[9] Venetian ceruse, or "Spirits of Saturn," based on white lead,
was widely used in the 16th century as a skin-whitener, but it
had virtually fallen out of use by 1906 because it was known
by then to cause hair loss and other nasty symptoms because
of the toxicity of the lead. (If lead piping in their baths played
a part in causing of the decadence of the Roman aristocracy,
imagine what ceruse did to the English nobility in the days
when the trend-setting Elizabeth I and Mary, Queen of Scots,
were enthusiastic users.) In the present instance, the poor
black casualties really have been condemned to death, albeit

It remained to individualize the white losses—which is to say, those suffered by our army.

Under the eyes of the scrutineers sent by all the Powers, forty thousand slips representing all the combatants, without exception—from the commanding general to the humblest infantryman—were put into a giant urn.

The regulations demanded that the draw by made by the innocent hands of a virgin canteen-waitress. The expeditionary force had kept two of them in reserve. They had engaged specially after an exceedingly scrupulous medical examination, and a surgeon-major first class had been specifically designated to watch over the integrity of their virtue.

Respectful of the rights of seniority, General Foiraubilles designated to represent chance the older of the two canteen-waitresses, but at the last moment, the young person in question confessed to having yielded to a corporal in the engineering corps during the night that followed the taking of Cirajoum. Her comrade, a petite blonde, blushing at so much honor, was, in consequence, led to the urn.

The first slip was opened; Captain Sylphe called out the serial number, ad a zouave emerged from the ranks. He was dead! He shouted "Vive la France!" twice and "Vive la République!" once, and in the midst of the acclamations of his brothers in arms, put on a long white smock fitted with a hood, which General Foiraubilles pulled up personally over the head of the dauntless soldier.

The second slip designated a brigadier in the dragoons. Captain Sylphe ordered the man to dismount from his horse, but the latter, with his right hand level with his helmet, claimed that a cavalryman ought to die on his horse. A discussion was engaged between the ambassadors present, which was threatening to take on the proportions of a veritable quarrel when the Marquis de Foiraubilles made the very apt observation that the French dragoons are a mixed corps, fighting on

---

slowly[i]—a fact of which the author eventually reveals his awareness.

foot as well as on horseback. The brigadier resigned himself to not being an equestrian cadaver, and put on his smock, shouting his regimental number.

Captain Sylphe announced that he was going to proceed with the draw for the fate of the wounded, when the English delegate, with perfect phlegm, pointed out that by applying the reckoning tables, in view of the number of their two thousand combatants, individually producing a one-ninth of a per cent mortality, still had the right to the death of a fraction of a Frenchman.

A Russian colonel pointed out the recurrence of that fraction, but in vain; it was necessary to yield to the obstinacy of the subject of His Most Gracious Majesty King Edward VII. It was agreed, however, that the case would be submitted to the appreciation of an international tribunal; in the meantime, the casualty, afflicted with regard to an indefinite part of his person, would assume a condition of provisional death.

The virgin hand of the young canteen-worker handed a third slip to Captain Sylph. The latter unfolded it and, tragically, handed it to General Foiraubilles, saying: General, I die for my country! Vive la France!"

"Vive la France!" repeated the vanquisher of Haricot VII, mechanically. Then, pulling himself together, he said: "My dear Sylphe, you shall be my son in law regardless. You're only provisionally dead!"

The British officer made the observation that Captain Sylphe need not put on the uniform of the deceased, but that it was indispensable that he adopt some distinctive mark. A gray dust-cover proposed by an American warrior won a unanimous vote. General Marquis de Foiraubilles enveloped his future son-in-law in it personally; the latter brandished his saber, swearing in an assured masculine voice to conduct himself officially as a dead man in all the circumstances of life, until a definition decision had been reached in his case.

The drawing of lots for the wounded and the nature of their wounds was free of any incident. Two artillerymen were deprived of the use of their right arms, six infantrymen lost their left legs, a sergeant in the cuirassiers received a wound in his lower back and an adjutant in the spahis paid for the glory of having defeated Haricot VII with an ear.

With its dead and wounded at the head, the French army returned to France; the Chambres voted all the necessary funds to celebrate General Foiraubilles and his harvesters of laurels worthily.

At Marseilles, in the midst of an indescribable enthusiasm, the shoulder-blades so gloriously recaptured were deposited with great pomp in the expiatory monument that the old Phocean city had erected to its unfortunate children.

With pride, the funeral oration pronounced by the Maire repeated the laudatory lines:

These bones were covered with the delectable meat
Which the great Haricot VII was pleased to eat.

A woman who had searched in vain for her son in the triumphal cortege cried out for him loudly. A staff officer went to her, reproaching her for her antipatriotic conduct, and added that there were six thousand mothers whose sons had also died of disease during the campaign. As the unhappy woman continued to moan and utter imprecations, a courageous citizen grabbed her by the throat to make her shut up. When his fingers relaxed their grip, the woman collapsed. She was dead.

An engineer of the P.L.M. Company had had the good idea of establishing metallic armatures on top of the locomotive and carriages making up the train of honor responsible for carrying General de Foiraubilles to Paris, which had been garnished at the last moment with flowers and foliage. Thus, the train seemed to run from Marseilles to Paris beneath an uninterrupted triumphal arch.

Everything had been calculated so that the victorious army would make its entrance on the first of September, the first anniversary of the Petitpaon Era.

85

The President of the Republic had claimed the privilege of taking center stage himself in the first apotheosis of his work.

Desirous above all of making it something original as well as beautiful, he had decided on the Place de la Concorde as its theater. The ordinary and extraordinary organizers of public celebrations had applauded the presidential choice, without the slightest hidden agenda of flattery. The name of the location was, in fact, a radiant symbol, concord being synonymous with peace in a rigorously exact fashion, and like peace itself, the result of an evolution as long as it was bloody, that corner of the Earth had been subject to many transformations. It had seen the hideous guillotine cause to fall, pell-mell, along with heads guilty of crimes, those circled with royal crowns and the heroic heads of those who had slaughtered one another in the dazzle of the first radiance of a humanity to which they had given birth.

Bernard Petitpaon was incapable of obedience to simple verbal attractions, however. He had wanted a grandiose centerpiece to heighten the glamour of the ceremony; that centerpiece he had found in the obelisk. The giant monolith, brother—perhaps elder—to the pyramids, which, in a fit of lyricism, Bonaparte had attributed to gazes forty centuries old in order to contemplate his unripe Grande Armée, had seduced Petitpaon as much by virtue of its so gloriously distant past as its twenty-three meter height. It was the pivot demanded by Bernard Petitpaon about which the entirety of France, in the person of her official and legal representatives, would rotate.

An extract of the people, the first magistrate of the Republic claimed for the people the right to the best possible view of the elect and the men invested by him with public functions. Putting his principles into action, he had, therefore, ordered the execution of a plan in which imagined the Obelisk serving as an axis for a series of circular steps on which, in protocolary order, the ministers, senators, députés would first take their places, and then the great State bodies, all fully constituted and reciprocally animated by a ferocious jealousy, eager to fill relative to one another the allegedly benevolent role of phagocytes, passionate devourers of their microbial relatives in the cause of the salvation of animal organisms.

It only remained to endow the symbolic installation with the soul constitutive of modern France. Of that soul, Bernard Petitpaon had penetrated all the arcana in their utmost and tenebrously democratic depths; hoisted to a supreme degree of initiation, he knew that mobility is the very essence of a free government veritably fond of equality and fraternity.

Without the slightest nuance of irreverence, he translated that by the formula dear to disabused lovers: *Tout passe, tout lasse, tout casse*; and, freighting the Parisian ship with a hint of pessimism, he Latinized: *Fluctuat at mergitor*, with a smile of serene satisfaction.[10] How could that soul be better expressed than by giving movement to the steps occupied by the representatives—varying in status but similarly tyrannical—of inconstant and perfidious universal suffrage, while the places reserved for the functionaries would be as immutable as them?

In consequence, a kind of conical stage had been constructed around the Obelisk, which it joined at about three meters from its summit. At that level there was a platform that an electric motor could turn in either direction; eleven armchairs destined for the ministers were installed there. The part of the cone fitted with the senatorial seats only rotated in one direction and with a velocity slightly less than half of that which animated the portion curulized by the députés, whose mandate, as everyone knows, lasts four years while in the Upper Assembly the unity of the legislature is nine years, for the

---

[10] The rhyme-scheme of the pithy French saying [Everything passes, everything wearies, everything breaks] does not translate, alas. Paris is frequently compared to a ship, and has a ship for its emblem, because the shape of the Île de la Cité makes easy to imagine it as a vessel floating on the Seine; the Latin quotation is a deliberate distortion of the ancient inscription *Fluctuat nec mergitur* [It floats and doesn't sink], removing the negative element.

87

security and tranquility of the conscripted fathers, whose status as aged parents does not always prevent them from being big babies.

"But where will Monsieur le Président sit?" Petitpaon's first confidant enquired, respectfully.

"Not on the bitumen or the wooden paving, for sure! The President ought to be highly placed, and he will be: the point of 'Cleopatra's Needle' will be my seat. However, as I don't deem it indispensable to give my contemporaries the spectacle of a presidential impalement, and, on the other hand, it would be as ridiculous as it would be dangerous to risk possible vertigo, you'll install a small round pulpit on that porphyry axis, similar to those that preachers employ in churches."

"Don't you fear, Monsieur le Président, that such a device might offend the clergy?" the political intimate objected.

"Drape it with red—that'll do the trick!" said Petitpaon, dismissively. "Oh, I forgot the essential symbol. It's necessary that the people of France see that I'm her servant, the slave of France. You will, therefore, establish immediately beneath me, and consequentially above the ministerial platform, a circular cage—immobile, of course, for it's destined for the trinity representative of the social synthesis: a priest, a soldier and a representative of finance. Those three men can impart to my pulpit whatever movement of rotation they see fit!"

The presidential plan was carried out in its most minute details. The platforms had been tested with a load of sandbags twice as heavy as the total weight of the ministers, senators and députés. No accident was therefore to be feared, and each stage obeyed its motor without hesitation.

The day before the ceremony, Bernard Petitpaon, equipped with a false nose and make-up in order to be utterly unrecognizable, had come to see a rehearsal. He had taken his place in the minuscule elevator that climbed the length of the Obelisk as briskly as possible. Ramses II was so bewildered by the spectacle that, in order to follow the stupefying ascension of the President of the French Republic, he forgot his homage to the god of Thebes.

From seven o'clock in the morning onwards, the expeditionary corps occupied the broad avenues opening on to the Place de l'Étoile. Before coming to stand with his staff under the vault of the Arc de Triomphe, where the landau of the dead and the brake of the wounded were waiting, as well as a horseman clad in an ample gray cloak who was none other than the fractionally defunct Alexandre Sylphe, General Marquis de Foiraubilles reviewed the troops placed under his command.

At ten o'clock, the first official carriages arrived in the Place de la Concorde, disembarking their picturesque contents: togas in garish colors, variegated uniforms, complicated accoutrements doubtless imagined in the joyous days of yore by court jesters and now gravely worn by all the administrative employees of various social causes prospering or vegetating in the world under the titles of empires, monarchies or republics.

In Paris more than anywhere else, a simultaneous influx of men, women and children to any point at the city merits the name of a crowd. A crowd, in fact, is not an indeterminate number of curiosity-seekers attracted toward a common goal; it is not a swarming populace running toward some ephemeral gratuity of bread and circuses; it is a gathering of human beings, rich or poor, of all ages and all conditions rubbing shoulders, at whim or hazard, without embarrassment or shame. A crowd sees, hears and thinks—which is to say that it is conscious. Certainly, like all seas, it has its tempests, which seem inexplicable; sometimes, terrible deep waves, whose sources escape observers at the surface, raise it up in titanic convulsions; but calm does not take long to be reborn, and all the heads soon reappear above the foam of the waves.

On this occasion, it was a matter of acclaiming the colors of France.

The Parisian crowd, augmented by an invasion of provincials and foreigners—moths attracted by the radiance of the City of Light—blocked the Champs-Élysées and the neighboring streets. Triple and quadruple cordons of troops and police hemmed in that buzzing multitude, pierced here and there by the shrill cries of women succumbing to sexual promiscuities.

Ministers, senators and députés installed themselves in accordance with protocol on the mobile steps above the great State bodies massed in a fan around the Obelisk on benches riveted to the ground.

Several hundred cannon shots announced that Bernard Petitpaon was leaving his house in the Faubourg-Saint-Honoré. In the eddies of the heavy surge of the cuirassiers of his escort, the presidential landau was perceived—or, rather, divined—by the thousands of eyes aimed at the gaping void of the roadway.

A few minutes later, a tricolor flag fluttered at the top of the Obelisk, over the red barrel from which protruded a black torso with a white shirt-front, surmounted by an ebony-haired head.

An immense acclamation greeted Bernard Petitpaon, who looked, in his French costume, like a magpie perching on the rim of its nest.

From the Concorde to the Étoile a continuous hedge of bugles sounded the rallying call.

On his chestnut thoroughbred, Captain Alexandre Sylphe, provisionally defunct for a fraction of his person, civilian as well as military, emerged from the immense arch raised to the glory of victorious French armies. His rank as an officer entitled him to the honor of appearing on horseback in front of the uncovered landau carrying the zouave and the brigadier of dragoons, the rest of his uniform as well as the body of his mount disappearing under the gray dust-cover that he could not take off in public without violating the treaties.

A large artillery brake followed, carrying the ten invalids, all in uniform, each having covered in white cloth the part of his person theoretically damaged on the African battlefield.

Next came the army. Preceding a classic staff, brilliantly composed, General Marquis de Foiraubilles, his bicorn hat decked with an impeccable ostrich feather, was astride a spirited but docile charger with a snowy mane and flanks.

Enthusiasm fraternized with delirium. To avoid the most timid false note capable of wounding, as in Marseilles, the harmony of the day, the authorities had imprisoned, for a lapse of time too short for it to be considered an infringement of individual liberty, the relatives and friends of the six thousand unfortunates whom disease and accidents had transported from the banks of the Niger to those of the Styx.

From all sides, crowns of laurels were thrown at the victorious general; a few fell under the feet of his horse, which sketched elegant avoiding steps, as if to excuse the impassivity of his master, eager to protect Republican susceptibilities obsessed by the specter of Caesar.

The cortege descended the Champs-Élysées and arrived at the border of the corridor leading to the space preserved between the base of the moving steps and the compact ranks of functionaries.

An immense clamor resounded. Bernard Petitpaon detached the tricolor flag fluttering above his head and waved it frantically, more than half of his body leaning out of his aerial pulpit. The ministers, who were rotating on their platform at top speed, heard him demand the Marseillaise several times over. The order to attack Rouget de l'Isle's work was given by General Croppeton, and, via the intermediary of several hundred parliamentary throats, reached the leader of the military bands massed between the members of the Institut and those of the Court of Cassation.

All a-quiver, with his brazen voice, which rendered the patriotic emotion gripping him even more vibrant, President Petitpaon intoned the famous hymn.

At a signal from General Foiraubilles, the wounded put their hands to their temples militarily, and the dead, including Captain Sylphe, made a gesture in the direction of the President of the Republic which signified that those who had just died for France were saluting him.

The senators and députés accomplished their rotations at their respective constitutional speeds, and when, among the crowd, a few groups recognized one of their chiefs in passing, there were cries of joy, renewed at each revolution.

Doubtless by virtue of timidity, the trio figuring, between the ministerial platform and the Executive tribune, the essential substratum of every social estate had not yet imparted the slightest movement to the presidential barrel. The priest, the soldier and the financier in the green-and-gold livery of the Maison Coffre, were mutually convincing one another of the value of their rights, and demonstrating to one another the absolute necessity of showing France that her Representative was nothing but a puerile plaything in their hands, at their entire discretion.

Their combined hands began to cause Bernard Petitpaon's station to rotate, and all three of them took a malign pleasure in abruptly stopping the barrel in its gyratory movement in order to launch it in the inverse direction—and the crowd applauded every time. Petitpaon, glued by centrifugal force to the rim of his pulpit, defended himself heroically against seasickness.

Infantrymen, artillerymen, cavalrymen and other services in full dress uniform—the entire army—filed around the Obelisk in order to reach the Jardin des Tuileries, where sumptuously-laid tables awaited them under gigantic tents.

On that day of rejoicing, the Government of the Republic could not forget those who had endured the same sufferings as its children, and run the same dangers; the horses and mules found hundreds of baskets filled with first-rate hay for their consumption. A dog of war, which had not quit the commanding general, any more than his shadow, for the entire duration of the expedition, took a place under the table of honor, and even gave Bernard Petitpaon a great fright by coming to sniff the presidential legs, stretched out opposite those of the Marquis de Foiraubilles, at overly close range.

As in any self-respecting banquet, a great deal was eaten and even more was drunk. There were allocutions and speeches, and so many toasts were drunk to the presidential health, that even by granting each of them an effect of a few minutes,

Bernard Petitpaon would have remained free of the slightest illness until his dying day.

The official personages withdrew in order to leave the martial joy to manifest itself without restraint. Drunkenness did not take long to overtake the majority of the guests. Outside, women gathered along the railings, attracted by an obscure force toward the soldiers. The latter, under the complicit eyes of their leaders, opened the gates; cries of hysterical fright resounded. Brutally seized by the soldiers in rut, of whom they were afraid as well as desirous, the women pleaded and howled, convulsively hugged to the breasts of men who carried them away at a crazy pace until the common collapse on to a bench, a table, a heap of straw, where an embrace left the couples momentarily inanimate.

With nightfall, the orgy took on the proportions of an antique bacchanal, It was Paris entire that was taking part in the celebration, in an unleashing of carnal madness and lust, amid the multicolored blaze of illuminations.

IV

In France, as elsewhere, one easily puts off serious matters until tomorrow, and when they assume the rank and title of public affairs, they are ordinarily postponed until a date that is purely and simply ulterior.

Thus, the Chambres did not resume their work until five days after the closure of the festivities.

The case of Captain Sylphe presented itself, threatening internal and external complications.

Two theses were put forward. The first, adopted by the military party and patriots conscious of the power of France, held that the young and brilliant officer was well and truly alive, the reason being that he preserved more than half his person intact. The second, defended by universal diplomacy and by French intellectuals committed by the letter of the treaty, was obstinate in making Alexandre Sylphe a definitive cadaver, alleging that a man deprived of two thousand two hundred and twenty-two ten-thousandths of his person—not to take the recurrence of the fraction any further—could not claim present existence, in that the partial substance held sway over the rest.

Personally, Captain Sylphe was quite indecisive and would have been placed in a cruel embarrassment if made responsible to taking the decision himself.

If he were declared dead, his brother, the sole close relative that remained to him, would become the definitive title-holder of the general treasury that the Government had granted him; deducting in advance half of what it produced, that was an income of twenty thousand francs for him, which, along with the heart of Madame Coffre and the little sweeteners afferent therefrom, might suffice amply for a man's happiness.

Reintegrated into the ranks of the living, he would, for matters of war, immediately be promoted to the rank of squadron-leader; he would marry Mademoiselle Hermine de Foiraubilles, for whom he was burning with a lukewarm conjugal flame, but whose hand would enable him to rise to the highest summits of the military hierarchy.

Those two alternatives rendered him as perplexed as Buridan's ass, immobilized, as everyone knows, by the equal attraction of two identical bales of hay—and if, aloud, he proclaimed his ardent desire to have General Foiraubilles for a father-in-law, he also confided to Madame Coffre his secret thirst to remain entirely hers.

Even when their hearts are not excited, all women like to hear about the passion they inspire, so Madame Coffre was delighted by the sighs of Captain Sylphe.

With her twenty years glorified by a perfect beauty, Emma Pulcelette, born of honorable but almost poor parents, had, in the course of an official soirée, made the conquest of the rich banker Hermann Coffre. The man in question, who could no longer count his millions, and whose fortune was linked to that of France, had passed forty without pausing in the presence of a woman for longer than the time necessary to extract from his wallet the talisman that opened the most virtuous doors to him, which he closed again immediately with the same discreet and rapid gesture. The encounter with the young woman had been a revelation to him, the hatching in his being of something he had never experienced. With all the precautions, delicacies and anguishes of a vulgar amorous individual, in the eyes of a family too dazzled to manifest any sentiment whatsoever, before God and men, he had taken Emma Pulcelette for his wife.

Wise demoiselles do not estimate gold as a chimera devoid of attraction; the enormous ingot of precious metal that Monsieur Coffre represented had produced on young Emma an effect analogous to that of Jupiter descending upon Danae in a cataract of nuggets. At first, the poor girl lost her senses therein; then, gradually, as her eyes became accustomed to the glare of wealth, she had perceived vague shadows in the picture of her happiness.

She wondered whether he was really a husband, that man who, after having himself announced, came into her bedroom with his hands full of flowers and jewelry, stammering excuses and returning swiftly to his business affairs. Was there, in consequence, something of which she was deprived and to which she had a right?

Adulated both for her beauty and her fortune, she incessantly trailed after her an inexhaustible procession of courtiers; the homages she received were those of a queen; she required a king. She selected an actor whom poets and dramaturges sought out in order to secure the triumph of love in the theater, as the target of various terrestrial and metaphysical relativities.

Hermann Coffre had observed the treason without complaint, as one does an incurable wound; he even affected an intangible indifference to safeguard male vanity—which is often the only love of which a man's heart is capable—in the eyes of the unfaithful wife and the gallery. He had taken mistresses, and, even in the presence of the lover, lauded the most secret charms of his wife, to which he referred, in his banking terminology, as her "liquidation."

Wearying as quickly as she had been smitten, to the extent of the most profound disgust, of her actor, who was playing the comedy of love in pitiful fashion to the entire city, Madame Coffre implored her husband's pity. The latter did not have the courage to refuse forgiveness of a lapse for which, in his conscience, he felt responsible, a woman of twenty—almost a child—having the right to the vigilant care of her spouse to defend her against others and herself. Monsieur Coffre took his wife back as one would take back an unfaithful mistress, because she is beautiful and voluptuous and one has a pronounced taste for her flesh.

Distraught, the unfortunate woman sought in a new amour, in vain, a remedy for her distress; then, her soul and senses perturbed, devoid of will, incapable of resistance, she yielded to any man who attacked her boldly. It was known that she had civilian and military lovers, advocates, physicians, artists and vulgar sporting heroes or men of the world.

However, whether because the joys dispensed by swordsmen were more intense or because their recruitment was easier, as well as their discreet dismissal—by virtue of discipline and the complaisance of the Ministry of War, ever-ready to recompense with a stripe or a medal any officer offering to quite Paris voluntarily after an expedition in Madame Coffre's bed—the banker's wife devoted herself exclusively to the army.

She began with generals, whose starry emblems caused her to desire embraces that were more virile although less elevated in the hierarchy; rank by rank she sampled the science of seasoned campaigners of amour and the impetuosity of conscripts of sensuality; for more than fifteen years, all units, including the specialist ones, beat the retreat of pleasure upon her senses.

Having reached the autumn of her life as a woman, on the brink of forty, experience had taught her that vice, like virtue, has a real advantage in seeking the *juste milieu*. For preference, she clasped to her bosom heads coiffed in kepis with three stripes, because captains, without yet having the hesitant gait of laggards fearful at every stage of not being able to achieve the goal, no longer have the so-often-deceptive ardor of adolescents.

Monsieur Coffre consoled himself as best he could by telling himself that his wife, who did not make him happy, was not making anyone else happy either; his self-esteem suffered less from knowing that she had lovers than from knowing that she had only one lover; in sum, he had no rival and could not be jealous of all men as a species.

Captain Sylphe, however, lingered, and the banker began to feel some hatred in his regard. To rid his bed of him, he had had him assigned as orderly officer to General Foiraubilles, of whom, according to custom, he had become the designated son-in-law—but the war, by provisionally removing the captain's official existence, cast his plan into disarray. A dead man, in fact, could not contract a legitimate union, and Madame Coffre had too tender a heart to close the door abruptly on an unfortunate soldier fallen victim to his professional duty.

Monsieur Coffre considered violence as a remedy always worse than the disease it was a matter of curing. Instead of resorting to manifestations as ridiculous as they would be futile, he limited himself to joining the party, in categorical fashion, of those whose deemed it just and necessary to maintain Captain Sylphe on the register of the living. Under cover of reasons of a patriotic order, he put pressure on the public powers for Captain Sylphe to recover his entitlements as a living man, which would permit him to marry Mademoiselle de Foiraubilles and force him to break with Madame Coffre.

As was customary, General Croppeton had the Cabinet castigated by one of those députés who, in parliamentary matters, play the same role as stimulators of the crowd in fairground wrestling booths. The orator seemed genuinely indignant to see France yielding to foreign pressure; he reproached the Government for lack of energy and summoned it, in grandiloquent terms, to declare its intention.

The Minister of Foreign Affairs, Henri Verbuis, replied that a France that was strong within would always be respected without, if it took for its only rule honestly considering treaties as inviolable and war as a measure of extreme rigor, only to be employed after the failure of all means of conciliation.

He made it known that the case of Captain Sylphe would be submitted to a tribunal of arbitration and that an accord could probably be reached that would give satisfaction to everyone, friends as well as enemies of France.

The majority applauded these declarations confidently, which left the present as it was and reserved the future.

Louis Méripal asked to speak and, as the rules of the Chambre safeguard all rights except the right to silence, President Perruquet corroborated with violet shakes of the handbell the appearance at the podium of Abbé Mortol, who, it appeared, had priority by right of inscription.

The abbé gave an unctuous explanation of the motives and reasons that would henceforth assure Petitpaon warfare the support of Catholics. He invoked the truth, momentarily hidden by God from his representatives, for a purpose whose mystery it would be sacrilegious to attempt to penetrate.

He declared that he was speaking on behalf of Cardinal-Archbishop Pecari, who had received precise instructions directly from the Holy Father, ensured by infallibility against the error of a long procession of miseries and pains visible and palpable only in the other world.

Taking as his witness the omnipotence of God, perfected to the point of having become capable of annihilating in an unappreciable lapse of time that which he had taken six days to edify, Abbé Mortol qualified Petitpaon warfare as the most radiant flash of enlightenment of all those that had traversed the Christian world since the most obscure times. He begged the Government not to dishonor France by sacrificing one of her noblest children, Captain Sylphe, to pretentions as injurious as they were misplaced.

"War if need be: war with Europe, war with the world! France will be victorious if God wishes it!" cried the bellicose ecclesiastic, quitting the podium, to which Louis Méripal climbed by the opposite staircase, avoiding the hands of the ushers trying to retain him in the hemicycle.

"What sinister hopes have made you retract your loud anathemas today, Monsieur Mortol? What odor of cadavers has brought back the briefly-distanced vultures?"

"It is God who, via my mouth...!" Abbé Mortol protested, from his bench.

"It's God who is shutting up via your mouth!" snapped Méripal, imperiously. "We know, anyway, what he wants, your God, in that he's just like all the other gods: monsters hatched in the dark abysms of the nightmares of the unknown! What he requires is bodies, bloodied to make them howl in their torture! It's souls to rip apart fiber by fiber, until death effaces them to plunge them in nothingness! Yes, you preach obedience, humility and resignation! And you make them into virtues—which you are careful not to practice—and you treat as crimes liberty, self-esteem and the spirit of revolt, because you know that you will be swept away by them, as dust is swept from the highway by the wind that watches over the fecund earth! You always talk about sacrifice..."

"Jesus died on the cross!" shouted a voice from the far right.

"And it's in the blood of that man, that man that you have led to theatrical torture in order to proclaim him God, that the Faith, the most formidable house of commerce, has been founded!"

Catholics, Protestants, Israelites, freethinkers and sectarians of every stripe remained as mute and motionless as statues.

"To make it prosper, Messieurs its inheritors, you need force! Flattering the vanity of the soldier, you have proclaimed your weakness before him, and, as his heart is simple, he has made himself your champion. He has replaced you on the fields of battle, braving Death for you who fear it, in spite of your Paradise to which it opens the door! Soon, dulled by the burden of his equipment, hallucinated by the miserable flame that you have lit in the depths of sanctuaries, the soldier has become the blind instrument of your ambition and your power. And the portion of wealth that you have not been able to detain in your own hands, you have confided to accomplices. Since the commencement of the centuries, priests have marched hand in hand with men of war and men of money. In their footsteps, roads have been changed into torrents in which black floods of blood run. Cut one another's throats—that has been your maxim!"

"The Gospel orders loving one's neighbor as one's brother," Abbé Mortol rectified.

"Lying words, like all those that emerge from your mouth! And it's not for you alone that I'm speaking, but for all the inventors of gods, the exploiters of the afterlife, the priests of all times and all religions, who soil the earth in order to render it hateful, so that no one will dispute its possession with you! The god that you Christians call the true and only God has only come along after many other gods; he has redoubtable competitors and he will have successors when his symbol is outdated in the attention of humans. Gods pass; the priest remains! And gods will pass into the hands of priests until life becomes beautiful enough to be venerated in isolation! On that day, the temples will crumble! The sun will give birth to flowers between their scattered stones! The only law will be happiness, and everyone will find it by freely following his own instinct!"

"The instinct of the brute and the criminal!" mocked a legislator of the ethical school.

"There are neither brutes nor criminals! It's because you have misappropriated the goals of life that they have gone astray. You have created darkness on the road, and crouched in the shadows, with a hooded lantern in hand, you wait for the traveler's foot to slip into some rut, or for his head to collide with another head; then, abruptly, you project the searchlight of your laws upon him. You take possession of his person and put him in prison, on the pretext that his eyes were unable to guide him. No, it is not an inviolable law for men to cut one another's throats. Why does humanity not rid itself this very day of the odious yoke that constrains them to pillage, murder and the inexpiable crime that is war?"

"Petitpaon warfare does not offer the slightest danger!" declared General Croppeton, spitting out his beard and moustache violently. "Even children could wage it! During the entire African campaign not a single accident occurred!"

"Do you recognize, then, that no hatred results from a difference of race or nationality?" Méripal interrogated.

"General Croppeton did not say that!" President Perruquet intervened.

"Then how do you explain that white men and black men, confronted with one another, did not tear one another limb from limb?"

"Discipline was in control!" General Croppeton declared, solemnly. "Besides which, it's not as so many individuals that men are enemies, but as so many collectivities obedient to the same laws, ranged under the same flag, pursuing the same goal..."

"What goal?"

"All those that the fatherland proposes! That of speaking more loudly than one's neighbor! Of having the right to make modifications to the land-registry of the world! Of being able to chastise those who take insult to a country as far as eating the flesh of its children!"

"And what vengeance did you extract from the cannibals?"

"France does not avenge herself, Monsieur," replied Henri Verbuis, aristocratically. "We vanquished Haricot VII. We maintained our discretion! We could have taken possession of his realm. We limited ourselves to recovering the remains of our unfortunate compatriots. The incident is closed, honor is satisfied. What more do you want?"

"And it's to recover those four shoulder-blades engraved with facetious verse that you caused the deaths of six thousand Frenchmen?"

"Diseases are not imputable to us!" said Croppeton, defensively.

101

"And that you spent five hundred millions?" Méripal continued, furiously.

"Consumption is the soul of commerce, as labor is the wealth of a people," thundered Pierre Phosphène. "Petitpaon warfare is an inexhaustible source of wealth, since it permits the utilization of all the resources of a country without shedding a drop of blood."

"We have what we need to maintain an army ten times as numerous!" agreed Thunasol.

"And thanks to the rigorous training of our soldiers," Croppeton continued, "to the perfection of our artillery and our methods of combat, we shall not take long to obtain a higher coefficient in the international casualty-reckoners."

Applause supported the President of the Council's words, while abuse and insults rose up toward Louis Méripal.

Very calmly, as if a complete change of direction had taken place within him, the latter concluded: "There are madmen whose dream it is necessary not to break. There are sleepwalkers who, in their hypnotic slumber, stand on the edge of the most dangerous precipices, sometimes for a long time, but who would fall at the slightest gesture made to awaken them. May your dream continue! May nothing come to trouble your slumber! Only remember that peoples who play with war are like children who are playing with fire. May the deadly work of armaments be undone! May the force of Petitpaon warfare not end in bloodshed!"

Louis Méripal came slowly down from the podium. Large tears were running down his cheeks. Abbé Mortol denounced that he was weeping in shame.

Before ending the session, President Perruquet put forward a motion ordered that the victory of Cirajoum be added to those inscribed on the sides of the Arc de Triomphe at the Étoile, but someone, in the midst of an indescribable enthusiasm, passed a motion for the removal of all those names, and their replacement by the names of the President of the Republic, the ministers, the senators and the députés who had opened the Petitpaon Era of the World.

V

Diplomacy is a bizarre and tenebrous art.

In order to practice it with distinction, it is necessary to renounce everything that is frankness and simplicity. A perfect diplomat is a man who disguises his thoughts to the point of absence, in the same way that he ordinarily accepts for truth the opposite of what he hears.

Like those animals to which nature forbids rectilinear progress, the diplomat cannot go straight toward the goal that he secretly wants to attain; his preoccupation to deceive others is so constant that he often falls victim to his own ruses.

In the Sylphe affair, it was important, above all, that France put everyone else off the track. The official newspapers reported and repeated that the glorious Captain was perfectly resigned to his fate and that he was awaiting the decision of the arbitration tribunal in title tranquility.

Insidious notes credited Mademoiselle Hermine de Foiraubilles with the intention of entering religion by taking the veil of "Novices of Love" if God stole her fiancé from her.

In the meantime, a plenipotentiary minister, charged with the instructions of the Government and sumptuous gifts for which Monsieur Coffre had insisted on paying, left for Cirajoum in a secrecy known only to a few tens of millions of readers of the newspapers who reported the fact over the surface of the continents. It was a matter of obtaining from Haricot VII a written declaration in which he admitted having abused the credulity of the arbitrator-evaluators in having a mortal coefficient of one nine-hundredth attributed to his warriors.

By fixing that coefficient at the infinitesimally inferior figure of one thousandth, only two French soldiers would have lost their lives, and Captain Sylphe would recover the full rights of his civil and military authority.

That plan, which Machiavelli would not have denied, had been imagined by Henri Verbuis; it was adopted by the Council of Ministers unanimously, plus the voice of Bernard

Petitpaon, enthused by the *coup de théâtre* that the revelation of the document in question would produce if the arbitration tribunal decided on the definitive death of Captain Sylphe.

King Haricot VII received the French envoy with all due respect. Military honors were rendered by the women, old men and children, the men in a condition to bear arms having been deprived of all official existence.

Under the layer of ceruse that coated them from head to toe, they could be seen wandering from hut to hut like white phantoms with black heads, and their fate appeared to them to be so sad that many of them allowed themselves to die, accusing the demons of the coconut trees of twisting their entrails.

Although the matter was not of any interest to him, the potentate refrained from immediately agreeing to what was requested of him. He feigned complete indifference to the presents, and only deigned to place a gray top hat with a broad red and gold band on his curly hair. By dint of eloquence, the diplomat succeeded thereafter in persuading him to put on a gendarme's shoulder-sash and a sub-prefect's épée, which, with knee-length boots and fencing-gloves, composed an outfit before which all his subjects prostrated themselves in admiration.

The promise of a certain quantity of tins of tuna similar to those that he was persuaded to consume under the pretext that they were human flesh, combined with the terrible fear that he felt in regard to a phonograph, which he took for the white men's god, whom the ambassador could cause to speak or shut up at will, convinced Haricot VII, after much procrastination, to set his seal on the parchment, which arrived in Paris just as the arbitration tribunal opened its sessions,

The discussion was long and obscure; each camp had its moments of emotion, in which triumph was as probable as defeat.

Around the green baize on which the existence of Captain Sylphe was being gambled, the most ludicrous nonsense was talked, thanks to the whole collection of interpreters charged with serving as points of intersection between the multiple languages present.

There was talk of the rights of people whom the universal deluge had briefly submerged and who emerged stronger than ever from that legendary bath. The intangible power of solemnly consented treaties was celebrated, and no words were found expressive enough to criticize adequately the aberration of people who did not fear being guilty of the crime of lèse-engagement.

Step by step, with all the fertility of his crafty imagination, our representative defended the honor and interests of France, but after a final examination of the diplomatic documents that linked Haricot VII with the rest of humankind, the tribunal, while adopting considerations extremely flattering to France, remaining above the paltriness of debates, nevertheless pronounced the definitive death of Captain Sylphe.

In the silence that followed the pronunciation of that verdict, the representative of France took out of his briefcase the declaration of Haricot VII, and read it out.

No sign of emotion or astonishment gave a glimpse of the thoughts of those diplomats, past masters in the art of misdirection and hiding their secret sentiments. It is true that the majority did not understand a single word of the French language, and that those who might have been able to understand had no intention of being the first to speak.

The interpreters did their best to translate the words of the orator, which arrived, after having passed through the English, Russian and Japanese languages, came back to English before being translated into Spanish, then Italian, then Latin, modern Greek and Occitan, all the way to the representative of a petty king in Tierra del Fuego.

That individual, whose colleagues avoided him as far as possible because of the musky odor that he exhaled with a violence wounding to the least delicate olfactory faculties, extended both his arms and pronounced a phrase that appeared in French after having gone through the same series of metamorphoses. It expressed the impossibility of the son of Tierra de Fuego considering the new proposal without obtaining orders from his sovereign. He added that his religion did not permit him to receive any communication other than from the mouth of his august master. For those reasons, he asked that the matter be postponed for a year in order to give him time to make the voyage to Tierra del Fuego.

The excellence of the pretext, admirable for prolonging for many months a mission full of advantages, could not escape men as alert as the delegates of the great nations. Unanimously, they pronounced in favor of the adjournment for a year, to the day—which is to say, until the following November the first, reserving the right to order a longer delay if it became necessary.

Telephonic, telegraphic and postal communications being authorized by the religions and laws of the majority of countries, all the members of the tribunal envisaged the possibility of remaining in Paris for a long time—a sojourn that appeared to them, in the context of their non-official dreams, as a paradise of sensual and other delights.

In consequence, the tribunal annulled the verdict that it had just pronounced and ordered Captain Sylphe to remain in his situation of provisional death.

VI

Along with all the properly regulated clocks in France, the Louis XVI pendulum clock placed on the mantelpiece of the drawing room of an apartment in the building bearing the number 27 in the Avenue de l'Observatoire, chimed four.

A man and a woman abruptly quit the sofa on which they had been sitting side by side.

The woman was tall rather than petite, brunette rather than blonde, pretty rather than ugly, and those who would have taken her for a young woman would have been exactly right, for the person was none other than Mademoiselle Hermine de Foiraubilles.

The man, a captain in the cuirassiers to judge by his uniform, would have answered "Present!" without hesitation to the call of the name of Alexandre Sylphe.

Those two individuals, one of whom surely loved the other, were waiting with an unequal impatience for the decision of the arbitration tribunal that would permit their union or render it impossible.

The Marquise de Foiraubilles, the General's wife, came into the drawing room, which was her own, and said, in a slightly tremulous voice: "Oh, my dear children! At this very moment your fate is being decided. And we don't know anything yet! Oh, there are minutes in life that last thousands of seconds, seconds that are hours. Where is the General, then? He ought to be here! I want to know!"

"Me too, Maman," said the young woman.

"And you, Alexandre?"

"What? Obviously, obviously! Nothing is more painful than uncertainty," the cuirassier sighed, falsely.

"And yet, to fear a misfortune is nothing compared with the accomplished, irremediable fact! What if the tribunal decrees your death?" said the General's wife, tearfully.

"No, Maman, that's not possible! No, it's not possible! Alexandre is my fiancé…I love him! I don't want him to be made into a dead man that I can no longer marry! And you love me, don't you, Alexandre?"

Alexandre pressed to his heart the person he called "his Hermine," while the Marquise countered her impatience by leaning out of one of the windows, from which her gaze plunged, trying to pierce the yellow foliage of the chestnut-trees in order to interrogate the sidewalk that the General would have to go along as he came home.

While the young woman was drinking, on the lips of her fiancé, the hope of a conjugal kiss and Madame de Foiraubilles was leaning recklessly over the window-sill, the drawing room door opened, giving passage to a man of about fifty, clad in a black frock-coat tightened at the waist and decorated on the left lapel by a large rosette of the Légion d'honneur.

The man's face was pale and his gray hair appeared when he removed his hat with a gesture of slow and solemn nobility.

"Kiss, my children! Kiss one another!"

The young people came apart; the Marquise turned round abruptly and snapped: "Well, Narcisse?"

The General's wife only called her husband by his forename in important circumstances: intimate effusions and capital emotions of tenderness or wrath.

Narcisse de Foiraubilles, who was a man of decision, as much in his capacity as a general who had been a commander-in-chief in the face of the enemy as that of the head of a family conscious of his sovereign and unchallengeable authority, declared in a firm voice: "Captain, you remain dead for a further year!"

"What a catastrophe!" moaned the Marquise.

"What, General? That's not possible!" the Captain exclaimed. "The tribunal was to decide whether I'm alive or dead."

"It hasn't decided one or the other." And the General related, in brief, what had happened.

"What a catastrophe!" the Marquise continued to wail.

"A catastrophe that will last a year, not a day longer! Civilians have been mocking military men long enough. Word of a Foiraubilles, if, in a year's time, the judgment of that tribunal isn't what we want it to be, I swear that things won't stop there! In the meantime, my children, continue to embrace one another as you were doing just now."

"O Papa!" said the amorous Hermine, tearfully. "Why can't we marry right away?"

"You're forgetting, Hermine, that I'm provisionally dead," observed Captain Sylphe, coolly.

"You'll be alive next year, my Alexandre!"

"Come on, daughter, no silliness! It's necessary to be patient. Twelve months soon pass."

"You love one another; you'll see one another every day," the Marquise put in.

"I want to get married right away!" declared the Captain's fiancée, in a resolute tone.

"Come on, my darling, that can't be. We wouldn't be able to find a priest to bless your union clandestinely."

"With money, one can get whatever one wants. I'll take responsibility for finding a priest," the recalcitrant lover insisted.

General Marquis Narcisse de Foiraubilles was obliged to get on his high horse, which involved sonorous oaths, to convince his daughter to go to her room.

Solemnly, the Marquise went to her future son-in-law, seized his shoulder-knots, passed one through the other, and pulled upwards sharply, saying: "Alexandre, if you're a man of honor, you won't undo that knot before the glorious and divine day when Hermine becomes your wife. Swear!"

"I forbid you to swear!" the General interjected.

"Why?" questioned the Marquise.

"Because I don't want the Captain to make an oath that he'll violate, this evening, tomorrow, next week, next month…within a year, at any rate. A Captain is a man! There's no need to blush at being a man! I pity Hermine if she marries a representative of the stronger sex capable of remaining in expectation for a year. 'The iron that doesn't work rusts!' one of our present Statesmen wrote, who has made work a religion.[11] In the same way, the virility that abstains becomes flaccid and devoid of energy. Deliver yourself, therefore, Captain, in accordance with your age and your temperament to the salutary simulacra of reproduction! Is not the most efficacious means of preparing for veritable combat taking part in grand maneuvers?"

---

[11] In fact, the quotation comes from a Jesuit rule-book, *Du Gouvernement des Communautés Religieuses* [On the Government of Religious Communities], but it would not be surprising had some contemporary parliamentarian borrowed it.

The Marquise, covering her face, went to join her daughter. The two men, left alone, looked at one another momentarily.

"Thank you, General, thank you," said the Captain, gripping his chief's hands.

"No, my boy, no, don't thank me. It's quite natural. Women are truly astonishing. Because nature constrains them to a fidelity that is sometimes, for them, equivalent to continence, they imagine that men...ha ha! It would be funny, if it weren't one more proof of the inferiority of women. Come on—salute the ladies and go console yourself! But no compromising the liaison, eh?"

"You can be tranquil, General," declared Captain Sylphe, with the most convincing simplicity—who, after having placed both cheeks within range of the tears generously secreted by the glands of the dames de Foiraubilles, mother and daughter, left the building with a genuine satisfaction, not without having first put on the gray dust-sheet without which he was forbidden, under penalty of the worst catastrophes, to show himself in public.

VII

When our eyes gaze into the shadows and divine rather than distinguishing objects, the imagination often lends them forms of an infinite multiplicity. It is our dream that gives life to that which surrounds us. If light surges forth, coming to clarify contours and colors, the world that we have created vanishes, slain by reality. It is doubtless for that reason that love, which is the most fragile and most beautiful of dreams, instinctively flees the daylight and the glare of chandeliers and lamps.

Fervent devotees of voluptuousness love to pray in the twilight hours, when the nocturnal veil half-envelops them; in the light that is drowning in darkness the gestures of tenderness turn blue with softness, and lovers belong entirely to one another, not seeking to read in one another's eyes the secrets hidden there: egotism on the part of the man, lies on the part of the woman.

Along the Column, whose summit could only any longer be made out confusedly, night was descending on the Place Vendôme.

Posted behind a bay window in the small drawing room adjacent to her bedroom, the banker's wife was gazing into that shadow, which entered slyly and which she could have thrown out with a gesture, by turning the commutator responsible for switching on the electric chandelier suspended from the ceiling. But like, and perhaps more than, the majority of women, Madame Coffre knew that semi-obscurity is propitious to the cult of amour.

As she had put on, for the benefit of Captain Sylphe, whom she was expecting, a charming pink silk peignoir garnished with lace, she refrained from dissipating the intimacy of the rendezvous by illuminating her boudoir, as she would have done to receive her husband.

Thought-transmission is a phenomenon so banal that there is no necessity to believe that Madame Coffre had heard the footsteps of Captain Sylphe when she ran to the door, her arms open, closing them immediately around her lover's neck.

"My Alexandre!"

"My Emma!"

"What a joy to see you again!"

"What happiness to find myself close to you again!"

Their tongues were occupied momentarily in translating their tenderness over all the accessible epidermal surfaces of their persons.

"My poor Alexandre, you're dead for another year!"

"Let's not talk about that! Am I not alive in your company?"

"For myself, I'm only alive next to your heart. All the same, it's very annoying that you're dead!"

"No! Why? On the contrary, that marriage, which I couldn't avoid, has become impossible."

"You don't love her, that little Foiraubilles?"

111

"I only love you, my Emma."

"Thank you, my Alexandre, my love! Oh, everything would be perfect if you could get rid of that dust-cover!"

"What prevents me from doing so, when we're alone?"

"That's true—but in public? Remember, my love, when you accompanied me to the theater, to fêtes? Everyone looked at us, and everyone said, in low voices: 'Monsieur Coffre, with all his millions, isn't loved by his wife!' I hate that man, who thought that I'd love him because he's rich! Love can't be bought! I bear the name of Coffre—that's quite enough."

"Come on, Emma, your husband is very good to you."

"Naturally, you're going to find excuses for him! Men are always in accord when it's a matter of putting a woman in the wrong. Speak, then! I shouldn't deceive him, should I?"

"But yes—on the contrary!"

"What—on the contrary? I should deceive him with everyone? Is that what you mean?"

"What's the matter with you, Emma? I take back what I said."

"Take off that frightful dust-sheet too! It seems to me that I'll no longer love you if I only see you decked out in that ridiculous envelope..."

"It's not my fault, though!"

"I don't hold it against you! But you're so handsome, squeezed into your dolman like a woman in her corset, with your bouffant trousers! Walk, my love, so that I can look at you. Let me admire you, my Captain!"

Sylphe, his back stiff and his knees braced in his varnished boots, strutted back and forth, glad to recover his prestige. Madame Coffre contemplated him with a tender expression; she could not help putting her arms around his neck.

"You see, my love, the uniform, for a man, is what beauty is for a woman."

"You're beautiful! You're a woman!"

"You're a soldier! You're a man, my warrior!"

Alexandre Sylphe drew Madame Coffre to the divan with the sure and measured gestures familiar to juvenile leads in dramas and comedies.

Their amorous duet was striking up its preparatory chords when a bell rang.

Madame Coffre stood up abruptly, mechanically readjusting the complex edifice of her hair. "That's all we need! The telephone!"

Irritated by the interruption to her amorous games, she seized the transmitter of the apparatus and interrogated abruptly: "What? What is it? Oh, it's you Joseph?"

Joseph was Monsieur Coffre's valet. The apartments of the two spouses were completely separate; they communicated by means of a private telephone, and the banker never came into his wife's apartment without warning her in advance.

"Tell Monsieur that I can't receive him at the moment."

Captain Sylph launched into a lively pantomime of protest, which Madame Coffre cut off with a significant shrug of the shoulders.

"Well, if you insist!" She pressed the call button. "All right, Joseph—tell Monsieur that he can come right away. I'm waiting for him!"

Joseph must have formulated a few reflections of respectful surprise regarding the contradiction between that order and the preceding one, for the irascible Emma launched an imperative: "Yes, let him come! Send him in!"

Alexandre Sylphe had precipitately put on his dust-cover again and installed himself in an armchair in the darkest corner of the room.

Hermann Coffre came in without noticing him and addressed his wife. "My dear, I've come to warn you that I won't be dining with you this evening. I'll be back very late."

"*Bon appétit*, and have a good time," said his thoughtful companion.

"Thank you," said the banker, who was about to retire when his eye discovered Captain Sylphe. "Oh, it's you, Captain. One can hardly see you there. Permit me to turn up the light..."

At arm's length, Alexandre Sylphe waited for Monsieur Coffre to offer him his hand. The two men exchanged the customary banal civilities.

"Well, Captain, you don't seem to have been unduly affected by the tribunal's decision, which extends your condition for a year?"

"What do you expect, Monsieur Coffre? War is war."

"And your marriage?"

"Postponed, inevitably."

"Mademoiselle de Foiraubilles will wait for you indefinitely, then?"

"She loves me," replied the heartbreaker, simply, without any false modesty.

"And do you love her?" asked Hermann Coffre, with an aggressive brutality.

Sensing Emma's eyes upon him, the Captain dared not answer "Yes," and as he could not say "No," he contented himself with remaining silent and lowering his head.

"You're quite right not to marry for love!" Hermann Coffre approved, emphasizing his words nervously. "If your wife loves you and you don't love her, it's her who will suffer and you who'll have the joy of having a heart at your mercy to lacerate."

"You're very poetic today, my love," Emma mocked, sarcastically. "Is it because you're dining out?"

"Perhaps, my love," Hermann Coffre relied, resuming his mask of total indifference. Sensing that he had said too much, he added: "What are you going to do during your year of waiting, Captain?"

"Oh, my dear Monsieur Coffre, there's no shortage of distractions in Paris. Not only your house, which is so hospitable to me..."

"Oh, you're exaggerating!" said the banker.

"No, no!" protested Alexandre Sylphe. "And I assure you that it's an amelioration of my fate—which, in any case, is not so very sad. My share of the funds granted to my brother will give me twenty thousand francs—that's more than a general's pay! Without this grotesque dust-cover, I'd be perfectly happy."

"How does it inconvenience you?"

"Oh, my dear Monsieur Coffre, one can see that you've never been a soldier, that you've never worn a uniform!" And to give pleasure to his mistress, he quoted the sentence she had used a little while before: "The uniform, for a man, is what beauty is, for a woman."

"But you're wearing it under that envelope, your uniform—one can tell!"

"But it can't be seen! I am, at this moment, like those plain-faced women of whom it is said: 'She's assuredly not beautiful, but she must have a good figure!' Very flattering! Which doesn't alter the fact that the woman can't find a lover."

"Unfortunate woman, especially if she's married!" Monsieur Coffre commiserated.

"Alas!" Emma sighed.

"Do you think it's amusing to circulate in this accoutrement? Everyone turns to look at me as I go by. They point at me, laughing, and I hear the words that have become my obsession: 'It's our provisional dead man!' If only I could give all those people a slap!"

"There are too many. Your two hands wouldn't be sufficient," the banker observed.

"Oh, after a few dozen duels to the death, they'd leave me alone, provisionally dead or not, but I can't fight, since I have no trace of official existence. To escape the street-urchins who grab the hem of my ridiculous livery, I'm obliged to travel in a closed carriage. To cap it all, I'm represented in a revue as the immortal dead man, under the pretext that in France, the provisional lasts forever. It's intolerable—enough to make one kill oneself for real!"

"Calm down, my friend, calm down!" the banker interjected.

115

"Oh, Monsieur Coffre, you've just given me a name the permits me to make a request of you—you called me your friend; you can't abandon me. Save me."

"Save you! Save you from what?"

"From this lamentable uncertainty. Am I dead? Am I alive? You're powerful, Monsieur Coffre—you can tip the balance for or against me at your whim."

Hermann Coffre looked long and hard at his wife and Alexandre Sylphe. Then, as if he had just made an inviolable oath to himself, he said: "Agreed, Captain. I'll ruin myself if I have to, but you shall be alive!"

And, either because he wanted to escape Alexandre Sylphe's protestations of gratitude or for some other reason, Hermann Coffre bowed to his wife, shook the Captain's hand and withdrew in great haste.

Left alone, the two lovers played an extra-conjugal scene for themselves, in the course of which Emma showed herself tyrannical and submissive by turns, and which Alexandre concluded by taking off his dust-cover before the rhapsodic eyes of his mistress.

The absence of Monsieur Coffre permitted them to dine together in private, and eat from the same plate. What happened thereafter lasted until midnight, the hour at which Alexandre Sylphe put on his dust-sheet again to return to his own domicile for a well-earned rest.

VIII

In accordance with ancient customs, Time is divided into slices of various sizes, which are mutually exclusive; thus, the months and the years only took their place on the calendar when their elders no longer figured there.

For people who do not follow the phases of the moon and who are not preoccupied with settlements of bills and debts or worldly duties—in brief, those who escape obsession with the date—days and weeks have a value that is intrinsically equal. The members of the arbitration tribunal found themselves temporarily classed in that privileged elite once they had received orders from their respective Governments to remain in Paris to await the resumption of the sessions, at which time they would receive further instructions.

The Minister Henri Verbuis put a young attaché at the disposal of each foreigner, with a mission to show them the treasures of Paris in their most favorable light.

First, there were visits to libraries and museums; the diplomats, united in a picturesque caravan that brightened up the quarters in which they appeared, gaped without the slightest enthusiasm at the books, paintings and sculptures in which France took the greatest pride.

At the Jardin d'Acclimatation, the representative of Haricot VII gazed without emotion at the animals of his homeland, and an American protested in the name of the League Against the Captivity of Ferocious Animals, of which he was a vice-president. The national manufactories and principal theaters only served as pretexts for the least flattering comparisons.

There was no doubt about it: France's guests were bored. What could be done to dissipate that unfavorable impression, which might have unfortunate repercussions throughout the world?

On the insistence of Abbé Mortol, Cardinal Pecari organized masses and vespers of sumptuous ostentation at Notre Dame; the delegates put candles out with their yawns. Lectures on the most elevated subjects given by the most qualified Masters turned the main hall of the Collège de France into a dormitory. A magnificent firework display at the top of the Eiffel Tower might perhaps have been applauded by the inhabitants of the Earth's planetary neighbors, but did not generate the slightest joy in the unsmiling company.

Out of ideas, Henri Verbuis confide his anxiety to Bernard Petitpaon. The latter listened, his brow furrowed, to the tale of the peregrinations and pleasures dispensed to the members of the international tribunal since the day when their functions had consisted of doing nothing.

"My dear Verbuis, have you ever been to Constantino-ple?"

"Never."

"All right—but let's imagine that your sympathetic person were to be transported there imminently. What would you desire to see, after a pilgrimage as rapid as it would be obligatory to a few mosques and other famous establishments?"

"The Sultan."

"The Sultan? All right. Ten minutes pause, a quick drink, you leave. It's spring; you've left Madame Verbuis in Paris..."

"Oh yes! Houris!"

"Exactly—houris! Or their equivalent. My dear Minister, diplomats aren't made of that insensible matter we call wood. These are men who, trusting in our universal renown, have arrived scenting festivities, as the warhorses of past centuries scented gunpowder—and you're treating them like young women! Have you left them to their own devices yet? No, you take them on excursions, expose them to the ill-treatment of the most notorious pedants of our era!"

"Oh!" protested the Minister of Foreign Affairs.

"There's no *Oh* about it. Between ourselves, do you know of anything more sinister than these nitpickers of texts, who, after having burning a hundred liters of oil over a single sentence, claim to be able to demonstrate to you that the author meant to express the exact opposite of what he wrote?"

"But these Messieurs are eminent professors, paid by the State," Verbuis objected.

"Paid by the State! Paid by the State! What does that prove? Every organism supposes parasites. Let's keep to ourselves those that we have the privilege of possessing and not think that even the sight of rare and savage animals might be capable of making our guests forget that which can only be found in Paris: Parisiennes!"

"In which case?" Verbuis interrogated.

"In which case, tell your young attachés that some fun is in order. There are places in Paris where one can have a good time, damn it! It's not difficult to find young, pretty girls..."

"Oh, my dear President, that's not the role of Protocol!" the Minister protested.

"If it were, your Protocol would be useful for something! Then again, I haven't finished. You're not unaware that Hermann Coffre is taking a very keen interest in Captain Sylphe?"

"I'm very well aware that Monsieur Coffre will bring down the Cabinet if he's not convinced that we're putting all our effort into restoring all the Captain's rights."

"Good! As I was saying to General Croppeton only this morning, it's vitally necessary that the decision of the arbitration tribunal is favorable to Captain Sylphe. We're fortunate enough to have the representatives of the powers for several months, and we're not profiting from that advantage. That's criminal, my dear Verbuis! Women are incomparable means of persuasion. Let's find each of the Foreigners a gracious and intelligent companion who will be able, at moments when the heart trumps all reason, to talk about the Captain, to obtain promises..."

"Oh! That's an idea of genius!" said Henri Verbuis, admiringly.

"My God, yes! It's up to you to realize it. Take the advice of our colleagues beforehand—that's more polite!"

In the Cabinet meeting that was hastily convened, Henri Verbuis presented Bernard Petitpaon's plan as if it were his own, which won him a veritable triumph. It was decided that nothing would be neglected to conquer the members of the tribunal. The young men whose delicate complexion or religious and moral principles were ill-adapted to a life of profligacy were relieved of their mission as guides and replaced by experienced roisterers, who took an oath not to fail in their duty.

Finally recognizing the Paris that they had so far only seen in their dreams, the diplomats amused themselves like schoolboys escaping the master's ruler. They were seen at the Bal Tabarin indulging in dances of the most frantic nature. At the Follies Bergère the Japanese delegate went up on stage to measure himself against one of his compatriots, a jiu-jitsu champion. At the Bal Bullier, in the midst of a circle of drunken students of both sexes, Haricot VII's spokesman picked a quarrel with a wooden negro whose spring-loaded abdomen served to measure the strength of pugilists, and ended up knocking him down while uttering his war cry.

In the great nocturnal establishments, the champagne flowed freely; noted hetaerae neglected their regular clients and only had eyes and ears for the enthusiastic and generous merrymakers. The wings of the theaters were devastated, and some directors, deprived of the entirety of their female personnel, were forced to revert to the suitably-embellished leotards of young adolescents.

Legend added to the reality, and whenever a street-urchin or a coachman perceived some staggering silhouette, he never failed to shout a sporting: "Hey there, diplomat!"

In the same way that debauchery often originates from too much virtue, however, excesses can bring about a return to temperance. Weary and worn out, the diplomats disappeared into the alcoves of their choice and when, on the night of the thirty-first of January and the first of January, Eternity changed its ultimate digit, all the members of the arbitration committee were at the discretion of one Parisienne or another.

Each of the amiable women in question received considerable subsidies drawn from the funds of the political police, whose cash-box Monsieur Coffre insisted on garnishing. Believing that they were loved for themselves, the noble Foreigners allowed themselves to indulge in confidences of which note was duly taken by the agents commissioned to that effect. However, out of human respect and to give satisfaction to the population of Parisiennes, who were very demanding in matters of official rejoicing, receptions were held at the Hôtel de Ville and the various Ministries, and the Palais de l'Élysée opened its most gilded reception rooms on several occasions.

An extraordinary gala illuminated the façade of the Lyrique Grand-Mondial, and as Bernard Petitpaon had announced that he would be present in person at the performance, veritable crimes were committed to force entry into the theater.

Until then, the President of the Republic had abstained from appearing at the Lyrique Grand-Mondial, which he had directed after having sung there. Either because he had shrugged off the yoke of courtiers ever ready to praise his high rank or because he would experience some joy in stepping back in his life, he not only decided that he would attend the gala, but expressed the desire that the performance would comprise a play in which he had once played the principal role.

Flatterers suggested to him the possibility of comparisons that, while doubtless being entirely to his advantage, might nevertheless be insulting.

"I shall applaud the young comrade," Bernard Petitpaon declared, "if he is, like me, a great singer and a good actor!"

The evening was epic.

Respectful of the art to which he had added luster and which had made him famous, Bernard Petitpaon arrived a few minutes before the curtain went up. In accordance with a custom as solemn as it was ancient, the director of the Lyrique Grand-Mondial came to meet him at the foot of the great staircase with a seven-branched silver chandelier in each hand; as they were very heavy and he was no athlete, he almost buckled under the burden several times, and only recovered his breath after seeing Bernard Petitpaon disappear into the presidential box.

Standing up, the President listened attentively to the Marseillaise, without which no ceremony is possible. After the regulation five or six ovations, he signaled to the leader of the orchestra to start the score.

The first chords of *Cincinnatus* covered with their majestic waves the stirring of the black coats and diamond-clad women, who hastily settled in their seats. Every note evoked a cherished memory for Petitpaon, all the dearer for having been buried in a distant past. His hand mechanically followed the cadence of the measure, and he was taken back to the first performance of *Cincinnatus*. He had been twenty-five years old; the author, Oscar Pistonnet, against winds and tides, cabals and perfidies, had confided to him the rude task of representing his hero. He relived the vertigo of finding himself alone, lost in the middle of the immense stage, waiting for the curtain to rise over the gulf of the auditorium.

He went pale, and his heart beat as if to burst when the character appeared whom he had once animated. The scenery had not changed; it was still the same Roman countryside under a luminous sky. The same plow seemed to be harnessed to the yoke of the same team of oxen, which were ruminating placidly without seeming unduly astonished by the slightly bizarre métier that they were following.

The artist, awaiting his cue, made sure of his breath and puckered his lips in order to moisten them, while following the conductor's baton with a furtive eye.

Hollowed out by an imperceptible hesitation in its first emergence, the voice affirmed its metal in order to launch with mighty lungs into the laborer's song. It was the titanic joy of the man who has tamed nature, opening the rebellious loins of the earth in order to fecundate them—and the music put so much power into that hymn of incessant victory over obscure forces that the protagonists of emperors, kings and anonymous Governments, come from the four corners of the world to play their parts in the tragicomedy of Captain Sylphe, blushed over the utter futility of their own métier.

Meanwhile, the drama unfolded, and when, at the end of the first act, the delegation of senators arrived to ask the man of the fields to quit his plough in the superior interest of the Republic, the entire auditorium gave Bernard Petitpaon a standing ovation.

Abruptly snatched out of his dream, the President looked down, trying to smile, but whether because his joy was too great or his vision of the past gripped him to profoundly, he dissolved in tears, covering his face with his hands.

After the second act, during which Cincinnatus, under the red mantle of his dictatorship, ensured the salvation of

Rome, Bernard Petitpaon asked the head of the Diplomatic Service to remained seated in the Presidential box and, preceding the director of the Grand-Mondial, his successor, he went down to the little door that led to the stage.

The scene-shifters were setting up the scenery for the final act, in the midst of that feverish agitation which has the appearance of chaotic disorder for the profane. In order not to get in the way of the operation, and also to contemplate at his ease the boards on which he had left so much of himself, Petitpaon hid behind a pillar.

Close at hand, a deep voice tried a vocal exercise. As if he thought that it had emerged from his own mouth, Bernard Petitpaon instinctively raised his hand to his throat. The director of the Grand-Mondial, who had seen the gesture and grasped its significance, reassured the President by introducing him to the actor who was playing the role of Cincinnatus.

Bernard Petitpaon took him in his arms and embraced him. "My boy, you are, after me, the artist who has understood the role with the greatest genius. Those who have not heard me have reason to judge you incomparable!"

The poor baritone, nonplussed by the effusive praise of his aged and illustrious colleague, started to weep, which caused Petitpaon to make the observation: "Watch out—you'll have a damp voice when you sing the third."

"Thanks you, oh, thank you, Monsieur le Président de a République Française!" stammered the employee of the Grand-Mondial.

"We're both Cincinnatus, and it's not because I've been the elder of the family that I'll forget my comrades!"

Petitpaon tried to make his exit from the circle that had gathered around him, but he was too late. All the cast members had come down to the stage for the third act. Everyone received the most hyperbolic compliments, and the President was in the process of kissing Cincinnatus' wife, with the standard precautions to avoid smudging her make-up, when the head of the Diplomatic Service surged forth from the tightly-knit ranks of the young dancers and chorus-girls.

Anticipating reproaches that he judged to be probably merited, the President simply said to the preventer of further embraces: "I'm coming!" And, following in the footsteps of the discreetly scandalized functionary, he returned to his box, to the renewed strains of the Marseillaise.

That evening, triumphant in every respect, was not the only one of its kind, so the diplomats sent dithyrambic narratives to their friends and acquaintances that bore fruit in the form of innumerable visitors. Trains, hectically multiplied, waited for days on end before finding a track free to get into Paris. In that vertiginous movement, accidents were so frequent that no one paid the slightest attention to them any longer, and hoteliers, with revolvers in hand, battled against the assaults mounted night and day on their establishments by hordes of travelers fleeing the stars.

In spite of the requisition of rural ovens and the mobilization of all the means of production, there were bread shortages in some quarters, and the streets were so crowded that traffic could no longer circulate. Food and everything else necessary to life reached fantastic prices, which were the palpable proof of an unprecedented commercial prosperity.

"This hasn't been seen since the Empire!" proclaimed Monsieur Jadis at the podium of the Senate, proposing a vote of thanks from the Upper Assembly to President Petitpaon, to whom France owed that incomparable renewal.

In that plenary exaltation, Captain Sylphe was relegated to the background of public attention. Cabaret singers gradually began to disdain the provisional dead man. People got used to his dust-cover. In Biarritz, where he went to join Madame Coffre, installed for the summer season in a sumptuous villa, he experienced the humiliation of being asked for his name by the porter.

At the Casino, the employee in charge of the observance of the sumptuary regulations designed to safeguard the traditional elegance of the Establishment mistook him for one of the Englishmen who refresh themselves by means of the exhi-

124

bition of picturesque costumes, the impeccability of which they make a strict law at home.

The inspector happened to be an old soldier, as testified by the ribbon of the military medal that he wore very apparently in the buttonhole of his frock-coat and his energetic and concise manner off speech. Confronted with the decline of Alexandre Sylphe's civil estate, the inspector was gripped by a veritable crisis of despair, begging the Captain to excuse his error. The latter was obliged to speak in the name of the authority that his rank conferred upon him to calm an emotion that he feared to re-engender by a further appearance at the pleasure-palace.

Hermine de Foiraubilles did not renounce her fiancé, and even though, under various pretexts, he only put in the appearances at her home indispensable to prevent the lapse of his courtship, the young woman, fortified by the paternal support that declared itself capable of smashing all resistance, considered the day on which the arbitration tribunal would ender its definitive verdict as that of her marriage.

IX

In France the dog days are for politics a kind of Divine Truce. Acts of violence, the culminating points of human passion, melt away in the burning rays of the sun like the snow on the mountains.

In any case, the majority of those to whom the people confer a representative mandate are worthy fellows, almost always in a much more placid humor than one might be led to believe by the bellicose attitudes that they stroke during parliamentary discussions, either for the edification of their electors or simply for their own pleasure. The man who brandishes an incessant tone of threat and terror at the podium becomes, on quitting it, the mildest of sheep, whose fleece yields to all-comers.

The perspective appropriate to every environment is something so essentially human that the most intransigent committees will judge with severity those of their members who permit themselves to speak in excessive terms outside the sacred boundaries.

For those who exercise it conscientiously, the profession of député is very taxing, and annual rest-cures are indispensable to maintain the condition of the lungs, stomach and brain, the organs generally overworked by the life that touches everything without getting into the depths of anything.

Amenable to the same treatment, Abbé Mortol and Louis Méripal, met up at the same thermal baths in the heart of the Pyrenees, and were inseparable companions for the twenty reglementary days. The Abbé only disappeared for a few minutes every morning on the pretext of going to celebrate a mass, whose brevity won Méripal's admiration.

"You can see that it's not diabolical to accomplish one's religious duties," the Abbé observed, without attempting to catechize his colleague.

"If your Lord likes rapid work, you must have a keen odor of sanctity in his regard," the hardened freethinker joked, without the slightest bitterness.

For both of them, the question of Faith was only skimmed in rare and light-hearted jokes; as for politics, they did not make the most distant allusion to it; it seemed that the two friends lost the very memory of the Palais Bourbon as they took the waters.

There were daily excursions into the mountains. One day, the Abbé slipped, and was beginning to slide down a slope toward a precipice when Méripal saved him from certain death by grabbing hold of the hem of his soutane.

"You ought to pray to God to watch over you more attentively," Louis Méripal said. "But for me you'd undoubtedly have perished."

"Don't think, my dear friend," César Mortol replied, with the unction, sharpened by a hint of irony, that is the characteristic of priests of good stock "that I want to diminish in any way your role as savior—I owe you my life, that's certain— but in sum, if I hadn't been dressed in the ample vestment of servants of Christ, you wouldn't have been able to catch hold of me! You can see that, by looking hard, one can find the hand of God everywhere, my dear atheist!"

Under various pretexts, for more than two weeks, in order to enjoy the exquisite and frank intimacy for longer, the two députés kept putting off the date on which they had originally been supposed to quit the Pyrenees, the Abbé to undertake a voyage to Rome and Louis Méripal to devote himself to personal affairs in Paris.

On the platform of the railway station from which trains were to carry them away in different directions, they eventually made their farewells. Neither of them dared say: "see you next month!" because they both knew that reentry into the Chambre would be the recommencement of the battle, bitter and merciless.

Sadly, Louis Méripal thought that the Abbé was going to obtain new weapons from the Pope, and César Mortol could already see the reckless orator scaling the podium in order to thunder against God and insult religion.

X

As they did every year, the Chambres reunited in mid-October in sessions qualified as extraordinary in order to distinguish themselves from the ordinary ones rightfully opened under the aegis of the Constitution on the first Tuesday of January. There was mild discussion of affairs described as "current," which had been in suspense for years immemorial to the legislators, and which served the Assemblies to sate their hunger on the eve of grave events.

The Sylphe affair was, in fact, of great importance, firstly for France, whose honor was invested in having the last word in the eyes of the world, and then for the Cabinet, because Monsieur Coffre had confided to General Croppeton that he had promised personally to put an end to the ridiculous provisional status imposed on the Captain.

"I understand," General Croppeton had agreed, "all the inconveniences of the situation. You're no more interested in the unfortunate Captain than I am, my dear Coffre. He's a military man in every sense of the word: noble heart, generous soul, tall stature, proud bearing, consummate cavalier, triumphant moustache! He's due to marry the daughter of my excellent comrade Foiraubilles, also a soldier!"

Monsieur Coffre had interrupted that flood of praise descending upon the head of his wife's lover: "Exactly! Captain Sylphe deserves to remain alive. I have made and will make any sacrifice necessary to have the tribunal rule in his favor; a verdict that condemns the Captain to definitive death will condemn you too. You know that I only have to make a sign to the Chambre and the Senate for my majority to bring you down."

"I know!" Croppeton had acquiesced, in a melancholy fashion, before racing to his natural inspirer, President Petitpaon.

The latter, after having articulated a few obnoxious epithets in regard to Coffre, had opined that it was necessary at any price to save the life of Captain Sylphe.

The Council of Ministers was convened to examine the dossiers established on the basis of information furnished by the ladies in "political service" with regard to the members of the arbitration tribunal. All of them had done their duty valiantly and as they had been instructed to be precise, the majority had entered into a luxury of the most suggestive details.

"It was only after having accorded him three rounds of favors, just as he was going to sleep, that I was able to extract a promise from him," informed the beauty to whom the representative of the Sublime Gate had fallen.

"The man is made of ice; I spent hours warming him up, and it was the same every time I wanted him to repeat his sworn promise to vote for the Captain," said the Companion of the Swiss delegate.

All the narratives had a pronounced perfume of the alcove or the dressing-room; there were secret penchants and vices that compelled unforeseen complications, men being ever the same in all latitudes.

To Pierre Phosphène, who waxed indignant at the erotic fantasies attributed to the representative of a vague South American Republic, Bernard Petitpaon made the observation that, as the victim did not appear at all surprised, it was necessary to believe that the Parisians who had instructed her in the science of lust must have anticipated and practiced the incriminating exercises.

"Besides which, everyone takes his pleasure where he finds it," concluded Petitpaon, philosophically. "Believe me, my dear Phosphène, let people love as seems good to them, and if the methods they employ don't appeal to you, don't adopt them, that's all! Keep the habits that are dear to you and abstain from trying to disgust others with those that don't impassion you. The essential thing in all of this is that the tribunal should proclaim the existence of Captain Sylphe. A contrary decision would be a disaster!"

"France can count on the unanimity of the diplomats," Croppeton affirmed.

"The boat that is bringing back the delegate from Tierra de Fuego arrives at Le Havre tomorrow," Henry Verbuis explained. "The tribunal will therefore be able to sit the day after tomorrow, the first of November, as was fixed. Two or three weeks will suffice, I'm certain, and nothing more will remain than to bring the diplomats together for a farewell banquet..."

"I'll make an appearance there," approved Petitpaon.

"We'll invite the ladies who have shown such complete devotion in the circumstances," said Charles Miraudel.

And, as the session ended, each of the ministers was already thinking about the toast he would propose to dazzle the diplomats and the quasi-widows that they were about to leave behind.

In the meantime, the diplomats were brushing their most severe frock-coats and rehearsing the principal poses of their employment before their bewildered companions.

It was with the expressions of sphinxes resuming the duty of guarding their secrets that they went, one by one, through the gates of the Palais des Affaires Étrangères, where the tribunal was sitting. All of them, having familiarized themselves with the French language during the year that had just gone by, decided that it would be the only one employed. It was a delicate tribute of gratitude to the country that had charmed them so amiably.

The representative of France thanked them in emotional terms, and only asked that they make an exception in favor or the Tierra-del-Fuegian, who was absolutely deaf to any language but his own. That eccentric individual required the complex intervention of interpreters.

A summary of the question was presented by the oldest of the members present, the Swedish delegate, a lushly-bearded old man of impressive bearing. As his delights had been poured out uninterruptedly from the mouth of a young Montmartrean very well-versed in argot, the worthy Scandinavian was very familiar with spicy language; for a septuagenarian novice, moreover, he handled it with a fine dexterity, enameling his discourse with exceedingly picturesque flourishes.

He recalled how, during the campaign in Cirajoum, Captain Sylphe has been killed, in the application of the official reckoning tables, in a recurring fraction of his person. He rendered homage to the prudent wisdom of the international arbiters who, faced with the unprecedented situation, had not hesitated to attribute to the captain the quality of provisional death while waiting for a conference to be convened to decide his case one way or the other.

He read the verdict rendered the previous year and which, based on the fact that in matters of human existence the part determines the whole, had decided the integral death of Alexandre Sylphe. He explained the reasons that had caused the postponement putting that verdict into effect, based on the fact that France had obtained from Haricot VII a declaration in which he confessed to having deceived the expert evaluators charged with determining the power of his engines of war.

The questions to be resolved were, therefore, as follows:

Firstly, does a victorious nation have the right to force a vanquished nation to admit an exaggeration committed in the evaluation of its armaments?

Secondly, should such an admission permit the victorious nation to obtain a retroactive diminution of its losses?

The Spanish delegate opened the debate by asking the representative of Haricot VII about the conditions in which his master had consented to adopt the coefficient of one thousandth for death instead of that of one nine-hundredth, which had been attributed to him.

The joyful black man set the broad keyboard of his teeth clocking. "The Master—may the god of the coconut trees watch over him and his wives—received gifts."

The ambassadors feigned profound amazement. The representative of France lowered his head to hide his shame.

Summoned to give details, the son of Cirajoum related that his Master—on whose behalf, every time he mentioned him, he called upon the grace of the god of the coconut trees— had been given a gray top hat. In a spirit of obsequious admiration, the native had obtained a similar one for himself, and he rang for an usher to ask that it be brought to him. He showed it to his colleagues triumphantly, making the observation that only the ribbon was different.

With forceful gesticulations, he evoked the shoulder-sash, the épée and the thigh-boots. "The Master—many the god of the coconut tress watch over him and his wives—is completely dressed with that!" said the negro, warmly wrapped in an ample mastic ulster, from which he was never separated. He also mentioned the tins of human flesh that the Master, under the eye of the god of the coconut trees, benevolent to him and his wives, had eaten with great pleasure.

"That means of corruption is unworthy of a civilized country!" put in the acolyte of an American dictator.

Amid a murmur of general approval, the spokesman of France invoked the absolutely constant usage, in matters of international relations, of the giving of gifts. He pointed out the small value and puerility of the latter. He attacked governments that "do not hesitate to favor vice by importing alcohol, which reduces men to the level of beasts, or opium, which plunges consciousness into a torpor akin to oblivion."

The desired riposte did not take long to arrive, launched by the German delegate, who, rightly or wrongly, felt that his country was being particularly targeted: "And you offer cannibals tins of human flesh!"

"France is ready to prove that the incriminated tins contained nothing other than tuna!" declared the diplomat by whom France was skillfully represented, solemnly. "They come from the Épicerie Potin. There were a gross of them. It will be easy to produce the invoice for the order!"

"I believe that we can accept an explanation as frank as it is clear," proposed the Russian plenipotentiary.

"I request the floor for a prejudicial motion," said the German, who did not want to admit defeat. "My august Master is moved by the fate that, in a moment of negligence, we reserved for the dead warriors of His Majesty Haricot VII. By forcing them to coat themselves with ceruse, we are condemning them infallibly to the grave, in a fashion as rapid as it is painful."

Explanations on that subject were sought from the subject of Haricot VII, who was smoothing the fur of his top hat one hair at a time.

"Yes, the demons of the coconut trees are twisting the entrails of the soldiers until they die! Nothing can be done against it!" the philosophical African concluded, laughing broadly, without ceasing to caress his hat.

"It's evidently deplorable to let those poor people die of saturnine intoxication," the old Scandinavian put in, "but we don't have to occupy ourselves with that matter."

"I agree," opined the German. "It was out of pure humanity that I raised the matter—but I won't insist."

"In that case, we can pass on to a vote on the articles," the Swede went on, getting bogged down in a subsequent sequence of argot terms.

"France has abused her victory," stated the pacific and pot-bellied Swiss.

"Without having any particular grievance against France, I deem it impossible to admit the possibility of a victor extracting from the vanquished a kind of retroactive withdrawal concerning all of part of its power," advanced the Russian.

"The reckoning tables established by universal agreement cannot be subject to retrospective modification by the simple whim of one of the parties," said the Italian.

Petitpaon warfare would no longer be possible if the results of a campaign were at the discretion of the belligerents," emitted the placid Belgian.

The representative of France rose to his feet. "Messieurs, it is not merely on the basis of a testimony, albeit obtained without the slightest constraint, that France asks you to pronounce. There are other arguments to weigh up. You will permit me to present them to you.

"When the arbiter-evaluators fixed at one nine-hundredth of a death the destructive force of each of His Majesty Haricot VII's soldiers, they based their calculations on the toxic energy of the poisons employed for the spears and arrows. Now, it is not the word of Haricot VII alone on which we intend to rely to prove that the poisons in question are quite harmless. We request the nomination of experts who will examine in their soul and conscience the murderous virtue of these supposedly toxic substances. It will not be difficult to demonstrate that the spears and arrows of which the soldiers of Haricot VII made use are simple pointed weapons, and can only occasion vulgar wounds. You should not refuse us the lowering of the coefficient that we are requesting!"

The plenipotentiaries looked at one another. Germany took the floor first to say that the French request seemed just to him. He was followed by the unanimity of the members of the tribunal, save for the envoy from Tierra de Fuego, whose

133

consultation was renounced in view of the difficulties of communication occasioned by his mother tongue.

An interlocutory injunction was therefore drafted, which called for the nomination of expert chemists, physicians, naturalists and physicists of all nations, with a mission to examine the martial equipment of Haricot VII *in situ*. A subsequent article ordered Captain Sylphe to maintain the state of provisional death until the pronunciation of a definitive sentence.

XI

In Paris, news spreads with a rapidity akin to instantaneity. From the place where it is produced, the slightest fact runs along the streets, follows the sidewalks, traverses the public squares and the gardens, climbs the stairways, hangs on to the narrowest balconies, traveling from mouth to mouth, and arrives immediately in the remotest corners in the depths of the most obscure outlying districts.

As often as not, that hectic course exaggerates it or diminishes it, always transforming it and causing it to appear under very different aspects.

Thus, in certain quarters, the decision of the arbitration tribunal was proclaimed as having restored all of Captain Sylphe's rights, while in some others, the rumor ran around that he had just been murdered.

It was scarcely two hours later when Herman Coffre, installed in Henri Verbuis' study, learned the news, which was communicated to him before the official statement had even been drafted. It caused him a veritable crisis of rage, and after having proffered terrible threats, he had himself driven home.

He took an enormous revolver from his desk and, without having himself announced, headed for his wife's apartment.

As he expected, he found Captain Sylphe there. Madame Coffre was at his knees. The disorder in their respective clothing indicated well enough the siesta *à deux* in which they had just been engaged.

Madame Coffre got up in order to gain a height advantage over her husband. "What is the meaning of this loutish behavior, Monsieur? Since when have you had the right to penetrate my rooms without asking me whether I will receive you? Leave me alone, please!"

Hermann Coffre carefully took out the revolver that he had placed in the pocket of his frock-coat, aimed the barrel at Captain Sylphe, and said, coldly: "Get dressed."

"But...," the captain stammered.

"You're behaving like a bandit!" snapped the tender Emma.

"Get dressed!" repeated Hermann Coffre, his finger on the trigger of his weapon.

The captain put on his boots, adjusted his braces and put on his dolman, which he buttoned slowly, attached his saber to his side and, with a movement of provocative dignity, put on his kepi, not forgetting to pay attention to the position of the Saumur label.

He took a step toward the armchair on which his dust-cover was lying. Hermann Coffre stopped him: "Leave it there!"

"But that's my dust-cover, my garment of provisional death," Alexandre Sylphe explained.

"I know," said Herman Coffre. "You're going out without it."

"You want to make me violate the treaties? That's a *casus belli* against France."

"I know. Go on! Get out! I'll follow you, and I advise you to do as I say. At the slightest sign of disobedience, I'll blow your brains out!"

Emma attempted to intervene, but, confronted by her husband's inflexible attitude, she limited herself to bursting into tears.

Captain Sylphe walked ahead of Hermann Coffre, who followed in his footsteps with a tranquil expression, with his right hand, holding the revolver, hidden under his frock-coat.

The concierge bowed so respectfully that he did not even notice Captain Sylphe's costume.

In the Place Vendôme, Monsieur Coffre hailed a fiacre, opened the door himself and got into it with Alexandre Sylphe, after having said to the coachman: "To the Ministry of Foreign Affairs! Stop at the main gate."

In the carriage, the revolver still threatening, Herman Coffre did not say a word.

The vehicle went alone the Rue de Rivoli, traversed the Place and Pont de la Concorde and came to a halt at the sidewalk on which a numerous crowd was standing, attracted by the desire to see the emergence of the diplomats.

In the middle of one group, Louis Méripal was talking, with animated gestures.

Without knowing what his furious guide wanted, Alexandre Sylphe got ready to get out.

"No, not yet," said Hermann Coffre.

"But what do you want of me?" demanded the captain, with a slight tremor in his voice.

"To obey," said the banker, laconically.

Half an hour went by. The idlers were still cluttering the sidewalk; the group in the middle of which Méripal was perorating had drawn closer to the carriage.

Suddenly, there was a stir in the crowd, whose members turned toward the gate. A few cries were uttered here and there. Policemen formed a hedge to protect the exit of the diplomats.

"Get out!" ordered Hermann Coffre, dryly.

The immediate proximity of a loaded revolver produced an effect on Captain Sylphe as powerful as it was disagreeable; the order did not have to be repeated. Jumping out of the vehicle, he collided violently with Louis Méripal, while Herman Coffre ordered his coachman to drive away at top sped.

The sight of a military uniform was to the revolutionary socialist député what the color red is to a bull. Believing at first that it was an attack, he struck the officer a formidable blow with his fist.

"Please! Please!" was the unfortunate man's only riposte. "I'm Captain Sylphe!"

"Captain Sylphe? The provisional dead man?" queried Méripal, recoiling instinctively.

Repeated by hundreds of mouths, that name and those words greeted the members of the arbitration tribunal as they appeared on the perron. Surprised, they stopped, searching for the meaning of that unusual manifestation.

In the crowd, two opposed currents had instantly formed, one in favor of Captain Sylphe, the other against him. His partisans, thinking that the challenge that he had come in person to throw down to the judges who had condemned him was very brave, took hold of him in order to carry him in triumph. His adversaries, with Méripal at the head, felt it their duty to abuse him loudly.

The diplomats went back into the conference room to deliberate on the action to take in the face of such an assault on human rights. They appointed a delegation who went to Henri Verbuis in order to obtain official information regarding the identity of the captain of cuirassiers whose name the crowd was howling all along the quay.

The Minister of Foreign Affairs did not want to submit France to the humiliation of an excessively dilatory response. He simply asked the representatives of the foreign Powers to wait for an hour or two, the time materially indispensable to obtain exact information.

That evening, after having telegraphed their respective governments of the forfeiture committed by France in the person of Captain Sylphe, who had not hesitated to show himself devoid of his uniform of a provisional dead man, not only in public but in the midst of a provocative demonstration, the ambassadors officially quit Paris.

XII

From the twelfth day of November onwards, to the great detriment of people afflicted with rheumatism who persist in wanting to get up early, the sun becomes extremely idle. It hesitates for a long time before passing the portal that the rosy fingers of dawn open up to it. Doubtless fearing to shed light events as frightful as those that were about to have France as a theater, it did not show itself to Paris on the day after the departure of the ordinary and extraordinary ambassadors.

The indescribable action of Captain Sylphe was equivalent, in fact, to a universal declaration of war, a manifest violation of treaties that could not leave any nation indifferent.

At eight o'clock the following morning, after half a day of perfectly understandable panic, the Government, holding in its elbows around the table presided over by Petitpaon, considered the situation.

The unanimity of the Council was in accord to declare that France was in a peril that necessitated the mass enlistment of all valid men.

"We'll enlist them all in a single corps," the assembly of ministers concluded, as they quit their seats.

"France is counting on you!" declared Bernard Petitpaon, standing up in his turn.

General Croppeton and Admiral Théhyx nearly came to blows in wanting to prove the superiority of the land army over the naval forces and the superiority of the naval forces over the land army.

Henri Verbuis put the question of allies on the table and recalled that war is only the opportunity sought by every country to cause its politics to triumph. The reasons of an economic order capable on ensuring the fidelity of engagements made by certain nations in respect of France were carefully weighed.

"Russia will march with us," explained the Minister of Finance, "because if we were defeated, the debt of fifteen billion that they owe us would pass into other hands, and the Russians know how difficult it would be for them to find people as amiable to their debtors as the French."

"The Tsar has always shown his gratitude for our good offices," declared Henri Verbuis.

"We're going to test the value of his amity!" snapped Phosphène.

"The sympathy of England in our regard won't be belied at this moment, when we enjoy several linked concerns," Henri Verbuis continued.

"I like those people, who don't get carried away and act immutably in their own best interests," Phosphène added. "As those interests are always easy to determine, with the English, one always knows exactly how things stand."

"In sum, which are the nations that will have the honor of finding themselves face to face with France?" asked Bernard Petitpaon.

"The big cheese is obviously Germany," declared General Croppeton. "All the bigger because she won't be alone."

"I fear, in fact, to see Austria at her side!" Henri Verbuis opined.

"And Italy? And Spain? And Greece?" queried Pierre Phosphène, making a list of States that did credit to his geographico-political knowledge.

"It's very difficult to say," explained the Minister of Foreign Affairs. "Everything depends on what happens at the beginning of the campaign. Many nations resemble, in fact, those individuals who put themselves, by definition and with a perfect regularity, on the stronger side."

"We'll begin by striking a great blow!" affirmed Croppeton.

"We ought to wait for the declaration of war," counseled Charles Miraudel.

"There's no need," Croppeton went on. "We've violated the faith of the treaties. That justifies any attacks directed against us by our enemies."

"Captain Sylphe's action was an act of madness. A madman isn't responsible for his actions," Miraudel objected.

"That's the very reason that renders France responsible instead of the Captain," Admirable Théhyx put on.

"Captain Sylphe has been apprehended, naturally. After having interrogated him myself, I've had him locked up in a

139

military prison," said General Croppeton. "A decision will be made in his regard later. Thus far, he hasn't said what motive drove him to behave in that fashion. We're lost in conjectures..."

He would have continued if Bernard Petitpaon had not cut him off. "There's no point in discussing facts of which we have no knowledge! It's a matter of defending ourselves, not philosophizing. I think it would be useful to study the coefficients attributed to each country and calculate the number of soldiers they can put into the field..."

General Croppeton took a large sheet of paper covered with figures out of his portfolio. He reminded them that the coefficient varied between zero and ten, and then read out, commencing with the land armies:

"France and Germany, ten for the dead and also for the wounded.

"England, Austria-Hungary, Russia, the United States and Japan, eight and a half for the dead and seven for the wounded.

"Italy and Spain, five for the dead and six and a half for the wounded.

"Greece, four and a third for the dead, five and a half for the wounded.

"Turkey, Sweden and Holland, four for the dead and three for the wounded."

The coefficient descended toward zero, passing through the South American republics, Bulgaria, China, Serbia, the principality of Monaco and the sovereign states of Central Africa. The kingdom of Haricot VII occupied one of the last places, with one nine-hundredth for the dead and one two-hundredths for the wounded.

At sea, England occupied the top place with ten all along the line; then came, on a footing of complete equality, Germany and France. After that there were the United States, Italy and Japan, followed by Russia, after which followed, successively, Spain, Turkey, Holland and Greece. Several powers, not possessing any ship capable of transforming its commercial habits into more bellicose operations, were absent from the list.

The calculations to which the general staffs of the Ministries of War and Marine had devoted themselves established that France, supported by Russia and England, could battle on fairly equal terms against a coalition formed by Germany, Austro-Hungary and two second order Powers selected at random from the world map.

That observation extracted from the depths of Bernard Petitpaon's lungs a "Vive la France!" of such beautiful sonority that the chorus of ministers, in repeating it, seemed no more than a dissonant echo.

The President of the Republic announced that, given the gravity of the situation, he had thought it his duty to draft a Message. He handed one copy to General Croppeton and another to Arthème Flopinte, those being the two ministers by means of whose mouths the document would be communicated to the Chambre des Députés and the Senate. And, sticking out his chest and holding his shoulders back, Bernard Petitpaon gave a model reading of his Message.

In rhythmic, almost musical prose, visibly written to give full value to the voice, the President asked of the patriotism of all citizens the deployment of the most energetic zeal.

He recalled that France would not have lived though the days that had put an unbreakable crown of glory on her head had she not found herself face to face with Europe.

He promised the heroes harvests of laurels—the laurels blooming in the fields of Bellona, which, thanks to him, Bernard Petitpaon, returned eternally green under the total exemption of spilled blood.

After an ultimate plea to everyone's civil and military duties. Bernard Petitpaon had added a final full stop, preceded by his autograph signature.

Multiple and patriotic handshakes were exchanged. The ministers divided into two groups. One, which had General Croppeton at its head, headed for the Chambre des Députés; the other, under the command of the Garde des Sceaux,

141

Arthème Flopinte, supported by Admiral Théhyx, went to the Senate.

The two Assemblies, their members in formal dress, all girdled by their sashes, were awaiting events in a state of nervousness near to overexcitement.

Either because their average age was younger, or because they were determined to pronounce, during the four years of their legislature, as many words as the senators in the nine years that their own lasted, or because their greater number incited them to noisier competition, the députés brought an unprecedented din to the Palais Bourbon, even in proportion to the Luxembourg.

Bernard Petitpaon's Message was welcomed by the Upper Assembly with a deference full of nobility and dignity.

A specialist in military questions asked Admiral Théhyx for a few clarifications of a technical nature.

The Admiral, after having deplored the fact that France was not ranked at the summit of the scale of naval Powers, explained the probable consequences of various foreign military stocks. As one senator did not understand the mechanism of coefficients, the Grandmaster of the Marine rendered it more palpable by taking examples; he asked his interlocutor to stand in, momentarily and successively, for representative of the most relevant nationalities, while he would retain the identity of the French himself.

"If you're German, we meet, in ordinary conditions and equivalent positions; there are equal numbers of dead and wounded on either side. But if you're English, Austro-Hungarian, Russian, Japanese or North American, there has to be ten of you to kill eight and a half Frenchmen or to wound seven of them."

"I get it," said the senator, following the table. "And if I were Italian or Spanish, there would need to be two of me to kill you and ten of me to wound six and a half Frenchmen."

"Exactly," approved Admiral Théhyx, to the applause of the Assembly.

"But what about the fractions?" asked the curious senator. "There was one of those in the war against Haricot VII, and it caused insoluble difficulties..."

"Insoluble? No! Nothing is insoluble in international matters. I would only ask the Senate not to forget that the addition of fractions always ends up forming a unity and that, in any case, if there are any at the end of a campaign, there can never be more than one fractionally dead or wounded man."

These explanations, followed by a few patriotic words, were deemed more than satisfactory by the near-unanimity of the Upper Assembly, which declared itself permanently is session in order to follow the menacing march of events step by step.

In the Chambre, the cries, invectives and thumbing of lecterns were in full flow when General Croppeton made his entrance to the hemicycle. The gestures commenced were not concluded; the most vehement insults died in the ardent throats of those proffering them.

In the midst of the sudden silence, before the immobility of députés changed into statues, General Croppeton climbed the steps of the podium, opened his portfolio and, by way of collecting himself, introduced his beard and moustache into his mouth several times. Having definitively spat them out again, he announced the reading of the Presidential Message.

The sentences cleverly orchestrated by Bernard Petitpaon lost their ring and their color; there was a formless sequence of words that only arrived very vaguely at the ears of those for whom they were intended. Nevertheless, the representatives of the people suspected the beauties hidden in the Presidential Message and applauded as if to break their hands.

During a calm, cutting through the ovation given to General Croppeton, who returned to the Government bench, a voice rose up: "I request the floor!" It was Louis Méripal.

Vociferations, howls and threats departed from all points of the Chambre, converging in the direction of the podium, toward which, walking backwards in order to confront the clamor, the socialist député slowly headed. He was pale. His eyes were shiny with a sharp gleam. He launched a "Citizens!" in a tremulous voice that emerged like a sob. His hands extended, he seemed to be pushing back the boos that were rising up in a frightful tumult.

After a quarter of an hour of superhuman efforts, he succeeded in making the following sentence heard: "I demand that formal charges be brought against Monsieur Coffre and his accomplice, Captain Sylph!"

In a stormy sea, the waves often decline, suddenly calmed, before the frail vessel that resists all their assaults. Thus the fury of the Chambre collapsed into a mute stupor before that man, insensitive to its violence.

Méripal repeated, slowly: "I demand that formal charges be brought against Monsieur Coffre and his accomplice, Captain Sylph!"

"What is this new infamy?" Abbé Mortol launched, like a harpoon.

Louis Méripal shrugged his shoulders in a gesture of arrogant pity. "Monsieur Coffre bought Captain Sylphe. He paid him."

"I would protest, if these words were not absurdity itself!" intervened General Croppeton. "I interrogated Captain Sylphe myself after his arrest. He swore to me on his honor that he was only obedient to his conscience..."

"Who is Madame Coffre!" concluded Méripal, with the gesture of an instrument of justice.

"Enough! Enough!" howled six hundred throats, taut with rage. "Throw out the blasphemer of the fatherland, who is now insulting women!"

"Masks off, hypocrites! Who among you is unaware the Captain Sylphe is Madame Coffre's lover? Well, Monsieur l'Abbé Mortol, who is their confessor—answer, then!"

"You do not have the right to talk about morality, you who do not believe in God!" replied Abbé Mortol, in a scornful tone.

"Which makes me moral! What importance would Madame Coffre's relationships with all the man on Earth have, if they did not result in a pile of ruins, a colossal litter of cadavers?"

"Only Petitpaon warfare will be practiced," declared General Croppeton, solemnly. "There will be no real death to deplore."

"And you don't count, of course, the countless victims of disease? Isn't it the case, Monsieur l'Abbé Mortol, that your God has prepared all his scourges, and that they will fall upon the troops that you call armies on campaign? The fatigue, the privations are holy things, are they not, since people die of them?"

Cries of "Enough! Enough!" punctuated the tumult, in the midst of which Méripal continued.

"The peoples, whom their oppressors carefully keep isolated from others, and whom they excite to reciprocal execrations by representing their neighbors as infidels that the true God commands them to exterminate like bloodthirsty barbarians, have looked at one another! And having looked at one another, they have recognized a similar face. Dazzled, they will hesitate momentarily before extending their hands and abolishing what their masters call frontiers and which are nothing, in reality, but a succession of fence-posts painted in different colors. A fatal moment! The masters who are on the lookout will see that gleam lighting up in the eyes of their slaves. They will tremble lest that radiation ignite the glorious conflagration in which all their thrones and scepters will perish. They will all unite to stifle it, and reanimate the fading hatred..."

"We don't hate anyone!" shouted General Croppeton, in a convinced tone.

"You don't hate anyone? But you maintain the simulacra of hatred against everyone! You no longer fight, but you keep your weapons, because you know full well that appearances are as powerful as realities...because you know full well that cannons and rifles often fire of their own accord!"

"I can offer my guarantee of respect for discipline!" declared Croppeton, authoritatively.

"We're not responsible for what's happening!" shouted Abbé Mortol, coming to the rescue.

"What? You're not responsible? But this war, again, is your work and that of your allies, Messieurs the priests. Oh, at first, Monsieur l'Abbé, you didn't understand what horrors were concealed by war practiced without blood, and you did everything you could to disrupt the comedy whose sinister end escaped you. Then you reflected, and you said to one another that since the billions would continue to emerge from the mouths of cannons, there was, in sum, no change in the formers state of affairs. You still had your implacable and faithful accomplice, hunger, which curbs life under the ignominy of its Caudine Forks.[12] Petitpaon warfare is still warfare, and the evils it engenders will perhaps surpass in horror everything of which your imagination could ever dream!"

"Explain yourself!" shouted a shrill voice.

"Explain myself? Is there any point, since you don't want to hear, since you don't want to see? Well then, listen carefully, the voluntary deaf and blind: I'm saying that the exact measure of all power is its oppressive and destructive force. To cause suffering—which is to say, to annihilate what there is of individual strength and beauty, to stifle under lies and hypocrisy the spontaneity that is the very spark of life— that is the goal that you have set out to attain. That objective you have surpassed, for effort, even the most cleverly meas-

---

[12] The "battle" of the Caudine Forks in 321 B.C. the story of which was recounted by Livy—probably as an item of didactic fiction rather than an account of actual events—went down in history as the first in which there was no fighting and no casualties. A Roman army trapped by Samnites in a narrow mountain pass in Campania had no alternative but to surrender, and the ensuing conflict was conducted by magistrates negotiating the terms, which obliged them to take into account long-term consequences normally ignored in the heat of conflict. As a former advocate, Austruy would have been familiar with the example and its relevance to his own parable.

ured, is the plaything of the milieu that transports it. For you, the people were passive matter, the flesh that one kneads to one's whim in the blood that flows through ever-open veins. But that source you have dried up! That flesh has become a block of marble on which your raptors' claws break! Life is the eternal diamond still darkened by the infamous matrix that you are, all of you whose breasts are like those sepulchers into which no ray of sunlight ever penetrates! Is it an apotheosis that you have sought in deploying the veils of mourning one last time over the world? Tomorrow, millions of men will be at odds!"

"You know very well that they won't do any harm!" proclaimed Pierre Phosphène.

"Yes, I know that you have consented to convert the most terrible weapons into puerile playthings! But to assure the campaigns a litter of cadavers worthy of the greatest battles you still have the burden of equipment, the fatigue of long marches, the complicity of bad weather, the scarcity of food and all the causes of physical decline from which you would rather protect horses than men. And if there are men who fall exhausted into ditches and whose trembling lips unconsciously repeat the name of God—imposed by the priest who is always there to pillage the agony of human wrecks—those men will once again be those weary of life, who go to death as toward the ideal bride, the only one capable of giving them the happiness that always flees them! But no, what you need are hearts that still beat, souls that still bleed, the youth in which faith in life is so pure and so strong that it cannot imagine the possibility of oblivion! Into those hearths where women weep for the departure of their husbands and sons, the priest will slither under the pretext of words of consolation! And the men who come back..."

"They will all come back, living or dead!" interrupted General Croppeton. "After each engagement, the arbiters will fix the losses. Lots will be drawn in each camp. The dead and the wounded emerging from the urns will immediately reenter into civilian life..."

147

"Where war awaits them in the same way!" snapped Louis Méripal. "Do you think that all those men will resign themselves to the role of dead men that you intend to impose on them?"

"Their existence will be assured by the generous recompenses that the Government will accord to their families," Thunasol explained. "We shall create as many new functions as are required. Everyone will have satisfaction."

"How? The hundreds of thousands of men that you have removed from all productive labor under the pretext of military service are not enough for you? You're now dreaming of a triple permanent army: that of soldiers, and that of functionaries, doubly paid since they will have to maintain the third army, composed of the fake dead and the fake wounded? It's famine that you're preparing with cheerful hearts! The day is imminent when people will be killing one another for a loaf of bread!"

"Our neighbors will be in the same condition," Henri Verbuis observed.

"They evil will only be more terrible! May my prediction never be realized! They are millions of victims whose death warrants you are signing by going to war with Germany!"

"We can't back down!" objected Croppeton.

"It's not a matter of backing down! According to what you call international conventions, Captain Sylphe has committed a crime; hand him over."

"Hand a Frenchman over to Foreigners—never!" protested Verbuis, vigorously.

"Hand him over!" repeated Méripal, emphasizing his words. "And hand over Monsieur Coffre too, who is the instigator of this act, accomplished in order to unleash world war."

"I declare my solidarity with Monsieur Coffre!" proffered Abbé Mortol.

"Your declaration is superfluous!" Méripal riposted. "We all know that you're part of the family! I demand that the Chambre order your immediate arrest! I accuse you, Monsieur

Coffre and Captain Sylphe of the crime of lèse-humanity! I demand that all three of you be handed over to Germany."

A frightful tumult was unleashed; half the députés rushed forward to attack the podium, threatening Méripal with their violently clenched fists.

The President, impotent to reestablish order, covered his head and quit the armchair. The session was ended.

Louis Méripal came down the steps of the podium slowly. The howling mob parted to let him pass and immediately reformed behind him. Whenever an insult reached his ears distinctly he turned round as if to catch sight of his insulter, and then resumed walking, coldly.

Still followed by the mob, he reached the exit. There, a severely dressed man approached him. "Are you député Louis Méripal?"

No sooner had Louis Méripal nodded his head affirmatively than his interlocutor struck him in the face with his glove. "I am General Marquis de Foiraubilles. You have just gravely insulted my future son-in-law, who is unable to reply to you. Here is my card."

"Very well, Monsieur," replied Méripal.

A formidable jostling broke out, which separated the two adversaries.

XIII

After being assured of the collaboration of the customary two friends and having given them instructions, General Foiraubilles went home to await Louis Méripal's seconds.

He did not reveal anything of what had just happened to the Marquise, who, in any case, was too distressed by what had happened to Captain Sylphe to notice her husband's nervousness.

It was not that the prospect of a duel troubled the General in the least. He was naturally brave and the possibility of losing his life had never appeared to him as a clear reality. However, as he was designated to take command of an army and the declaration of war was imminent, without admitting it to himself, he was hoping to see his adversary duck out.

He was weighing up the reasons capable of causing Méripal to decline any encounter when the doorbell rang, interrupting his reflections. A soldier from the logistics corps, who served France by performing the not-very-military functions of valet with regard to the general, handed his master two visiting cards.

They announced Méripal's witnesses. The Marquis experienced a vague disappointment and gave the order to send the Messieurs in.

One of them coldly explained the mission with which they had been charged. The general gave them the names of his friends and the address at which they would be able to contact them immediately. After a correct exchange of bows, the bell was rung, which caused the orderly to reappear and show the two Messieurs out.

The conversation between the seconds was brief. Méripal's declared that their client had no desire to fight, upon which the Marquis de Foiraubilles' stated that the matter would be closed on receipt of a letter of apology signed by the député. In the face of such an inappropriate claim, Méripal's friends limited themselves to replying that he, in the incontestable capacity of the offended party, chose pistols, and that it only remained to fix the time and place of the encounter.

Sensing that a decent retreat was impossible, the general's witnesses accepted that the encounter would take place the following day at eight a.m., at the foot of the stands on the racecourse in the Bois de Boulogne.

For the Marquis de Foiraubilles the night was a double sentry duty. With a view to his duel he brought out his testament and added the final clauses to it. As he had already been in mortal danger hundreds of times, and had thought it necessary every time to affirm the expression of his last will, it formed a veritable volume. Then, as he counted on neither being killed nor wounded, and France had confided an army to him, he went over the secret mobilization papers heaped up on his desk, one by one.

At six o'clock in the morning, General Marquis de Foiraubilles washed his hands and face in cold water; he went to kiss his wife and daughter; he put so much expression into his conjugal kiss and his paternal kiss that the two poor women realized in an eruption of tenderness that he was bound for the dueling-field. They wept, while he remained tragic and stiff in his black frock-coat, militarily buttoned up.

Seven o'clock chimed. He drank a cup of chocolate in the company of his seconds, who had come to fetch him. His last word, which he pronounced on the landing, was for France, at whose disposition he would be once again, if it pleased God, before midday sounded.

At eight o'clock precisely, the General's landau reached the winning-post that saluted the annual arrival of the winner of the Grand Prix de Paris.[13]

A few paces away, Louis Méripal was calmly smoking a cigar in the company of his seconds. He asked one of them to go and ask the Marquis de Foiraubilles' seconds whether they judged it necessary to take the ceremony to its conclusion. As he had spoken quite loudly, the General had heard what he said, so he immediately replied that "nothing could stop the fight once he had scented powder."

"Let him also sniff the bullet—that would be more complete!" said Méripal to his witnesses, with a smile.

The adversaries were set twenty-five paces apart, the places and weapons having been allocated by lot.

"Ready!" said the director of the combat. "One!... Two!... Three!"

A double detonation resounded.

Genera Marquis de Foiraubilles collapsed on the grass.

---

[13] Prior to the institution of the Prix de l'Arc de Triomphe in 1920 the Grand Prix de Paris, run at Longchamp in July, was the most important flat race in the French calendar.

His seconds and the physician ran to him and lifted him up. He had received the bullet full in the forehead.

Louis Méripal tried to approach, but one of the General's witnesses said, brutally: "Go away, Monsieur! Your presence is unnecessary."

The General was placed in the ambulance that had been prudently brought to the terrain. On examining him more attentively, the physician observed that the bullet had not penetrated the skull, and had only made a small circular wound that was quite superficial.

The doctor was so astonished that such a wound should have occasioned death that he interrogated the patient's pulse. It was weak but regular; the heart was beating slowly; the breast was rising with an imperceptible rhythmic movement.

"The General isn't dead!" declared the physician, as the carriage went through the gate in the fortifications.

He therefore set about administering injections of ether, while one of the seconds introduced the contents of a bottle of smelling salts to the Marquis' nostrils and the other but his fingertips.

Nothing had any effect. Tractions of the tongue produced no result either.

"But the General isn't dead!" pronounced the physician, again. "He's breathing! As long as a man is breathing, he isn't dead! This coma can't be prolonged, though!"

Further attempts were made, without the slightest change.

As the carriage approached the Avenue de l'Observatoire, the physician concluded that the shock had produced a commotion resulting in a total and progressive paralysis, whose termination could only be resolved by death, within a few hours at the most.

It was necessary to prepare the Marquise de Foiraubilles for the fatal news. One of the seconds took responsibility for the painful task; it was agreed that the carriage would wait for ten minutes on the Boulevard Montparnasse in order to give him time to accomplish his mission.

The first shock was terrible. The dolor of the General's wife and Hermine was heart-rending. Puling herself together, however, the Marquise asked to see her husband's body, which the physician, assisted by nurses and the concierge, had just installed in a bed.

The pallor of the forehead made the wound seem redder.

The General's wife uttered a scream and fell backwards, her arms outstretched. The physician ran to her. He lifted her up momentarily and made a pious sign of the cross; there was one cadaver more in the room.

"Ruptured aneurism!" he declared.

Abbé Mortol, who had just arrived, recited the prayer for the dead and employed all the consolations of religion to soften Hermine's despair; at twenty years of age, in a single day, she had been orphaned of her father and mother.

XIV

The morning of the third of November was not only marked by the death of Madame a Marquise de Foiraubilles and that of her husband the General—who, although he was still holding back his last sigh, was considered nonetheless as a cadaver by the great men of the art who came running to lend reinforcements to their illustrious colleague. His orderly officers had, in consequence, taken off the General's civilian garments in order to deck him out in his finest dress uniform.

With his moustache well waxed and his eyes carefully closed, therefore, he was waiting in his bed, his ostrich-plumed bicorn between his hands, folded over his breast, for his soul to abandon his body definitively to fly to the ethereal spaces of Valhalla—for General Marquis Narcisse de Foiraubilles was a brave warrior, and a good master in the belief of his valet, who deposited the pearls of his tears on the marble of the night-table.

As midday chimed in all the belfries in France a dispatch from the special commissioner at Pagny-sur-Moselle brought it to the attention of his hierarchical superiors that a train packed with German soldiers had just crossed the frontier.

"That imbecile shouldn't have let it pass!" cried the Minister of the Interior, Charles Miraudel, picking up his hat in order to go to see General Croppeton. The latter was already in conference with Henri Verbuis, who had received an official telegram from the German government informing him of the opening of hostilities and notifying him of the names of the arbiters.

"Which way is the train heading? Is it going in the direction of Verdun or toward Nancy?" demanded General Croppeton, his nose in a map.

"I don't know," Miraudel confessed.

"It's hardly worth the trouble of having special commissioners!" complained Croppeton, shrugging his shoulders.

"The train didn't even stop for the customs," Miraudel said, in self-justification.

"As long as it doesn't get as far as Paris!" the President of the Council of Ministers thought aloud—a reflection interrupted by a strident telephonic appeal.

Further dispatches had been received at the Ministry of the Interior. The Director of the Cabinet informed his chief that train after train was now going through the frontier stations at top speed.

"Catastrophes are going to occur!" cried the Minister of Public Works, entering breathlessly. "These people are mad! They're going through in spite of the signals on red!"

"What do you expect in a time of war!" said Croppeton, swallowing his beard. "What if we were to blow up the tracks?"

"All the trains would be derailed, colliding with one another. You'd kill thousands of men! Petitpaon warfare doesn't give you the right!"

"The case hasn't been anticipated!" put in a new arrival, Admiral Théhyx.

"Telegraph the order to blow up the tracks, bridges and tunnels, then!" said Croppeton, enthusiastically.

"I believe that it would be more prudent to refer the matter to the President of the Republic!" put in Pierre Phosphène, less effervescent than usual. "Reprisals are to be feared!"

"That's true," replied the Ministers present, putting on their hats in order to go to the Élysée.

Bernard Petitpaon was alone. He was eating lunch, and as emotion constituted an incomparable aperitif and the morning had been particularly fecund in tragic events, he was eating with a very hearty appetite. He interrupted the play of his jaws to give the order to have the Ministers shown in.

After apologizing for receiving them in the dining room, he asked General Croppeton to what he owed the honor of an unexpected visit.

In a few words, the General brought Petitpaon up to date with the situation and asked his opinion regarding the opportunity to blow up the tracks and the engineering works on the railway.

"What? Accidents, with wounded, perhaps dead? Veritable wounded and dead? Do you want to revive the bloody and barbaric customs of ancient warfare? Are we, yes or no, fully in the Petitpaon Era?"

"We are," said the ministerial chorus, meekly.

"Well then, be worthy of it, and don't compromise the vigils of my genius so lightly!" Petitpaon thundered, introducing a large slice of mutton into his mouth, which he chewed up with four thrusts of his jaws. "And if you haven't had lunch yet, sit down! There's enough to go round, isn't there, Maître d'Hotel?"

The domestic bowed in a reverence of solemn affirmation, and brought forward seats for each of the guests.

"You were saying, General?" said Petitpaon, to open the conversation.

"The Germans are heading for Paris at full steam!"

"Bravo! Bravo!" judged Petitpaon, serving himself with wine.

"What?" said Croppeton, astonished.

"Bravo! A hundred times, a thousand times bravo! They're in the process of committing an irreparable tactical error."

"Oh! Do you think so?" said Admiral Théhyx, bewildered.

"Certainly! By abandoning their country and venturing into our territory, their putting us on the defensive—which is to say, giving us the choice of the time and place of battles. It's necessary not to lose sight, General, of the advantages resulting from our positions on the terrain, and the skillful opportunism of our movements is capable of far overcoming the slight superiority that a few soldiers more gives our enemies."

"You're sure of victory?" General Croppeton put in.

"Obviously! And if there are people who doubt it, they must be thrown in prison. Confidence is to a soldier what the mainspring is to a watch. Suppress them, and arrest the lot! This is what will happen: the enemy armies penetrate into France; they go forward, and keep going forward. We retreat, retreat incessantly. We're ungraspable! You understand? Ungraspable! The enemy persists in our pursuit; we draw it after us through France!"

"But we can't allow Paris to be taken!" objected General Croppeton.

"Why not? The enemy won't be able to hold it. And it will be immobilized for some time within our walls, which will be an unexpected stroke of luck and a further guarantee of success. Reflect, then, that while they abandon themselves to these new delights of Capua, the Russians will have time to install themselves in Berlin! Then, with all possible precautions, we'll cut off the retreat of the German armies and slowly, methodically, with an irresistible movement, we'll drive them back to the ocean, where the English fleet will be waiting for them."

"It's a plan that even Hannibal couldn't have conceived!" said Croppeton, admiringly.

"Nor Napoléon!" put in Pierre Phosphène.

"Nor Caesar!"

"Nor Tamerlane!"

"Nor Alexander!"

"Nor Togo!"[14]

"Nor Carnot!" the Ministers proclaimed, simultaneously, each of them launching the name that seemed to him to established the most flattering comparison.[15]

Petitpaon thanked his admirers by drinking to their health. "I had another idea, but I admit that it's inferior to the one I've just voiced: we drive the Germans all the way to the Pyrenees and, with a supreme effort, we throw them into the arms of the Spaniards, who don't have any reason not to side with us."

"It's marvelous in its audacity!" Croppeton ecstasized.

"But it's less reliable. Let's stick to the ocean and the English. My dear Verbuis, it's necessary to send an absolutely reliable man to London in order that our plan doesn't go awry."

"I'll go myself!" declared the Minister of Foreign Affairs.

"Good!" Petitpaon approved. "Now, General, you need to take the necessary measures immediately to ensure that no French corps comes into contact with the enemy. As it's necessary to think of everything, I believe it's wise to assume Paris in its possession. Needless to say, in that case, we'll transport the seat of government elsewhere. It's therefore necessary to evacuate all our troops from the city..."

---

[14] Togo Heihachiro was the Japanese admiral whose forces destroyed the Russian fleet at the Battle of Tsushima in 1905.

[15] Sadi Carnot, the fourth President of the Third Republic, assassinated in 1894, had earlier been charged with organizing French resistance in the north of the country during the Franco-Prussian War of 1870. Given the outcome of the war in question, the comparison is not as flattering as its predecessors.

"In troubled times, it's difficult to ensure order with police forces alone," observed Charles Miraudel. "I think it would be prudent to keep thirty or thirty-five thousand men in reserve to be prepared for all eventualities."

"The African army, composed of battle-hardened soldiers on whom we can rely, merit being designated for that post of honor," said Croppeton. "It will be complete once it has a new commander."

"That Méripal had to go and kill the Marquis de Foiraubilles!" groaned Admiral Théhyx.

"Is he dead yet?" Petitpaon asked, for the sake of politeness.

"I don't know," Croppeton replied. "An hour ago he was still breathing, but so feebly that the physicians thought that the end was nigh. Since he can't pull through, it's to be hoped that he dies today. He can be buried tomorrow with the Marquise. That will save time and money, for a start; then too, I'm sure my old comrade would be glad to make the journey to Père-Lachaise side by side with the dear companion of his life."

"Let our good wishes open the gates of Père-Lachaise to him, then!" Petitpaon granted, with a gesture of benediction. "Croppeton, you can nominate his successor; I'll ratify your choice in advance."

"Thank you—but out of deference to my old companion in arms, will you permit me to wait, before making that nomination official, until we've accompanied him to his final dwelling?" Croppeton interceded.

"As you please!" Petitpaon approved. "But to get back to the African army, it would be useful, I think, to concentrate it in a single barracks."

"I don't know of any in Paris large enough," Croppeton objected.

"There's the Grand Palais des Champs-Élysées," suggested Pierre Phosphène.[16]

"Yes, it would be easy to adapt it," agreed Croppeton.

"Perfect, perfect!" Petitpaon applauded. "It's very central, and if the Germans enter Paris, they'll never think of going to look for soldiers in the temple of the Liberal Arts! Do what's necessary to install the little army in that ideal location as soon as possible."

"It'll be done within three days," promised General Croppeton.

In spite of the gravity of the questions that had just been discussed, the Ministers, following Petitpaon's example, had lunched comfortably. As a satisfied conscience ensures a good digestion, they congratulated one another for having done merit to the fatherland.

After having lit a cigar and taken their leave of the President of the Republic, they went their separate ways, each hastening to wherever his duty or his function summoned him.

XV

After having created, in war, the surest and most terrible source of anguish, human beings were quite naturally seized by the desire for a diversion, temporary at least, so they invented palaver.

Indeed, the best means of escaping the reality of something is to talk about it, for speech is a magical garment that

---

[16] The edifice in question, constructed for the Exposition Universelle of 1900 and inspired by London's Crystal Palace, was still new when the story was written; Austruy had no way of knowing that it would be employed as a military hospital during the Great War, or that the Nazis would put on propaganda exhibitions therein during World War II, although modern readers might think that those developments add a little extra irony to the story. Nowadays, Chanel holds annual fashion shows there.

disguises forms, modifies colors, makes what which one desires seem closer at hand, and blurs with a fog sounds that one wants to flee. Anyone who proffers plaints and screams in pain only hears his plaints and screams; he escapes the brutal consciousness of his distress and his agony.

It is thus that every man belonging to a nation, susceptible of taking part in a war that has just broken out, experiences a need to make speeches of varying grandiosity about the prospect of eventualities.

The French all possess, in various doses, parcels of oratory genius, and a large number of southerners, justly claiming a very legitimate affiliation with Cicero, Demosthenes or one of their principal rivals, are past masters of the art of talking well and at great length.

That day, so well-supplied with important and tragic events, could not leave eloquences ever-ready to manifest themselves indifferent. In all parts of France they held forth with an incomparable generosity. Accents of terror were manifest in inflections of a natural kind, which the impetuosity of improvisation deprived of all restraint.

In cafés, on street corners, in public squares and on their doorsteps, citizens proclaimed loudly what were, in the circumstances, the elementary duties of Government.

Old men, with a fleeting gleam traversing their dull eyes, told the young about the memorable battles that they had witnessed, and, as the "conscripts" never testify sufficient enthusiasm for their pompous narrations, the "veterans" bemoaned the disappearance of noble and generous ideas.

"Once, not only did people get themselves killed for their fatherland, but their hearts beast faster when they talked about it. Young people nowadays, when they hear the name of France pronounced, blush as if it were that of their mistress."

"Nowadays, one doesn't blush at either one of them," replied some disrespectful adolescent. "Go home and don't let the fires that your rheumatism needs go out! Don't worry; we'll do our duty as you did yours, and later, when we're your age, we'll also say to those who will be the young that the past was much better than the present. The links that form the chain of the generation are all the same size and made of the same metal. Everyone prizes the link that his own fingers have molded, just as everyone thinks himself superior to his neighbor. We love the fatherland, we'll continue to love it, and we'll defend it until it no longer has an essential reason for being, in the same way that on the day when bread is no longer indispensable we'll sow roses and lilies instead of wheat."

The young men meant what they said, and that evening, from the north, the south, the east and the west of the territory, before having received the order to mobilize, they set forth to join up at the various points assigned to them.

Thus, on the morning of the fourth of November, France was not only in a state to defend herself, but also to attack her adversaries.

Russia, which is a country with a very large surface area and lacks rapid means of communication, required a further fortnight to prepare herself.

As for England, her steamships were under pressure, only waiting for the signal to set forth to sail useful waters.

In any case, there was no urgency. The German military trains were still crossing the frontier at hectic speeds, and there was scarcely time, as they approached, to move French trains transporting passengers terrified by the mere idea of a possible crash into the sidings.

No one knew as yet the destination of those carriages packed with enemies, who were insolently smoking their long pipes at the windows, and did not even make the token gesture of tipping their pointed helmets at the guards energetically brandishing signals to stop. They went passed like phantoms, heading northwards, coming southwards again, wandering incessantly all along and through the départements of the east.

Before going to the funeral of the Marquis de Foiraubilles, General Croppeton had convened a Council of War in order that some enlightenment might pierce the thick obscurity of those mysterious maneuvers.

The unanimous opinion was that nothing should be done until further information arrived.

It was, therefore, relieved of any immediate care that General Croppeton, followed by one of his orderly officers, disembarked from his coupé in front of the building inhabited by the spouses Foiraubilles while alive.

An enormous crowd, attracted by the funeral preparations, was cluttering the sidewalks and the roadway, in spite of the energetic invitations to move on issued by the police on duty.

During the night, certain symptoms had given the physicians hope that it was all over for the General, and that by delaying the Marquise's funeral by twenty-four hours it would be possible to load a double coffin into a single hearse. Dawn had arrived; the general persisted in his condition, which was no longer life but was not yet death.

The most resolute physicians hesitated to have him put in a coffin, impressed as they were by the long list of false cadavers woken up by the jolts of the funereal carriage or the impact of the earth thrown to cover their grave. Furthermore, a corresponding member of the English Society for the Prevention of Premature Burial had got involved and had taken active steps to prevent any imprudence.[17]

It had therefore been decided to transport the body of the Marquise to Père-Lachaise in a provisional coffin, which would wait there for her husband to come to join her in order to have the simultaneous honor of a definitive sepulcher.

---

[17] The London Association for the Prevention of Premature Burial was founded in 1896 by William Tebb and Walter Hawden; the movement remained active until the 1930s, when the practice of embalming became sufficiently widespread to make sure that anyone scheduled for burial or cremation was well and truly dead. It is not obvious why it was not replaced by an Association for the Prevention of Premature Embalming.

The master of ceremonies asked whether the flowers and wreaths should be placed on the carriage. A grave discussion as held on that subject by the relatives and friends. Many of those supreme testimonies of admiration and sympathy had, in fact, been addressed to the general and not to his spouse, but the Marquise's family argued forcefully that the poor woman had perished a victim of her conjugal love, and that, on the other hand, the funeral of Narcisse de Foiraubilles had been put off to a date that might be sufficiently distant for the flowers to have faded completely when the moment came to utilize them. It was better, therefore, from all points of view, for the present cortege to take advantage of them.

This reasoning triumphed, and it was under a multicolored mountain of bouquets and beribboned sprays that the Marquise drew away forever from the house in which she left a husband asleep beneath the wing of Death and a daughter of twenty years who was weeping all the tears in her body.

The pall had confided its cordons to military and political personalities of the highest rank.

With the family marched General Croppeton, in full dress uniform, his breast constellated by civilian and military medals.

In groups, the crowd arranged itself in their wake, and under a gray sky that threatened rain, descended slowly toward Notre-Dame, between a double hedge of curiosity-seekers, which included the two dead men of the African war, buried in their ample white vestments.

Cardinal-Archbishop Pecari had decided to officiate. Clad in his sacerdotal vestments, assisted by a curate who was holding a fully-loaded aspergillum, he was waiting under the porch of his church, his whole body agitated by a senile tremor.

When the mortal remains appeared of the great believer, snatched away, if not in her prime, at least very brutally and without preliminary warning, Monseigneur Pecari rectified his stance. His chin, which, in his youth, had been a "nutcracker" but which now merely drooped, sought the angle most expressive of the divine authority his rank and titles conferred upon him. With gestures of haughty unction he blessed the coffin and delivered himself, without haste but also without slowness, to the accomplishment of the rites.

When the ceremony was over, the body was replaced on the flower-decked hearse, the cordons of the pall were taken up again by the important individuals, and the crowed re-formed in procession.

A final blessing from the Cardinal-Archbishop seemed to liquefy the large black clouds in a diluvian torrent. Although the objective of all that water, following the ineluctable law of gravity, was to rejoin the earth, it first saturated the garments and the bodies that barred its route, aided by the umbrellas hoisted by some over others, which channeled in, without wasting a drop, over the heads and shoulders of the followers.

The most thoroughly-soaked, on arrival at the threshold of Père-Lachaise, were the officers and others whose wearing of a uniform forbade the usage of the bourgeois defense made illustrious by Louis-Philippe, but which did not save him from revolution—which is a sign of the wrath of the people, as rain is a sign of the wrath of God.

XVI

At the exit from the ceremony that marked, for the Marquise de Foiraubilles, the first step toward the paradise reserved for her by her piety, Monsieur Coffre offered to take General Croppeton back to his house in the Rue Saint-Dominique in his carriage.

Endowed with the flair of an exceedingly subtle artilleryman, the General understood that that proposition on the banker's part was a polite way of expressing his desire to have a chat with him.

A soldier never runs away; Croppeton, therefore, climbed without hesitation into the silver and gold coupé of which the financier was doing him the honors, and in which Abbé Mortol was already seated.

The door had hardly been closed by the footman than Monsieur Coffre, after having devoted a few remarks to his patriotic apprehensions, started on the much longer chapter of the fears of the disorder and pillage that individual property might have to suffer at the hands of scoundrels and revolutionaries of all kinds, untiringly on the lookout for circumstances propitious to their evil exploits.

General Croppeton raised the stakes of the banker's terrors. He recalled, one by one, the darkest days of our history, in which the populace had been excited by sinister troublemakers.

"Like that Louis Méripal!" spat Abbé Mortol, disgustedly. "Don't you think that we have the right to have men like that assassinated?"

"To whom are you talking, my dear Abbé," the Minister approved. "Believe me, a country has to sink very low to permit a Méripal to measure himself against a Foiraubilles!"

"And to kill him," added Monsieur Coffre.

"Yes, to kill him, along with his wife, the poor Marquise—and who can tell whether her daughter, the unfortunate Hermine, might not also die of grief?" commiserated Abbé Mortol.

"The General was wrong to fight a duel with his murderer," opined the banker.

"Obviously! He should have blown his brains out like a dog. That Méripal isn't even a dog. As you said only yesterday, my dear Abbé, dogs sometimes go to mass when they accompany their masters, while Méripal has never been into a church."

Abbé Mortol approved discreetly, and said: "It requires dictatorship, a state of permanent siege, the saber always raised, to reduce to silence the atheism that is the cause of all crimes!"

"It's sure that with a few firing-squads," growled Croppeton, "we'd finish with it quickly and for good."

"In sum, what measures are you counting on taking to safeguard our property and persons during the disarray that every war brings?" enquired Monsieur Coffre, anxiously.

General Croppeton made a vague gesture, which might have signified that he was leaving it to the grace of God.

Monsieur Coffre probably did not think celestial power capable of replacing a well-organized police force, for he launched into bitter recriminations against what he called the ingratitude toward him, who had so often put considerable capital at the disposal of works of social conservation and who was still ready to make all the sacrifices necessary to assure order in Paris.

As the carriage had traversed the Champs-Élysées and was passing in front of the Grand Palais, General Croppeton interrupted the banker's complaints. "Stop the carriage, I beg you. A few minutes should suffice for you to render account that the Government has done its duty—all of its duty."

Slightly nonplussed, Monsieur Coffre pressed a button hidden in the quilting. The coupé immediately stopped. The General got down, and invited Monsieur Coffre and Abbé Mortol to follow his example. Guiding his companions, he went into the Grand Palais, waving away with an imperious gesture a guard who rushed to block the entrance.

Soldiers of the engineering and logistics corps were unloading ammunition-wagons in which beds and camping equipment of all sorts were heaped up. General Croppeton exchanged a few brief remarks with an officer who appeared to be commanding the operation; then, drawing his two companions to one side, he unveiled the plan that had been elaborated the day before in the Council of Ministers.

Gradually, Monsieur Coffre's face cleared. He listened with a kind of approving delight to the voice explaining the precautions taken in case of rioting.

"Tonight, thirty-four thousand men will enter here," General Croppeton explained. "They install themselves with their arms and baggage, the artillery with its equipments and the cavalry with its horses on the ground floor, while the in-

166

fantry will occupy the first-floor galleries. The army consists of proven soldiers; it's the one that defeated Haricot VII. To deflect the attention of the population, because it's important that all this remain somewhat mysterious..."

"Very good! Very good!" approved Abbé Mortol. "Mystery is an invincible force. All durable things rest thereon..."

"Like Eternity," said Monsieur Coffre, smiling.

"...Troop movement will commence at nightfall," General Croppeton continued. "In the midst of the multiple comings and goings, the regiments of the African army, all in barracks in Paris or the suburbs, will set out to march to this destination, which only their colonels know. When the last man is inside, the doors will be carefully closed and bolted—for it's important that not the slightest contact is established between the inside and the outside. It only remains to ensure the provisioning of the troops..."

"I'll put twenty million francs at your disposal," Monsieur Coffre offered. "That's my contribution to the defense of the fatherland."

"Thank you. That money will be transformed into provisions—but it's necessary that the provisions reach the soldiers without any breach of the rules of the strictest discretion."

"That seems to me to be complicated, not to say impossible," said Abbé Mortol sententiously.

"Complicated perhaps, but the world impossible was long ago struck out of the dictionary that the Ministry of War uses when France is at stake. Our information service has had the good fortune, in fact, to discover a kind of subterranean tunnel linking the Seine to the basements of the Palais. The competent services immediately undertook the necessary explorations and, at present, it has recognized that the route in question, which is about four hundred meters long, is practicable in all its parts.

"Without losing a moment we've requisitioned the Naval Construction Yards at the Point-du-Jour in order to put into action the plan that we've submitted to a most distinguished engineer. The plan consists of fitting the boats that I intend to use for the subsistence service of the Grand Palais with four wheels. Those boats, manned by naval officers and sailors to whom France can confide its most cherished interests in complete security, will be loaded with foodstuffs at some point on the two banks, inside or outside Paris; under cover of darkness, in silence and secrecy, they'll be brought to the mouth of the tunnel; there they'll be moored to a steel cable moved by electricity, which will pull them out of the water, and they'll roll as far as the location beneath our feet on rails that soldiers of the engineering corps are busy laying now..."

Abbé Mortol and Monsieur Coffre were so literally mute with admiration that they did not pronounce a single word, allowing General Croppeton to continue his explanation.

"We've anticipated everything—absolutely everything—to make sure of the blindest devotion of this army, which will, if need be, safeguard public order. The rations will be doubled; all silent, or, at least, not very noisy games will be permitted, and as it's necessary to envisage the possibility of a long sequestration and young soldiers, even when well-nourished, don't adapt well to the privation of certain pleasures—which are no longer those of our age, my dear Coffre—the catering corps will recruit an entire battalion of special canteen-girls.

"The Cythera battalion!" the banker joked.

"Exactly. It's the Devil's part, my dear Abbé; God's will be all the more beautiful for it, for I've instructed the military chaplains to multiply religious exercises to the maximum."

"You have a thousand good reasons, General," Abbé Mortol approved. "Prayer will temper their souls. A soldier who does not have piety is unworthy of the uniform."

"Permit me to ask," advanced Monsieur Coffre, "whether munitions of war have been distributed to this army?"

"This very morning," the Minister affirmed.

"My dear Abbé, I hope you'll share my opinion: don't you think that it would be as well to provide these soldiers with normally loaded cartridges and to make sure that the artillery, on whom we're relying for the salvations of our persons and property, are equipped with murderous shells?

"But of course! It's entirely necessary to be able to exterminate, if the occasion arises, all fomenters of disorder and rebellion. An army that is not intended to fight the enemy, but to chastise guilty nationals, cannot be content with the theoretical effects of Petitpaon warfare. Its bullets must be veritably capable of puncturing torsos. It's necessary that its machine-guns can reduce all those who raise their voices to silence."

"If you think it would be useful," said Croppeton, already convinced.

"But it's indispensable!" proclaimed the banker and the priest, in unison.

"Very well—I'll give orders in consequence," approved General Croppeton, drawing his two companions toward the exit door.

XVII

Although responsibilities in governmental matters are very often taken on with a light heart by those on whom they fall, General Croppeton was in a state of very painful perplexity. His sleep, haunted by atrocious nightmares, showed him the soil of the fatherland bruised by German boots; one night, he uttered a terrible cry that woke up his aides de camp and brought them running. They found their chief sitting on his bed, angrily lashing out with his fists into empty space while uttering frightful oaths punctuated with fragmentary sentences; "Jeanne d'Arc expelled the English! I'll expel the Germans!"

He was still lashing out, and the tassel of his night-cap, disturbed by the violence of his movements, struck him in the face—which made him think that his enemies were returning the blows that he was striking.

His orderly officers had enormous difficulty bringing him round and dissipating his patriotic hallucination.

Returned to reality, the Minister of War started weeping like a baby and ordered that he was not to be left alone for the briefest interval,

Meanwhile, Petitpaon did not want to let go of the plan he had conceived, and as he had the entire Council of Ministers with him, General Croppeton was only able to march against the German in his dreams, and in words.

In vain, dispatches arrived in heaps from all points in the east. The populations were alarmed by the sight of the Germans circulating freely without encountering a single obstacle, as if they were at home in a conquered country.

Now the trains were stopping in mid-country; the soldiers were getting off, pillaging the farms and villages and returning to their trains laden with booty, to recommence the same operation further along the line.

"Are they respecting the women?" Petitpaon enquired, in the course of the daily meeting of the Council of Ministers.

"I don't know! They're not complaining, at any rate," replied Charles Miraudel.

"Good!" said Petitpaon. "In spite of everything, the Germans are wrong to attack private property. The laws of war oppose it."

"But force permits it!" Croppeton concluded. "Since you think it best to adopt a plan that consists of not engaging with the enemy, I believe we can use the same strategy and send our soldiers into Germany. The reciprocity of pillage will enable the populations to be patient."

Bernard Petitpaon put his head in his hands to appeal to his genius. The latter hastened to come to his aid, and replied: "The idea is acceptable in principle, but it's necessary to be careful that our soldiers don't come into contact with the enemy."

"Orders will be given to ensure an irreproachable reconnaissance service," promised General Croppeton.

"It's easy for scouts to cast light on all the movements of an adversary," said Admiral Théhyx, supportively, who was very enthusiastic about Petitpaon's plan. "What a day it will be, Messieurs, that sees the enemy caught between the iron barrier of our army and the oceanic wall of fire. Our fleet and the allied fleet will be there, hand in hand! In their turn, our mariners will cry: 'Fire first, Messieurs les Anglais!'[18] Be certain that it will be in the state of cadavers that we see the Germans return to the frontier."

"On reflection, I wonder whether it might not be wise to enter into Germany by passing through Belgium," suggested Bernard Petitpaon.

"We'd be violating a neutral territory!" protested Henri Verbuis.

"Oh, that territory has been violated so many times!" said Petitpaon, with a slightly scornful grimace. "Belgium reminds me of a woman I had in the Grand-Mondial company. Several times in the space of a few years she claimed to have been raped. Every time she changed her name in order to reclaim a virginity that didn't take long to fall prey to a further accident. Thus, the present kingdom of Belgium is a land predestined to the role of battlefield, and it isn't the badge of neutrality she wears in her hat that will prevent European armies from meeting at the inevitable crossroads of their plains. The Belgians don't like war, in the same way that the lady I just mentioned didn't like love. The lady had to be taken by force; Belgium has to resign herself to people fighting on her soil. Nevertheless, I don't have any pretension to impose my opinion upon you. It's up to you, General, to direct operations as you see fit. Everyone to his own trade! How many men and France put on foot?"

"About four million, all good soldiers, well-armed and well-equipped," replied the Minister of War.

"In theory, Russia can mobilize nearly three million," Henri Berbuis added. "Her Government has given me that

---

[18] The reference is to Voltaire's (fictitious) account of the battle of Fontenoy in May 1745, when the Comte d'Anterroche of the Garde Française was said to have invited the English to shoot first after being taunted by Sir Charles Hay.

assurance. In that country, though, it isn't just the calendar that's in retard. I fear that the Russian army won't be able to enter the campaign for two or three months, and even then, it's necessary not to rely on it too much."

"All the more reason for not encountering the Germans right away," affirmed Petitpaon. How many are they?"

"Our spies have unanimously fixed their number at four million five hundred thousand," Croppeton replied. "We'll have England with us; on land, she can put more than five hundred thousand combatants at our disposal."

"I hope so! We're the ones who need to set the enemy up for the ocean thrust!" exclaimed Petitpaon. "Will Austria-Hungary and Italy march against us in considerable proportions?"

"I don't believe so," said Verbuis. "The Hungarians are perfectly indifferent, not to say hostile, to the plans of the Emperor of Austria. As for the latter, he's afraid of ending up as the turkey of the farce and he'll tell himself that if he augments the power of his brutal ally any further, he'll reserve a terrible insecurity for the future. Nevertheless, I think that Austria won't dare separate itself from Germany—but the aid she'll lend won't exceed half a million men. The Italian nation nurtures sentiments of genuine affection with regard to her Latin sister. Her governments have been able to distract the people temporarily, but gallophobia has been a political trampoline whose springs are as broken today as the puppets quivering on top of it. Italy will remain neutral, and I think many of its children will hold out their hands to us individually..."

"Vive Garibaldi!" put in Pierre Phosphène, who had not yet manifested his presence.

"Adding up the totals," put in the Minister of Finance, Thunasol, a great lover of figures, "I find in land troops, seven and a half million combatants on the French side and five on the German..."

"We'll have the victory without the fleets!" proclaimed Bernard Petitpaon.

"We'll have numerical superiority, even if the Russians only contribute a quarter or a fifth of what they've promised," Thunasol continued. "In view of the figures of the various coefficients, and allowing for a generous margin of errors..."

"We won't make any," Croppeton affirmed.

"Our laurels will be all the greener!" Thunasol continued. "I simply want to establish that even by attributing to us all the factors of inferiority, we're still sure of victory..."

"On condition that the other countries don't get involved!" observed Miraudel.

"None of them can have any interest in taking sides for or against us," said Henri Verbuis. The United States are busy forming Trusts of their own products. It's too young a country to think about conquests that could only impoverish Europe, and Europe isn't yet old enough to be transformed into colonies of the New World. The Japanese are busy meditating on the costs of victory. Their country has been exsanguinated by the losses suffered in the last war, which wasn't a Petitpaon war..."

"Certainly not!" put in the President.

"All the other countries, like Spain, Greece, Sweden, Denmark and Portugal are too fearful of a shock that would compromise their already-unstable equilibrium to get mixed up in a business that the great nations will settle by themselves."

Abbé Mortol had asked for Captain Sylphe to be released provisionally, but Louis Méripal had protested so violently against such a measure that General Croppeton had not dared to put it into execution.

According to the expectations of the most competent specialists, the great battles would not take place before the end of December.

"Victory will be the New Year's gift that we'll offer to France!" Petitpaon declared.

XVIII

In his study, which journalists fond of imagery called the tabernacle of the war, General Croppeton was talking about the progress of events in the company of Monsieur Coffre, who had come to ask for a captain of zouaves whom he had encountered in his wife's apartment for two consecutive weeks to be sent on campaign.

"Your slightest desire in an order, my dear friend," said the Minister, signing the officer's service order.

By virtue of a sentiment of delicacy rare in a soldier more habituated to maneuvering on battlefields than in the labyrinths of psychology, General Croppeton never made the slightest allusion capable of implying that Madame Coffre might also have an interest in the officers of whom the banker was appointing himself the protector.

"Oh, my dear friend, if only everyone took as much interest as you do in army matters," he confided to Monsieur Coffre. "You allow yourself to be approached by our most brilliant officers. You weigh their merits, you appreciate their value and when you've observed the existence of an elite subject, you hasten to make me party to your discovery. Quickly, an encouragement, a stripe, a medal, with a posting of confidence. It's France who profits from it..."

Several times, Monsieur Coffre wondered whether the chief of the army might be making fun of him, and suffered a moment of anxiety with regard to his head, at which Croppeton might be taking potshots, to assure himself that the symbolic horns had not really grown there. He had ended up convincing himself of the complete absence of irony in the general, who took his candor far enough to talk about Captain Sylphe.

"He's still in prison, the poor fellow! There's one for whom Fortune has been a cruel stepmother! A Captain at twenty-eight, almost as in Revolutionary times, much appreciated by his superiors, adored by his inferiors, collecting with the same ease a flower from a lady's corsage, a palm in con-

174

tests of horsemanship and a laurel on the battlefield, Alexandre Sylphe considered his future as a starry certainty! Alas, all that is broken, annihilated under the walls of Cirajoum. It was in the condition of provisional death that France saw her predestined son return. Of his act of despair, all those who have a heart in their bosom that beats militarily cannot help but approve! However, Méripal has dared to say that you drove Captain Sylphe to that manifestation, which is quite naturally explicable by the decision of the arbitration tribunal, destroying, along with his life, all his hopes of happiness, his imminent union with Hermine de Foiraubilles. As misfortunes never come singly, Captain Sylphe's protest was followed by the sad death of the Marquise and the plunge into lethargy of my excellent comrade Foiraubilles..."

"How is he today?" asked Monsieur Coffre, who had followed his loquacious interlocutor with a captive attention.

"He hasn't made a movement all night. Yesterday, it was permissible to hope that he was finally about to come out of his coma. He opened his mouth. The trainee from the Val-de-Grâce in service at his bedside took advantage of it to make him swallow and almost complete meal: soup, eggs, cold meat, cheese and dessert. My comrade appeared to have eaten with appetite; he thanked those who had served him, kissed his daughter, picked up his bicorn, replaced it on his breast, closed his eyes again, and hasn't budged since..."

"At least he's not dead!" concluded Monsieur Coffre.

"Evidently not, since he can eat. The physicians are amazed. Their art does not record any analogous case in its annals. They cannot, therefore, offer a prognosis regarding his condition, whose termination has given rise to the engagement of large agers. Personally, even though I'm Foiraubilles' friend, I've bet a hundred louis against a thousand francs that he won't last the week..."

An orderly officer came in and waited at arm's length for his chief to ask him the cause of his irruption.

"What is it?"

"It's a secret matter, General..."

"Speak. Monsieur Coffre has a right to know everything; we have nothing to hide from him. He's the vital fiber of the war, since he's France's banker. Speak!"

"General, the Admiral in command of the provisioning of the Grand Palais had just informed Monsieur le Ministre de la Marine, who instructed me to inform you, that grave and thus-far inexplicable events interrupted the services in the course of last night. It was around midnight; the first boat, laden with fresh meat, arrived at the mouth of the tunnel; it was immediately moored to the traction cable; the captain gave the signal, as usual to start the electric capstan; nothing happened. He gave the signal again, in vain. The captains of the boats that arrived at regular intervals were no more fortunate in their attempts. At daybreak, the boats were obliged to return to their ports of origin without having been able to unload anything."

General Croppeton inveighed against the Navy, whom he accused of wanting to play one of their familiar tricks on the land army. He asked why no sailor had gone into the tunnel to see what was happening.

The orderly officer replied that the orders specifically forbade such a maneuver, the personnel of the fleet being prohibited, under any pretext, from communicating with the troops in the Grand Palais. He cited the installation of a small pontoon on which, directly adjacent to the quay, the mariners were to await the return of their empty boats.

General Croppeton ordered the officer to disguise himself as an angler, in order not to attract attention, and to go see what was happening inside the Grand Palais.

In the meantime, Abbé Mortol arrived. The Minister brought him up to date with hat he had just learned. The three men formulated hypotheses as to the possible causes of that interruption in the service provisioning the "supreme army."

Croppeton put the responsibility on the Navy, the eternal insubordinate, which must have been guilty of some capital negligence, which a formal investigation would surely discover.

Monsieur Coffre wondered whether it might not have been a protest against the poor quality of the subsistence, and insisted that all the necessary sacrifices had to be made to give full and complete satisfaction to the inhabitants of the Grand Palais.

Abbé Mortol leaned toward a revolt fomented by a few godless and undisciplined soldiers. The troublemakers were preventing the arrival of food in order to be able to persuade their dutiful comrades that the Government wanted to let them die of starvation.

The situation had not been clarified by these conjectures when the officer reappeared to report on his mission. His disguise as an angler was so exact that the concierge of the Ministry had not recognized him and had not wanted to let him pass. He was as pale as someone who has just suffered a violent shock.

Without circumlocutions, militarily, he related what he had seen.

The officers and soldiers were lying in their beds and seemed to be profoundly asleep. He had tried to wake up a general and several men. All had remained inert, as if dead.

In their turn, Croppeton, Monsieur Coffre and Abbé Mortol went pale. They looked at one another, and simultaneously asked one another the same question.

"What is this new misfortune?"

After having affirmed that it was necessary not to panic, the Minister declared that he was leaving in order to take account with his own eyes of what was happening at the Grand Palais.

"We'll go with you!" said Monsieur Coffre and Abbé Mortol, in unison.

The Minister was in civilian clothes, so he only had to take off his medals to ensure himself of an anonymity that was rendered complete by the presence at his side of the angler, who accompanied him.

Monsieur Coffre was wearing a soft hat that changed his very Parisian physiognomy sufficiently into that of some maître d'hôtel. Abbé Mortol could not take off his soutane, so he kept it on, and headed for the indicated point of the bank on his own.

The four individuals slipped into the tunnel successively. They had forgotten to bring a lantern. Monsieur Coffre burned a few matches that guided them as well as could be expected through the dark section of the tunnel to the extremity, at which the fully-armed man on guard was asleep at his post.

They passed by without stopping, took their places in the elevator that took them up into daylight, beneath the immense glazed atrium, in a matter of seconds.

The orderly had not been mistaken; the entire army was sleep. Cuirassiers, spahis, cavalrymen, hussars, dragoons, artillerymen—in sum, all of those whose inseparability from the most noble of human conquests had lodged on the ground floor—were lying in their beds, not far from their mounts, which were also fast asleep.

"But why are they sleeping like this?" groaned Croppeton, shaking officers and soldiers at random, all clad in complete campaign uniforms.

"They're drunk!" whispered Abbé Mortol in Monsieur Coffre's ear.

"Since they have all their equipment," the latter observed, "sleep must have overtaken them in the middle of some maneuver..."

"An equipment review, of course!" muttered Croppeton. "Suppose you help me to wake them up instead of delivering yourselves to contemplation? You probably think that you're a real angler, don't you? You have the brain for it!"

The orderly officer put his right hand to the brim of his straw hat, but the resultant military salute produced a deplorable effect.

"You're ridiculous! Come on, wake that cuirassier!"

The means of extracting a cuirassier from his sleep does not figure in any theory. The angler attempted to proceed by intimidation: "Stand up, Cuirassier!"

He repeated the injunction energetically: "Stand up! Cuirassier!" But the man continued to snore in the chrome steel carapace, which vibrated when the note emerging from the man's throat corresponded to the pitch of its diapason.

"Leave him! You can see that he's a brute!" Croppeton intervened. "Help me to shake this artilleryman, who seems less deeply asleep than the others!"

And the Minister, aided by his picturesque acolyte, inflicted frantic gymnastics on the cannoneer, whose limbs fell back inertly on the bed as soon as they were left to themselves.

"That's a bit much!" muttered Croppeton, striking the sleeper's face vigorously with his closed fists. The latter showed no hint of emotion.

"Perhaps these soldiers are ill?" hazarded Monsieur Coffre, whose temples were moistened by anguish.

"They've been poisoned!" Abbé Mortol concluded.

"Quickly—fetch a physician...physicians. Lots of physicians—all the physicians you can bring!" Croppeton ordered his aide-de-camp. "Go on! At the double! Hurry up!"

The angler ran to the cage of the elevator and disappeared.

The Minister of War, Abbé Mortol and Monsieur Coffre went up to the first floor. The infantrymen were asleep, like their comrades on the ground floor. Multiple attempts to wake them made at various point of the gallery produced no result.

Then the three men went back downstairs, without exchanging a word that might have distracted the intensity of their thoughts, and sat down on empty beds to await the arrival of the physicians.

Only a few minutes went by before General Croppeton leapt abruptly to his feet and howled in a hoarse voice: "I can feel that I'm going to sleep too! My God, protect me! Protect me, my God!"

His two companions ran to him, and after an energetically-administered massage the Minister sighed: "Oh, thank you, my God! It was a false alarm! Oh, I was so frightened!"

The physicians emerged from the cage of the elevator with the precipitation of wild beasts alerted to the fact that it was meal-time. Medical orderlies of various ranks, and some even devoid of rank, disembarked in their turn with boxes of various forms, which seemed to be very heavy, to judge by the difficulty with which they were being transported.

It was the entire Military Council of Health, which the valiant orderly had found in session and had brought, along with its natural auxiliaries, porters of cases of instruments and pharmaceuticals. Alarmed by the spectacle offered to their eyes, the representatives of the curative art—whom it was not surprising to see in the uniform of the corporation whose talents boast of being murderous—saluted before proceeding hierarchically with a summary examination of a few patients.

The meninges encircled in the oak-leaf crowned kepi of a Medical Inspector refused to formulate a diagnosis in advance of a preliminary autopsy, and this opinion, which was complicated by the necessity of analyses whose results demanded a delay of several years, was that of all the echelons of the hierarchy.

The responsibility of making a decision fell upon the Minister of War, who weighed the full gravity of ordering an autopsy on thirty-four thousand bodies that were perhaps only temporarily unconscious. He was already thinking about taking the advice of the sage guardian of the Constitution when a junior orderly started gesticulating and shouting, his right arm extended and the thumb and forefinger united: "Tsetse! Tsetse!"

"A madman now!" groaned General Croppeton, definitively depressed.

The junior orderly continued to utter his lamentable: "Tsetse! Tsetse!"

An Aide-Major headed toward the man and seized his wrist in order to examine what he was holding between his thumb and index finger. "Tsetse! Tsetse!" he howled, fleeing. "Don't let it go! Don't let it go!"

The oak-leaved kepi ran forward, only to recoil immediately and imperatively demand a surgical kit, in which he rummaged rapidly. He took out a large veil of white gauze, with which he enveloped his head carefully, knotting it around his neck. He slid his hands into rubber gloves and advanced toward the junior orderly at a deliberate pace, whose wrist he seized in his turn.

He stood in contemplation for a few minutes, and then uttered, in a grave tone: "Certainly! Yes…no possible doubt. Tsetse! Tsetse!"

His thumb and index finger delicately pinch the extremities of the fingers of the humble servant of Science, as if to collect something.

The operation must have been crowned with success, because the Medical Inspector came back to the Minister and, removing his veils with his left hand, he displayed his right hand, saying: "Here's the guilty party, Monsieur le Ministre. This fly is a variety of tsetse: *Glossina palpalis*, to give it the scientific name to which it has a right. This fly pullulates in the tropical regions of Africa; the banks of the Niger are particularly infested with them. It's the fly responsible for carrying the terrible trypanosome that is the cause, little recognized until now,[19] of the strange malady that the indigenes designate by terms that all translate to what we call sleep: *koulala* in Loango and Bangala, *auyo* in Pahouin, *nelawan* in Yoloff, *sonorhodimi* in Bambara…"

---

[19] Although the responsibility of tsetse flies in spreading the animal disease *nagana* had been recognized by David Livingston in the 1850s, it was not until 1895 that the trypanosomes causing the disease were identified, and not until 1901 that similar trypanosomes were first observed in human blood; Aldo Castellani was the first to suggest their responsibility for sleeping sickness in 1902, when he observed them in cerebrospinal fluid. When Austruy wrote this story the transmission was still thought to be purely mechanical; the complex life-cycle of the parasite was not elucidated until 1909.

"What's that?" Croppeton interjected.

"Native dialects, Monsieur le Ministre," replied the doctor.

"I'm not asking you to talk native, but to tell me what disease has struck these men."

"They have *mtoga*, otherwise known as sleeping sickness."

"That's why they're asleep?" Croppeton put in.

"Exactly, Monsieur le Ministre. The protozoan penetrates into the cerebrospinal fluid and provoke ravages there that it's hard to believe can be produced by something so infinitesimally tiny. The infection passes through three distinct phases..."

"You don't think these men are faking?" General Croppeton interjected.

"Impossible, Monsieur le Ministre! The symptoms are indisputable, and the presence of the *Glossina palpalis* that I've just presented to you completes the basis for the certainty of my diagnosis."

"So these men who are asleep...?" Croppeton enquired.

"Will be awakened by Death," completed the scholarly doctor, gravely. "Science hasn't yet been able to reckon with the redoubtable trypanosome, which it has known for two short a time. The newcomer is profiting from our surprise..."

"What are we going to do?" General Croppeton wailed, lamentably, toward Abbé Mortol and Monsieur Coffre.

"We'd do well to get out of here!" opined Monsieur Coffre.

"Indeed, Messieurs, your presence here is not indispensable, and you're exposing yourself needlessly to the bite of the redoubtable *Glossina palpalis*. Withdraw, then; I'll stay here with my personnel, and I'll set up the bases of field hospital. These soldiers aren't dead yet...they might wake up from time to time to eat. It would be unworthy of France to let them die of starvation."

"Perhaps they'll recover!" said Abbé Mortol hopefully. "I'll have Cardinal Pecari order prayers to that effect."

"Anything's possible!" said the physician, with a pitying smile with regard to the efficacy of archiepiscopal paternosters.

The Minister, framed by Abbé Mortol and Monsieur Coffre and followed by his orderly officer, had already taken a few steps toward the elevator when the Medical Inspector caught up with him. "I forgot to tell you, Monsieur le Ministre, that the horses and mules are sick too..."

"I can see that," said Croppeton, brutally.

"They're afflicted with *nagana*, which is the soliped sleeping sickness. It's transported from one organism to another by another variety of tsetse, *Glossina morsitans* or *pallipides*..."

The General did not listen to the rest of the lecture, in haste as he was to confer with Petitpaon.

The conversation was one of the most dramatic. The President's senses almost betrayed him, but he pulled himself together in the name of France, and even had the presence of mind to make a connection between General Foiraubilles' coma and the one into which the garrison of the Grand Palais had fallen.

He declared that it would be wise, in order to avoid the contamination of Paris, to transport the Marquis de Foiraubilles to join his brothers in arms afflicted by the same disease. The operation was carried out in secret the same day.

The General was installed in the center of the atrium, on a four-poster bed surmounted by a huge tricolor awning with gold trimmings—and a black horse with a red velvet saddle, harnessed in according with the protocol for the mount of a commander-in-chief was stationed at the bottom of the bed.

XIX

Bernard Petitpaon's anticipations were partly realized. It was indeed on Belgium that the armies of the two coalitions converged in order to find a battlefield worthy of them, but the Germans refused to fall into the trap of distancing themselves from their frontiers. The "ocean stroke" thus remained to the count of its inventor, who reserved the option of bringing it into play later if the opportunity presented itself subsequently.

Throughout the month of November and a part of December the Germans continued the maneuver that consisted of exiting their homeland via Alsace and Lorraine in order to reenter it via the Prussian Rhineland, passing through Belgium. It was a circular voyage that their military trains accomplished, and since the violated nation did not make any complaint heard, it was supposed that the booty stolen by the Germans went, at least in part, to buy silence from the brave Belgians, who are never at a loss when it comes to banking.

Responding to the supplications of Bernard Petitpaon, General Croppeton had made superhuman efforts to contain the ardor of the French troops, impatient for the promised victories.

The populations visited by the enemy did not hide their discontentment; they accused the Government of being disinterested in their fate. On several occasions, in fact, meetings were held in which the word treason was pronounced, and as politics does not lose its rights in any circumstances, the adversaries of the Republic counseled the inhabitants to defend themselves, since the masters of France had abandoned them.

Trans were stoned; at Hirson, in the département of the Aisne a stick of dynamite placed on the track exploded, fortunately after the passage of the train, for the accident might have had grave consequences for a large number of soldiers.

Meanwhile, a French army had reached the upper Rhine, the left bank of which it descended with such prudence and skill that its presence had not yet been detected. The secret plan was to go as far as Cologne in order to cut off the retreat of the Germans who, in all probability, would remain stuck in Belgian territory by the surprise of such a mysterious attack.

Following the example of very great men of war, General Croppeton wanted to remain free in his movements and not be bound by a sequence of operations whose ensemble is often contrary to the utilization of unexpected advantages furnished by the enemy as a result of imprudence or poorly executed maneuvers. He therefore refrained from anticipating what he would do once he had cut off the German retreat.

On an immense map pinned to a table he had planted little flags representing the positions of the different armies. As soon as a telegram arrived one of the orderly officers would quickly stick a flag bearing the number of men, horses and artillery pieces at the point indicated by the information.

The British standard floated over Dover with an inscription of five hundred thousand men, ready to cross the Channel with their cannons, munitions and baggage, all fully assembled. England was, therefore keeping her promises with the rigorous exactitude of a bank.

The Russian flag remained fixed at St. Petersburg, which meant that our powerful allies had not yet completed their campaign preparations.

The Austrian banner indicated a million combatants on the frontier lines, while Italy and the other countries bore question marks in their indicative flags, signifying that nothing was known about them.

For France and Germany the general staff had operated in accordance with authentic—or supposedly authentic—mobilization plans, at least with regard to our neighbors. The areas of the two countries had been turned into skimmers by the innumerable small flags necessary to identify each combat unit. General Croppeton contemplated that eloquent bristling with admiration, murmuring: "There are two veritably great nations, worthy of measuring themselves against one another."

Gradually, in small stages, like travelers in no hurry to get to the destination where a rendezvous has been arranged for a long time and where they are sure to meet up, the first arrivals having to wait for the laggards, the little German and French flags drew nearer to Belgium.

Day by day, Bernard Petitpaon was brought up to date with that progress, which did not surprise him at all.

"I told you so! Great days happen in Belgium!"

185

"Damn! It's just that there's Waterloo!" observed Croppeton, chewing a few hairs from his beard.

"Do you think, then, that all Waterloos are the same?" cried the President. "The Usurper was vanquished there in summer; the Republic will be victorious there in winter. I tell you, personally, that we'll have a dazzling Waterloo, which will leave far behind the Waterloo of which historians have the habit of speaking. And I wish the Germans a Cambronne as energetic as ours!"[20]

"They surely don't have one of them!" Croppeton articulated, scornfully.

The English, invited to cross the Channel, occupied the entire coast from Dieppe to Calais, their tents causing belief in an invasion of bathers who had mistaken the season—for that mid-December, the temperature was so rigorous that many soldiers froze to death.

Scattered cases of cholera appeared in the French corps massed in the quadrilateral formed by Alençon, Chartres, Beauvais and Caen. The sanitary services loudly proclaimed that the disease remained limited to a few isolated individuals, but in lower voices they anticipated the beginning of a formidable epidemic, impossible to check.

---

[20] General Pierre Cambronne's Guards were cut off at Waterloo and left in a hopeless position. The rumor was put around that when he was invited to surrender he replied; "The Guards do not surrender—they die!" In fact, the remaining Guards did surrender, and the counter-rumor went around was what he had actually said was "Merde!" which can be loosely translated as either "Oh shit!" or "Fuck off!" He always maintained— very plausibly, in view of the fact that he was seriously wounded at the time—that he did not say anything at all, but the latter anecdote was widely adapted by litterateurs, who followed the example of Victor Hugo in signaling obscenities too indecent to print as "*le mot de Cambronne*" [Cambronne's word].

Following the opinion of General Croppeton, the Council of Ministers, and Petitpaon himself, thought that it would be best to get the war over with as soon as possible, in order to devote themselves subsequently entirely to the struggle against the terrible scourge.

For identical reasons, the Germans, in whose ranks cholera was also causing great ravages, sought battle. In consequence, they did not wait for the Austrians to join forces with their army based in Westphalia, ready to march as soon as the signal was given against the French headquarters established in Aix-la-Chapelle.

That army was, therefore, to see its retreat cut off by the German forces that were occupying very strong positions in Luxembourg and the province of Liège. It was necessary to hasten to its rescue without counting on the support of the Russians, who announced that their preparations had been somewhat delayed by unforeseen events. Nevertheless, five hundred thousand men had embarked at Kronstadt on rapid transports destined for Kiel, whose canal they would cross in order to reach the north of France and join up with us. Volunteers from Italy, Spain, Greece, the United States and the four corners of the world, out of sympathy for France, had joined our armies, which they augmented by a hundred thousand men.

The mathematician Thunasol had carried out very meticulous calculations, and he affirmed that, in the case of a general engagement, the opposed forces would be exactly equal, the volunteer soldiers, by their number and their valor, balancing out the slight inferiority caused by the English and Russian coefficients.

"But then there'll be neither victor nor vanquished," remarked General Croppeton.

"Come on, General, don't you have confidence in the soldiers of France?" President Petitpaon criticized. "Given equality, the content will evidently be hot, but we'll be victorious if our arbiters do their duty with conscience and firmness. Can we count on them?"

"They've been chosen from among the generals with the longest energetic past..."

"You're sure that past hasn't worn them out? Will-power is a string that weakens in old age. It might perhaps have been preferable to designate as arbiters young officers full of ardor and impetuosity."

"My dear President, when I was in command in Algeria, I often had occasion to study the mores of apes—the apes which, by virtue of their intelligence, would perhaps be superior to humans if they were provided with a soul and speech. Those cunning and prudent quadrumanes live in colonies, and I always noticed that the role of sentinel was played by the oldest ape in the band. It had lost much of its native agility; its eyes no longer had the same acuity; and yet, it was on him that communal security relied. That's because the old ape had the experience that permitted him to distinguish the fortuitous and innocent approach of a traveler from the veritable danger of hunters. In the same way, our arbiters, grown old in harness, will give voice, perhaps less brilliantly, to far more solid arguments. Our enemies have understood that so well that they've appointed centenarians."

"What about the English? And the Russians?" asked Petitpaon.

"The English have similarly sought among the remotest ancestors. As for the Russians, the age of their Grand Dukes isn't counted by the number of their years but the favor they enjoy with the Tsar. The arbiters of the other Powers are all at least nonagenarians."

"In that case, you've chosen well," Petitpaon approved. "I'll finally be able to contemplate my work on a stage-set worthy of it." And suddenly, as if he were taking a great resolution, he declared in a profound voice: "I want to witness the battle in person."

"What, you, Monsieur le Président? A civilian? To see the fire, it's necessary to be military..."

"I can wear a uniform as well as anyone else."

"You don't have the right to get yourself killed!"

"Who mentioned getting myself killed, my dear General? I would have that right if I sought to use it, but I know my duty to France too well to go into combat, seeking the possibility of a death that is only natural for a soldier. I simply want to be a spectator, to taste the joy of the artist before the creation of his brain and his genius. I shall leave tomorrow to join the main body of the army. Ask Verbuis to notify the German government of the purely esthetic character of my presence on the terrain of hostilities..."

"Your departure might provoke troubles in Paris," Croppeton reasoned, feeling close to vertigo at the idea of being deprived of the comforting tutor that Bernard Petitpaon was to him. In vain he cited the danger of cholera. The President of the Republic replied, with a good deal of justification, that the disease was as rife in Paris, and he left the next day for Valenciennes, where gigantic military honors were rendered to him by three million soldiers.

It was the twentieth of December. The cold prevented the digging of graves for the countless victims of cholera, but the physicians were sure that the frozen cadavers would not enter into putrefaction, and that, in consequence, there was no danger in leaving them exposed for some time on the ground.

New alarms arriving from the army of the Rhine, which feared being surrounded, begged the generalissimo of the French forces to move forward as rapidly as possible, while it fell back toward Belgium, pushing before it German corps derived of any hope of retreat.

The international arbiters had established their headquarters in the vicinity of Wavre, which was the almost certain point of the imminent encounter.[21]

---

[21] Wavre was the location of a battle fought simultaneously with Waterloo, in which Maréchal Grouchy engaged retreating Prussian troops. Afterthought suggested that if he had disobeyed the order he had received to do that and taken his troops to Waterloo instead (the gunfire of which was audible) Napoléon would probably have won.

The French, with Bernard Petitpaon at their head—who confessed that he was more emotional than he had been when the curtain went up at the first performance of *Cincinnatus*—reached Nivelles on the twenty-fifth of December.

The advance guard stopped in order to rally the laggards, and resumed its march the following day.

"It's hotting up! It's hotting up!" repeated Petitpaon nervously, his teeth chattering with cold and emotion.

In fact, the enemy and almost captive forces were installed on the plateau of Mont Saint-Jean, facing up to French detachments that had retreated before the compact mass of four million Germans.

"It really is the battle of Waterloo recommencing!" said Bernard Petitpaon, on horseback alongside the commander-in-chief.

Spies signaled the departure of the bulk of the German army from Ottignies, where it had been camped for forty-eight hours.

According to the most plausible predictions, battle would be engaged on the twenty-eighth or twenty-ninth of December.

Bernard Petitpaon, seething with ardor, wanted the forces to get to grips as soon as possible, because he was impatient to return to Paris, his arms full of laurels. The strategy for which the high command assumed responsibility resisted any desire for precipitation, and preferred to accumulate to the French side all the advantages resulting from the application of the most savant and most sure methods of combat.

On the morning of the twenty-ninth of December, a Tuesday—the day of Mars, the god of war[22]—curious skirmishes began the action, under the marveling eyes of Petitpaon and those of the arbiters, a dozen and a half of whom had decided to go up in a tethered balloon. From the height of that incomparable observatory, the slightest detail could not escape them.

---

[22] In France, Tuesday is *mardi*.

In the two camps, the cannons began to thunder furiously. The balloon's gondola danced on the aerial waves raised by
the uninterrupted commotions, but the arbiters, conscious of
the importance of their role, remained heroically at their post,
aiming with great dexterity at the key points of the battle the
objective lenses of photographic apparatus designed to record
documents that would become extremely precious if disputes
emerged in the course of the regulation of losses.

Night fell and became black so rapidly that the arbiters
were unable to agree on the exact positions of the belligerents,
several units of which, having come into overly intimate contact, were confused without distinction of nationality.

At La Haye Sainte,[23] the French and Germans were prepared to bivouac pell-mell in the fraternity of a similar fatigue
and an equal hunger when, from the heights of Mont-Saint-
Jean, a gigantic light sprung forth over the plain. Cannon reo-
pened fire noisily. Powerful electric searchlights had been put
in service by the German army at the beginning of the campaign, which were able to make the darkest night into clear
enough day to guide the fire of cannons over a distance of
several kilometers.

The German and Austrian arbiters, along with the secret
partisans of our enemies, could not retain a cry of joy, for that
maneuver assured their arms an indisputable advantage. The
French arbiters had a moment of anguish, quickly passed. A
cloud of complete opacity surged from the ground, raising a
curtain of unbreachable darkness between the two armies.

The German artillerymen, afraid of firing on their own
brothers, ceased fire.

The nocturnal truce being ensured, this time, since the
French had responded with shadow to the attempted illumina-

---

[23] A walled farmhouse that became a crucial position during
the battle of Waterloo, over which Napoléon and Wellington
fought ferociously. Troops led by Maréchal Ney eventually
took it, but too late; the final attack launched therefrom was
beaten back and the battle lost.

tion of the enemy, the arbiters returned to the ground to file their documents and observations and take a well-merited rest.

The next day, at dawn, the battle recommenced with a new ardor.

At dusk, the arbiters held a rapid council in their gondola. By a unanimous decision, they declared the battle finished and ordered the immediate cessation of hostilities.

Bernard Petitpaon immediately returned to Paris.

A complicated and delicate work of accountancy commenced. The general staffs of the two armies were invited to furnish statements of men and munitions before and after the battle, with supporting evidence. The arbiters, installed at the Belle Alliance,[24] devoted the entire month of January to their operations, while cholera claimed forty thousand victims a day in each camp.

On the first of February, by unanimous accord, they fixed the number of the dead at four millions, to be equally shared between the two armies, and the figure of the wounded at five million, also equally divided between the French and the Germans.

The arbiters had, therefore, done things on a grand scale. To reduce the duration of the drawing of lots to a minimum, it was agreed that each serial number drawn out of the urn should be applicable to all the regiments taking part in the action.

Two canteen-girls, one French and one German, of virtue guaranteed by seals placed on them at the beginning of the campaign, represented hazard with their innocent hands.

The first numbers drawn in each camp created an absolutely unforeseen complication. The majority of the designated

---

[24] The inn that was Napoléon's headquarters during the battle, where he and Blücher met to signify its end. Blücher wanted to call the battle the Battle of the Belle Alliance, but Wellington, who had spent the last night of the battle in the village of Waterloo, insisted that it should be the winner's command post, not the loser's, that had the honor in question.

dead really had been reduced to the state of cadavers by chol-era. Ought they or ought they not to be counted in the number of the four million dead?

The drawing of lots was suspended in order to take ad-vice from the arbiters, who declared unanimously that in order to die, even theoretically, it was necessary to exist. It was therefore necessary to continue the designations until the totals of two million dead were attained in each army.

The canteen-girls went back to work. Untiringly, they drew small pieces of paper folded in four from the urns. After three weeks they stopped; there were still a great many slips in the urns, but there no longer remained a single man to call "Present!" at the appeal of any serial number whatsoever.

The accountants had only been able to register eighteen hundred thousand designated dead men in each camp. It was therefore necessary not to have any wounded at all. Adding in the effects of the cholera, there was a total figure of three mil-lion four hundred thousand soldiers that it was necessary to take away. The civilian populations in France and Germany had been so rudely tested by the scourge that entire provinces were almost completely depopulated.

As the first days of March arrived, the armies broke up to return to their respective countries.

XX

France and Germany were thus obliged, as the interna-tional treaties required, to lay down their arms.

The Germans had begun to pile up in the fields rifles, sa-bers and revolvers, when the rumor ran around that the French, in spite of the orders of their officers, were refusing to do the same. They said that they needed them to defend them-selves, and the unfortunates, maddened by the cholera that was creating enormous gaps in their ranks, did not understand that their weapons could do nothing against the disease.

The Germans picked up their rifles, sabers and revolvers again, and got ready to return to their own country in good order, without a word of anger against the cholera, which had not spare them either.

The return of the French army resembled a formidable rout. In complete confusion, the regiments fled, aimlessly and hopelessly, full of the invasive horror or oblivion, driven by the instinctive need to distance themselves from the victims who fell by the thousand on the road. Irritation, muted and contained at first, soon burst forth. Threats were made by the soldiers against their leaders, whom they held responsible for all their troubles.

While the German army allowed itself to be guided passively to isolation camps, the French Government had conceived the plan of embarking all the soldiers whose despair was to be feared on warships at Le Havre. A sea cruise might perhaps impede the propagation of cholera through France, and, in any case, would remove the danger of a possible revolt.

The plan remained secret, because the generals feared a mutiny by the troops. As the advance guard approached Le Havre, however, it was necessary to make the embarkation order known. The officers took infinite precautions. They talked about the maternal solicitude of the Republic. They tried to demonstrate that it was a measure indispensable to halt the giant progress of the cholera that was threatening to make France into a desert.

A long murmur went up. Cries rang out: "Treason! Treason! The Government wants to throw us in the sea! To Paris! To Paris!"

In less than an hour, it was the entire army—the twelve hundred thousand survivors—that was repeating like maniacs: "To Paris! To Paris!"

No human force could have contained those men, convinced that their leaders were slyly sending them to their death. In a formidable surge, the cavalry at the head, the army marched on Paris, blindly driven toward the city where the masters of the Republic were—who, they believed, could save or doom them in accordance with their whim.

Populations fled before that whirlwind, which destroyed everything in its passage.

As soon as they became known in Paris, these events provoked a frightful panic. All those who could flee, abandoning the sick and the helpless, loaded up their most precious wealth and set off at hazard for the Midi.

Panicked, General Croppeton and his colleagues raced to the Élysée to beg Bernard Petitpaon to save the situation.

Violent recriminations were proffered against the malign destiny that had struck with sleeping sickness the thirty-four thousand well-armed men who would have been able, by a brutal and sudden intervention, strike a great blow against the enfevered imagination of the revenants of Waterloo, who were no more than three days' march from Paris.

Bernard Petitpaon proposed to set himself at the head of the Ministers and go to meet the soldiers, who, in his opinion, were more to be pitied than blamed.

"That would be madness!" cried General Croppeton. "We'd be marching to certain death, and in the present circumstances, we don't have the right to yield to the attractions of a beautiful gesture! To get ourselves massacred would be an unpardonable crime!"

"But we won't be massacred!" Petitpaon protested. "Those unfortunates are worthy men driven astray by suffering! I'll talk to them! I'll explain to them that it isn't the Government's fault that cholera has tested them so cruelly and that they've died for the fatherland. I'll tell them that France considers them the best of her children and will take such good care of them that they'll soon forget their status as dead men!"

And Bernard Petitpaon, warming up, launched into an improvisation that underlined his unique qualities as a Statesman.

"We'll create three hundred thousand new collection agencies; four hundred thousand tobacconists or subsidiary post offices; a million posts in the civil service, from which the heirs of the victims of the war will be able to choose. We'll centuple the duties with which we complicate the tax system in order to ensure work for the assessors and collectors; we'll improved administrative mechanisms vastly in order to provide a perfect justification for the humblest of posts—for what it's necessary to avoid is that the State might be suspected of granting the slightest salary without demanding serious and assiduous work in return. Under the Republic, a citizen ought not to be one of those pensioners, whether rich or starving, that have been the shame of monarchies. The honor of all is the dignity of each. The wellbeing of the dead will be ensured by the labor of the living, and France will continue to march on the road of glorious liberty and beneficent progress!

"New needs require new institutions; we'll found a Ministry that will supervise the dead in the slightest detail of their material and moral life. And Messieurs, why shouldn't we authorize these victims of Petitpaon warfare to group together in a vast association, as ancient combatants once did? Do you think that if we go to announce to these soldiers, whose very names must leave no further official trace, that the Government of the Republic will grant them a civil personality, that they won't cheer us, and that we won't reenter Paris in triumph, carried on their shoulders?"

After having protested his personal bravery for a second time, General Croppeton persisted in believing that it would be the most elementary wisdom to barricade themselves in as solidly as possible and await events, of which he did not augur anything good.

Bernard Petitpaon still required to be persuaded, but he ended up yielding to Croppeton's reasoning, while the latter repeated mechanically: "Oh, if the Africans would only wake up! If the Africans would only wake up!"

Everything that Paris possessed of police agents, municipal guards and men susceptible of being out in uniform was requisitioned and placed around the Élysée.

On the twenty-fifth of March several squadrons of cavalry entered Versailles. They called a halt there, firstly in order to rest and secondly to await the rest of the army, which had already been reduced to less than half a million men.

In all the quarters of Paris, fear gave rise to bloody disorder. In the same way that the vertigo of nothingness leads the sick to commit suicide, the fear of danger drives men to kill one another. With the imminent arrival of the army came the threat of cholera and in order to escape it, many people sought death in the battles they fought against one another night and day with ferocious savagery, turning the streets and squares into charnel houses.

The Chambres, fearful of popular fury, were no longer sitting; the majority of senators and députés were carefully concealing their identity. In the best-informed milieux it was said that Abbé Mortol was undertaking a retreat with the Archbishop whose exemplary piety ought to bring France back to divine compassion.

Only Louis Méripal continued to live in the open, without trying to hide his person or his ideas from anyone. He threw himself into the most violent riots, not to strike blows but to try to dissipate the delirium that was transforming men of the calmest and most placid humor into crazed brutes.

On the evening of the second of April, in the Grenelle quarter, he interposed himself between two bands of fanatics who were each accusing the other of wanting to provoke troubles with an inadmissible aim. Horribly mutilated bodies were trailing their debris along the roadway.

Méripal pronounced words of peace and love: "Why not love one another, brothers whom terror has driven apart?"

Cries of "Kill him! Kill him!" replied

A young man clad in a smock and blue overalls launched himself forward to seize him by the throat. "You too are a traitor to the people's cause! You too have deceived us, Citizen Méripal! It's in order to drink our blood that you want to prevent us from shedding it as we like! Our blood belongs to us, Citizen Méripal! You shan't drink it! No, you shan't drink it, you miserable traitor!"

A fight began. Méripal attempted to escape from the grip of his attacker; he received a formidable blow from a club on the head and collapsed. A melee broke out between the men and the women who all wanted to strike him. A woman tried to put out his eyes with a crochet hook. She howled that Méripal was the cause of all the troubles that had occurred and that it was necessary to punish him for insulting God. Three times the iron stem was on the brink of plunging into his orbit; three times it was deflected by the jostling—and the woman, returning to the charge, vociferated further insults and further threats.

Finally, he fainted, and when he recovered consciousness he was alone in the darkness.

Instinctively, he stood up. Slowly, he wiped away the blood that was running down his forehead. He tried to walk; his legs could hardly carry him. Leaning on the walls of houses, staggering like a drunkard, he drew away without knowing where he was going.

XXI

Swollen by the bleaching dawn, the veils of night floated, refreshing the Earth.

In his agonized flesh, Méripal shivered. His breast rose slowly, very slowly, as if the morning air were penetrating into it without any summons issuing therefrom.

His crossed arms, trying to rejoin his body, trailed on the ground. His hands, with groping fingers, came to clutch at his throat, which they seized with a convulsive movement, as if to rip it and make the renascent breath of life enter more rapidly.

Abruptly, his eyelids opened, uncovering his eyes, which filled with light that was vanquishing, one by one, the fleecy clouds remaining on the horizon.

At each of the gasps that distended his jaws in long yawns, his breathing became deeper and more regular.

Forerunners of consciousness, which was returning as the daylight whitened, tremors ran over his body.

Suddenly, out of the cloud, like a cup overflowing, sunlight appeared in a pale gold foam, streaming over the face of the moribund.

His frightened eyes remained fixed momentarily, and then began blinking in a rapid flutter.

Instinctively, his hands rose up to protect them, but they fell back, inert, on his forehead, reopening the wound crusted with a black clot.

The blood began to flow again, reddening his hands, which, in an abrupt movement, extended forwards at the end of stiff arms.

The sun shone upon them, filtering in dark red darts between the bloody fingers.

Perhaps without seeing them, Méripal looked at them; they clapped together; a few drops of blood fell on his face, which contracted. His lips came together as if to attempt to articulate a few words, while his arms, vanquished in their effort, fell back alongside his body.

To flee the assaults of the sun, his head inclined on to his right arm, and suddenly, with a great surge, his left arm described the arc of a circle, dragging the body with it, which lay down on that side.

Méripal remained immobile for a long time. He seemed to be asleep when he folded up his elongated legs and, bracing himself on his elbows and knees, he made an effort to get up. His head fell back heavily. He began again, and then again, still in vain, but his obscure desire ended up triumphing over his weakness; he propped himself up in a sitting position, his arms extended backwards supporting his body, slightly inclined backwards.

Consciousness of life returned to him. Several times, he drew in large draughts of air, and gazed fixedly at the sun rising in a fiery flood over the horizon.

He leaned forward; he rested his hands on his knees; only then did he perceive the blood with which they were covered.

Suddenly, the memory of the atrocious scene surged forth: the savage aggression of the crowd whose fury he had tried to calm; and so much sadness penetrated him that he no longer thought about his wounds and forgot the dolors of his body, bruised all over.

He wept, and his tears, running down his cheeks, swept away the clots of blood stuck to his beard.

Words came to his lips, translating distant thoughts.

"The people didn't hear my voice. They didn't understand my words. They accused me of lying and imposture. I talked to them about love and generosity; they replied with hatred and ferocity. I told them that all men are brothers and that nothing ought to divide them; they rushed at me and struck me, uttering cries of rage.

"Why don't they hear my voice? Why don't they understand my words? Why do they accuse me of lying and imposture? But I haven't lied! I'm not guilty of imposture, though!

"The imprecations of that woman are still resonating in my head. She tried to put my eyes out with a crochet-hook, howling that I'd offended God and was the cause of all the misfortunes. She struck my furiously in the name of that Jesus who also died for having said things that weren't understood...

"Every new dawn is a shroud for the man who divines it and is the first to proclaim it: those who don't see it treat as a criminal the prophet whose gaze is clearer and whose thought is freer...

"In the subsequent course of time, the chimera becomes a reality: the dawn illuminates the Earth with its full clarity; by then, forgetfulness has taken the name of the precursor of the radiant day. His memory, sometimes, doesn't die entirely, and it's as a god that people adore him...why doesn't humankind have faith in itself? Why don't people have confidence in people? Why must life always be soiled by hatred and lies? It would be so beautiful, in the splendor of the sunlight!"

Louis Méripal, his face raised in the flood of light, remained in ecstasy.

Suddenly, he looked around fearfully, as if he were searching for something. He put himself on his knees and, turning round, placed his ear against a bronze door.

He listened, trying to define the sounds that he could hear.

The heavy panels drew apart.

In order not to fall into the gap that opened before him, Méripal placed both his hands on the ground with the fingers splayed.

An extraordinary spectacle appeared to him. Against a background of helmets and breastplates, gold and steel, which the sun lit up with a great flamboyance, stood a jet black horse mounted by a general in full dress uniform. Two men, a priest in a soutane and an old man with long white side-whiskers, were holding the bridle of the horse to either side

Louis Méripal uttered a cry. It was General Foiraubilles, framed by Abbé Mortol and the banker Hermann Coffre.

The three individuals exchanged a few words.

The Abbé let go of the bridle of the horse and, brandishing the heavy iron cross he was holding in his right hand, said: "Ride over the body of this wretch! It's Méripal! Louis Méripal, the murderer, the revolutionary, the atheist! Forward, General! Crush him! Crush him! The blood of the enemies of religion is agreeable to God!"

Hermann Coffre, his hat in his hand, had stood aside in order to put himself out of range of the kicks of the horse, unnerved by the sound of bugles.

General Foiraubilles, his sword naked, high in his right fist, spurred his horse violently, which bounded sideways. With thrusts of his spurs he drove it forward.

In vain, Lois Méripal had tried to get up; on his knees, he had instinctively extended his arms forwards. The horse came right up to the man and abruptly, ears pricked and limbs stiff, stopped in order to sniff the obstacle; its quivering nostrils shot warm breath into Méripal's face.

General Foiraubilles made an appeal with energetic legs. The beast reared up, and, as if it were afraid of falling on the man kneeling on the ground directly under its fetlocks, it recoiled, insensible to the spurs that were streaming with blood.

The horse's defenses triumphed over the brutal will of the rider, who was nearly thrown out of the red velvet saddle several times. Pale and panting, he stiffened his legs convulsively against the foam-flecked flanks.

Doubtless to exteriorize and intimate prayer, Abbé Mortol made the sign of the cross and approached Méripal, gripping the heavy crucifix by its extremity.

His eyes staring, widened by the horror of his impotent weakness, Louis Méripal begged: "Don't kill me! Don't kill me!"

The grim voice of Abbé Mortol proffered, three times: "God wills it! God wills it! God wills it!"

The heavy cross fell with a dull thud on Méripal's skull. He fell backwards.

Abbé Mortol went back to General Foiraubilles, seized the bridle of the horse and brought it back to Méripal's cadaver, which Herman Coffre was trampling furiously. The general's horse cleared the inert body of Louis Méripal in a single bound.

The trumpets and bugles burst forth loudly.

On that radiant spring morning, the African army, miraculously extracted from its slumber, emerged from the Grand Palais under the guidance of Abbé Mortol and Hermann Coffre in order to reestablish order in Paris and put an end to the regime that had permitted itself to raise its voice, in the name of wicked liberty, and that of Louis Méripal, of whom it would have been impossible to rediscover the slightest trace after his corpse had been trampled by the feet of thirty-four thousand soldiers.

XXII

Between soldiers, as between the remainder of men, dangers run in company create tight and powerful bonds. The individuals who have simultaneously seen the mask of an identical death are mutually smitten by a fraternal amity.

Thus, the African army, woken up at the same moment from the same sleep, which might have been the last for them, formed a kind of great family united by a blind affection, external to any idea of discipline.

No one was able to say exactly what had happened.

All the efforts of the physicians had failed; the most bizarre cares had been lavished, but the terrible trypanosome of the *mtoga*, or sleeping sickness, had done its work. It had penetrated into the cerebrospinal fluid of the unfortunates, who had nothing left to do but die, science being only able, at the most, to soften their agony.

Abbé Mortol had convinced Hermann Coffre to accompany him to the Grand Palais to attempt a supreme maneuver: divine intervention.

The banker only had a very relative confidence in God, but Abbé Mortol had given proof of sovereign skill so many times that Monsieur Coffre allowed himself to believe that he might achieve the awakening of the African army so ardently desired by the partisans of public order.

Very advantageously known to the guards and the men of the rescue services on duty at the Grand Palais, Abbé Mortol and Herman Coffre had installed themselves alone at General Foiraubilles' bedside on the evening of the first of April. Until midnight, the Abbé had remained at prayer, the collar of his overcoat raised against the chill, for the moon's rays, on limpid nights like the one on which the scene unfolded, illuminate but do not warm. Herman Coffre privately offered God the sacrifice of a certain number of his millions if he would deign to render life to the brave men of whom there was such an urgent need.

The fervor of the prayer and the sincere promise of the handsome sum remained vain. The General did not budge.

Discouraged, the two men began talking in whispers, Coffre begging the Abbé to find a means, to try again, making the firm offer of a hundred million francs to subsidize the work of piety.

Until dawn appeared they invoked all the horrors of the situation, with its frightful consequences: for Coffre, ruination; for the Abbé, the annihilation of religion.

After one last exhortation from Coffre, the Abbé leaned over the General's breast.

"His heart's beating!" Slowly, he repeated the hopeful words: "His heart's beating!" Then, as if gripped by a sudden folly, he started shaking the inert body furiously and crying out: "Get up, General! Get up! God wills it! God wills it!"

An enormous oath emerged from the general's throat.

Frightened by that resurrection, the two colleagues threw themselves off the stage.

General Foiraubilles rolled his frightened eyes around him and, getting out of bed, shouted in a loud voice: "It's getting light! On your feet, everyone! Bugles, sound the reveille!"

Abbé Mortol and Hermann Coffre had fallen to their knees and were weeping frantically.

A bugle sounded a vibrant appeal under the metallic vaults with panes of glass, instantly repeated by a hundred more.

In a matter of minutes, in the midst of a gigantic hubbub punctuated by the whinnying of horses, which had also woken up, the regiments formed up in accordance with the order indicated by the processions of different weapons.

Abbé Mortol took the bridle of the horse caparisoned in red and gold, respectfully held by a soldier of the logistics corps, and presented it to General Foiraubilles.

The general, the priest and the banker undertook a brief and intimate conference, at the exit from which Narcisse de Foiraubilles set his foot in the stirrup held by Hermann Coffre and hoisted himself on to his horse.

A brief command had made the heavy bronze battens pivot on their hinges, revealing the lamentable wreck of Louis Méripal's body.

The arrival at the Élysées was not at all tragic. Bernard Petitpaon having not yet got up, Abbé Mortol and Hermann Coffre penetrated into his bedroom, followed by a platoon of zouaves.

Invited to resign his functions immediately, the President initially declared that he preferred immediate death.

"You've chosen a bad time to steal liberty! This morning, in my person, the Republic has woken up with an intense thirst for martyrdom. Before your injunctions and your threats, this head, as you can see, will not bow! Cut it off! It will fall with an ineffable patriotic joy! Shed my blood! It will put on your hands the ineradicable stains of the most universal of deluges. Plunge into my breast, identified with that of the Republic, those bayonets drawn at the same time from their sheaths and the path of duty! Kill me! Kill me, then!"

In response to a second demand made in a curt voice by Abbé Mortol, Bernard Petitpaon recalled grandiloquently the services that he had rendered to France.

"I am the man who has put on the wound of war the dressing of my marvelous conception! Thanks to me, men can measure themselves against one another in total security! Ingratitude cannot be my recompense!"

"All that's theater!" put in Monsieur Coffre, shaking his head.

After a third summons followed by a "Take aim!" that leveled a dozen rifles against him, Petitpaon had a complete change of mind; he quit his bed in the capacity of a simple citizen, entirely won over to the new states of affairs, by which General Marquis Narcisse de Foiraubilles became Emperor of the French, under the name of Narcisse I.

The days that followed were devoted to a repression that was severe and bloody. Eight hundred thousand men, not counting women and children, were massacred in Paris and the great cities of France alone.

The greater part of the army returned from Belgium had joined the African soldiers and all of them formed a guard around Narcisse I, of an incomparable devotion and heroism.

God, as a humble servant of all financial and religious interests, lent a very visible hand to that imperial instauration by putting an abrupt end to the cholera epidemic.

In response to his the plea of his daughter, whose heart had remained faithful to Alexandre Sylphe, the captain had been released from prison. Provided with the title of Prince, in the midst of the enthusiastic manifestations of a people glad to have found a brutal and magnificent master again, he led the heir to the throne of France to the altar of the metropolitan church of Notre-Dame.

Abbé Mortol and Monsieur Coffre were witnesses to the marriage, in the company of representatives of the royal families of Europe.

In the cortege, Madame Coffre appeared on the arm of an officer in the navy, from the bosom of which she was now recruiting her admirers.

The celebrations lavished to solemnize these events terminated with a gala performance at the Lyrique Grand-Mondial, at the head of which, by express imperial command, Bernard Petitpaon had been placed again.

In accordance with tradition, the director of the Lyrique Grand-Mondial had to receive the Head of State with his fists charged with two silver chandeliers with seven branches.

Bernard Petitpaon did not fail in his duty, and the figure he cut as a porter of the symbolic flames, at the foot of the great staircase of marble and gold, must have satisfied the Emperor fully, for he immediately placed around his neck the sash of the Ordre du Narcisse, which he had just created.

Thus the Petitpaon Era came to a close.

As it was the first of September, its third year, to the day, had just come around. Like all failed trials, Bernard Petitpaon's attempt had run into yet another complication in the difficult problem of world peace.

MIELLUNE

Enclosed today in a narrow circle of mountains, the small town of Miellune[25] once rose up in the center of a plain that extended cultivated fields, meadows and woods around it, all the way to its horizons.

In a remote epoch, abolished from human memory, in the middle of the night, a mighty clap of thunder disturbed the slumber of the inhabitants.

In spite of the cold, windows were precipitately opened, and in their frames, filled with the hesitant gleam of night-lights, wan apparitions surged forth: the heads of men, wrapped in handkerchiefs knotted at the four corners, or coiffed in conical bonnets terminating in a tassel whose weight caused it to angle in front of frowning foreheads; the heads of women with bushy hair, which hands moved away from faces, or carefully braided into plaits wound around skulls in tight spirals.

In the distance, at irregular but brief intervals, muffled detonations succeeded one another, and the houses shook on their foundations.

Through the darkness of the streets, instant interrogations were launched, to which similar interrogations responded.

The season did not permit the explanation of a storm. All the ridiculous human forms that had invaded the windows, attempting to take account of what was happening, were fixed in a tragic immobility.

---

[25] Nowadays, when used as a common noun, *miellune* signifies "honeymoon." In 1908, however, that term had not yet been imported into French with a meaning equivalent to its English significance, so its use here as the name of a town was an improvisation.

Suddenly, a sinister cry, emerging from the top of a tall house, denounced a conflagration. Immediately, the same cry emerged from every mouth, proclaiming the name of fire in tones of fear and resignation.

The questions became more specific, rising from floor to floor all the way to the roofs, where, through narrow skylights, heads devoid of bodies seemed to emerge from walls. The names of all the neighboring towns were uttered successively by those whose elevated position invested them, in such circumstances, with the role of sentinels.

Then the citizens, habituated to not missing any opportunity to give proof of courage and devotion, and the functionaries, professionally obliged to demonstrate their zeal, got dressed precipitately, lending a distracted ears to the exhortations to prudence lavished by their wives, frightened of being left alone but nevertheless flattered by the thought that, the following day, the newspapers would glorify the conduct of heroes whose names they had the honor of bearing.

Soon, the "Saviors of Miellune," obedient to an ancient command, found themselves gathered in the main square of the town. There they awaited the arrival of their leaders, delayed by the donning of regulation uniforms, accompanied by numerous complicated accessories.

Exercising the authority conferred upon them by a silver salamander embroidered on a dark cap, one of the latecomers proceeded with a roll call of the Saviors of Miellune, lined up in two rows. After having traced a few figures in a notebook, he went to join a small group formed of men similarly dressed in dark caps decorated with a silver salamander.

An animated discussion began, which died away on the appearance, on the far side of the square, of a black horse, led on a bridle by a man carrying a smoky torch. It was the commandant's mount.

The latter did not take long to appear, his eyes full of sleep, widened in an expression of comical anger against the evil hazard that had constrained him to dress precipitately in the green dolman with the garish golden Brandenburg fasteners, which his numb fingers had not yet succeeded in doing up.

At his approach, all hands, with an automatic rigid movement, bore their thumbs directly to the salamanders of the caps. The commandant suspended the battle of his fingers against the fastenings of his dolman momentarily and returned the salute of his men, whose hands immediately fell back into the row.

Taking turns, descending through the ranks, each of the officers rendered an account of the mission incumbent on him by virtue of the laws and regulations in vigor. The chief approved with a nod of the head or uttered a kind of grunt that seemed to cover the officer's obsequiousness with confusion.

These explanations furnished, the commandant let slip an oath directed at his Brandenburgs, obstinate in not hooking on to the metal clips, and ordered a maneuver. Twenty men went into the house in front of which they were arrayed, and soon emerged again, having opened a large coaching entrance, dragging and pushing a large coat laden with ropes, hoses and engines of various kinds, all useful in conflagrations.

A stool was brought forward with great precaution. The commandant was hoisted up on to his horse, still held by the man with the smoky torch.

After having imposed silence on an officer who seemed to want to inform him as to the probable location of the fire, with a grand gesture of his right arm, prolonged by a light sword, the commandant indicated the direction to take. The troop of Saviors of Miellune moved off, escorted at a respectful distance by a variegated troop. Poor wretches barely covered in thin garments surged like phantoms out of the shadows where the police had forced them to hide; merrymakers enveloped in furs came out of establishments consecrated to nocturnal pleasures, streaming with light.

The gates of the town were soon crossed, revealing a terrifying spectacle: on the horizon, in broad sheets, flamboyant clouds were rising, aspired by the darkness in which they were lost, clearing the way for new clouds, which launched forth in their wake in a vertiginous whirlwind.

The detonations redoubled in violence; as his horse was showing increasingly frequent signs of agitation, the commandant of the Saviors of Miellune, judging it unnecessary to risk a fall in such critical circumstances, dismounted.

He was giving orders for a detachment of men to depart on reconnaissance when the appeals of voices arrived, borne by distant echoes.

The commandant, his two arms extended, instructed everyone to maintain the strictest silence, and while the simple Saviors in the ranks held their breath, the officers tormented their ears with their gloved hands, directing them in the direction from which the sounds seemed to be coming.

A young lieutenant leaned toward his chief, murmuring a few words in a very low voice, accompanied by an indication given by his extended arm. The old man made a gesture of incredulous astonishment; then, as if enlightened by a sudden vision, extending his own arm in the direction determined by his subaltern, he said: "You can never tell where a sound is coming from. It's quite simple, though. A noise always follows a parabola from the place where it is emitted to the place where it is perceived. You're at one of the two points; it isn't difficult to find the other. Lieutenant!" With severity, he addressed a young officer whose cap was ornamented by the silver salamander. "...Assuming that the cries you perceive emerge from human throats at a velocity of four hundred meters a second, which is the scientifically established mean, how far away are the people uttering those desperate appeals in our direction?"

The lieutenant lowered his head to reflect and took out his chronometer. Then, timidly, in order not to allow by lack of a response a new and brutal interrogation, he said: "Three kilometers, Commandant."

"With lungs like yours, that's possible. When I was your age, I had a voice that could be heard distinctly five kilometers away."

"But that voice has never cried 'Help!'" the lieutenant replies, respectfully.

"Who, me? Cry 'Help!' You haven't looked at me, then, Lieutenant? Know that..."

But a lamentable fit of coughing shook the larynx from which formidable sounds had once emerged. The commandant tried several times to inform the lieutenant of what his excessive youth did not know, but before the flamboyant gusts that were unfurling a wall of fire on the horizon in gigantic bounds, he interrupted himself in order to observe: "But that's not a fire!"

And as if his words were an expected signal, the cries, now very close, launched distinct exclamations: "Hell is overflowing! Flee! Flee! The Earth is burning! Flee! Flee!"

An entire cohort of men and women came to collide with the Saviors of Miellune.

Those poor creatures, crazed, with incomprehensible words punctuated with gasps that shook their throats, contracted by terror, implored aid and assistance. To the questions that were addressed to them they replied which strident cries of fright, extending their arms behind their heads, which they dared not turn for fear of being further assailed by the nightmare they were fleeing.

Eventually, the commandant, using all his authority, succeeded in extracting a few explanations from the unfortunate fugitives. He learned that a catastrophe had just reduced Fleursat, the charming neighbor of Miellune, to a mass of ruins. The Earth had risen up in the midst of a formidable din and flames had sprung forth from gaping crevices, reducing anything that came into contact with them to ash.

The commandant, understanding the gravity of the situation and judging an intervention on his part futile, gave the order to return to Miellune in order to put himself at the disposal of the governor.

The latter, in full uniform, was waiting in the main square for the return of scouts that he had sent forth in all directions.

He listened to the story of the swallowing of Fleursat from the commandant's mouth.

One by one, the scouts returned; each of them, at a similar distance from the gates, had seen a wall of flame looming up ahead of him.

The governor, in whom the responsibility of the situation and the measures to be taken was incumbent, slowly turned around several times as if in search of inspiration from the ruddy circle of clouds.

A long time of immobile reflection having passed, with a grand gesture, he made the heroic decision to return to his palace.

Surrounded by his principal functionaries, he made his way through the crowd, whose members were shouting naïve supplications in his direction, so powerful, in times of danger, is the prestige of the great men whose role, it seems, is to protect from the elements themselves the humble folk bound defenselessly to the yoke of passive obedience.

Men and women rubbing shoulders in the square, at the hazard of the only veritably spontaneous fraternal equality devoid of any hidden agenda, which is the consciousness of common peril, kept their eyes fixed invincibly on the windows of the Council Chamber, as if the bright patches with which the black façade of the monument was holed had the power to calm their anxiety.

Out of respect for their masters, whose will was the only thing that could ensure their salvation, the inhabitants of Miellune were waiting in bleak silence when the sky suddenly brightened, invaded by floods of molten metal.

Livid beneath these incandescent reflections, faces contracted into frightful grimaces; from all throats, gripped by a similar peril, the same cry escaped, inarticulate in its sinister tone.

Traversed by a sudden subconscious thought, those people, calm and confident until then, rushed to assault the broad marble perron that led to the palace.

Bodies were crushed against the bronze doors, immutable under the furious pressure.

Among heart-rending appeal from the wounded, there were invectives of revolt and hatred against those behind the walls, who had abandoned the people to their misery.

Stones were thrown angrily at the windows, the broken glass of which fell on skulls from which blood flowed.

The unfortunates, not knowing who to blame for the frightful destiny, began fighting one another, striking mortal blows.

A window opened on a first floor balcony. Its frame of light filed with a tall silhouette. Immediately, the crowd became still and silent.

The nearest had recognized the governor; an acclamation saluted him. All arms were extended toward him.

In a slow and forceful voice, he spoke.

"Inhabitants of Miellune, you whose name has become a synonym for courage and steadfastness, will you fail your blood? The combined forces of the entire universe, raised against you, would be powerless to move you, but you are going to tremble before events that are still inexplicable? It is not death that you fear, I know; it is the mystery that troubles you—the mystery that the night will hide for a few more hours. Have patience; the day will come..."

"And what if the day doesn't come?" shouted a shrill voice from the crowd.

"If they day doesn't come?" the governor repeated, uncomprehendingly.

"Yes! What if we perish in darkness, without ever seeing the sun again?" the voice went on.

"But that's impossible! That cannot be! I swear to you that it's impossible," the governor affirmed.

"Why is it impossible?" questioned the obstinate challenger.

Not wanting to compromise his authority in perilous arguments, the Statesman vehemently denounced the criminal behavior of the prophet of doom.

"By what right do you accuse then sun of turning away from us? Are you, then, party to the secrets of destiny? You know, however, that talking about death brings it closer! Beware! If Miellune has some misfortune to deplore tomorrow, the cadavers will rise up to curse you! You are a public danger!"

"We're all going to perish! It's the end of the world!" howled the voice, repeating the words in a tragic lamentation, soon drowned out by cries of: "To death! To death!" which surged from the foot of the balcony on which the governor was waving his arms desperately.

A formidable turbulence stirred the crowd, excited by a furious need for murder. "To death! To death!" howled a thousand throats, strangled by fear, and while the governor prudently disappeared, a frightful melee broke out in the square, traversed by savage vociferations and brief cries of pain.

The flames seemed less ardent now; their summits stood out in gray arabesques dancing high in the sky, streaked in places by light transparent patches.

Those who had not yet been felled by their wounds were attacking one another too furiously to notice the gradual emergence of daylight. They did not even hear the loud blasts of trumpets sounding the charge. Without seeking to flee, they tumbled pell-mell beneath the hooves of horses.

It was the Miellune Guard clearing the square. Sabers stabbed bodies lying on the ground and were then lifted up, bloodied, in the fists of the riders.

A fanfare of trumpets brought the troop to form up in front of the façade of the palace. The officers circled the square on their whinnying horses, whose nostrils were flaring at the odor of blood.

The order had been carried out. There were a few wounded, still capable of movement, to be finished off, and then the governor could come out of his palace in total security

Indeed, he appeared at the top of the perron. After having displayed signs of violent irritation against the cadavers, he summoned the officers, to whom he distributed curt orders.

Each of them, taking a few cavalrymen with him, departed in a different direction.

It was a matter of ascertaining, in the fullest and most precise detail, the effects of the cataclysm, in order to discover its cause and combat it with appropriate weapons.

A few hours later, as the midday sun was shining vertically down on Miellune, the officers set foot on the bottom of the perron one by one and went into the palace anxiously.

All of them had recorded similar observations in their notebooks, which they read in turn to the Supreme Council, chaired by the Governor, now clad in a flamboyant red and gold uniform.

At a distance of even kilometers, all around the center of the town, marked by the palace, an uninterrupted line of craters was launching torrents of fire.

"We're cut off from the rest of the world!" observed the governor, with a gesture of despair, which he immediately repressed in order to ask: "What is the nature of this fire?"

"Of a burning nature, Governor!" replied the longest-serving of the high-ranking officers.

And although the carefully-gathered explanations all indicated ingenious and subtle minds, none could provide the slightest clarification.

The officers were asked to withdraw in order to permit the Council to deliberate in secret.

A scientific discussion was immediately engaged between two famous geologists. One affirmed on his honor as a scientist that only volcanoes could vomit forth fire like that; the other swore to his great gods that the fire in question was descending from the sky in an invisible form to rebound on impact with the earth in terrifying sprays.

They went on thereafter to envisage, hypothetically, the possible consequences of the facts, whose mysterious cause did not exclude the alarming reality. The physician who was the Director of Social Conservation summarized them in a few neat and brief sentences.

"Firstly, Miellune might be destroyed by burial under the lava and various materials projected from the craters." He cited the example of several towns disappeared in that fashion in various epochs of the world.

"Secondly, assuming that the first danger is averted, Miellune is threatened by being burned at a distance by the simple radiance of the flames." Calculations, hasty but established on the most serious bases, demonstrated the possibility of this atrocious alternative with exactitude.

"Thirdly, if the volcanoes only launch flames and imponderable fumes and the radiant heat, by reason of the distance from the source of various obstacles susceptible of interrupting its ardor, is tolerable, we're separated from the rest of the world, and consequently condemned to die of starvation after an interval of variable duration."

They argued for a long time for and against each of these three hypotheses, supported in such learned fashion.

The third, adjourning death, naturally rallied the unanimity of votes, and a triple salvo of applause greeted the governor's conclusions, as reasonable as they were optimistic:

"It's certain that the volcanoes only possess a temporary activity. Our duty is, therefore, to make every effort to gain time. By employing all our strength, we shall act as a prudent administration and be equally worthy of the fatherland and ourselves."

When the consoling enthusiasm had died down, the governor said: "It's necessary now to think about the people and make provision against the violence that they are sure to direct against us and against one another, if we give them the leisure."

"All disorder requires severe repression!" declared an apoplectic old man, whose moustache had whitened on the battlefield. "Thus, last night, we should have calmed the crowd with cannons."

"The cavalry didn't spare a single one of the demonstrators," the governor observed.

"Perhaps so," the implacable soldier continued—without provoking the slightest emotion, an exclamation of "Murderer!" was uttered by a thin and grim individual sitting at the extremity of the table—"but dying is nothing; everything is in the manner of being killed. Cannons have moralizing effects on a population to which men cannot lay claim, even mounted on horses and armed with sabers. With regard to civilians, a charge is almost a brawl. A salvo of artillery is an execution. That's a nuance of which it's salutary not to lose sight."

"I agree," the governor acquiesced, laconically. "Now, let's proceed with celerity, and in an orderly manner. What should we do first?"

"Pray," said a soft voice to the governor's right.

The Bishop of Miellune was a little old man, trembling all over in his quilted coat, carefully buttoned over his violet soutane. All eyes turned toward him.

"It's necessary to pray to the Lord and thank him for having deigned to render possible the expiation of our sins..."

"Miellune is counting on you. Pray for her," said the governor, deferentially. "Permit us, my lord, to devote the present moment to more urgent decision..."

"They have my blessing in advance," the prelate promised.

"In order not to die, it's necessary to live, and to live, it's necessary to eat," the Director of Social Conservation advanced, authoritatively.

"That's indispensable," approved the whole assembly, in chorus.

"For a lapse of time whose duration we can't determine, we'll have to count entirely on the provisions of food presently existing in Miellune. The most elementary prudence commands the requisitioning of everything, to the last grain of wheat. Everything that has nutritive value will be locked in warehouses placed under strict guard. Under the supervision of the administration, on a daily basis, each person will be allocated the amount strictly necessary to his alimentation; I propose that the ration should be proportionate to the weight of the beneficiary."

"In the name of equality, I protest!" said the emaciated interrupter from the extreme left, rising to his feet. "I represent the people! I will not fail in my duty! I protest!"

The most scientific considerations militate in favor of my proposal," the orator continued, coldly. "It's obvious that a tall fat man requires more nourishment than a small thin one. The most conclusive experiments have proved..."

"What you're not saying," the demagogue cut in, "is that your experiments would also have proved that with equal nourishment the fat would get thinner and we, the thin, would get fatter. What! A unique opportunity has presented itself to arrive at the equality that you state to be the goal of your dreams and your efforts, and you intended to perpetuate that age-old injustice?"

"To each according to his needs," pronounced the governor sententiously.

"Exactly!" snapped the hot-heated egalitarian. "But in the name of liberty and justice you ought to let each person judge his needs. Enough talk of acquired rights that are nothing but the criminal consecration of iniquities and spoliations! Thus, I, whom am thin because I've never been able to eat enough to sate my hunger, even in the womb, my mother being too poor..."

"The asceticism of your person is the secret of your empire over the people!" someone put in. "It's necessary to be thin in order to speak on behalf of the emaciated."

"The emaciated are more respectable than the stout!"

"We have the same respect for both," said the governor. "It's a matter of deciding whether the distribution of food to the inhabitants will be made per head or in proportion to their weight."

"It's necessary to adopt the most economical policy," opined one Council member.

"It's still us, the children on the people, who are going to pay for the rich!" said the flag-bearer of social equilibrium, indignantly.

"Charity won't lose any of its rights. All prayers will be said gratuitously," insinuated the Bishop, whose frail voice was lost in the vehement and bitter argument.

"Let the partisans of the *per capita* regime raise their hands," the governor pronounced.

All hands were raised in a movement of perfect unanimity.

"Which doesn't alter the fact that the rich are still the rich," groaned the champion of pauperism, not completely satisfied by the integral adoption of his proposal.

"I put to the vote the following motion," the governor continued. "The members of the Supreme Council may have delivered to them personally the quantities of food that they judge appropriate..."

"I invite the Council to address to the Governor the expression of their gratitude for that idea, whose wisdom and fecund consequences we all appreciate," put in a zealous supporter of the ruling power. "We have assumed the responsibility of public affairs. We owe it to Miellune! Let us make an engagement of honor to nourish ourselves well. Impotence of the brain always leads to the debilitation of the body. Let us remain strong in the face of destiny!"

Periods of bold lyricism were proffered in the midst of general enthusiasm. It seemed that sight had been lost of the reality of the facts when the representative of the sacrificed classes demanded, on their behalf, posters by means of which the people would be enlightened as to what was happening.

A proclamation was therefore drafted in which appeal was made to the energy and self-composure of everyone. Emphasis was placed on the eminently temporary character of the situation. The governor promised honorific distinctions to those who made themselves illustrious by their zeal and devotion.

The Bishop asked to signal the gratuity of prayers, which was granted to him.

"What about the requisition of foodstuffs?" someone asked.

"It's better not to make any allusion to that," the governor opined. "Dissimulations are numerous enough in the advertisement."

"The people have a right to know everything—we have a duty not to hide anything from them," protested the champion of plebeian interests. "When do you intend to carry out the requisitions?"

"Immediately! All the operations will be concluded by tomorrow morning," declared the governor.

"Well, then," concluded the demagogue, "have no fear of announcing the requisitions frankly and honestly, but make arrangements for the posters not to be made public until tomorrow. Thus, the people won't be able to complain and the general interest will be safeguarded."

This idea, deemed to be ingenious, was adopted without any discussion.

The session had been long and laborious. The governor declared it lifted. The members of the Council left the palace to return to their respective domiciles. As much because of the prestige with which they had an obligation to surround themselves as the fear of ever-possible aggression, they had themselves escorted by armed soldiers.

In the distance, in the fading daylight, the sinister glare of the flames increased. With that, the anguish appeased by the sight of the sun returned.

On all sides, cries went up, isolated at first and then grouped. As on the previous night, the crowd instinctively flocked toward the governor's palace.

Soldiers were blocking the streets opening into the square. They resisted he human flood as best they could. Under the pressure, their ranks opened, unmasking cannons, whose work was as terrible as it was rapid.

In the meantime, in the deserted houses, the requisitors removed everything that appeared to them to be edible. The terror was so intense that no one had even thought about hiding their provisions.

As the governor had promised, by dawn, the administrative warehouse contained everything in Miellune that could be suspected of having the slightest nutritional value.

The second appearance of the sun installed in the most pessimistic hearts the definitive hope of life.

Sensations and sentiments carry the seeds of their own reaction, which is manifest sooner or later, in proportion to their exaggeration.

In the town, shaken a few hours earlier as if by the effects of a frightful agony, there was an explosion of delirious joy.

To give themselves courage, those who were still trembling began to heap derision on the volcanoes, terrible only by virtue of the complicity of the night. Some mocked the ephemeral nature of their activity, and everyone ended up observing the decrease of the eruption.

The first posters were put up in the midst of a lively movement of curiosity; their reading provoked ironic shrugs of the shoulders and pitying smiles, so much did their content seem to be in tune with public enthusiasm.

That enthusiasm left no room for the most timid protest against the requisitioning of food, which terror had prevented from attracting attention.

Musicians had the idea of going to fetch their instruments, and, singing to the accompaniment of catchy marches, crowds headed for the warehouses where the first distribution was to take place.

Rich and poor received equal rations eaten by all with similar appetite.

In the square and the streets, under the tender gaze of parents, dancing caused the daughters of the people to swoon in the arms of young representatives of the aristocracy, while opulent heiresses blushed at the unprecedented pleasure of feeling themselves frankly pressed against plebeian breasts.

With nightfall, a vague anxiety came to brush many minds again, but on that third night, in order to humiliate the volcanoes and render them ridiculous, it was decided to bring forward the magnificent firework display promised for the imminent festival of Miellune's foundation.

Roman candles crackled, nailing fugitive stars in the sky; sunbursts rotated vertiginously, to the applause of the delighted crowd, which launched implausible threats at the volcanoes. Meanwhile, existence reasserted another of its rights; egotism, which is its most general and most absolute manifestation, immediately showed itself under the cover of preoccupations of a material order.

The authorities were asked whether all possible measures had been taken to achieve the best employment of objects of alimentation. Questions multiplied seeking to determine the time for which nourishment was assured.

Demands were not long in being made, formulated by those who now declared themselves to be the victims of the requisitions. To these complaints of spoliation the governor turned a deaf ear.

Then, some people offered to buy food with their money. That trafficking could not be officially sanctioned. Nevertheless, a very active commerce was established between the poor, who sold the best part of their rations, only keeping just enough to prevent them from dying of starvation, and the rich, who hid those provisions in the most secret locations in their houses.

The mechanism of social life, momentarily interrupted, resumed its march, driven by all the motives derivative of human nature or born of needs acquired by several centuries passed in a state of advanced civilization.

Hierarchy reformed of its own accord. Imperious characters, who commanded because they liked to be in command, recovered their ascendancy over the weak and the humble, seemingly grateful to those who were saving them the trouble of regulating their own activity.

The terror of the first hours and the releases of the intoxication of being alive had caused religion to be completely forgotten. The words of priests resumed falling from the height of pulpits in violent anathemas against Miellune, which, by its impiety and misconduct, had attracted punishment. Prayers and penances were ordered, to which everyone submitted, some by virtue of authentic faith, others out of vague fear of a possible and perhaps omnipotent God.

During one of the Bishop's sermons, snow began to fall in thick flakes. The prelate immediately proclaimed it as undeniable proof of celestial intervention. Meekly, the crowd proclaimed the miracle, and gave a harsh beating to an impious individual who insisted that the meteorological phenomenon, frequent enough in winter, was entirely natural.

As if revitalized by a second youth, the administration manifested itself in a recrudescence of fastidious zeal with regard to the public.

Impediments to the satisfaction of a desire fortify that desire with the effort expended in triumphing over those impediments. It is thus that fiancés, in order to obtain the celebration of their union, see their tenderness increased by the multiple steps and formalities necessitated by the application of rules whose origin has long been buried in sanitary forgetfulness.

The quotidian routines of existence functioned with all the regularity desirable by the adherents of the distinctive virtues of banal and puerile sociability obligatory in all small towns.

The incessant inevitable contacts that everyone suffers and no one can avoid were aided by the homeopathic remedy of mundane duties—visits, balls, meetings held on the pretext of propagandistic or charitable efforts and all the other servitudes that relieve human beings, however careless of their reputation, of the most fugitive particle of corporeal and moral liberty.

In salons, unified by the fashions of the day, conversations manifested their habitual scorn for subjects demanding some attention and were consecrated to the thousand trivia that fill, to the point of obstruction, the butterfly minds of chattering ladies whose husbands resemble dull and colorless fowlers.

While the masters were killing time and exchanging the most malevolent remarks with regard to one another, the domestics devoted themselves lazily to their duties, full of satisfaction when, in the evenings, they had hermetically closed the shutters behind which one could forget the volcanoes, whose flames were no longer visible.

Although the governor had reduced the rations, the food-supplies were running low. All the horses had been eaten, with the exception of those ensuring military or administrative function. The authorities had already foreseen their imminent diminution. A committee examined the entitlements of each one; some owed a temporary salvation to the protectors they had the honor of pulling or carrying. As the exigencies were becoming more pressing, the judges became more pitilessly rigorous, and soon, there were no horses left in Miellune but the governor's. The whole town was familiar with them: covered with cloths embroidered with Miellune's coat-of-arms they wandered along the boulevards, led on the bridle by pikemen; thin and hungry, while all heads were bared as they passed by, they extended avid lips toward the low branches of the trees, which were beginning to come into bud.

Forty days had passed since the terrible night; they had thus arrived in the month of March. The certainty of an imminent end to present misery caused the privations to be supported without overmuch complaint. Fine words and the threat of a few hours in prison sufficed to calm irritated individuals capable of disturbing public order.

One morning, a rumor ran around Miellune, which posters immediately confirmed and specified. The authorities informed the population that enough food remained for another forty-five days, and in consequence, the last distribution would be carried out at midday on the thirtieth of April.

Hope is like those birds that cross seas. Their flight is so forceful that, to them, it seems that the air is aiding their effort. Suddenly, in the calm of the clouds, the bird stops falls like an inert mass into the waves. It is because fatigue has gradually overtake it. Every wing-beat has used up a little energy, and in the air, one point of resistance similar to all the rest has sufficed to vanquish the exhausted organism.

Thus human beings go, supported by the dreams that animate their thoughts, careless of the obstacles whose debris interrupts the monotony of the route, abridging the difficulty and the tedium. Their brisk stride, certain of the promised end, suddenly buckles; the travelers roll in the dust, inert. Reality, with a slow and painless bite, has eaten away the hope, and it has died, charging frail shoulders with an excessively heavy weight.

The government's laconic warning, even though people were prepared for it and in spite of the forty-five day respite it contained, toppled the edifice built by the interest of living, and massively reinforced by hypotheses and deductions.

While some protested against the brutality of the communication, others criticized administrative negligence. What was Miellune if not a town besieged? Why had no one attempted to get through the ring of fire? Glorious sieges were recalled in which heroes had traversed enemy lines surely more perilous than that of the volcanoes.

Fathers of families called upon the devotion of bachelors whose right to exist was doubtless less undeniable than their own, the fact of not being officially recorded with a wife and children being a social crime.

The love of sacrifice flourishes in a soul without it being possible to identify its seed, and it is not the thirst for glory and appetite for recompense that drive individuals to action whose glamour increases with their temerity. Scorn for life seems to be a normal reaction to the fear of dying. In an atmosphere paled by cowardice, reckless courage is born like a star in the night.

Appeals to sentiments of pride and vanity, the promises of enormous sums and extraordinary distinctions, the engagements of priests reserved places of honor in the other world for those who would risk their lives for common salvation, did not find the slightest echo.

The people demanded the official designation by the drawing of lots of one of the soldiers whose blood belong to the fatherland by contract. The governor acquiesced.

The reluctant hero was a hussar, who immediately advanced his quality as a cavalier to decline any pedestrian mission. The military code being formal on that point, there could be no thought, according to the most authorized jurists, of violating one of its most essential articles. The hussar was, therefore, entirely assured as to his fate when a councilor with an ingenious mind found the legal solution to the quandary.

"Since he's a cavalier, let's give him a horse!"

The palace stables only had four remaining. The others had been slaughtered in order to be eaten a few hours before the maladies caused by the progressive starvation to which they had been subjected had consummated their natural death.

The governor had more than affection for the survivors; being part of the dignity of his responsibility, they were a large fraction of himself. He could not, however, withhold them from the patriotic objective that was about to be pursued by the hussar, perhaps fatally.

According to humans, animals do not enjoy free will; their destiny can only be determined by blind chance. In consequence, a committee was formed to elect the most qualified charger. After several laborious sessions, the question of the coat was declared to be the most important of all, and without discussion, the committee-members voted for a burnt chestnut on which the reflection of the flames had the most beautiful effect.

In accordance with the calendar officially adopted, which counted down the time remaining until the thirtieth of April, it was on day thirty-three that the first sortie was attempted.

The hussar had put on his dress uniform. Before climbing into the saddle he received, along with the governor's accolade, the rarest and most envied insignia of decoration. His colonel embraced him as if he were his own son, after having, moved by a very paternal solicitude, emptied the regulation cartridges, the contents of which risked explosion on contact with the fire.

The twelve strokes of midday were sounding as the cortege, composed of all the functionaries and citizens of note, moved off, to the vibrant and disorderly strains of multiple bands, to leave the town. The entire population, in a compact double hedge, acclaimed the imminent hero, whose vague eyes gazed ten paces ahead, in conformity with the theory of his armaments.

A young woman, struck by a thunderbolt, ran forward, braving the reactions of the horse, and, seizing one of the rider's legs—which nearly tipped him out of the saddle—pressed it frantically to her heart, crying that no other man would be her husband.

Close by, a couple was weeping tenderly; they were the sudden fiancée's father and mother. They counted among Miellune's wealthiest; they had amassed an enormous fortune in the transformation of the mortal envelopes of rabbits and other furred and feathered animals into hats, muffs and sumptuary objects as useless as they were varied.

Several years before, Philémon Sphéroboul had abandoned the effective management of Sphéroboul & Co., in which he nevertheless conserved major interests. The time that was left to him by his concern with the fine fare that had made him the arbiter of all culinary difficulties, and the satisfaction of his penchant for the fine wines and varied liqueurs that he consumed on a daily basis to the point of the least discreet inebriation, he devoted to imagining extravagant fashions that he attempted to launch, to the undissimulated joy of his fellow citizens.

Naturally, he enjoyed an incomparable popularity, but the solemnity of the moment prevented anyone from paying any attention to him.

A captain disengaged the hussar's leg as gallantly as he could, whereupon the young woman went to join her tears to those of her authors.

Slowly, they marched toward the furnace, whose radiation increased to the pint of not permitting another forward step.

The governor addressed a few words to the hussar, whose head was turning back continually toward Miellune.

The Bishop also spoke to him, on behalf of omnipotent God, and made him bend down to kiss the amethyst in his ring.

Trumpets sounded the charge. The horse emitted a long whinny; the neck-cloth extended over its bristling mane, its eyes bloodshot and its nostrils flared, it launched forward with an abrupt surge on its hamstrings, and it set off at a furious gallop, further exasperated by its rider's spurs as is legs instinctively tightened about the animal's flanks.

Time has the value one gives it. At that speed, the time required to reach the furnace could not have surpassed fifty seconds, but it was centuries that detailed their duration for the spectators of that patriotic enterprise.

Instead of shrinking in accordance with the laws of perspective, the man and the horse were magnified as they drew away.

Suddenly, the giant group came to a stop. The animal, whose ardent cost was streaming with a hectic glare, bucked several times, projecting a fantastic silhouette on the fiery sky. Arms widespread, the rider fell to the ground; his mount, relieved of all servitude, disappeared into the flames with a mighty leap.

The hussar got up, spun around several times, tottering, and, as fast as his legs could carry him, stiffened as they were by tight leather trousers, started running toward the crowd, whose amazement as such that it opened to let him pass.

He was waving his arms in front of his face as if to ward off danger. His moustache and hair had been singed; his garments were smoking. In a hoarse voice he cried: "Where is she? I want to see her! Where is she?"

The poor devil was remembering the young woman who, a few moments before, had spontaneously offered him her heart. She had probably forgotten him already. His haggard eyes perceived her and, without anyone thinking of stopping him, he threw himself upon her and hugged her in his arms.

The parents intervened. Impotent to extract the young woman from that wild embrace, they tried to arouse the crowd against the hussar, denouncing the indignity of his conduct, accusing him of desertion, of having voluntarily separated himself from his horse in order to bring trouble and dishonor into the best family in Miellune.

Philémon Sphéroboul displayed, beneath the turned up brim of the octagonal top hat that he was about to make fashionable, a broad moon-shaped face crimson with irritation—all that remained approximately human in his person—along with an implausibly developed belly, behind which, buckled by effort, short legs were splayed to describe a polygon of insufficient support. The neck had disappeared; the arms could not move away from the trunk save for the elbows and the hands, with stout red fingers, emerging with difficulty from sleeves sealed by large shiny cufflinks.

From his body, coated with an obscene and triumphant lard, a nasal voice emerged: "I am Philémon Sphéroboul, the guide and servant of the world of fashion..."

Booing greeted these words, and cries of "Down with Sphéroboul!"

One member of the audience, with a gesture of defiance directed at the howling crowd, placed a hand on Sphéroboul's shoulder, in order to show solidarity with him. He was tall, thin and twisted, as if he had passed through a fantastic rolling-mill. His face was sad and pale, dotted with a few yellow hairs. In imitation of his future father-in-law, he wore an octagonal top hat, which a blow from a cane knocked to the ground, exposing a dull, wrinkled cranium afflicted by a sickly baldness, edged by a thin demi-crown of hairs separated from one another as if by a repulsive force. The individual's ugliness tended to the prodigious.

His name was Percepointe. The dead languages he taught seemed to have caused all the usual appearances of life to flee from his person. Bleakly, he inclined his angular silhouette over Sphéroboul like a giant heron looming over an enormous pumpkin.

Folantin Percepointe had been engaged to Jenny Sphéroboul for several years. The marriage had not taken place, delayed by multiple mournings, as can occur in families as numerous as those of the Percepointes and Sphérobouls. In any case, unlike most young women, Jenny was in no hurry to savor the joys of marriage, and whenever Folantin, at the moment he judged propitious during the two hours of his implacably quotidian courtship, indulged himself in a gesture translating his sentiments, he received a magisterial slap in the face, for which the mother of the bourgeois Amazon apologized with heartbreaking tears.

The physician of the two families had declared in vain that the nature of the Sphérobouls, predisposed to plumpness, would be very fortunately corrected by the gaunt temperament of the Percepointes; Jenny, with all the piquancy of the brunette grace of her twenty years, dreamed of a husband less ingrately edified and more expert at amorous talk in the Miellunese language, the only living one so far as she was concerned.

The cavalier, corseted in azure and helmet in gold, going forth on a magnificent horse the color of fire to the heroic adventure of deliverance, had dazzled the heiress of the Sphérobouls. In order to protect Folantin Percepointe, her parents, had been careful not to take Jenny's inflamed gesture seriously—according to them, it was merely further evidence of an adorable heart ready for sacrifice.

Now the soldier had come back, after a fall that had dragged the best of Miellune's hops down with it—and it was that man, incapable of staying on a horse, who had the impudence to embrace the daughter of Philémon Sphéroboul, the former head of the house of Sphéroboul, the foremost in the city! Was there no longer any justice, then?

The lame lady in question arrived under the auspices of a captain leading a squad of gendarmes. The hussar was apprehended, tied up and taken before the governor, who gave the order to lock him up in anticipation of a court martial.

Philémon Sphéroboul had recaptured his daughter. She administered two slaps to Folantin Percepointe, whose cheeks happened to be in the vicinity of her hand.

That family tragicomedy had not advanced public affairs. The people were demanding violently, for a new attempt, the three horses that remained in the palace stables. After much argument, the governor ordered that they should be brought. An hour later, the palfreys were presented, bridled and saddled. The governor was about to proceed with a triple drawing of lots when a very moving scene occurred.

Abandoning the tails of his frock-coat to the Sphérobouls, who were trying to hold him back, Folantin Percepointe demanded the honor of mounting one of the horses. He did so with nobility ad simplicity, his eyes turned toward his fiancée.

Doubting the equestrian talents of the professor of dead languages, the governor refused his offer, but the crowd, transported by that gesture of abnegation, offered Folantin Percepointe a long ovation, before the significance of which it was prudent to bow.

Two young men, electrified by Percepointe's example, ran forward to complete the trio of heroes to whom Miellune was about to confide its last three horses.

It was decided not to sacrifice them simultaneously. In spite of his pleas, Folantin Percepointe was kept for the supreme effort, if that one still remained necessary.

The first two failed. One after the other, the riders were unsaddled when they reached the line of fire. Unluckier than the hussar, however, they were unable to get up; their bodies agitated briefly, crackling like hot parchment, then stiffened and no longer moved.

The frightened horses, their flanks beaten by the stirrups, had continued their course.

Folantin Percepointe's role assumed a dramatic capital importance. Fully conscious of his responsibility and intent on pleasing his fiancée, he had put on a hussar's uniform. The undershoes of his overly short trousers extended over his ankles; his dolman floated around his body, and his helmet rested on his ears, maintained by a short chin-strap whose blackness cut through the saffron-speckled collar of his beard.

Sincere eyes do not stop at external appearances. No one saw the grotesque aspects of that caricaturish figure. The whole crowd doffed their hats to Folantin Percepointe.

After having embraced his present and future parents, transformed into fountains of tears, and making a supreme bow to offer his life to Jenny—who, with a finger in her mouth, was too absorbed by distant thoughts to notice his gesture—he climbed on to his mount, evoking an image of instantaneously-growing ivy.

The piebald horse seemed to suspect what was expected of it. It departed at a stolen pace, progressively elongating its stride to a trot, reserving the gallop until the last hundred meters.

Contemptuous of all esthetics, Percepointe had let go of the reins in order to attach both hands to the pommel of the saddle. His upper body oscillated in acrobatic disequilibrium. His trousers, the undershoes having snapped, left his wading-bird legs bare above the feet adorned with brilliant spurs.

But an equestrian miracle was about to burst forth; man and horse disappeared, making a breach in the flamboyant wall that immediately closed up again.

They had got out of Miellune!

A cry of joy resounded; they would come back with news of the outside world! Communications had been reestablished. Miellune had vanquished its isolation.

The idea did not occur to anyone that Percepointe and his mount might have perished in the flames.

It was, therefore, only necessary to await their return.

Night fell, rendering the volcanoes their terrifying aspect. The governor suggested that the population return to Miellune. He set the example, leaving two men on guard with orders to send word as soon as Percepointe appeared.

The night passed, and then the following day, followed by another night, and then another day, and so on, until the calendar marked day three—which meant that three times twenty-four hours had still to elapse before the thirtieth of April.

A panic broke out, which threw outside the town a crazed host of men and women carrying their children. That stampede, in which the strong trampled the weak in the attempt to gain a few places, raced headlong into the blaze. The upright bodies sizzled momentarily and fell, blackened and unrecognizable.

In the meantime, in Miellune, prudent and sage individuals demanded an energetic intervention by the governor.

An attempt was made to construct a balloon. It rose up a hundred meters and fell back. A stupid circle surrounded the nacelle, the wicker of which allowed a few shreds of the mangled body of the pilot to leak through its mesh.

Supplicant appeals implored Percepointe not to abandon Miellune.

A madman ran through the streets stopping the clocks, which he accused of causing time to move on.

The final distribution of food was solemnly made. The Bishop had insisted on sanctifying it with a benediction susceptible of summoning divine attention to the absolute necessity of a miraculous renewal of the exhausted supplies.

The prodigal consumed their ration immediately in ostentatious haste; the miserly carried theirs home without bringing it to their mouths; children cried out to their mothers, who wept at the thought of the morrow, when the poor little ones would reach out in vain.

The physicians had organized meetings in order to popularize scientific means of combating starvation. It was necessary to avoid any unnecessary expenditure of energy in order to lower vital consumption to a minimum. They cited the example of marmots, whose total abstention from nourishment could last several months, thanks to a complete immobility in a dark and tightly enclosed space.

Entire families made themselves cozy in their bedrooms in order to attempt to hibernate.

As the physicians affirmed that an organism can live on its reserves until the loss of half its body weight, the fat excited a sentiment of envy mingled with admiration.

Philémon Sphéroboul, whose adipose development had attained proportions unknown among the most fortunate of his fellow citizens, became the object of a respect pushed to idolatry; everyone knew that he would be the last survivor. His person became an object of pilgrimage; people came to contemplate him installed in the depths of an armchair, his two hands placed over his abdomen in a pious gesture, as if to testify his affectionate gratitude to it.

At first Sphéroboul had seemed touched by these marks of consideration, vengeance for the jokes and gibes formerly addressed to his overly advantageous form. Soon, however, he began to dread becoming an object of public jealousy stretched to the point of changing into violent hatred. He lowered the blinds behind his windows in order to render himself invisible, and no longer left his house.

Three days passed; to save them from the further tortures of hunger, mothers strangled their children before committing suicide. Victims of hanging were swinging from the gibbets of street-lights; wells filled up to the brim with the bodies of those who had a preference for asphyxia. All methods of suicide were employed, from poison to jumping from monuments.

On the fourth day, a considerable crowd gathered outside Sphéroboul's house. The latter, imagining that the return of his future son-in-law was the reason for the demonstration, got up and appeared on the sidewalk.

Arms, vigorous in spite of the enforced diet to which their owners had been subjected, took possession of him. Seized by a convulsive trembling, he stammered supplications: "Don't hurt me! It's not my fault that I'm fat! Don't eat me, I beg you! Don't eat me!"

Arms hoisted him up on to shoulders. Utterly terrified by the thought of being transformed into victuals, he begged for mercy, without hearing anything. In the meantime, it was explained to his wife, already bewailing the grief of her widowhood, that in a few minutes, she would be saluted with the name of Empress, the unanimous will of Miellune being to proclaim Philémon Sphéroboul, marked by God with all the signs of preeminence, Emperor.

The crowd carried the improvised emperor all the way to the palace, where the governor received him with multiple marks of the most humble administrative deference, under the menacing gaze of the leader of the public procession.

Philémon Sphéroboul, still too overwhelmed to make use of his tongue, paraded a long fugitive gaze around him. When his heartbeat had slowed down somewhat, he was able to articulate a few words in a muffled voice pierced with an intense satisfaction.

"I'm not going to be eaten, then?"

"To eat its master, its Emperor, would constitute a crime of which even a tribe of cannibals would not render itself guilty," the governor replied, curving his back at an exceedingly acute angle. With manifestations of infinite respect, he begged His Majesty to deign to follow him.

Sphéroboul, completely reassured as to the outcome of the adventure, followed in his footsteps, traversing a series of solemnly decorated rooms.

They arrived via a narrow corridor at a wall, which opened under the pressure of a small instrument that the governor handed to Sphéroboul, terrified to enter the darkness of the subterranean tunnel gaping before him.

With a gesture of the most fervent loyalism, the servant, still completely devoted to the master of the moment, yielded to him the secret of the State reserves, which he alone knew.

There were varied provisions there for several years. By the light of a small lamp, the governed presented them to Sphéroboul. The later contemplated them for a long time with the affection of someone rediscovering beings very dear to him. His hand caressed devotionally the tawny hams and the marmoreal slabs of lard sparkling with grains of salt. His gaze pierced earthenware terrines and tins concealing succulent conserves. He could scent the perfume of truffles dormant in the bosom of *foie gras* so clearly that his salivary glands swelled up in order to blossom generously over the precious imagined alimentary bolus.

Still ignorant of the elementary rules of protocol, and entirely subservient to his emotion, which suddenly caused his role to seem endowed with perfect authenticity, he hugged the governor to him, trying to kiss his cheeks, but his excessive abdominal preeminence prevented him from realizing that osculatory manifestation.

He apologized for that in a flood of speech into which the governor was scarcely able to insert a few comments at respectful intervals.

"You Majesty might well have the prudence to have his table set up here. I beg him to accord me the signal favor of serving him.

Philémon Sphéroboul protested and, remembering that he was a good husband and father, said: "No, no! You'll sit down with us! My wife and my daughter..."

"Long live the Empress and the Princess!" The governor bowed deeply.

"...Will take care of the cuisine; that's their job!" Sphéroboul declared, simply, and then proposed: "Shall we have a bite to eat?"

"May Your Majesty's desire be granted!" said the governor, uncovering a little table with a single place-setting.

"Sit with me—I demanded it!" ordered Sphéroboul, whose eyes were shining with imminent gastronomic satisfaction.

"Out of obedience," the governor acquiesced, unhooking a ham, which joined packets of biscuits and several bottles of old wine in front of the Emperor.

Fasting is an infallible aperitif. The one endured by Sphéroboul had developed an already-powerful appetite to improbable proportions. The imperial guest ate frenziedly, with all the elasticity of his violently distended jaws, imparting a few admiring words at intervals, when his mouth was not absolutely full.

"Astonishing!... Superior!.... Exquisite!... Divine ham!... Glory!... Pickles!... Unique biscuits! Perfect!... Wine?... Nectar!... Velvet!... Eternal poem!... Eat!... Eat!... Veritable joy!... Life is nothing without eating and drinking!... I owe you happiness!... Thank you!... Thank you!"

"Your Majesty is too kind," the governor protested, amazed by that ingestive verve.

"Thank you!... Thank you!" burbled Sphéroboul, whose congested face took on the appearance of a stop sign. He demanded pâtés, more ham, absorbed the contents of several tins, complained of the excessively reduced format of the biscuits, and, after emptying another bottle, stopped, panting, with just enough breath left to confess that he felt better, in a tone of the utmost sincerity.

"Would Your Majesty deign to think about his coronation?" asked the governor.

"No," admitted Philémon Sphéroboul, with no false shame. "I'm entirely devoted to my digestion."

"May it be kind to You Majesty!" the governor wished.

"It will be!" exhaled Sphéroboul, closing his eyes. With his two hands placed on is abdomen in an expression of infinite gratitude in his own regard, he went to sleep, invaded by the wellbeing that only boas among the animals and fervent gastronomes among humans are able to savor fully.

The governor could only respect his master's torpor. A shrewd courtier, he thought about the awakening, and with a thousand precautions he placed a cup full of odorous liquid on a table. The imperial nostrils quivered. The eyelids rose imperceptibly. Devotedly, hands picked up the cup, brought it to the lips, and Sphéroboul, tilting back his head, drained it with the piety of a priest emptying the sacred chalice.

The governor took advantage of that to utter a deferential "Sire," which attracted a muffled reply.

"What? What? My name is Sphéroboul, Philémon Sphéroboul…I'm a merchant, a rich merchant…"

The governor had to call upon all the force of his eloquence to make his interlocutors grasp the status of Emperor to which the will of the people had raised him.

"What an excellent idea!" Sphéroboul approved, incontinently naming as prime minister the man he knew as such a magnificent Amphitryon. And his intoxication, emerging from the period of somnolence, agitated grandiloquent gestures, accompanied by speeches of an entirely unprecedented imperialism.

"My people will rejoice in my happiness. They will echo all my joys. Those who complain will be judged as criminals, because I don't want anyone to be miserable. Let's drink to the health of the people!"

And, matching action to words, he poured himself a generous draught, which he swallowed with a sonorous cluck of pleasure. The prime minister thought it a good opportunity to talk about the coronation. Sphéroboul ordered an immediate celebration. In a few picturesque phrases he settled the features that seemed most important to his hallucinated brain.

"I don't need ceremonial garb. My pearl-gray trousers are brand new. My white waistcoat is fashionable and my frock-coat unstained. My octagonal top hat will be a revelation for all of Miellune! The Bishop will do the rest. Follow me, my dear Prime Minister."

The laws of equilibrium are indulgent to corpulent drunkards. His center of gravity remaining faithful in spite of a few wobbles, Philémon Sphéroboul went back along the narrow corridor and through the entire series of solemnly decorated rooms. When he arrived in the main hall, where he recognized his wife and daughter sitting in two armchairs, behind which the functionaries and most important people of the town were standing, he waved his hat, shouting with all the force of his lungs: "Vive Miellune!"

A formidable acclamation: "Vive Philémon!" replied to him.

"Let the people in!" he ordered.

The ushers opened the doors. The crowd rushed into the room, where only a small free space remained around the stage supporting the red armchair destined for the emperor.

The latter demanded assistance to climb the steps. Short of breath, hiccupping, he spoke, expectorating his optimistic and tenacious will.

"My people will rejoice in my happiness. They will echo all my joys. Those who complain will be judged as criminals, because I don't want anyone to be miserable..."

"Sire, I beg you, don't let my poor children die of hunger!" sobbed a woman, dragging herself on her knees to the foot of the stage.

"Your children won't die!" Sphéroboul affirmed, without the slightest hesitation.

A triple salvo of applause burst forth, resounding with: "Long live Philémon I!"

Excited, Sphéroboul continued: "You won't die either! We aren't going to die! No one will die! Down with death! Long live life!"

Infected by the Bacchic delirium, the transported crowd repeated: "Down with death! Long live life! Long live the Emperor!"

The Bishop presented a vast crown to the latter. Sphéroboul took it, and, with an august gesture, put it over his hat. He demanded a cane, which he began to twirl with the grace of a drum-major's apprentice.

"I want, as a gift of my joyous advent, to marry my daughter this very day."

"You're forgetting, Philémon, that Monsieur Folantin Percepointe hasn't yet returned," put in Madame Sphéroboul, while Jenny made gesture of protest.

"I hope that he doesn't come back!" declared the Emperor, in whom thoughts induced by the wine incited forgiveness of weaknesses of the heart. "The Princess will marry for love!" Turning to an officer whose sleeves were braided with stripes, he said: "I'll give the hussar who made my daughter's heart beat the title and rank of Duke of Miellune. Go fetch him, and after having dressed him in an appropriate uniform, bring him here. The Bishop will bless the union right away. I have spoken!"

The Sphéroboul ladies embraced tearfully—tears of dread on the part of the mother, anxiously wondering how this improbable escapade was going to end, and tears of joy on the part of the young woman, blushing at the idea of becoming a Duchess as well as a wife.

The ceremony only lasted a few minutes. The hussar rolled his frightened eyes and begged for mercy. The extravagant scene seemed to him to the one specified for capital punishments by the Military Code, the daily reading of which had horrified the nights of his imprisonment.

Philémon I continued the exercise of absolute power by ordering his minister to show the young couple the way to the private apartments. With the Empress on his arm, he closed the march, in the midst of frenetic applause.

Every day, the Emperor came to offer the people the comforting spectacle of a continuous inebriation. He went through the streets on his son-in-law's arm, without pomp and without a crown, coiffed in his immutable octagonal hat.

He called out to his subjects in a familiar fashion, anxious about their health, asking them whether there was anything they lacked.

"I want my happiness to be yours! I won't tolerate the slightest of those shameful maladies called hunger and thirst among you! I'm counting on you not to be afflicted by them!"

And they all replied that they were neither hungry nor thirsty, and that their happiness was perfect.

The imperial will was manifest with regard to the volcanoes. Philemon I enjoined them to consider themselves simply as natural and uncrossable frontiers, thanks to which Miellune formed a world within the world. The volcanoes no longer allowed a groan to escape; their flames, during the day, resembled an opaline mist copper-tinted by the sun; by night, Miellune slept beneath a vault with a dark summit, which brightened as it spread out to stream to earth in a luminous flood.

Time passed. The privation of nourishment not only did not cause any death, but did not occasion the slightest suffering. The most elementary laws of nature seemed to have drowned in Sphéroboul's gastronomic excesses. An indescribable bliss had penetrated minds and bodies. The voluptuousness of life, calm and profound, succeeded the anguish of death, the vertigo of which has led so many desperate people to commit suicide.

The Director of Social Conservation was disturbed by that abnormal state of affairs, which science could not explain. He had established a voluminous report in which thousands of strictly monitored cases of absolute dieting not followed by the most minimal loss of weight were recorded.

That work had been handed to the Emperor by his minister's own hands, during dessert at a copious dinner. Its reading had provoked such fits of hilarity in Philémon I that his digestion was effectuated in the midst of various troubles.

"Would I have the right to fatten myself if my subjects were victims of the slightest thinning?" he had exclaimed to the Bishop, who had come to ask for imperial approval of the mandate prepared in order to announce solemnly that the terrestrial paradise had been rediscovered with all its attributes.

"Indeed, Bishop, not only have I revoked the injunction made to man to earn his bread by the sweat of his brow, but also..."

"God..." the worthy ecclesiastic had attempted to insert.

"I have dried up that inconvenient sweat and have determined that bread will no longer have any utility," the autocrat continued. "My volcanoes are sufficient to all needs. Go mandate that to your faithful!" And with a baroque gesture, he had sent the prelate away.

It really was as Sphéroboul had said; all the needs of life were satisfied of their own accord. Miellune was living in the primordial state of the world when Eve had not yet transgressed the divine commandment.

The Bishop, in a spirit of excessive prudence, went by night to pour a corrosive liquid at the feet of a few apple trees that seemed ready to flower in the palace gardens. The poor trees withered. Thus, a Miellunese woman afflicted by the evil of curiosity would not have found any forbidden fruit to bite, and paradise would not run the risk of being lost for a second time.

For it really was paradise.

In the vicinity of the fires that surrounded it, Miellune enjoyed a climate so mild that clothes had become perfectly unnecessary. Philémon I rendered their suppression official and obligatory, walking around completely naked with his wife, his daughter and his son-in-law, all without the slightest veil. He had even decided to abandon his octagonal top hat because it reminded him of one of the abolished sumptuary needs. Only a crown, the insignia of his rank, ornamented his head.

The struggle for existence, having become pointless, arrested all its manifestations. All the people plunged into the contemplation of their own happiness; they applied themselves to savoring it without letting the slightest fraction escape.

The very idea of death, as a natural term of existence, was lost, and no one was astonished when the Bishop declared that the mere fact of living in paradise conceded immortality.

Weeks, months and years went by in that inalterable and quiet immobility. Everyone remained identical to himself, without aging in body or in thought. There no longer being any death, no births occurred. The word "desire" had lost all significance and no one would have been able to respond to the provocation of the formulation of one.

Philémon I had exhausted the secret provisions a long time ago. He did not even retain the notion of regret, for his alcoholic delirium had followed the laws of eternity, which made him drunk and stuffed forever.

Time had become an expression of which scientists, ever the victims of their mania for explaining the inexplicable, tried in vain the reconstitute the meaning.

They had also attempted to establish a scientific demonstration of the nutritive value of the volcanoes. Radioactivity, they said, is an essential and constitutive property of all bodies. Its intensity varies naturally from one body to another. It constitutes, in a way, the soul of matter. That soul radiates around it activities that condense into emanation.

Chemists described the properties of the emanation, which presents itself in the state of a gas whose existence is recognized in mineral waters and, in very great quantity, in the vapors issuing from craters. That emanation reacts by exterior contact to produce new substances. It is thus that argon results from the action of the emanation on water, lithium and neon from the reaction of the emanation on a salt of copper.

Reacting upon the carbon dioxide in the air, the emanation produces tropheon, the nourishing—or, rather, dynamogenic—properties of which are such that all aliments become unnecessary to the organism that breathes it. However, experiments established that tropheon, remaining in the state of a gas mixed with the air, is only capable of repairing the losses of organisms, without ever being able to impart any growth or any augmentation of weight. Thus was unveiled the mystery of the immutability of the human body.

It was then that an audacious mind had conceived the project of polymerizing the tropheon into a liquid, the nutritive energy of which would be so greatly multiplied that its absorption would cause growth and fattening. The laboratory work had not yet given any result, and the tropheon was obstinate in remaining diffusely faithful to the atmosphere, in spite of the charming name of bouloteon that the chemist had promised it on the day on which it consented to liquefy in some flask or other.

The prime minister had thought it his duty not to hide these attempts from his master. Philémon I was transported to the scientist's domicile. With a furious whirling of his insepa-rable cane he had broken flasks and retorts in order to put an immediate stop to the experiments, which he declared to be a threat to the security of paradise.

Time, which is only one of the innumerable aspects of the relative, is annihilated in the bosom of eternity, a simple reflection of the absolute. In consequence, only a god, enjoy-ing the plenitude of his faculties, would have been able to say whether it was years or centuries that the inhabitants of Miellune saw file past in days and nights, the black and white squares of the chessboard of the inconceivable.

The fact is that no one attempted the impossibility of de-limiting the limitless. With forceful oaths, the emperor en-joined those measurers of the infinite to put away their meas-uring-sticks and respect his desire to live in tranquility, with-out seeking a quarrel with an unknown from which only nasty surprises could be expected.

Past, present and future, in confusion, reigned with an unfailing authority that identified beings and things to them-selves. Existence was a bottomless lake without shores, with a motionless and polished surface, like a mirror in which the skies were reflected.

Images being a reality with as much entitlement as the objects that give birth to them, and as the sky is not imagined as desert of a god, Miellune promised its emperor that summit. Philémon Sphéroboul installed himself there without vertigo, totalizing his nudity by removing his crown, which he gave to his son-in-law. His cane alone remained among the attributes of his terrestrial power; in order to enhance its power, he forbade his subjects—even the lame—to make use of such an instrument.

Apart from that restriction, everyone enjoyed liberty to the extent of the most extreme fantasies. Their full exercise found all the more facility because, all needs being suppressed, their satisfaction did not require the slightest effort or give rise to the shadow of an anxiety.

Amour, having no objective, had thus fallen into desuetude. Men and women lived side by side without desiring one another. Assorted couples exalted their tenderness by absorbing themselves in a reciprocal motionless and mute contemplation.

Hunger was perpetually sated by the inspiration of tropheon, so obsession with the pleasures of the table had been so radically abolished that no taste-bud was able to evoke the slightest memory.

Voyages, the object of which is to go in search of unprecedented sensations by means of the frequentation of new horizons, had lost their essential value, for even madness, which is one of the poles of human reason, would be unable to displace itself infinitely.

Thanks to the suppression of these difficulties, money, the habitual notation of the difficulties of relationship between human beings, did not attract the slightest attention.

As for dreams, in the bosom of which flowers stillborn of the exiles from Earth might have bloomed, like vacillating bouquets in the mouths of chimeras, weary of cradling their own reality, they had been extinguished to the last drowsy echo.

Thus lived Miellune.

Thanks to Sphéroboul, it had entered into eternity.

Thanks to him, it was to emerge therefrom.

One day, the god-emperor, in one of the rooms of the palace, found himself face to face with an individual who was holding a cane in his right hand. He was identical to him in every respect: the same implausibly developed abdomen, held

245

up by similarly-curved short legs, like him in a state of complete nudity.

Philémon Sphéroboul did not intend to be disobeyed. The sight of that cane irritated him. He spoke sharply to the intruder, who made no reply, although his mouth opened, articulating words composed of the same syllables as those he heard.

"I'll teach your mute tongue to speak!" the god-emperor howled—and he raised his cane. The other cane made the same gesture, simultaneously. Frightened, Sphéroboul threw himself backwards. Gripped by a twin fear, his adversary also recoiled. That retreat emboldened Sphéroboul. He stared at the temeritous individual, who did not lower his eyes in response.

Suddenly, furiously, he cried: "The wretch isn't content to carry a cane! My word, he's fatter than me!"

Buffeted by a murderous jealousy, he dipped his head in order to charge—but that abrupt movement broke his equilibrium; his abdomen dragged the rest of his body to the floor.

Painful efforts brought him back to his knees.

He was alone.

"He's gone!" he observed, reassured. And his eyes, certain of not encountering the enemy, paraded around with satisfaction.

Suddenly, he uttered a cry: "There he is coming back! He's crawling toward me, the traitor!"

The emperor stood up, attentively following the movements of his adversary, whose heaviness made him anxious. At the same instant, they found themselves on the semicircle of their short legs. Then closing his eyes, Sphéroboul launched himself forward, cane raised. The blow made such a racket that Philémon Sphéroboul fell unconscious after having shouted: "I've killed him!"

When he came to, before having recognized his wife, his daughter and his son-in-law, who had come to his aid, he repeated: "I've killed him! That'll teach him to be fatter than me! I've killed him!"

The Empress and the Duchess of Miellune tried in vain to explain to him that he had not killed anyone and that he had only broken a mirror, which was his strict right as emperor and god. As the Duke of Miellune did not appear to be giving a sufficiently enthusiastic approval to that license, however, his imperial mother-in-law snapped at him violently: "Naturally, you don't agree with me, good-for-nothing!" And she told him that if he persisted in not rendering her a grandmother, she would repudiate him and expel him from the family.

Under that threat, the unfortunate son-in-law looked at his wife, lowered his head and made no reply.

Philémon Sphéroboul went to bed with a delirious fever of the worst sort. He summoned his minister and said to him: "My dear prime and only minister, go right away to that scientist who was manufacturing bouloteon. I need bouloteon—a lot of bouloteon—because I want to get fatter, so fat that no one can dream of being as fat as me!"

When the minister gave his august master an assurance that his plumpness would always be unequaled, Sphéroboul stopped him and said, bitterly: "You're saying that to flatter me; that's what a good servant does. I thank you for that delicate thought, but I've already found a rival. I killed him." And he narrated the scene of the encounter.

The scientist, who had been continuing his experiments in secret, had just obtained the result that he had been seeking for such a long time at the very moment when the minister, the bearer of the imperial will, arrived at his home. A small round-bottomed flask had ended up half-full of a liquid that was surely bouloteon. The honest and devoted minister brought it back in all haste to his master.

The latter emptied it in a single draught and, getting out of bed, went to sit down in front of a mirror in order to give himself the joy of following the assimilatory progress of his digestion.

Alas, how frightened he was when he saw the skin of his belly, so shiny and so taut, wither and wrinkle like the rind of a fruit from which the vital sap has been removed.

He howled that he had been poisoned. Weeping, begging, apologizing for having taken the title of god, he offered his cane in sacrifice against the certainty of the salvation of his life.

In order to escape a just punishment, the scientist, the author of the terrible mistake, had fled Miellune like a madman, and when an attempt was made to catch up with him in order to take possession of his person, he was seen to disappear into the flames.

The Bishop ordered public lamentations in honor of the god-emperor, whose person, in the wake of that unfortunate ingestion of false bouloteon, had diminished by fifteen pounds.

Not daring to annul the holocaust of his cane, Sphéroboul had taken the imperial crown back from his son-in-law.

That loss of fifteen pounds had plunged him into a black depression. He sat motionless in an armchair, his desolate eyes staring at his abdomen, whose wrinkles denounced the internal catastrophe. The shame of showing himself in that pitiful state was such that he did not leave the palace, in spite of the exhortations of his family, who feared that an even greater diminution might result from that regime of claustration.

The prime minister eventually vanquished his master's resistance by proving to him that the palace, by virtue of its central situation, which made it the point most distant from the volcanoes, was the location poorest in tropheon. Philémon Sphéroboul consented to go to respire the richer atmosphere that his health demanded.

As much out of personal vanity as pride in his rank, he did not want to show his sickly body to his subjects; he asked his wife for his clothes.

To the general bewilderment, he appeared in a black frock-coat, peal-gray trousers and a white waistcoat. By virtue of a reminiscence of his sumptuary tastes, infallible in determining the harmony of a costume, he put on his octagonal top hat again. Solemn and dignified, he went out of Miellune every day to take his tropheon cure.

An example set at such a high level could not fail to be imitated. As if by enchantment, the fashion of getting dressed returned. Soon, even partial nudity was first decreed to be ridiculous, and did not take long to become a fault giving rise to severe criticism.

The physicians decided to resume their forgotten role; they prescribed tropheon cures. There were regimes to follow day and night. The prescription specified the exact distance of the volcanoes at which patients had to station themselves, the distance naturally being proportional to the energy of the treatment.

But jealousy did not take long to awaken in the heart of the god-emperor. Fearing that he might see the tropheon profiting one of his subjects more than himself, he declared it his exclusive property and forbade anyone to leave Miellune in order to go in search of it. He graciously surrendered that which could be obtained within the walls, reserving the rest for his personal use.

Most things only have value by virtue of the difficulties that surround their possession. Solely by virtue of its prohibition, the exterior tropheon acquired an immediate and tyrannical importance. Procuring it became the unique and constant goal of everyone.

In order to attain it, the old instincts surged forth one by one from their immemorial slumber. Guided by the intelligence acquired in the course of ages consumed, they put themselves at the service of renascent appetites.

There were ingenious and stubborn ruses designed to deceive Sphéroboul's surveillance, the latter having been advised by his minister to recall to activity the soldiers formerly sacked because of their flagrant lack of utility. They mounted guard around Miellune and tried to drive back the tropheon thieves by force. As they were permitted to breathe while they were on sentry duty, the tropheon thus abandoned to them constituted an inestimable salary.

The prime minister had spoken to his master very truthfully, for everyone wanted to be a soldier in order to breathe the famous tropheon at closer range.

By way of precaution and to leave the greatest margin possible to a fattening morally prejudicial to his own person, the emperor-king made the selection from his subjects in order of thinness. The first who had the honor of taking the title of Tropheonic Guard was a skeletal individual whose bones were obviously near neighbors of his skin.

The uniforms of presphéroboulian times—to employ the term consecrated by the emperor-king, desirous of fixing the consequence of his advent—were exhumed, and proclaimed the bellicose cacophonies of their colors very loudly.

The Tropheonic Guards, having sworn an oath to ensure without weakness and distraction the accomplishment of the imperial will, showed an inflexible rigor. Men, women and children obtained no mercy from them. Brutally, they were driven back inside when they tried to reach the forbidden zone.

Attempts at corruption failed; violence against the soldiers was punished by imprisonment a location devoid of air, and consequently deprived of tropheon. That detention made the convicts thinner, which exasperated their desire. Recidivism became so frequent that the number of prisoners threatened to surpass that of their guardians.

By virtue of conjugal weakness, the emperor-king granted the capricious whims of the empress, who first demanded of her son-in-law interminable sessions even closer to the volcanoes than the most radical regime that would have been prescribed by the physician least careful of the life of his client.

The Duke of Miellune had obeyed without a murmur, because he respected his mother-in-law even in thought. The latter, observing that the tropheon cure in question was not leading her to the status of grandmother, to which she aspired more ardently every day, embarked on the martyrdom of her son-in-law. The god-emperor blindly made himself the humble artisan of that process.

Successively, the Duke saw himself stripped of several of his prerogatives, of which the principal one, immediately placed before that of wearing an entirely gilded uniform, was being able to leave Miellune day and night and approach the volcanoes in complete liberty.

Of bourgeois descent, the empress would have thought it in poor taste to reveal the intestinal dissents of the family to the people, so the Duke continued to wear his entirely gilded uniform and enjoy the right to walk outside the town. His shrewd mother-in-law contented herself with having him put in charge of the palace dungeons. That appointment only permitted him to leave the subterrains during the hours of night consecrated to sleep.

Every evening, the Duke rejoined the Duchess, and, under the angry gaze of the Empress, went back to their apartment with her. As the rarefied air of the subterrains did not sustain him sufficiently, he spent his nights on the balcony soliciting the tropheon he lacked. In the meantime, the Duchess bewailed her solitude in the depths of her alcove.

To her mother, who interrogated her regarding her red eyes, the Duchess replied evasively, but the Empress out her finger on the truth in concluding, disdainfully: "Your husband is like your father. All men are alike!" And before descending to his post, the Duke was subjected to a scene in which the least flattering epithets and insults were offered to him in profusion.

One evening, he came back pale, his eyes cold and his brow furrowed.

Frightened by that expression, which was unfamiliar to her, the poor Duchess asked her husband: "Are you ill?"

"No," he replied, somber and bleak.

"What's the matter?"

"Nothing. I've just decided to kill your mother, and your father too."

"Why?"

"Your mother, because she's a nasty woman. Your father, because he's her husband. That's it."

251

"Duke, you mustn't do that."

"Duchess, you know very well that I don't want to cause you any pain. If you insist, I won't kill the nasty woman or her husband."

The Duchess took the Duke in her arms and embraced him recklessly. The Empress came in and caught sight of that effusion, of the cause of which she was unaware.

"How stupid you are, my poor child, to throw the flowers of your tenderness in the face of that..." She searched for the name of the animal synthetic of all physical and moral flaws, but as it had disappeared from Miellune and its memory, going back to presphéroboulian times, had been effaced, the Megaera was unable to find the evocative syllable. She concluded her sentence by spitting on the floor and stamping on the saliva furiously.

The young couple fled before that savage manifestation.

In their room, the Duke and Duchess allowed the tears to flow in which dolors drown and hot anger and virile resolution dissolve.

In the middle of the night, the Duke and Duchess, holding hands, left the palace. As everyone was asleep and they were walking on tiptoe, no one noticed their departure.

Weary of persecution and ill-treatment, the Duke had decided to leave Miellune. The Duchess, as infatuated with her husband as in the early days of their marriage, had succeeded in bending his determination to depart alone; she had obtained his agreement that they would not be separated.

As they went by the Tropheonic Guards rendered them honors and watched them draw away in the direction of the volcanoes. The respect they had for their master extending to the members of his family, they neither exchanged the slightest criticism nor permitted themselves to make any privately.

The next day, at dawn, the Empress was, as was her habit, on sentry duty at the young couple's bedroom door. She would have considered it as a failure of duty to let a single day go by without insulting her son-in-law, who, forced by the topography of the location to pass that way, could not escape her aggressive matinal demonstrations.

Outside the closed door, the mother-in-law savored the bitter joy of sensing her bile acidify, in order to spring forth more forcefully when her victim appeared.

That day, the wait was neverending. Exasperation shook the Empress with convulsive tremors. Her haggard eyes became bloodshot; foam whitened the corners of her lips; she stimulated herself with menacing gestures.

Finally, in a paroxysm of fury, roaring, she hurled herself against the door that was obstinate in not opening. By deference or weakness, the panel gave way without a shadow of resistance.

The customary "Wretch!" was swallowed by her contracted throat at the sight of the empty bed and the deserted room. She uttered the cry of a famished beast whose pretty has escaped, at the very moment when its fangs sensed the warmth of its flesh.

Then her maternal entrails performed a somersault. "My daughter! My daughter! Where's my daughter?"

Philémon Sphéroboul, the god-emperor, brought running by the outburst of that racket, stood there mutely, which attracted vehement invective to him.

The tenderness of mothers sometimes occasions brief truces in the ardor of their gendrophobia. The Empress, having become Madame Philémon Sphéroboul, mother of Jenny, once again, asked, breathless with anxiety: "Where are they? Where are they?"

An instantaneous investigation, led by the prime minister in person, furnished the response: the Duke and Duchess had left Miellune during the night and had disappeared into the flames.

The stupor of despair was followed by the need to accomplish important and definitive actions. By means of a few brief questions, the Empress informed herself of the route taken by the fugitives. Turning toward the god-emperor, she said: "Come with me."

"Where?" Sphéroboul thought he ought to ask.

"To join them. Come on, let's go!"

The Emperor pronounced blurred fragments of incomprehensible phrases, while his spouse took him by the hand.

In the square, all that Miellune counted of living beings had gathered, or the news of the event had spread from house to house; everyone wanted to see what could not fail to happen.

The god-emperor appeared on the perron. His octagonal top hat, surmounted by the crown, gleamed with countless reflections. His frock-coat had never seemed so solemnly black, nor his waistcoat whiter; as for his trousers, their pearl-gray was mirrored, without a shadow, in the dazzling polish of his shoes. His right hand was supported by his cane—the offering of which he had revoked, in the misfortune that had struck him—and his left hand rested on the folded forearm of the Empress, whose silhouette was drowned by the plats of a long dark veil.

The Tropheonic Guards, assembled by a fanfare of trumpets, in full dress uniform, were arranged in a double row, holding back the curious. Their band played a slow march with muffled sonorities.

The Emperor and Empress, escorted by the prime minister and the dignitaries of the court, filed slowly away. The musicians fell into step behind them, then the troopers, and finally, in disorder, the crowd, with old men with curved backs, and women dragging children hanging on to their skirts or clutching them in their arms against their breast.

It did not occur to anyone to ask where they were going. They all followed their god-emperor because a mysterious force attached their steps to his; it was like an accomplishment of the fatality before which human consciousness is effaced.

And the procession, which was neither a joyful procession nor a sad procession, emerged from the town, serenely, under the giant wing of destiny, its members protecting their eyes from the glare of the sun, whose vertiginous abyss opened directly above their heads.

Philémon Sphéroboul, on his short bowed legs, rolled his formless body toward the unknown of the volcanoes in order to obey his wife, obsessed to the point of the annihilation of her will by the mystery that her child had just penetrated. And that obscure attraction being the human law, on Earth as in Heaven, Miellune, which had been paradise, was changed into a desert in which no breath of life palpitated.

Outside, the worlds had continued to play their parts more or less harmoniously in the concert of universal gravitation. The disappearance of Miellune had captivated public opinion momentarily, but it had not taken long to be impassioned by another event.

When the volcanoes, whose existence was temporary, were extinguished, bold explorers had climbed their craters, raised into mountains. They had found the ruins of the town that had been called Miellune.

By restoring its name, they made it once again a place propitious for the settlement of humans.

The new Miellune, haloed by the aureole of cosmic martyrs, became established as the primary place of pilgrimage for scientists, sterile by nature and consequently happy to objectivize themselves in blind and hazardous reconstitutions.

And life, in the depths of that hollow valley, flourished as before at a point on a plain of infinite horizons.

THE REPUBLICAN JUNGLE

At the price of indescribable efforts and unspeakable suffering, Humans had obtained complete domination over their eternal companion, Nature.

Intoxicated by their victory, they exploited the activity of the slave—who, when she was free, had kept redoubtable occult forces at bay—to the point of exhaustion.

Sensing their liberation, slyly, in a slow but obstinate revolt, those forces rose up against humans, gradually eroding and crumbling the imperious block of their sovereignty. Surprised, humans lowered their eyes interrogatively toward Nature. She, as of old, before humanity had invented the languages of the present day, replied to humankind:

"What folly, my master, was yours! Have we not been forged to fuse our double existence into one alone? Was I not your eternal ally? Had our fidelity not been marked with an unbreakable seal? Side by side, have we not struggled against our common enemies, the elements? Has not each of their defeats circled your head with a new crown? Without jealousy, have I not glorified myself in your triumphs? Why, when the list was closed and the goals of which you had dreamed ceased to be tangible, did you turn the thrust of your genius against me? Your cruelties surpassed dementia: you have afflicted me to the extent of my partial destruction. Now the elements, confronted my by death-throes, are fomenting their revenge against you. My brother, I beg you, let me forgive you for your ingratitude. Hold out our hands to me. Lift me up again. Stem the blood flowing from my wounds. The life that you can render me, I will employ in its totality for your defense against the enmity of the elements."

Thus was revealed the religion of the revival of Nature. Being utilitarian and making a complete abstraction of the entities usually appointed to reign over souls—which is to say, not offering any competition to the multiple enterprises already created with regard to the afterlife, the new religion, without demanding a single martyr, came close to drowning at its birth in the delirious enthusiasm of its first devotees.

Of the ministerial cells that form the great administrative hive, that of Agriculture is especially consecrated to the relationships established between the Government of the Republic and Nature. The politics of the moment, combined with the personality of the Minister in office, incessantly modified the exercise of the tacit concordat.

The agricultural superintendent serves as the master of arms of the important families in the bureaucratic divisions of the three kingdoms. He holds the Almanach de Gotha of the great species. He is the one who, without appeal, consecrates the nobility of fur, feather and scale. By his order, horses, bovines, pigs and sheep figure in the golden book of breeding. Under his control he holds poultry, fish, birds, and even the silkworm. His role is to whiten lilies, gild wheat and blacken truffles. The world of vegetables is submissive to his recognition. In accordance with his will, he makes and breaks the amorous careers of stallions. With a sign he exalts or debases the trees of forests. He reigns in full authority, fattening the souls of penguins where they slumber, far away.

In the course of the present year, one of the most fortunate with which the Third republic has provided the French people, relations between the Minister of Agriculture and Nature have been very cordial, in spite the fact, that the harvests over the major part of the territory, as happens every year, have heavily inclined toward deficit. Because the earth has suffered, by turns, aridity and excess of water, the fruits have not kept the promises of the flowers.

The evil, always in the process of becoming chronic, is known in its source and its cause. It only remains to find the practical remedy and its application.

If Agriculture lacks strong arms, the Chambre des Députés is extremely rich in orators promised to rustic labor. An oratory instrument, late but arriving vigorously, speech has dethroned the plow.

For several years, the group of the "Laborers of the Palais Bourbon" had for its president and founder the honorable Parisian depute Philémon Singeoreille.[26] The Marais quarter knew the hazard of having given him birth. Until his twentieth year came round, the Parisian fidelity of Philémon Singeoreille had been total; never, in body or mind, had he crossed the fortifications. The exigencies of conscription dispatched him to a banal southern sub-prefecture, all of whose houses, including the barracks, lived cheek by jowl with the countryside, detailed in gardens, cultivated fields, woods or meadows.

Parisians are curious by nature. Military life has its leisures. Philémon Singeoreille consecrated his to discovering Nature, of which the first sight had struck him at a distance with stupefaction.

He wrote enthusiastic accounts of it to his relatives and friends. His destiny determined that he should only encounter incredulity. No one responded to the challenge of "Come and see!" with which he slapped skeptics when he first went home on leave. In the regiment, his companions considered him with

---

[26] Singeoreille translates as "monkey ear." Austruy must have been fond of the name because he reattributed it, in full, to a different character in "Un Samsâra" (1932; tr. in the third volume of the present set as "A Samsara").

bewilderment. He received pressing and reiterated injunctions from his superiors to cease his simulation of a native imbecility or an acquired cerebral derangement.

Following the example of a few other human beings, Philémon Singeoreille had a soul. That soul was the soul of an apostle. It supported reproaches and mockery with an unshakeable calm.

When the hour of his liberation arrived, Philémon Singeoreille's first civilian action took the form of an announcement to his father and mother of his engagement to a young country girl encountered in the course of a rural exploration.

"Why not a foreigner?" asked Père Singeoreille, indignantly, who, in his anger—that of a Parisian wounded in the most intimate fiber of his pride—transformed into Gallo-Roman subsoil his shop selling porcelain and faience, until then run with a sacrosanct tenderness conjointly with his spouse, whose more conservative fury, if it spared plates and jugs, was no less demonstrative with regard to a project that was provincial to a point beyond implausibility.

Young Philémon, with his filial hands, had helped his authors pick up the debris of the victims of their imperative manifestations, after which he had persisted so heroically in his determination that, a few months later, after the civil and religious formalities, he installed his wife in the porcelain and faience shop, scrupulously dusted for the occasion.

The parents quickly laid down their arms before their rural daughter-in-law, who glorified the prestige of the capital by a perpetual widening of both eyes. The Singeoreille spouses conceived a personal pride on that basis. Moved by a praiseworthy sentiment of reciprocity, they lent such an indulgent ear to Philémon's stories that the following summer, taking advantage of the sequential days of the National Festival, both couples embarked for the destination of the minuscule subprefecture that had initiated Philémon.

The latter's spouse took pride in doing the honors of the familial domain for her in-laws. Gradually, she abandoned herself to the customary sentiments, and blushed discreetly on going into her maidenly bedroom with her husband. She showed the Parisians around the barns, the poultry-yard and the stables, but the second day constrained her to renounce, for lack of strength, taking part in the frenetic races that precipitated them from the woods to the vineyards via the ploughed fields and the meadows.

Philémon, alone, paused for a few moments to suffer, without letting too much impotence show, the reproaches of his mother-in-law, offended at not retaining the attention of her visitors to a greater extent.

Even superalimented by excitement, human strength has its limits. They were close to being reached when the third of the days of leave was completed. The last express train saw the Singeoreilles collapse on to its banquettes, reduced to the state of parcels improbably compressed by the excess of a customary crowd always very safely anticipated. In a slumber neighboring on turpitude, the neophytes of nature smiled blissfully at the jolts of the train.

The next day, the shop of the Golden Salad Bowl raised its shutter again, in accordance with a habit that went back to Louis-Philippe. In spite of appearances, however, there was no longer an identity between the past and the present; the Singeoreilles had been possessed by Nature. They no longer talked about anything but her, even to their clients. All their thoughts were of her. That possession became so complete that one morning, Père Singeoreille, embracing the porcelain and faience with a scornful gesture, asked his wife this question:

"Isn't this transformation of the earth into basins and salad bowls a crime? Does man have the right to inflict sterility on what nature has conceived to give birth to plants and trees?"

Mère Singeoreille replied with a long gaze of negative anguish.

The old shopkeepers did not take long to confess their desire to retire to the bosom of nature as soon as "the little ones" had acquired sufficient experience. In the meantime, they begged their son's pardon every day for having so grossly and so unjustly misunderstood him. They reread the first letters he had written as a soldier, tearfully.

In such a favorable atmosphere, Philémon's proselytizing zeal was revived. It was urged on by his family that the heir presumptive of the Golden Salad Bowl reappeared in the neighborhood café. The proprietress, with whom he had entertained, concurrently with the other regulars, a platonic flirtation, welcome him with a moist gaze and recommended, in the finesse of her taste, a new aperitif liqueur.

Under our sky, less clement than that of ancient Hellas, the estaminet replaces the Agora. Orators gripped by the disease of eloquence find a podium there with ever-ready echoes. There is no question of a political, military or social order that can resist definitive demonstrations registered in black pencil on marble table-tops.

More often than not, victory in multiquotidian card games constitutes the sole recompense of these benevolent legislators, but it sometimes happens that their audiences send them, furnished with regular powers, to sit in a representative assembly in which their universal ignorance soon takes on the allure of infallible doctrine.

Three years in the café established Philémon Singeoreille as a candidate. His associates, having become his disciples, grouped around him as a committee. At their head, in the very heart of the capital, Philémon Singeoreille deployed the standard of Nature, of whom he proclaimed himself the pioneer of regeneration.

The enthusiasm of the quarter crystallized in the foundation of the "Circle of Laborers," every member taking an oath to employ body and soul for the election of Philémon Singeoreille. A minuscule plow, schematically tattooed on the palm of the right hand, commemorated the solemnity of the oath and constituted an infallible sign of solidarity.

A few months later, on the occasional of a partial election, the name of Philémon Singeoreille, multiplied by the unanimity of citizens qualified to nominate a député, emerged from the urns.

The victorious "laborers" led their elected representative to the Palais Bourbon in procession. The people of Paris cheered them. Neophytes spontaneously joined their ranks. Believing it to be a revolutionary demonstration, the guards on duty closed the gates of the Palais. The concierge opened them wide again to Philémon Singeoreille on the mute presentation of the plow inscribed in the palm of his right hand.

An indescribable ovation saluted his entry into the hall of sessions. The fresh hatchling of universal suffrage went to his bench under the indicative smile of the ushers responsible for the bodily separation of honorable gentlemen on days of parliamentary tempests. Applause was born of hands too distant to shake his as he passed by. As soon as he was seated, the President wished him an admiring welcome, congratulating the miraculous coincidence of his appearance with the precise moment when discussion was commencing of a projected law intended to ordain means appropriate to endure the refurbishment of forests, the dearest question of all to Nature's servant knights.

As if Nature herself were preparing to listen via the ears of his new colleague, the orator scheduled to speak first in the debate went up to the podium sketching in the direction of Philémon Singeoreille the gesture of homage and sacrifice habitual to gladiators, toreadors and all those who make a profession of immolating themselves under the eyes of crowds.

The Deluge—an accident tainted with clericalism, and in consequence inapt to impress Republican minds—was passed over in silence, to the benefit of the strictly laic inundations that had desolated France in rationally historical times. In a sonorous evocation, in which his voice strove to attain the noise of devastating cataracts, the orator summoned to the vengeful bar of the representatives of the French people the authors responsible for the incriminated catastrophes:

"Advance, woodcutters with frenzied axes! Listen to me! From my mouth emerges the voice of humanity kneeling in the conscience of sincere repentance. Blind artisans of irreparable evils, return to us the legions of green trees that impose on aquatic life, outside of which everything is annihilation, a regular rhythm! Now, on the flanks of the denuded mountains, the snow no longer sleeps its provident slumber. The slightest wind chases it in avalanches toward the rivers, which howl outside their beds the submersion of plains that will be haunted thereafter by the specters of thirst.

"All of you, who weep for those dead of aridity or drowning, open your eyes. The assassinated flora demands your grief. Its mourning ought to be borne blacker than that of the dearest human beings. But there is still time to think of the salvation that is contained entire in the verb of hope and redemption: *reforest!* Let us apply that admirable verb to all times, to all fashions, to all persons! Men, women, children, rich, poor, strong and weak, let us conjugate it with the same ardor. Let us charge with high treason everyone who does not bring his tree to the Fatherland!"

The vehemence of the tirade rebounded from all the benches in vigorous echoes translated by the appeals of throats, the stamping of feet, the rattling of lecterns, the clapping of hands and the thousand other means by which the sovereign people simultaneously express their agreement or their anathema in the hectic microcosm of their representation.

Cries cut through the chaos of the tumult: "Vive la République! Vive la France! Long live the forests! Down with the axes!"

Several times, vibrant cries were heard of "Vive Singeoreille!"

The new occupant of the podium, who waited until the noise had calmed down somewhat before speaking, offered to cede his turn to his colleague, desired by the entire Chambre, but the President, invoking the hour, belated for an intervention as capital as that of the leader of the "laborers" could not fail to be, asked the orator to develop his amendment, proposing to the assembly to hear Philémon Singeoreille at the beginning of the next day's session.

Unanimous applause approved the President's decision.

The députés listened in relative silence to the speech, in the question was raised of climactic anarchy and the profligacy of the atmosphere. Demonstrations of joyous sympathy greeted the accusation of anonymous guilty parties of having trampled underfoot the rose of the winds and fomenting the saddening disappearance of the four seasons, now confused in an inconsistent sequence of months devoid of character and virtue.

The conclusion necessarily led to the remedy, already commended, of reforestation. He added to it a system of scaled subsidies—rather ingenious, according it its promoter—to bring the treetops into rapid conjunction with the sky.

The goal of eloquence is to force attention. Whoever consents to listen is ready to be conquered, especially in a political assembly in which opinions automatically polarize to the right or the left, according to whether they are emitted by a partisan or a adversary, and without giving the slightest weight to the arguments posed for or against the adoption of a thesis.

However, advanced minds and conservative minds found themselves entirely in agreement on the principle of reforestation; only its realization raised an infinite number of problems, opening innumerable divergences of view, which each of the députés reserved the privilege of exposing in the pell-mell of amendments and counter-proposals by which the Chambre tries honestly to take the place of the general interest by juxtaposing the eminently dissimilar elements of interests particular to each electoral circumscription.

In sober but energetic terms, the representative of an electorate whose territory was reputed to be the wettest on France demanded a text protective of official pluviometers, those modest but indefatigable auxiliaries of atmospheric science.

"Inscribe in the law an article punishing with severe penalties any person convicted of tampering with the free functioning of pluviometers! France has a right to know exactly how much water falls upon her, because, Messieurs, as water is the mother of humidity, humidity is the blood of the earth!"

The orator vituperated against the violators of pluviometers, which, in a bold move, he called the baptismal fonts of Agriculture. Opening a voluminous dossier relating the details of an investigation that he had made in numerous départements, he supported his accusations with evidence.

"In one town, which I shall not name, to protect its honor, do you know what I found in the bosom of the instrument reserved for the most noble and moist useful of sciences?"

"A goldfish!" replied a voice from the extreme right.

"Yes, my dear and esteemed colleague! Exactly! A goldfish! And you don't find it fantastic that the sky should send goldfish to earth?"

"It proves that God is a Republican!" the right-winger retorted, gravely.[27]

"It proves, above all, that there are inferior consciences, corrupt minds for whom nothing is sacred!" riposted the man at the podium, hotly.

Ironic applause burst forth in a tempest. The députés, becoming once again the schoolboys that most of them had once been, uttered the various onomatopeias by means of which humans affirm their fraternity with a host of animals.

In the din, which the presidential hand-bell augmented instead of calming, the accusatory speech against the enemies of pluviometers continued, violent and picturesque, citing the fabulous errors of statistics.

"So, Messieurs, in my home town of Cancale, I wanted to keep watch on the national pluviometer personally. My surveillance was secret and precise. On the morning of my first

---

[27] I have translated *poisson rouge* [goldfish] literally, although the elimination of the word "red" spoils this item of weak repartee. Translating it as "red herring" would have preserved the wordplay, but at the expense of accuracy. It is not obvious why the French deem goldfish to be red, but nor is it obvious why we deem them to be gold.

inspection the pluviometer was full. That evening, at dusk, it was empty! The same thing happened for fourteen days running!"

"It's the pluviometer of Tantale!" put in a piercing voice.[28]

"Of Cancale!" rectified a basso-profundo echo.

"The result, Messieurs, is that my arrondissement is, in the eyes of the administration, the least aqueous place in France, when in reality it rains there continually..."

"Make a motion for obligatory umbrellas!" suggested a facetious honorable gentleman.

Running out of wit, weary of laughter, the entire Chambre, turning toward Philémon Singeoreille, sang in formidable chorus: "Until tomorrow!"

The leader of the "Laborers" had shared very ostentatiously in his colleagues' hilarity. The latter conceived a satisfaction therefrom that increased the sympathy they already experienced for his person.

Great legislative sessions do not lose out in any respect to artistic, theatrical, sportive or worldly solemnities. On certain days, the Palais Bourbon is the place where it is necessary to be seen, under pain of not being recognized as an active participant in Parisian Society, into which one enters either by the violence of a scandal or rights acquired by a slow and laborious incorporation, which anoints Parisiennes of the most varied personalities, over which a discreetly posed question mark suddenly become more precise in a summons to appear before an examining magistrate. Philémon Singeoreille's debut, trumpeted by the newspapers as if it were a music hall attraction, had drawn to the Chambre, in addition to the regular clientele, a crowd in whom ancestral rustic tastes abolished by generations of strictly Parisian residence had suddenly reawakened.

---

[28] I have not translated Tantale as Tantalus out of respect for the rhyming echo.

The regulation of the day's schedule having been rapidly expedited, the President pronounced the sacramental phrase impatiently awaited: "Monsieur Philémon Singeoreille has the floor," which he followed with a few kind words of welcome.

At the assured pace of a soldier marching to victory, Philémon Singeoreille traversed the hemicycle and climbed the steps of the podium with a measured agility.

He commenced by confessing the violence done to his timidity by the inconceivable audacity of speaking before the masters of French eloquence.

A stammer located in the center, sympathizing heartily with that oratory precaution, greeted it with a halting and mulish "He...he...he...," which a colleague charitably completed as "Hear hear!"—approved by an "Exactly!" projected in a hazardous jet from the throat of the sufferer.

The orator entered into his subject like a hussar to a conquered town.

"The soul of Nature soars, immensely, over this assembly. Invisible to our eyes, she is present in our hearts! An august communion that raises us all to the height of those trees whose tops you were able to contemplate yesterday, so eloquently raised from the podium that I am occupying today with the unique and essential concern of simple words and sincere thoughts."

Invocations of simplicity and sincerity are always much appreciated by people dedicated without weakness to emphasis and imposture; the députés applauded them in the person of Philémon Singeoreille, who continued in the same fashion.

"The evils of deforestation you know! I could revive, with an emotional scalpel, the horror of the mountain are the agony of the plain, both of which are dying, preceding us, perhaps not by very much, into extinction. I shall not do that. I shall go straight to the remedy. It resides in this single word: *reforest*. Infinitive of our dream, you are no chimera!

"Before me, I see a younger brother of Pegasus causing young shoots to spring from the earth with a luxuriant hoof, the younger sisters of clear springs. I see hectic branches hugging trunks with inextricable embraces. I see our forests becoming virgin again, as if they had never known the frightful kiss of the woodcutter's ax. It is not an illusion cradled by the palpitations of the breeze, a false hope born of the greenery of foliage! It is a reality, which France has placed in the benevolent carpals of your hands.

"On your will depends the resurrection of the queen of waters, our ancestral sylvan. You want, I know, to be anointed as the legitimate fathers of our territorial renaissance. The greatest gestures are concretized in the briefest formulae. Who has not read on the edges of enclosures the inscriptions before which poachers sometimes pause: *Beware of wolf traps*. Well, Messieurs, in order for our work to be complete and fecund, it is sufficient to change that threat into a pact of alliance; it is sufficient that, henceforth, on the edges of forests devastated by the pitiless Attilas of commerce and industry, one reads: *Beware of wolves*.

"But what am I saying? Wolves? Obviously, Messieurs, wolves—but also lions, tigers, bears, snakes and elephants. All the representatives of an imprudently calumniated fauna must answer "Present!" to our appeal, which is the appeal of the Fatherland. France, Messieurs, is dying of the incomprehension of wild beasts. We have one foot in the grave because we have misunderstood their protective role.

"Oh, Messieurs, we believe too easily that Nature is impenetrable; her secrets have, however, been delivered. To the man who can see and comprehend, she sometimes reveals the most complex cogs of her infinite mechanism. Thanks to native dispositions and special circumstances, it has been given to me to see, and I have understood: in my sleep, haunted incessantly with thirst for the public good, the vast spaces of Africa, Asia, America and Oceania, as well as a few corners of Europe, have appeared to me.

"I have seen them populating themselves with that giant fauna—carnivorous or vegetarian, what does it matter?—as the same time as the trees that are also giants are born and grow, the paternal pillars throughout the centuries of those countries in whose bosom the attributes of virgin forests soon pullulate, barriers perpetually raised against the deforestation that causes the baldness of Nature as the loss of hair causes human baldness.

"I have seen and understood, Messieurs, that the ensemble of beings and things follows a rigorously mutual and essentially reciprocal process. Everything is in the one; the one is in everything. Thus, the animal is born and lives with the forest, as the forest is born and lives with the animal. I take as witnesses the dreaming lions seated at the feet of baobabs, the tigers swaying in flowery hammocks on elastic lianas.

"Let us ensure the existence of those inseparable twins, and we shall have accomplished the grandiose work that French soil awaits! The animals first! The vegetal will follow, in accordance with the mysterious and fatal law. Let us obey the primordial instincts. Let us contemplate the effects, still palpable on the soil of unexplored continents. Let us evoke those colossal forests that go in harness with the great fauna! Let us think of the relationship that links the splendor of woods o the quality of their residents. Let us not forget the magisterial formula: *such animals, such trees!* Let the scale of ferocity be the hierarchy of our appeal. Let us reconstitute the jungle in the service of the Republic!"

"Long live the Republican Jungle!" clamored the assembly triumphantly, transported by enthusiasm for an idea whose grandeur its members sensed.

"Let us repeat three times, like the sovereign words of antique theurgies, that cry of hope! Let is magnify its advent! Let us salute it as a definitive and unretractable step on the moving ground of progress! Souls of all ideals, hearts of all doctrines, voices of all parties, vibrate in that victorious unison of capital salvation!" Philémon Singeoreille concluded, in an inflamed peroration.

The Chambre took on the unaccustomed appearance of an assembly of the faithful gathered around their pontiff. Half a thousand mouths repeated the solemn words in the tone of a prayer, which does not count on violence in order to be heard.

After a silence, a voice demanded immediate discussion of the proposal dignified with the name of "the Philémon Singeoreille law." Five hundred hands were raised to approve the proposal.

A rapid colloquium was established between the President and the orator, who, before descending from the podium, handed the President a text, which the latter immediately read:

"Proposal of a law intended to restore virginity to the forests:

"Article One. The forests will be reintegrated in their estate and their destination.

"Article Two. From the date of the promulgation of the present law, the existing forests, and plantations in the locations of vanished forests, will have for residents ferocious or assimilated animals, the list of which will be fixed by decree.

"Article Three. The present law will entail the opening of a credit of a billion francs to the Ministry of Agriculture with a view to the acquisition of couples of animals in sufficient number to ensure the instantaneous increase of the selected species, the organization of services, and the execution of the works necessary for their immediate accommodation in the rigorously virgin forests and plantations envisaged in article one.

"Article Four. The present law is applicable to France and its colonies."

The President concluded: "I invite the Chambre to appoint its committee." His voice was drowned out by a frightful concert of reproach.

"No committee! A vote by raised hands! Immediate adoption by unanimity! Long live the Republican Jungle! Vive la France!"

Desirous of associating himself personally with that demonstration, the President agitated his hand-bell frantically, shouting at the top of his voice, with foam on his lips, impotently: "Silence, Messieurs!"—a cry reverberated in noble *basso profundo* echoes by the ushers.

Silence fell, as it sometimes does in the paroxysms of storms. The Minister of Agriculture, standing at the government bench, as finally able to get in a few words.

"The Government associates itself enthusiastically with the prestigious proposal of Monsieur Philémon Singeoreille."

Shouting, acclamations and various noises burst forth again. The voice of the President was scarcely audible in a brief calm, howling as he leaned over stenographers with haggard ears: "It is from similar minutes that Eternity is made!"

The reappearance of Philémon Singeoreille at the podium reestablished the silence that the Presidential objurgations had been unable to obtain.

"With a heart suspended by emotion, I thank the Chambre for carrying my brainchild so gloriously over the bulwark. I deem it to be healthy, well-conformed and called to the highest destiny, but permit me to oppose energetically its spontaneous adoption, flattering as it might be. My dear colleagues, takes as a model, if you will, the she-bear, who, with an indefatigable tongue, kneads in definitive relief the malleable forms of her cubs. Each of you is a torch which ought to shine its light upon the common endeavor. I insist on a discussion, point by point and in all its details, of the proposition that I have the honor of submitting to you."

A brief ovation, as vibrant as a drum-roll, closed that declaration, which invited all the members of the Chambre to leave the imprint of their real presence on that session, henceforth and already historic.

"The Minister of Agriculture has the floor," the President pronounced.

In order to give more solemnity to what he was about to say, the Minister climbed the steps of the podium. Head held high, his gestures broad and his voice assured, he commenced:

"Messieurs, the sun only rises rarely on a day comparable to the once that we have the signal honor of living today, thanks to the genius of one of our number. I shall, for posterity, name our colleague, the infinitely honorable Monsieur Philémon Singeoreille."

The Minister allowed the salvo of applause earned by that perambulatory remark to pass.

"Far be it from me to present to you the economy of a project whose vertiginous grandeur you have understood, and which you have already unanimously approved. I ask its henceforth-illustrious author to do me the honor of coming to take his place beside me during the discussion that he has demanded, with an intention for which, on behalf of the entire nation, I thank him with all gratitude."

Almost carried by his colleagues, Philémon Singeoreille was installed to the right of the Minister of Agriculture, who kissed him on both cheeks in a patriotic accolade.

In the meantime, innumerable pieces of paper were transmitted by way of interested parties or that of the ushers to the President's desk. Save for the members of the Government and Philémon Singeoreille, all the deputes, without exception, asked for a turn to speak, opening the perspective of five hundred and twenty-eight speeches whose authors had the columns of the *Journal Officiel* in mind.

Without apparent emotion, the President called upon the first name inscribed.

That honorable gentleman limited himself to celebrating in florid terms the narrow correlation established between the value of a country and the power of its fauna.

Another came forward, who tried to calculate the volumetric relationship that might exist between the vegetal and the animal. Becoming confused in his equations, he proclaimed a result that gave one cubic meter of flesh belonging to animals of average ferocity per cubic centimeter of ligneous matter of various species.

There was one who, in gripping images, saluted the creation of that double army of which animals and trees were going to be the faithful soldiers, destined to become the heroes of the sacred cause of reforestation.

Delights flourished in the imminent promise of conquests subsequent to those of the horse, of which nothing could nevertheless ever dethrone the supreme nobility.

In the sentimental order, wishes fell from the podium for every Frenchman, no matter what might emerge in the unknown of the future, to retain for the dog the first place in his heart.

Orators were enthusiastic to represent the neighborhood of ferocious beasts as the best and most efficacious school of courage and firmness.

Some sounded a melancholy note in requesting the assembly to address a fraternal adieu to the present landscapes that were the accustomed visages of old France.

Among the listeners, Philémon Singeoreille was perhaps the only one to lend an attentive ear to that interminable procession of hollow words and grotesque phrases, which faded away in the ever-more-active comings and goings established between the session hall and the corridors leading to the bar.

Everyone was waiting for the veritable start of the discussion, of which these speeches were merely the inoffensive hors-d'oeuvre, incapable of sating the hunger of experienced députés intent on playing a role susceptible of capturing public attention.

After observations carefully garlanded with rhetoric had identified the possible danger of tubercular illness in tropical animals transplanted to cold climes, legitimate esthetic preoccupations became manifest, provoking the first interruptions.

It was a matter of deciding whether or not the presence of monkeys in the Republican Jungle was desirable. The arguments for and against were eloquently presented.

"The monkey is the purest representative of primitive beauty," a pharmacist asserted.

"It is the decadent instrument of synthetic ugliness!" retorted a priest. "A monkey is a human without a soul!"

"I remind you of the respect due to ancestors, with the inscription of an official warning!" said the President, severely, to applause from the left and murmurs from the right. By way of conciliation, he added: "In any case, monkeys are external to the debate; they probably cannot be considered as ferocious."

"The Government reserves its opinion," put in the Minister of Agriculture. "An intermediate order ought to decide."

"I agree entirely with the Minister," the President capitulated, courteously.

The debate became animated when an orator advocated the employment of French wolves to the formal exclusion of foreign wolves. A socialist, a zealous partisan of internationalism, interrupted violently.

"The wolves of France are not true wolves. They prowl around habitations in the indubitable search for easy prey, and perhaps also in the debased hope of some handout.

"You are slandering the French wolf despicably! I defy you to say that you have ever seen one put out its hand!" thundered the orator.

"They're domesticated," the socialist contented himself with adding.

"In matters of Government," the Minister of Agriculture declared, "it's as well not to hesitate to examine the reactive impacts of ideas and facts, as well as their consequences. Thus, it is necessary to envisage that it might be necessary to grant to animals coming to France in conformity with the dispositions of the present law, certificates of naturalization. Personally, and without engaging the responsibility of the Government in any fashion, I deem that many foreigners, men and women, have been able to acquire French nationality without having rendered to the Nation services comparable to those we expect of these animals..."

"On behalf of the revolutionary group, I ask the Government what its intentions are with regard to the social status of the animals. My friends and I dare to hope that they will be more fortunate than the members of the human family and that no inequality of rank and treatment will be imposed upon them."

"Personally, I am an irreducible adversary of castes and privileges. However, first of all, it seems to me to be difficult to realize the unity of regime with regard to individuals recruited from various latitudes, representing multiple species whose needs are far from being the same. There are infinitely troubling problems therein, and extremely complicated questions," the Minister argued.

The partisan of one rule for all, once and for all, cut in brutally, as if he were demanding the verdict of the Last Judgment: "Equality! Equality! Equality!"

"Equality is a lie," put in a right-winger.

"I beg you, my dear colleague, not to charge lying with the testimony of your scorn," implored the President. "You know that lying is the most energetic homage rendered by humans to the truth. I'm truly saddened that this debate, departing from such a high point, should be descending to the level of base moral brawling."

The moral brawl nearly degenerated into a material brawl during the intervention of a professor of mimetics. That scientist, the spokesman of one of the black elements of the French people and black himself, developed his theory of the interplay of environmental influences, calling the attention of the Chambre to the adaptation of colors that would doubtless be realized externally by the inhabitants of the Republican Jungle.

"It's high time that you did the same!" shouted a center-leftist whose legitimate wife, it was notorious in parliament, had an intractable weakness for ebon adultery.

"Black is better than yellow," insinuated the native, in the smile of his white teeth.

"I forbid you to insult me!"

"We're talking about colors! You started it!" The negro continued to smile, flattered by the publicity given to his good fortune.

"It's lucky for the *maison*/is a good *encornaison*!"[29] sang the extreme left in chorus, as the unfortunate Republican tried in vain to shut them up by waving his fists.

---

[29] I have left *maison* [house] untranslated, in order to preserve the rhyme with the non-existent word *encornaison*, which obviously refers to fitting with [cuckold's] horns.

"The least gracious epithets were exchanged in the tumult inexplicably unleashed by that minuscule incident. The President shook his hand-bell and called for order. Between two repetitions of the chorus he attempted, with no more success, to talk about the majesty of the assembly. Without persisting further, as it was getting late, he embarked on a simulacrum of consultation, for the benefit of the drafter of the official record, with a view to suspending the discussion until the next day's session, and, putting on his hat, abandoned the armchair whose occupation is indispensable to the legal standing of debates.

The newspapers celebrated, with all due pomp, the sumptuousness of that parliamentary day, with the promise of even more admirable days to come. That stimulation of curiosity, checked as it was by the official notification of the absolute exhaustion of places available to the public, bore its fruit. There was a mass exodus in the direction of the Palais Bourbon of Parisians, ever ready to accept martyrdom in order to satisfy their need to witness a notorious and gratuitous spectacle. The people of Paris readily consider that presence as an active participation in events to which they are witnesses. Perhaps many revolutionary actions, especially those that have the streets and public places for their theater, are the simple result of that natural propensity, produced by curious vanity.

In a crowd, the individual loses himself to the extent of losing sight of himself, and as for his soul, it dissolves into the collective soul, composed not only of the sum of all the individual souls but also of innumerable reactions of those souls to one another. Those reactions escape the control of the subjects who experience them. They are manifest as a force comparable to cold and heat. Those who believe that they dominate it are, in fact, its most servile slaves. Without lightening their burden, they charge their neighbors with the weight of their own chains.

To put oneself at the head of a crowd is to abdicate one's individual soul unreservedly; it is to push obedience to the collective soul to the point of annihilation. In the same way, in a block of metal, the molecule sensitive to temperature wrongly believes that it is imposing on the aggregate by its own will the variations to which it is subject, and it is expressing an elementary truth under a paradoxical appearance to say that leading a crowd is following it.

Sometimes, one sees clouds in the sky hot on one another's heels, racing recklessly toward a certain point on the horizon. Suddenly the clouds stop, immediately resuming their rush toward a different point, no less certain, to judge by their urgency in approaching it. The clouds are the playthings of the wind, as crowds are the playthings of the atmosphere born of the collective soul. Some clouds interrupt their progress to precipitate them successively toward the four points of the compass; some crowds, set in movement in one direction, turn aside to throw themselves to the right or the left, or even to go backwards, sometimes with a sudden and utterly inexplicable violence.

Toward midday, a hundred thousand people, without the slightest preliminary agreement, found themselves gathered in a compact mass in the Place de la Concorde, the bridge of which was blocked by police forces. Violent eddies, precursors of a stampede, were agitating the crowd. The guardians of the peace were preparing to defend their pass of Thermopylae when the human tide, perhaps deceived by the sight of the church of the Madeleine, the other Greek temple with a colonnade similar to that of the Palais Bourbon, surged into the Rue Royale.

In the meantime, the President of the Chambre invited his colleagues to calm down, reminding them that the most moving pages of national history are those that require to be read with the most self-composure. Having said that, he gave the floor to Adrien Rezon.

Adrien Rezon was a former lion-tamer. The last representative of a family already illustrious in that arena, he had long been the unrivaled hero of the fairground. His popularity had exceeded the bounds of glory. While still young, his father having been mauled by his favorite lion before an audience petrified with horror, he had gone into the cage and, after a tense battle, had reclaimed the bloody body, already inert, from the furious beast. Slightly pale, an unknown man had come up to him, shaken his hand and, without a word, handed him a wallet. He was an Englishman who had been following the menagerie for twenty years in the daily hope of seeing the tamer eaten, and thought it only equitable to pay that supplement for the realization of his dream.

The contents of the wallet served to pay for a funeral for Père Rezon such as had never been seen in the circus world, which turned out in its entirety to pay its last respects to the greatest of its own. Immediately behind the hearse came the lion Brutus, lying motionless in his crepe-veiled cage, limp-maned, his half-closed eyes fixed on his master's coffin.

That same evening Adrien Rezon had donned the white culottes and black dolman, put on the high boots of varnished leather, and without a weapon, strictly bare-handed, he had presented his wild beasts to staged benches crammed to breaking-point with a public amazed by his boldness.

His silhouette became legendary. Everyone knew his black hair, falling in curls over his shoulders, and his carefully-waxed beard and moustache, causing the mat pallor of his face and the fulgurant gleam of his gold-flecked gray eyes stand out.

But everything passes and lassitude afflicts the most refined pleasures. After years of frenetic infatuation, the vogue quit the menagerie in favor of other attractions. The most spectacular parades were impotent to retain attention. The personality of Adrien Rezon could not longer succeed in arresting the flow of strollers outside his tent. The crowd that had idolized him seemed not to know him any longer. Out of need as much as self-respect, Adrien Rezon had continued to work, often before rare devotees and the Englishman, who, having seen the father eaten, legitimately nursed the hope of seeing the son eaten.

Difficult days had come. The beasts had grown old; they perished and were not replaced. Finally, via the newspapers that consecrated stubs of articles to him akin to obituaries, it was learned that Adrien Rezon had retired. A modest auction sale dispersed his materials. The zoological gardens graciously welcomed the surviving borders, with the exception of the lion Brutus, which Adrien Rezon took with him to the rural corner of his native Auvergne where the old family house stood, fortunately restored during the prosperous days.

There, Adrien Rezon led the existence of a sage, kneading pellets of bread amalgamated with a little meat, with which he fed the now gout-stricken companion of his triumphant evenings, which he now carried, wrapped in blankets to the shadiest corner of the gardens in the hours of bright sunlight.

The man had changed too; the curls of his hair, his beard and moustache had become snowy; the flame of the gold-flecked eyes had gone out; his emaciated face seemed sculpted in old ivory.

A prophet in his own land, surrounded by the esteem and affection of all, Adrien Rezon wanted nothing more than to spend the time remaining to him in that retreat, when the electors of the arrondissement, faced with the prospect of making a selection between a physician and an advocate equally qualified to make a député and each furnished with an equal number of partisans, came to him to ask him to accept a candidacy offered with the certain guarantee of success. Adrien Rezon had refused flatly, putting forward his incompetence and alleging, in addition, the impossibility of leaving Brutus. The latter had died in his master's arms, removing the pretext of amity, while the first invoked was rendered inadmissible by a convincing argument formulated by one of the ambassadors on behalf of them all:

"You know animals too well, Monsieur Rezon, not to understand humans and their petty affairs."

More concerned to defend the interests of his electors that to make an impact on their imagination, Adrien Rezon only manifested himself in the Chambre by brief and always judicious interventions. However, by virtue of his career, he could not avoid taking part in the debate on the "Singeoreille law."

His head, emerging in a symphony in complete white from the upright collar of a black jacket similar to a dolman, the former animal-tamer began: "Messieurs and dear colleagues, it is a friend—I almost said a brother—of beasts who does not want to let the debate concluded without making their voice heard. I have lived with them for so long, and I have loved them so much, that my speech, I hope, will not betray them

"I have no need to remind you of the interest a master has in treating his servants well, and far be it from me to suppose for a single instant that the government is capable of failing in the duty to ensure an appropriate existence to the animals. I would like to pay some attention to their morality, because among the beasts, morality has a greater importance than it has among humans. We have, in fact, been the prisoners of frontiers, laws, conventions and prejudices for so many generations that not the slightest memory of liberty remains to us outside of the three syllables of its name, which we are pleased to repeat without giving any real significance to them. Wild beasts, on the other hand, have not had time to lose the sense of their liberty—which rends their exile and their captivity infinitely sad.

"That exile and that captivity are useful to us. Let us accept the necessity without remorse and without hypocrisy. It is not humans, the inventors of war, in which they massacre one another with unusual refinements of cruelty, that it is necessary to reproach for egotism. Human beings are animals, perhaps, in sum, the best and worst of them all. As such, they are submissive to the universal and ineluctable law of blood, which dictates that death is the ransom of life.

"To be born is to kill. To exist is to destroy. To grow is to eat. Let us therefore yield to the necessities of our role, without which we could neither be nor subsist; but let us be

280

content to have pity for our victims; let us also respect their souls. I have known strange subtleties in them, which pierce instinct as a ray of light pierces the darkness.

"How many times I have read, in the somber golden eyes of my beasts, thoughts that were neither of anger nor of hatred, but of resigned acquiescence to a role similar to the one I was playing myself. How many of them, gentle and affectionate in intimacy, understood that in order to satisfy the excitement-loving public they had to show themselves in their terrible aspect, roaring with all their might, with menacing expressions. How many marks of tender repentance my old lion Brutus testified to me before his death for the minute of aberration that cost my father his life...

"Believe the old animal-tamer who later became your colleague: animals have a heart that knows how to love, and perhaps better than the human heart. You should not charge them with unnecessary pain. Let them know that it is not for our pleasure alone that you make them suffer and you will obtain all their devotion.

"That is all that I want to say to you."

Adrien Rezon came down from the podium as simply as he had gone up to it. Polite applause accompanied him to his bench.

After him, there was the flood of those who no longer had the ear of the Chambre for having exceeded those, albeit robust, of the deputes: those who took the podium for a gymnastic apparatus designed to develop the torso and fortify the vocal cords. For them, an orator is a man who emits sounds. They talk for the sake of hygiene, in the manner of an exercise in physical culture, which, for the most part, they neglected in their youth in parallel with their education. They seem happy and satisfied to feel their lungs dilate, their vocal cords vibrate and their temples stream with sweat. The victims of that eloquence do not appear to worry about it, just as, in a declamation class, no one pays any attention to the sonorous efforts of the pupils, or, in a Turkish bath, no one is astonished to see the sweat glands of his companions in the steam working hard.

As in a pot-pourri of celebrated works, speeches succeeded one another without any thematic linkage or consequence. The greater number treated the material conditions of the animals, relative to which Adrien Rezon had had confidence in the Government. The central heating of natural and artificial caves was envisaged, as well as the creation of vast refrigeration establishments, with the aim of giving equal satisfaction to tropical beasts and polar bears.

One député declared that it was necessary to be prudent and that from now on it was necessary to take the future under consideration. He therefore proposed to fix an age-limit and a number of years of service, after which every animal having met the required conditions would be gratuitously repatriated.

Another, a dyed-in-the-wool realist, criticized dreamy and sentimental animals, in particular the nostalgic giraffe. He favored their absolute proscription from the Republican Jungle.

A former magistrate, who was reputed to be a devotee of the wings of the Opéra, embarked on the reading of a study of the amorous season among animals. It seemed to him to be appropriate to keep it open every year, while leaving the usage of it to the free appreciation of interested parties. He recalled that in that matter, only humans knew no unemployment, and without withdrawing their crown as the monarchs of creation, he proclaimed them the emperors of amour. He celebrated his own erotic glory, of which he gallantly left a part to woman. He quoted Latin verses exhumed from licentious texts.

A chorus to the right translated them in its own manner by singing a well-known verse: "Blonde hair, silky thread/that grows in the head/in a mat that teaches vice/to climb to paradise."

After that interlude, the discussion entered the domain of application, and it was then that particular interests collided with one another and came into conflict. One representative of a honey-producing region opposed the importation of bears, sworn enemies of hives because of their fondness for the work of bees. Another undertook the defense of his electoral rabbits.

The exotic Noah's ark was searched in every corner of its holds. Every one of its guests had its detractors, all armed with plausible and legitimate local reasons.

Philémon Singeoreille looked in amazement at his neighbor, the Minister of Agriculture, who smiled at the host of amendments that submerged his proposal, and remained speechless when he heard the pronunciation "The Government proposes the appointment of a committee."

That was what the assembly decided, with a unanimity inclusive of the vote of Philémon Singeoreille, who learned with a keen satisfaction of his designation as a committee-member.

For three-quarters of a century the creation of the Republican Jungle served as a trampoline in every election. Not one candidate failed to make it the capital item in his program. Not one profession of faith omitted a formal engagement on its subject.

At the debut of every new legislature, every four years, in synchronicity with the bissextile years, Philémon Singeoreille renewed his proposal. The Chambre appointed a committee, which undertook its task so conscientiously that the mandate of its members expired before the report necessary for the plenary discussion could be completed.

Finally, Philémon Singeoreille did, on the very eve of the day when his faithful electors were about to celebrate his centenary. No one after him thought themselves cut out to continue his unfinished work, and the project of the Republican Jungle joined in oblivion numerous parliamentary initiatives that likewise might have merited a better fate.

SF & FANTASY

Adolphe Alhaiza. *Cybele*
Alphonse Allais. *The Adventures of Captain Cap*
Henri Allorge. *The Great Cataclysm*
Guy d'Armen. *Doc Ardan: The City of Gold and Lepers*
G.-J. Arnaud. *The Ice Company*
Charles Asselineau. *The Double Life*
Cyprien Bérard. *The Vampire Lord Ruthwen*
S. Henry Berthoud. *Martyrs of Science*
Aloysius Bertrand. *Gaspard de la Nuit*
Richard Bessière. *The Gardens of the Apocalypse*
Albert Bleunard. *Ever Smaller*
Félix Bodin. *The Novel of the Future*
Louis Boussenard. *Monsieur Synthesis*
Alphonse Brown. *City of Glass; The Conquest of the Air*
Emile Calvet. *In a Thousand Years*
André Caroff. *The Terror of Madame Atomos; Miss Atomos; The Return of Madame Atomos; The Mistake of Madame Atomos; The Monsters of Madame Atomos; The Revenge of Madame Atomos; The Resurrection of Madame Atomos; The Mark of Madame Atomos; The Spheres of Madame Atomos*
Félicien Champsaur. *The Human Arrow; Ouha, King of the Apes; Pharaoh's Wife*
Didier de Chousy. *Ignis*
Jules Clarétie. *Obsession*
Michel Corday. *The Eternal Flame*
André Couvreur. *The Necessary Evil*; *Caresco, Superman; The Exploits of Professor Tornada* (3 vols.)
Captain Danrit. *Undersea Odyssey*
C. I. Defontenay. *Star (Psi Cassiopeia)*
Charles Derennes. *The People of the Pole*
Georges Dodds (anthologist). *The Missing Link*
Harry Dickson. *The Heir of Dracula*
Jules Dornay. *Lord Ruthven Begins*
Alfred Driou. *The Adventures of a Parisian Aeronaut*
Sâr Dubnotal *vs. Jack the Ripper*
Alexandre Dumas. *The Return of Lord Ruthven*
Renée Dunan. *Baal*
J.-C. Dunyach. *The Night Orchid; The Thieves of Silence*

Henri Duvernois. *The Man Who Found Himself*
Achille Eyraud. *Voyage to Venus*
Henri Falk. *The Age of Lead*
Paul Féval. *Anne of the Isles; Knightshade; Revenants; Vampire City; The Vampire Countess; The Wandering Jew's Daughter*
Paul Féval, *fils. Felifax, the Tiger-Man*
Charles de Fieux. *Lamékis*
Louis Forest. *Someone is Stealing Children in Paris*
Arnould Galopin. *Doctor Omega; Doctor Omega and the Shadowmen* (anthology)
Judith Gautier. *Isoline and the Serpent-Flower*
H. Gayar. *The Marvelous Adventures of Serge Myrandhal on Mars*
Léon Gozlan. *The Vampire of the Val-de-Grâce*
G.L. Gick. *Harry Dickson and the Werewolf of Rutherford Grange*
Edmond Haraucourt. *Illusions of Immortality*
Nathalie Henneberg. *The Green Gods*
V. Hugo, P. Foucher & P. Meurice. *The Hunchback of Notre-Dame*
Romain d'Huissier. *Hexagon: Dark Matter*
Jules Janin. *The Magnetized Corpse*
Michel Jeury. *Chronolysis*
Gustave Kahn. *The Tale of Gold and Silence*
Gérard Klein. *The Mote in Time's Eye*
Fernand Kolney. *Love in 5000 Years*
Paul Lacroix. *Danse Macabre*
Louis-Guillaume de La Follie. *The Unpretentious Philosopher*
Jean de La Hire. *Enter the Nyctalope; The Nyctalope on Mars; The Nyctalope vs. Lucifer; The Nyctalope Steps In; Night of the Nyctalope; Return of the Nyctalope; The Fiery Wheel*
Etienne-Léon de Lamothe-Langon. *The Virgin Vampire*
André Laurie. *Spiridon*
Gabriel de Lautrec. *The Vengeance of the Oval Portrait*
Alain le Drimeur. *The Future City*
Georges Le Faure & Henri de Graffigny. *The Extraordinary Adventures of a Russian Scientist Across the Solar System* (2 vols.)
Gustave Le Rouge. *The Mysterious Doctor Cornelius* (3 vols.); *The Vampires of Mars; The Dominion of the World* (w/Gustave Guitton) (4 vols.)
Jules Lermina. *Mysteryville; Panic in Paris; To-Ho and the Gold Destroyers; The Secret of Zippelius*
André Lichtenberger. *The Centaurs; The Children of the Crab*

Jean-Marc & Randy Lofficier. *Edgar Allan Poe on Mars; The Katrina Protocol; Pacifica; Robonocchio; Return of the Nyctalope;* (anthologists) *Tales of the Shadowmen 1-10*

Xavier Mauméjean. *The League of Heroes*

Joseph Méry. *The Tower of Destiny*

Hippolyte Mettais. *The Year 5865*

Louise Michel. *The Human Microbes; The New World*

Tony Moilin. *Paris in the Year 2000*

José Moselli. *Illa's End*

John-Antoine Nau. *Enemy Force*

Marie Nizet. *Captain Vampire*

C. Nodier, A. Beraud & Toussaint-Merle. *Frankenstein*

Henri de Parville. *An Inhabitant of the Planet Mars*

Gaston de Pawlowski. *Journey to the Land of the 4th Dimension*

Georges Pellerin. *The World in 2000 Years*

Ernest Pérochon. *The Frenetic People*

Pierre Pelot. *The Child Who Walked on the Sky*

J. Polidori, C. Nodier, E. Scribe. *Lord Ruthven the Vampire*

P.-A. Ponson du Terrail. *The Vampire and the Devil's Son; The Immortal Woman*

Edgar Quinet. *Ahasuerus*

Henri de Régnier. *A Surfeit of Mirrors*

Maurice Renard. *The Blue Peril; Doctor Lerne; The Doctored Man; A Man Among the Microbes; The Master of Light*

Jean Richepin. *The Wing; The Crazy Corner*

Albert Robida. *The Adventures of Saturnin Farandoul; The Clock of the Centuries; Chalet in the Sky; The Electric Life*

J.-H. Rosny Aîné. *Helgvor of the Blue River; The Givreuse Enigma; The Mysterious Force; The Navigators of Space; Vamireh; The World of the Variants; The Young Vampire*

Marcel Rouff. *Journey to the Inverted World*

Han Ryner. *The Superhumans*

Angelo de Sorr. *The Vampires of London*

Brian Stableford. *The New Faust at the Tragicomique;The Empire of the Necromancers (The Shadow of Frankenstein; Frankenstein and the Vampire Countess; Frankenstein in London); Sherlock Holmes & The Vampires of Eternity; The Stones of Camelot; The Wayward Muse.* (anthologist) *News from the Moon; The Germans on Venus; The Supreme Progress; The World Above the World; Nemoville; Investigations of the Future; The Conqueror of Death*

Jacques Spitz. *The Eye of Purgatory*

Kurt Steiner. *Ortog*
Eugène Thébault. *Radio-Terror*
C.-F. Tiphaigne de La Roche. *Amilec*
Louis Ulbach. *Prince Bonifacio*
Théo Varlet. *The Golden Rock. The Xenobiotic Invasion; The Castaways of Eros; Timeslip Troopers* (w/André Blandin); *The Martian Epic* (w/Octave Joncquel)
Paul Vibert. *The Mysterious Fluid*
Villiers de l'Isle-Adam. *The Scaffold; The Vampire Soul*
Philippe Ward. *Artahe*
Philippe Ward & Sylvie Miller. *The Song of Montségur*

MYSTERIES & THRILLERS

M. Allain & P. Souvestre. *The Daughter of Fantômas*
A. Anicet-Bourgeois, Lucien Dabril. *Rocambole*
A. Bernède. *Belphegor*; *Judex* (w/Louis Feuillade); *The Return of Judex* (w/Louis Feuillade); *The Shadow of Judex*
A. Bisson & G. Livet. *Nick Carter vs. Fantômas*
V. Darlay & H. de Gorsse. *Arsène Lupin vs. Sherlock Holmes: The Stage Play*
Séamas Duffy. *Sherlock Holmes in Paris*
Paul Féval. *Gentlemen of the Night; John Devil; The Black Coats ('Salem Street; The Invisible Weapon; The Parisian Jungle; The Companions of the Treasure; Heart of Steel; The Cadet Gang; The Sword-Swallower)*
Emile Gaboriau. *Monsieur Lecoq*
Goron & Emile Gautier. *Spawn of the Penitentiary*
Rick Lai. *Shadows of the Opera: Retribution in Blood; Sisters of the Shadows: The Curse of Cagliostro*
Steve Leadley. *Sherlock Holmes: The Circle of Blood*
Maurice Leblanc. *Arsène Lupin vs. Countess Cagliostro; Arsène Lupin vs. Sherlock Holmes (The Blonde Phantom; The Hollow Needle); The Many Faces of Arsène Lupin*
Gaston Leroux. *Chéri-Bibi; The Phantom of the Opera; Rouletabille & the Mystery of the Yellow Room; Rouletabille at Krupp's*
Richard Marsh. *The Complete Adventures of Judith Lee*
William Patrick Maynard. *The Terror of Fu Manchu; The Destiny of Fu Manchu*
Frank J. Morlock. *Sherlock Holmes: The Grand Horizontals; Sherlock Holmes vs Jack the Ripper*

Jean Petithuguenin. *The Adventures of Ethel King*
Antonin Reschal. *The Adventures of Miss Boston*
P. de Wattyne & Y. Walter. *Sherlock Holmes vs. Fantômas*
David White. *Fantômas in America*
Pierre Yrondy. *The Adventures of Thérèse Arnaud*

SCREENPLAYS

Mike Baron. *The Iron Triangle*
Emma Bull & Will Shetterly. *Nightspeeder; War for the Oaks*
Gerry Conway & Roy Thomas. *Doc Dynamo*
Steve Englehart. *Majorca*
James Hudnall. *The Devastator*
Jean-Marc & Randy Lofficier. *Royal Flush*
J.-M. & R. Lofficier & Marc Agapit. *Despair*
J.-M. & R. Lofficier & Joël Houssin. *City*
Andrew Paquette. *Peripheral Vision*
Robert L. Robinson, Jr. *Judex*
R. Thomas, J. Hendler & L. Sprague de Camp. *Rivers of Time*

NON-FICTION

Stephen R. Bissette. *Blur 1-5. Green Mountain Cinema 1; Teen Angels*
Win Scott Eckert. *Crossovers* (2 vols.)
Jean-Marc & Randy Lofficier. *Shadowmen* (2 vols.)
Randy Lofficier. *Over Here*

ART BOOKS

J.-M. Lofficier & D. Taylor. *Tongue Lash*
Jean-Pierre Normand. *Science Fiction Illustrations*
Raven Okeefe. *Raven's L'il Critters; Rave's Faves*
Randy Lofficier & Raven Okeefe. *If Your Possum Go Daylight...*
Daniele Serra. *Illusions*